Iden Ford

Laurie R. King is the Edgar Award–winning author of five contemporary novels featuring Kate Martinelli, eight acclaimed Mary Russell mysteries, and four stand-alone mysteries, including the highly praised *A Darker Place*. She lives in Northern California.

www.laurierking.com

BY LAURIE R. KING

A Darker Place

Folly

Keeping Watch

Califia's Daughters (writing as Leigh Richards)

MARY RUSSELL MYSTERIES

The Beekeeper's Apprentice

A Monstrous Regiment of Women

A Letter of Mary

The Moor

O Jerusalem

Justice Hall

The Game

Locked Rooms

KATE MARTINELLI MYSTERIES

A Grave Talent

To Play the Fool

With Child

Night Work

The Art of Detection

ties ensure a lively adventure in the very best of intellectual company."

—The New York Times Book Review

"The game's afoot. And a lively, well-plotted game it is."

—The Philadelphia Inquirer

"I report that Laurie R. King's *A Letter of Mary* delights me as much as its two predecessors in what I must hope will be a long, unfolding series. . . . I thoroughly enjoyed this book; I also admired it."

—The Boston Globe

"Audacious . . . amazing . . . an intellectual puzzler, full of bright red herrings and dazzling asides . . . Not the least of King's many accomplishments in her Russell books is the ability to make us believe that Holmes was a real person, and that he loved and was loved by a remarkable young woman."

—Chicago Tribune

The Moor

"There's no resisting the appeal of King's thrillingly moody scenes of Dartmoor and her lovely evocations of its legends."

—The New York Times Book Review

"Mary's description of how she thinks through all the elements of a mystery—so deep in thought as if she were in a trance—is excellent."

—Salon.com

"*Dazzling* may be the word to describe King's latest Mary Russell–Sherlock Holmes adventure. . . . Add King's devilishly clever plot and eccentric characters, her ability to achieve a perfect balance between serious mystery and lighthearted humor, and the charm with which she develops the captivating relationship between Holmes and Russell, and the result is a superbly rich read that would please Doyle himself."

—*Booklist*

"Erudite, fascinating . . . by all odds the most successful re-creation of the famous inhabitant of 221B Baker Street ever attempted."

—*Houston Chronicle*

THE
BEEKEEPER'S
APPRENTICE

❧

Or On the Segregation
of the Queen

❧

A Mary Russell Novel

LAURIE R. KING

Picador

Thomas Dunne Books
St. Martin's Press
New York

www.picadorusa.com

Picador® is a U.S. registered trademark and is used by St. Martin's Press under license from Pan Books Limited.

For information on Picador Reading Group Guides, please contact Picador.
Phone: 646-307-5259
Fax: 212-253-9627
E-mail: readinggroupguides@picadorusa.com

Chapter epigraphs are from Maurice Maeterlinck, *The Life of the Bee*, copyright © 1901 and 1928, published by Dodd, Mead & Co., New York, 1970.

Library of Congress Cataloging-in-Publication Data

King, Laurie R.
    The beekeeper's apprentice, or, On the segregation of the queen / Laurie R. King.
    p. cm.
    ISBN-13: 978-0-312-42736-8
    ISBN-10: 0-312-42736-0
    1. Holmes, Sherlock (Fictitious character)—Fiction.   2. Russell, Mary (Fictitious character)—Fiction.   3. Private investigators—England—Fiction.   4. Women detectives—England—Fiction.   5. Young women—England—Fiction.   6. England—Fiction.   I. Title.

PS3561.I4813 B44 1994
813'.54—dc20   93043522

First published in the United States by St. Martin's Press

10   9   8   7   6

For another M.R.,
my mother,
Mary Richardson

THE
BEEKEEPER'S
APPRENTICE

❊ EDITOR'S PREFACE ❊

THE FIRST THING I want the reader to know is that I had nothing to do with this book you have in your hand. Yes, I write mystery novels, but even a novelist's fevered imagination has its limits, and mine would reach those limits long before it came up with the farfetched idea of Sherlock Holmes taking on a smart-mouthed, half-American, fifteen-year-old feminist sidekick. I mean, really: If even Conan Doyle hungered to shove Holmes off a tall cliff, surely a young female of obvious intelligence would have brained the detective on first sight.

However, that doesn't explain how this story came into print.

It began several years ago, when the UPS delivery woman came barreling down the driveway and, somewhat to my surprise, began to unload not the order of vegetable seeds I was expecting but a very large, heavily strapped cardboard box that must have stretched UPS's weight restrictions to the limit, because she had to use her dolly to maneuver the thing onto my front porch. After questioning her to no avail and checking carefully that the address on the box was indeed mine, I signed for it and went to get a kitchen knife to cut the tape. I ended up cutting considerably more than the tape, and when I had finished hacking away the cardboard I was ankle-deep in scraps; that knife has never been the same.

Inside was a trunk, a large and much-abused, old-fashioned metal traveling trunk, complete with stickers from hotels familiar and unlikely. (Could there be a Ritz in Ibadan?) Someone had thoughtfully fastened the key into the padlock with a length of Scotch tape, so I removed the tape and turned the key, feeling somewhat like Alice confronted with a "Drink me" bottle. As I stood looking down at the jumbled contents, my curiosity began to take on alarming overtones. I rapidly pulled back my hand and stood away from the trunk, thoughts of madmen and stalkers standing out in my mind like newspaper headlines. I went down the stairs and around the house fully intending to call the police, but when I went in the back door I stopped to make myself a cup of coffee first, and when it was in the cup I walked through the house to look cautiously out the window at the dented metal and the gorgeous purple velvet that lay inside it, and I saw that one of the cats had curled up on top of the velvet. Now, why a sleeping cat should cause fears of explosive devices to fade so quickly I cannot think, but it did, and I was soon on my knees, elbowing the cat out of the way to examine the contents.

They were very strange. Not taken by themselves, but as a collection, there was neither rhyme nor reason: some articles of clothing, including the beaded velvet evening cloak (with a slit near the hem), a drab and disreputable man's bathrobe or dressing gown, and a breathtaking gossamer wool-and-silk embroidered Kashmiri shawl; a cracked magnifying lens; two bits of tinted glass that could only be a pair of peculiarly thick and horribly uncomfortable contact lenses; a length of fabric that a friend later identified as an unwrapped turban; a magnificent emerald necklace, a weight of gold and sparkle that rode my throat like wealth personified until I unhooked it and carried it inside to thrust beneath my pillow; a man's emerald stick-pin; an empty matchbox; one carved ivory chopstick; one of those English railway timetable books called ABC for the year 1923; three odd stones; a thick two-inch bolt rusted onto its nut; a small wooden box, ornate with carving and inlay depicting palm trees and jungle animals; a slim, gold-leaf, red-letter King James New Testament, bound in white leather that had gone limp with use; a monacle on a black silk ribbon; a box of newspaper clippings, some of which seemed to deal with crimes committed, and an assortment of other odds and ends that had been pushed in around the edges of the trunk.

And, right at the bottom, a layer of what proved to be manuscripts, although only one was immediately recognizable as such, the others being either English-sized foolscap covered top to bottom with tiny, difficult writing or the same hand on an unwieldy pile of mismatched scrap paper. Each was bound with narrow purple ribbon and sealed with wax, stamped *R*.

Over the next couple of weeks I read through those manuscripts, all the time expecting to find the answer to the puzzle of who had sent them to me, waiting for it to leap out like some written jack-in-the-box, but I found nothing—nothing, that is, but the stories, which I read with equal parts enjoyment and eyestrain.

I did try to trace the shipper through UPS, but all the agent at the New York office where the parcel had originated could tell me was that a young man had brought it in, and paid cash.

With considerable puzzlement, then, I folded the cloak, dressing gown, and manuscripts away and stashed the trunk in my closet. (The emeralds I put in a safe-deposit box at the bank.)

There it sat, month in and month out, for some years, until one bleak day after a too-long series of bleak days when nothing would grow under my pen and money pressures loomed, I remembered with a stir of envy the easy assurance of the voice from the manuscripts in the back of my closet.

I went to the trunk and dug out one of the piles of paper, took it to my study to read again, and then, motivated by despair as much as the roof that was leaking around my ears, set about rewriting it. Shame-faced, I sent it to my editor, but when she rang me some days later with the mild comment that this didn't read like my other stuff, I broke down and confessed, told her to mail it back to me, and went back to staring at a blank page.

The following day she called again, said that she'd had a consulta-tion with the firm's lawyer, that she really liked the story, though she wanted to see the original, and that she'd like to publish it if I were willing to sign my life away in waivers should the actual author appear.

The battle between pride and roof repairs was over before it began. I do, however, have some self-esteem, and still considered the narra-tives in my possession, as I said, farfetched.

I don't know how much truth there is in them. I don't even know if they were written as fiction or fact, though I cannot rid myself of the feeling that they were meant as fact, absurd as it may be. However, selling them (with disclaimer) is preferable to selling that gorgeous necklace I will probably never wear, and surely if selling the one is ac-ceptable, so is the other.

What follows is the first of those manuscripts, unadorned and as the writer left it (and, presumably, sent it to me). I have only tidied up her atrocious spelling and smoothed out a variety of odd personal short-hand notations. Personally, I don't know what to make of it. I can only hope that with the publication of what the author called *On the Segregation of the Queen* (such a cumbersome title—she was obvi-ously no novelist!) will come, not lawsuits, but a few answers. If any-one out there knows who Mary Russell was, could you let me know? My curiosity is killing me.

—Laurie R. King

As the result of no small effort in the stacks of the University of California library I have identified the quotations with which the author prefaced her chapters. They come from a 1901 philosophical treatise on beekeeping by Maurice Maeterlinck, entitled *The Life of the Bee*.

❖ PRELUDE ❖

Author's Note

To this spot a sort of aged philosopher had retired. . . .
Here he had built his refuge, being a little
weary of interrogating men. . . .

DEAR READER,

As both I and the century approach the beginnings of our ninth
decades, I have been forced to admit that age is not always a desirable
state. The physical, of course, contributes its own flavour to life, but
the most vexing problem I have found is that my past, intensely real to
me, has begun to fade into the mists of history in the eyes of those
around me. The First World War has deteriorated into a handful of
quaint songs and sepia images, occasionally powerful but immeasur-
ably distant; there is death in that war, but no blood. The twenties
have become a caricature, the clothing we wore is now in museums,
and those of us who remember the beginnings of this godforsaken
century are beginning to falter. With us will go our memories.

I do not remember when I first realised that the flesh-and-blood Sherlock Holmes I knew so well was to the rest of the world merely a figment of an out-of-work medical doctor's powerful imagination. What I do remember is how the realisation took my breath away, and how for several days my own self-awareness became slightly detached, tenuous, as if I too were in the process of transmuting into fiction, by contagion with Holmes. My sense of humour provided the pinch that woke me, but it was a very peculiar sensation while it lasted.

Now, the process has become complete: Watson's stories, those feeble evocations of the compelling personality we both knew, have taken on a life of their own, and the living creature of Sherlock Holmes has become ethereal, dreamy. Fictional.

Amusing, in its way. And now, men and women are writing actual novels about Holmes, plucking him up and setting him down in bizarre situations, putting impossible words into his mouth, and obscuring the legend still further.

Why, it would not even surprise me to find my own memoirs classified as fiction, myself relegated to cloud-cuckoo-land. Now there is a delicious irony.

Nonetheless, I must assert that the following pages recount the early days and years of my true-life association with Sherlock Holmes. To the reader who comes upon my story with no previous knowledge of the habits and personality of the man, there may be some references that pass by unseen. At the other end of the spectrum are the readers who have committed whole sections of the Conan Doyle corpus (a particularly appropriate word here) to memory. These readers may find places at which my account differs from the words of Holmes' previous biographer, Dr. Watson, and will very probably take offence at my presentation of the man as being someone totally different from the "real" Holmes of Watson's writings.

To these latter I can only say that they are quite right: The Holmes I met was indeed a different man from the detective of 221B Baker Street. He had been ostensibly retired for a decade and a half, and was well into his middle age. More than this, however, had changed: The world was a different place from that of Victoria Regina. Automobiles and electricity were replacing hansom cabs and gaslights, the telephone was nosing its obtrusive self into the lives even of village people, and the horrors of war in the trenches were beginning to eat at the very fabric of the nation.

I think, however, that even if the world had not changed and even if I had met Holmes as a young man, my portraits of him would still be strikingly different from those painted by the good Dr. Watson. Watson always saw his friend Holmes from a position of inferiority, and his perspective was always shaped by this. Do not get me wrong—I came to have considerable affection for Dr. Watson. However, he was born an innocent, slightly slow to see the obvious (to put it politely), although he did come to possess a not inconsiderable wisdom and humanity. I, on the other hand, came into the world fighting, could manipulate my iron-faced Scots nurse by the time I was three, and had lost any innocence and wisdom I once may have had by the time I hit puberty.

It has taken me a long time to find them again.

Holmes and I were a match from the beginning. He towered over me in experience, but never did his abilities at observation and analysis awe me as they did Watson. My own eyes and mind functioned in precisely the same way. It was familiar territory.

So, yes, I freely admit that my Holmes is not the Holmes of Watson. To continue with the analogy, my perspective, my brush technique, my use of colour and shade, are all entirely different from his. The subject is essentially the same; it is the eyes and the hands of the artist that change.

—M. R. H.

Book One

APPRENTICESHIP

The Beekeeper's Apprentice

❧

❧ 1 ❧

Two Shabby Figures

The discovery of a sign of true intellect outside
ourselves procures us something of the emotion Robinson Crusoe
felt when he saw the imprint of a human foot on the
sandy beach of his island.

I WAS FIFTEEN when I first met Sherlock Holmes, fifteen years old with my nose in a book as I walked the Sussex Downs, and nearly stepped on him. In my defence I must say it was an engrossing book, and it was very rare to come across another person in that particular part of the world in that war year of 1915. In my seven weeks of peripatetic reading amongst the sheep (which tended to move out of my way) and the gorse bushes (to which I had painfully developed an instinctive awareness) I had never before stepped on a person.

It was a cool, sunny day in early April, and the book was by Virgil. I had set out at dawn from the silent farmhouse, chosen a different direction from my usual—in this case southeasterly, towards the sea— and had spent the intervening hours wrestling with Latin verbs, climbing unconsciously over stone walls, and unthinkingly circling hedgerows, and would probably not have noticed the sea until I stepped off one of the chalk cliffs into it.

As it was, my first awareness that there was another soul in the universe was when a male throat cleared itself loudly not four feet from me. The Latin text flew into the air, followed closely by an Anglo-Saxon oath. Heart pounding, I hastily pulled together what dignity I could and glared down through my spectacles at this figure hunched up at my feet: a gaunt, greying man in his fifties wearing a cloth cap, ancient tweed greatcoat, and decent shoes, with a threadbare Army rucksack on the ground beside him. A tramp perhaps, who had left the rest of his possessions stashed beneath a bush. Or an Eccentric. Certainly no shepherd.

He said nothing. Very sarcastically. I snatched up my book and brushed it off.

"What on earth are you doing?" I demanded. "Lying in wait for someone?"

He raised one eyebrow at that, smiled in a singularly condescending and irritating manner, and opened his mouth to speak in that precise drawl which is the trademark of the overly educated upper-class English gentleman. A high voice; a biting one: definitely an Eccentric.

"I should think that I can hardly be accused of 'lying' anywhere," he said, "as I am seated openly on an uncluttered hillside, minding my own business. When, that is, I am not having to fend off those who propose to crush me underfoot." He rolled the penultimate r to put me in my place.

Had he said almost anything else, or even said the same words in another manner, I should merely have made a brusque apology and a purposeful exit, and my life would have been a very different thing. However, he had, all unknowing, hit squarely on a highly sensitive spot. My reason for leaving the house at first light had been to avoid my aunt, and the reason (the most recent of many reasons) for wishing to avoid my aunt was the violent row we'd had the night before, a row sparked by the undeniable fact that my feet had outgrown their shoes, for the second time since my arrival three months before. My aunt was small, neat, shrewish, sharp-tongued, quick-witted, and proud of her petite hands and feet. She invariably made me feel clumsy, uncouth, and unreasonably touchy about my height and the corresponding size of my feet. Worse, in the ensuing argument over finances, she had won.

His innocent words and his far-from-innocent manner hit my smouldering temper like a splash of petrol. My shoulders went back, my chin up, as I stiffened for combat. I had no idea where I was, or who this man was, whether I was standing on his land or he on mine, if he was a dangerous lunatic or an escaped convict or the lord of the manor, and I did not care. I was furious.

"You have not answered my question, sir," I bit off.

He ignored my fury. Worse than that, he seemed unaware of it. He looked merely bored, as if he wished I might go away.

"What am I doing here, do you mean?"

"Exactly."

"I am watching bees," he said flatly, and turned back to his contemplation of the hillside.

Nothing in the man's manner showed a madness to correspond with his words. Nonetheless I kept a wary eye on him as I thrust my book into my coat pocket and dropped to the ground—a safe distance away from him—and studied the movement in the flowers before me.

There were indeed bees, industriously working at stuffing pollen into those leg sacs of theirs, moving from flower to flower. I watched, and was just thinking that there was nothing particularly noteworthy about these bees when my eyes were caught by the arrival of a peculiarly marked specimen. It seemed an ordinary honeybee but had a small red spot on its back. How odd—perhaps what he had been watching? I glanced at the Eccentric, who was now staring intently off into space, and then looked more closely at the bees, interested in spite of myself. I quickly concluded that the spot was no natural phenomenon, but rather paint, for there was another bee, its spot slightly lopsided, and another, and then another odd thing: a bee with a blue spot as well. As I watched, two red spots flew off in a northwesterly direction. I carefully observed the blue-and-red spot as it filled its pouches and saw it take off towards the northeast.

I thought for a minute, got up, and walked to the top of the hill, scattering ewes and lambs, and when I looked down at a village and river I knew instantly where I was. My house was less than two miles from here. I shook my head ruefully at my inattention, thought for a moment longer about this man and his red- and blue-spotted bees, and walked back down to take my leave of him. He did not look up, so I spoke to the back of his head.

"I'd say the blue spots are a better bet, if you're trying for another hive," I told him. "The ones you've only marked with red are probably from Mr. Warner's orchard. The blue spots are farther away, but they're almost sure to be wild ones." I dug the book from my pocket, and when I looked up to wish him a good day he was looking back at me, and the expression on his face took all words from my lips—no mean accomplishment. He was, as the writers say but people seldom actually are, openmouthed. He looked a bit like a fish, in fact, gaping at me as if I were growing another head. He slowly stood up, his mouth shutting as he rose, but still staring.

"*What* did you say?"

"I beg your pardon, are you hard of hearing?" I raised my voice somewhat and spoke slowly. "I said, if you want a new hive you'll have to follow the blue spots, because the reds are sure to be Tom Warner's."

"I am not hard of hearing, although I am short of credulity. How do you come to know of my interests?"

"I should have thought it obvious," I said impatiently, though even at that age I was aware that such things were not obvious to the majority of people. "I see paint on your pocket-handkerchief, and traces on your fingers where you wiped it away. The only reason to mark bees that I can think of is to enable one to follow them to their hive. You are either interested in gathering honey or in the bees themselves, and it is not the time of year to harvest honey. Three months ago we had an unusual cold spell that killed many hives. Therefore I assume that you are tracking these in order to replenish your own stock."

The face that looked down at me was no longer fishlike. In fact, it resembled amazingly a captive eagle I had once seen, perched in aloof splendour looking down the ridge of his nose at this lesser creature, cold disdain staring out from his hooded grey eyes.

"My God," he said in a voice of mock wonder, "it can think."

My anger had abated somewhat while watching the bees, but at this casual insult it erupted. Why was this tall, thin, infuriating old man so set on provoking an unoffending stranger? My chin went up again, only in part because he was taller than I, and I mocked him in return.

"My God, it can recognise another human being when it's hit over the head with one." For good measure I added, "And to think that I was raised to believe that old people had decent manners."

I stood back to watch my blows strike home, and as I faced him squarely my mind's eye finally linked him up with rumours I had heard and the reading I had done during my recent long convalescence, and I knew who he was, and I was appalled.

I had, I should mention, always assumed that a large part of Dr. Watson's adulatory stories were a product of that gentleman's inferior imagination. Certainly he always regarded the reader to be as slow as himself. Most irritating. Nonetheless, behind the stuff and nonsense of the biographer there towered a figure of pure genius, one of the great minds of his generation. A Legend.

And I was horrified: Here I was, standing before a Legend, flinging insults at him, yapping about his ankles like a small dog worrying a bear. I suppressed a cringe and braced myself for the casual swat that would send me flying.

To my amazement, however, and considerable dismay, instead of counterattacking he just smiled condescendingly and bent down to pick up his rucksack. I heard the faint rattle of the paint bottles within. He straightened, pushed his old-fashioned cap back on his greying hair, and looked at me with tired eyes.

"Young man, I—"

" '*Young man*'!" That did it. Rage swept into my veins, filling me with power. Granted I was far from voluptuous, granted I was dressed in practical, that is, male, clothing—this was not to be borne. Fear aside, Legend aside, the yapping lapdog attacked with all the utter contempt only an adolescent can muster. With a surge of glee I seized the weapon he had placed in my hands and drew back for the coup de grâce. " 'Young man'?" I repeated. "It's a damned good thing that you did retire, if that's all that remains of the great detective's mind!" With that I reached for the brim of my oversized cap and my long blonde plaits slithered down over my shoulders.

A series of emotions crossed his face, rich reward for my victory. Simple surprise was followed by a rueful admission of defeat, and then, as he reviewed the entire discussion, he surprised me. His face relaxed, his thin lips twitched, his grey eyes crinkled into unexpected lines, and at last he threw back his head and gave a great shout of delighted laughter. That was the first time I heard Sherlock Holmes laugh, and although it was far from the last, it never ceased to surprise me, seeing that proud, ascetic face dissolve into helpless laughter. His amusement was always at least partially at himself, and this time was no exception. I was totally disarmed.

He wiped his eyes with the handkerchief I had seen poking from his coat pocket; a slight smear of blue paint was transferred to the bridge of his angular nose. He looked at me then, seeing me for the first time. After a minute he gestured at the flowers.

"You know something about bees, then?"

"Very little," I admitted.

"But they interest you?" he suggested.

"No."

This time both eyebrows raised.

"And, pray tell, why such a firm opinion?"

"From what I know of them they are mindless creatures, little more than a tool for putting fruit on trees. The females do all the work; the males do . . . well, they do little. And the queen, the only one who might amount to something, is condemned for the sake of the hive to spend her days as an egg machine. And," I said, warming to the topic, "what happens when her equal comes along, another queen with which she might have something in common? They are both forced— for the good of the hive—to fight to the death. Bees are great workers, it is true, but does not the production of each bee's total lifetime amount to a single dessert-spoonful of honey? Each hive puts up with having hundreds of thousands of bee-hours stolen regularly, to be spread on toast and formed into candles, instead of declaring war or going on strike as any sensible, self-respecting race would do. A bit too close to the human race for my taste."

Mr. Holmes had sat down upon his heels during my tirade, watching a blue spot. When I had finished, he said nothing, but put out one long, thin finger and gently touched the fuzzy body, disturbing it not at all. There was silence for several minutes until the laden bee flew off—northeast, towards the copse two miles away, I was certain. He watched it disappear and murmured almost to himself, "Yes, they are very like *Homo sapiens*. Perhaps that is why they so interest me."

"I don't know how sapient you find most *Homines*, but I for one find the classification an optimistic misnomer." I was on familiar ground now, that of the mind and opinions, a beloved ground I had not trod for many months. That some of the opinions were those of an obnoxious teenager made them none the less comfortable or easy to defend. To my pleasure, he responded.

"*Homo* in general, or simply *vir*?" he asked, with a solemnity that made me suspect that he was laughing at me. Well, at least I had taught him to be subtle with it.

"Oh, no. I am a feminist, but no man hater. A misanthrope in general, I suppose like yourself, sir. However, unlike you I find women to be the marginally more rational half of the race."

He laughed again, a gentler version of the earlier outburst, and I realised that I had been trying to provoke it this time.

"Young lady," he stressed the second word with gentle irony, "you have caused me amusement twice in one day, which is more than anyone else has done in some time. I have little humour to offer in return, but if you would care to accompany me home, I could at least give you a cup of tea."

"I should be very pleased to do so, Mr. Holmes."

"Ah, you have the advantage over me. You obviously know my name, yet there is no one present of whom I might beg an introduction to yourself." The formality of his speech was faintly ludicrous considering that we were two shabby figures facing each other on an otherwise deserted hillside.

"My name is Mary Russell." I held out my hand, which he took in his thin, dry one. We shook as if cementing a peace pact, which I suppose we were.

"Mary," he said, tasting it. He pronounced it in the Irish manner, his mouth caressing the long first syllable. "A suitably orthodox name for such a passive individual as yourself."

"I believe I was named after the Magdalene, rather than the Virgin."

"Ah, that explains it then. Shall we go, Miss Russell? My housekeeper ought to have something to put in front of us."

It was a lovely walk, that, nearly four miles over the downs. We thumbed over a variety of topics strung lightly on the common thread of apiculture. He gestured wildly atop a knoll when comparing the management of hives with Machiavellian theories of government, and cows ran snorting away. He paused in the middle of a stream to illustrate his theory juxtaposing the swarming of hives and the economic roots of war, using examples of the German invasion of France and the visceral patriotism of the English. Our boots squelched for the next mile. He reached the heights of his peroration at the top of a hill and launched himself down the other side at such a speed that he resembled some great flapping thing about to take off.

He stopped to look around for me, took in my stiffening gait and my inability to keep up with him, both literally and metaphorically, and shifted into a less manic mode. He did seem to have a good practical basis for his flights of fancy and, it turned out, had even written a book on the apiary arts entitled A *Practical Handbook of Bee Culture*. It had been well received, he said with pride (this from a man who, I remembered, had respectfully declined a knighthood from the late queen), particularly his experimental but highly successful placement within the hive of what he called the Royal Quarters, which had given the book its provocative subtitle: *With Some Observations Upon the Segregation of the Queen.*

We walked, he talked, and under the sun and his soothing if occasionally incomprehensible monologue I began to feel something hard and tight within me relax slightly, and an urge I had thought killed began to make the first tentative stirrings towards life. When we arrived at his cottage we had known each other forever.

Other more immediate stirrings had begun to assert themselves as well, with increasing insistence. I had taught myself in recent months to ignore hunger, but a healthy young person after a long day in the open air with only a sandwich since morning is likely to find it difficult to concentrate on anything other than the thought of food. I prayed that the cup of tea would be a substantial one, and was considering the problem of how to suggest such a thing should it not be immediately offered, when we reached his house, and the housekeeper herself appeared at the door, and for a moment I forgot my preoccupation. It was none other than the long-suffering Mrs. Hudson, whom I had long considered the most underrated figure in all of Dr. Watson's stories. Yet another example of the man's obtuseness, this inability to know a gem unless it be set in gaudy gold.

Dear Mrs. Hudson, who was to become such a friend to me. At that first meeting she was, as always, imperturbable. She saw in an instant what her employer did not, that I was desperately hungry, and proceeded to empty her stores of food to feed a vigorous appetite. Mr. Holmes protested as she appeared with plate after platter of bread, cheeses, relishes, and cakes, but watched thoughtfully as I put large dents in every selection. I was grateful that he did not embarrass me by commenting on my appetite, as my aunt was wont to do, but to the contrary he made an effort to keep up the appearance of eating with me. By the time I sat back with my third cup of tea, the inner woman satisfied as she had not been for many weeks, his manner was respectful, and that of Mrs. Hudson contented as she cleared away the débris.

"I thank you very much, Madam," I told her.

"I like to see my cooking appreciated, I do," she said, not looking at Mr. Holmes. "I rarely have the chance to fuss, unless Dr. Watson comes. This one," she inclined her head to the man opposite me, who had brought out a pipe from his coat pocket, "he doesn't eat enough to keep a cat from starving. Doesn't appreciate me at all, he doesn't."

"Now, Mrs. Hudson," he protested, but gently, as at an old argument, "I eat as I always have; it is you who will cook as if there were a household of ten."

"A cat would starve," she repeated firmly. "But you have eaten something today, I'm glad to see. If you've finished, Will wants a word with you before he goes, something about the far hedge."

"I care not a jot for the far hedge," he complained. "I pay him a great deal to fret about the hedges and the walls and the rest of it for me."

"He needs a word with you," she said again. Firm repetition seemed her preferred method of dealing with him, I noted.

"Oh, blast! Why did I ever leave London? I ought to have put my hives in an allotment and stayed in Baker Street. Help yourself to the bookshelves, Miss Russell. I'll be back in a few minutes." He snatched up his tobacco and matches and stalked out, Mrs. Hudson rolled her eyes and disappeared into the kitchen, and I found myself alone in the quiet room.

Sherlock Holmes' house was a typical ageless Sussex cottage, flint walls and red tile roof. This main room, on the ground floor, had once been two rooms, but was now a large square with a huge stone fireplace at one end, dark, high beams, an oak floor that gave way to slate through the kitchen door, and a surprising expanse of windows on the south side where the downs rolled on to the sea. A sofa, two wing chairs, and a frayed basket chair gathered around the fireplace, a round table and four chairs occupied the sunny south bay window (where I sat), and a work desk piled high with papers and objects stood beneath a leaded, diamond-paned window in the west: a room of many purposes. The walls were solid with bookshelves and cupboards.

Today I was more interested in my host than in his books, and I looked curiously at the titles (*Blood Flukes of Borneo* sat between *The Thought of Goethe* and *Crimes of Passion in Eighteenth-Century Italy*) with him in mind rather than with an eye to borrowing. I made a circuit of the room (tobacco still in a Persian slipper at the fireplace, I smiled to see; on one table a small crate stencilled LIMÓNES DE ESPAÑA and containing several disassembled revolvers; on another table three nearly identical pocket watches laid with great precision, chains and fobs stretched out in parallel lines, with a powerful magnifying glass, a set of calipers, and a paper and pad covered with figures to one side) before ending up in front of his desk.

I had no time for more than a cursory glance at his neat handwriting before his voice startled me from the door.

"Shall we sit out on the terrace?"

I quickly put down the sheet in my hand, which seemed to be a discourse on seven formulae for plaster and their relative effectiveness in recording tyre marks from different kinds of earth, and agreed that it would be pleasant in the garden. We took up our cups, but as I followed him across the room towards the French doors my attention was drawn by an odd object fixed to the room's south wall: a tall box, only a few inches wide but nearly three feet tall and protruding a good eighteen inches into the room. It appeared to be a solid block of wood but, pausing to examine it, I could see that both sides were sliding panels.

"My observation hive," Mr. Holmes said.

"Bees?" I exclaimed. "Inside the house?"

Instead of answering he reached past me and slid back one of the side panels, and revealed there a perfect, thin, glass-fronted beehive. I squatted before it, entranced. The comb was thick and even across the middle portion, trailed off at the edges, and was covered by a thick blanket of orange and black. The whole was vibrating with energy, though the individuals seemed to be simply milling about, without purpose.

I watched closely, trying to make sense of their apparently aimless motion. A tube led in at the bottom, with pollen-laden bees coming in and denuded bees going out; a smaller tube at the top, clouded with condensation, I assumed was for ventilation.

"Do you see the queen?" Mr. Holmes asked.

"She's here? Let me see if I can find her." I knew that the queen was the largest bee in the hive, and that wherever she went she had a fawning entourage, but it still took me an embarrassingly long time to pick her out from her two hundred or so daughters and sons. Finally I found her, and couldn't imagine why she had not appeared instantly. Twice the size of the others and imbued with dumb, bristling purpose, she seemed a creature of another race from her hive mates. I asked their keeper a few questions—did they object to the light, was the population as steady here as in a larger hive—and then he slid the cover over the living painting and we went outside. I remembered belatedly that I was not interested in bees.

Outside the French doors lay an expanse of flagstones, sheltered from the wind by a glass conservatory that grew off the kitchen wall and by an old stone wall with herbaceous border that curved around the remaining two sides. The terrace gathered in the heat until its air danced, and I was relieved when he continued down to a group of comfortable-looking wooden chairs in the shade of an enormous copper beech. I chose a chair that looked down towards the Channel, over the head of a small orchard that lay in a hollow below us. There were tidy hive boxes arranged among the trees and bees working the early flowers of the border. A bird sang. Two men's voices came and receded along the other side of the wall. Dishes rattled distantly from the kitchen. A small fishing boat appeared on the horizon and gradually worked its way towards us.

I suddenly came to myself with the realisation that I was neglecting my conversational responsibilities as a guest. I moved my cold tea from the arm of my chair to the table and turned to my host.

"Is this your handiwork?" I asked, indicating the garden.

He smiled ironically, though whether at the doubt in my voice or at the social impulse that drove me to break the silence, I was not certain.

"No, it is a collaboration on the part of Mrs. Hudson and old Will Thompson, who used to be head gardener at the manor. I took an interest in gardening when I first came here, but my work tends to distract me for days on end. I would reappear to find whole beds dead of drought or buried in bramble. But Mrs. Hudson enjoys it, and it gives her something to do other than pester me to eat her concoctions. I find it a pleasant spot to sit and think. It also feeds my bees—most of the flowers are chosen because of the quality of honey they produce."

"It is a very pleasant spot. It reminds me of a garden we once had when I was small."

"Tell me about yourself, Miss Russell."

I started to give him the obligatory response, first the demurral and then the reluctant flat autobiography, but some slight air of polite inattention in his manner stopped me. Instead, I found myself grinning at him.

"Why don't you tell me about myself, Mr. Holmes?"

"Aha, a challenge, eh?" There was a flare of interest in his eyes.

"Exactly."

"Very well, on two conditions. First, that you forgive my old and much-abused brain if it is slow and creaking, for such thought patterns as I once lived by are a habit and become rusty without continual use. Daily life here with Mrs. Hudson and Will is a poor whetting stone for sharp wit."

"I don't entirely believe that your brain is underused, but I grant the condition. And the other?"

"That you do the same for me when I have finished with you."

"Oh. All right. I shall try, even if I lay myself open to your ridicule." Perhaps I had not escaped the edge of his tongue after all.

"Good." He rubbed his thin dry hands together, and suddenly I was fixed with the probing eye of an entomologist. "I see before me one Mary Russell, named after her paternal grandmother."

I was taken aback for a moment, then reached up and fingered the antique locket, engraved MMR, that had slipped out from the buttons of my shirt. I nodded.

"She is, let us see, sixteen? Fifteen, I think? Yes, fifteen years of age, and despite her youth and the fact that she is not at school she intends to pass the University entrance examinations." I touched the book in my pocket and nodded appreciatively. "She is obviously left-handed, one of her parents was Jewish—her mother, I think? Yes, definitely the mother—and she reads and writes Hebrew. She is at present four inches shorter than her American father—that was his suit? All right so far?" he asked complacently.

I thought furiously. "The Hebrew?" I asked.

"The ink marks on your fingers could only come with writing right to left."

"Of course." I looked at the accumulation of smears near my left thumbnail. "That is very impressive."

He waved it aside. "Parlour games. But the accents are not without interest." He eyed me again, then sat back with his elbows on the chair's armrests, steepled his fingers, rested them lightly on his lips for a moment, closed his eyes, and spoke.

"The accents. She has come recently from her father's home in the western United States, most likely northern California. Her mother was one generation away from Cockney Jew, and Miss Russell herself grew up in the southwestern edges of London. She moved, as I said, to California, within the last, oh, two years. Say the word 'martyr,' please." I did so. "Yes, two years. Sometime between then and December both parents died, very possibly in the same accident in which Miss Russell was involved last September or October, an accident which has left scar tissue on her throat, scalp, and right hand, a residual weakness in that same hand, and a slight stiffness in the left knee."

The game had suddenly stopped being entertaining. I sat frozen, my heart ceasing to beat while I listened to the cool, dry recitation of his voice.

"After her recovery she was sent back home to her mother's family, to a tight-fisted and unsympathetic relative who feeds her rather less than she needs. This last," he added parenthetically, "is I admit largely conjecture, but as a working hypothesis serves to explain her well-nourished frame poorly covered by flesh, and the reason why she appears at a stranger's table to consume somewhat more than she might if ruled strictly by her obvious good manners. I am willing to consider an alternative explanation," he offered, and opened his eyes, and saw my face.

"Oh, dear." His voice was an odd mixture of sympathy and irritation. "I have been warned about this tendency of mine. I do apologise for any distress I have caused you."

I shook my head and reached for the cold dregs in my teacup. It was difficult to speak through the lump in my throat.

Mr. Holmes stood up and went into the house, where I heard his voice and that of the housekeeper trading a few unintelligible phrases before he returned, carrying two delicate glasses and an open bottle of the palest of wines. He poured it into the glasses and handed me one, identifying it as honey wine—his own, of course. He sat down and we both sipped the fragrant liquor. In a few minutes the lump faded, and I heard the birds again. I took a deep breath and shot him a glance.

"Two hundred years ago you would have been burnt." I was trying for dry humour but was not entirely successful.

"I have been told that before today," he said, "though I cannot say I have ever fancied myself in the rôle of a witch, cackling over my pot."

"Actually, the book of Leviticus calls not for burning, but for the stoning of a man or a woman who speaks with the spirits—*iob*, a necromancer or medium—or who is a *yidōni*, from the verb 'to know,' a person who achieves knowledge and power other than through the grace of the Lord God of Israel, er, well, a sorcerer." My voice trailed off as I realised that he was eyeing me with the apprehension normally reserved for mumbling strangers in one's railway compartment or acquaintances with incomprehensible and tiresome passions. My recitation had been an automatic response, triggered by the entry of a theological point into our discussion. I smiled a weak reassurance. He cleared his throat.

"Er, shall I finish?" he asked.

"As you wish," I said, with trepidation.

"This young lady's parents were relatively well-to-do, and their daughter inherited, which, combined with her daunting intelligence, makes it impossible for this penurious relative to bring her to heel. Hence, she wanders the downs without a chaperone and remains away until all hours."

He seemed to be drawing to a close, so I gathered my tattered thoughts.

"You are quite right, Mr. Holmes. I have inherited, and my aunt does find my actions contrary to her idea of how a young lady should act. And because she holds the keys to the pantry and tries to buy my obedience with food, I occasionally go with less than I would choose. Two minor flaws in your reasoning, however."

"Oh?"

"First, I did not come to Sussex to live with my aunt. The house and farm belonged to my mother. We used to spend summers here when I was small—some of the happiest times of my life—and when I was sent back to England I made it a condition of accepting her as guardian that we live here. She had no house, so she reluctantly agreed. Although she will control the finances for another six years, strictly speaking *she* lives with *me*, not I with her." Another might have missed the loathing in my voice, but not he. I dropped the subject quickly before I gave away any more of my life. "Second, I have been carefully judging the time by which I must depart in order to arrive home before dark, so the lateness of the hour does not really enter in. I shall have to take my leave soon, as it will be dark in slightly over two hours, and my home is two miles north of where we met."

"Miss Russell, you may take your time with your half of our agreement," he said calmly, allowing me to shelve the previous topic. "One of my neighbours subsidises his passion for automobiles by providing what he insists on calling a taxi service. Mrs. Hudson has gone to arrange for him to motor you home. You may rest for another hour and a quarter before he arrives to whisk you off to the arms of your dear aunt."

I looked down, discomfitted. "Mr. Holmes, I'm afraid my allowance is not large enough to allow for such luxuries. In fact, I have already spent this week's monies on the Virgil."

"Miss Russell, I am a man with considerable funds and very little to spend them on. Please allow me to indulge in a whim."

"No, I cannot do that." He looked at my face and gave in.

"Very well, then, I propose a compromise. I shall pay for this and any subsequent expenses of the sort, but as a loan. I assume that your future inheritance will be sufficient to absorb such an accumulation of sums?"

"Oh, yes." I laughed as I recalled vividly the scene in the law office, my aunt's eyes turning dark with greed. "There would be no problem." He glanced at me sharply, hesitated, and spoke with some delicacy.

"Miss Russell, forgive my intrusion, but I tend towards a rather dim view of human nature. If I might enquire as to your will . . . ?" A mind reader, with a solid grasp of the basics of life. I smiled grimly.

"In the event of my death my aunt would get only an adequate yearly amount. Hardly more than she gets now."

He looked relieved. "I see. Now, about the loan. Your feet will suffer if you insist on walking the distance home in those shoes. At least for today, use the taxi. I am even willing to charge you interest if you like."

There was an odd air about his final, ironic offer that in another, less self-possessed person might have verged on a plea. We sat and studied each other, there in the quiet garden of early evening, and it occurred to me that he might have found this yapping dog an appealing companion. It could even be the beginnings of affection I saw in his face, and God knows that the joy of finding as quick and uncluttered a mind as his had begun to sing in me. We made an odd pair, a gangling, bespectacled girl and a tall, sardonic recluse, blessed or cursed with minds of hard brilliance that alienated all but the most tenacious. It never occurred to me that there might not be subsequent visits to this household. I spoke, and acknowledged his oblique offer of friendship.

"Spending three or four hours a day in travel does leave little time for other things. I accept your offer of a loan. Shall Mrs. Hudson keep the record?"

"She is scrupulously careful with figures, unlike myself. Come, have another glass of my wine, and tell Sherlock Holmes about himself."

"Are you finished, then?"

"Other than obvious things such as the shoes and reading late by inadequate light, that you have few bad habits, though your father smoked, and that unlike most Americans he preferred quality to fashion in his clothing—other than the obvious things, I will rest for the moment. It is your move. But mind you, I want to hear from you, not what you have picked up from my enthusiastic friend Watson."

"I shall try to avoid borrowing his incisive observations," I said drily, "though I have to wonder if using the stories to write your biography wouldn't prove to be a two-edged sword. The illustrations are certainly deceptive; they make you look considerably older. I'm not very good at guessing ages, but you don't look much more than, what, fifty? Oh, I'm sorry. Some people don't like to talk about their age."

"I am now fifty-four. Conan Doyle and his accomplices at *The Strand* thought to make me more dignified by exaggerating my age. Youth does not inspire confidence, in life or in stories, as I found to my annoyance when I set up residence in Baker Street. I was not yet twenty-one, and at first found the cases few and far between. Incidentally, I hope you do not make a habit of guessing. Guessing is a weakness brought on by indolence and should never be confused with intuition."

"I will keep that in mind," I said, and reached for my glass to take a swallow of wine while thinking about what I had seen in the room. I assembled my words with care. "To begin: You come from a moderately wealthy background, though your relationship with your parents was not entirely a happy one. To this day you wonder about them and try to come to grips with that part of your past." To his raised eyebrow I explained, "That is why you keep the much-handled formal photograph of your family on the shelf close to your chair, slightly obscured to other eyes by books, rather than openly mounting it on the wall and forgetting them." Ah, how sweet was the pleasure of seeing the look of appreciation spread over his face and hearing his murmured phrase, "Very good, very good indeed." It was like coming home.

"I could add that it explains why you never spoke to Dr. Watson about your childhood, as someone so solid and from such a blatantly normal background as he is would doubtless have difficulty understanding the special burdens of a gifted mind. However, that would be using his words, or rather lack of them, so it doesn't count. Without being too prying, I should venture to say that it contributed to your early decision to distance yourself from women, for I suspect that someone such as yourself would find it impossible to have an other than all-inclusive relationship with a woman, one that totally integrated all parts of your lives, unlike the unequal and somewhat whimsical part-nership you have had with Dr. Watson." The expression on his face was indescribable, wandering between amusement and affrontery, with a touch each of anger and exasperation. It finally settled on the quizzical. I felt considerably better about the casual hurt he had done me, and plunged on.

"However, as I said, I don't mean to intrude on your privacy. It was necessary to have the past as it contributes to the present. You are here to escape the disagreeable sensation of being surrounded by inferior minds, minds that can never understand because they are just not built that way. You took a remarkably early retirement twelve years ago, apparently in order to study the perfection and unity of bees and to work on your magnum opus on detection. I see from the bookshelf near your writing desk that you have completed seven volumes to date, and I presume, from the boxes of notes under the completed books, that there are at least an equal number yet to be written up." He nod-ded and poured us both more wine. The bottle was nearly empty.

"Between yourself and Dr. Watson, however, you have left me with little to deduce. I could hardly assume that you would leave behind your chemical experiments, for example, though the state of your cuffs does indicate that you have been active recently—those acid burns are too fresh to have frayed much in the wash. You no longer smoke ciga-rettes, your fingers show, though obviously your pipe is used often, and the calluses on your fingertips indicate that you have kept up with the violin. You seem to be as unconcerned about bee stings as you are about finances and gardening, for your skin shows the marks of stings both old and new, and your suppleness indicates that the theories about bee stings as a therapy for rheumatism have some basis. Or is it arthritis?"

"Rheumatism, in my case."

"Also, I think it possible that you have not entirely given up your former life, or perhaps it has not entirely given you up. I see a vague area of pale skin on your chin, which shows that some time last summer you had a goatee, since shaven off. There hasn't been enough sun yet to erase the line completely. As you don't normally wear a beard, and would, in my opinion, look unpleasant with one, I can assume it was for the purpose of a disguise, in a rôle which lasted some months. Probably it had to do with the early stages of the war. Spying against the Kaiser, I should venture to say."

His face went blank, and he studied me without any trace of expression for a long minute. I squelched a self-conscious smile. At last he spoke.

"I did ask for it, did I not? Are you familiar with the work of Dr. Sigmund Freud?"

"Yes, although I find the work of the next, as it were, generation more helpful. Freud is overly obsessed with exceptional behavior: an aid to your line of work, perhaps, but not as useful for a generalist."

There was a sudden commotion in the flower bed. Two orange cats shot out and raced along the lawn and disappeared through the opening in the garden wall. His eyes followed them, and he sat squinting into the low sun.

"Twenty years ago," he murmured. "Even ten. But here? Now?" He shook his head and focussed again on me. "What will you read at University?"

I smiled. I couldn't help it; I knew just how he was going to react, and I smiled, anticipating his dismay.

"Theology."

His reaction was as violent as I had known it would be, but if I was sure of anything in my life, it was that. We took a walk through the gloaming to the cliffs, and I had my look at the sea while he wrestled with the idea, and by the time we returned he had decided that it was no worse than anything else, though he considered it a waste, and said so. I did not respond.

The automobile arrived shortly thereafter, and Mrs. Hudson came out to pay for it. Holmes explained our agreement, to her amusement, and she promised to make a note of it.

"I have an experiment to finish tonight, so you must pardon me," he said, though it did not take many visits before I knew that he disliked saying good-bye. I put out my hand and nearly snatched it back when he raised it to his lips rather than shaking it as he had before. He held on to it, brushed it with his cool lips, and let it go.

"Please come to see us anytime you wish. We are on the telephone, by the way. Ask the exchange for Mrs. Hudson, though; the good ladies sometimes decide to protect me by pretending ignorance, but they will usually permit calls to go through to her." With a nod he began to turn away, but I interrupted his exit.

"Mr. Holmes," I said, feeling myself go pink, "may I ask you a question?"

"Certainly, Miss Russell."

"How does *The Valley of Fear* end?" I blurted out.

"The *what?*" He sounded astonished.

"*Valley of Fear.* In *The Strand.* I hate these serials, and next month is the end of it, but I just wondered if you could tell me, well, how it turned out."

"This is one of Watson's tales, I take it?"

"Of course. It's the case of Birlstone and the Scowrers and John McMurdo and Professor Moriarty and—"

"Yes, I believe I can identify the case, although I have often wondered why, if Conan Doyle so likes pseudonyms, he couldn't have given them to Watson and myself as well."

"So how did it end?"

"I haven't the faintest notion. You would have to ask Watson."

"But surely you know how the case ended," I said, amazed.

"The case, certainly. But what Watson has made of it, I couldn't begin to guess, except that there is bound to be gore and passion and secret handshakes. Oh, and some sort of love interest. I deduce, Miss Russell; Watson transforms. Good day." He went back into the cottage.

Mrs. Hudson, who had stood listening to the exchange, did not comment, but pressed a package into my hands, "for the trip back," although from the weight of it the eating would take longer than the driving, even if I were to find the interior space for it. However, if I could get it past my aunt's eyes it would make a welcome supplement to my rations. I thanked her warmly.

"Thank you for coming here, dear child," she said. "There's more life in him than I've seen for a good many months. Please come again, and soon?"

I promised, and climbed into the car. The driver spun off in a rattle of gravel, and so began my long association with Mr. Sherlock Holmes.

I FIND IT necessary to interrupt my narrative and say a few words concerning an individual whom I had wanted to omit entirely. I find, however, that her total absence grants her undue emphasis by the vacuum it creates. I speak of my aunt.

For just under seven years, from the time my parents were killed until my twenty-first birthday, she lived in my house, spent my money, managed my life, limited my freedom, and tried her worst to control me. Twice during that time I had to appeal to the executors of my parents' estate, and both times won both my case and her vindictive animosity. I do not know precisely how much of my parents' money she took from me, but I do know that she purchased a terrace house in London after she left me, though she came to me nearly penniless. I let her know that I considered it payment for her years of service, and left it. I did not go to her funeral some years later and arranged for the house to go to a poor cousin.

Mostly I ignored her while she lived with me, which maddened her further. She was, I think, gifted enough herself to recognise greatness in others, but instead of rejoicing generously she tried to bring her superior down to her own level. A twisted person, very sad, really, but my sympathy for her has been taken from me by her actions. I shall, therefore, continue to ignore her by leaving her out of my account whenever possible. It is my revenge.

It was only in my association with Holmes that her interference troubled me. It became apparent in the following weeks that I had found something I valued and, what was worse in her eyes, it offered me a life and a freedom away from her. I freely used my loan privileges with Mrs. Hudson and had run up a considerable debt by the time I came into my majority. (Incidentally, my first act at the law offices was to draw up a cheque for the amount I owed the Holmes household, with five percent more for Mrs. Hudson. I don't know if she gave it to charity or to the gardener, but she took it. Eventually.)

My aunt's chief weapon against my hours with Holmes was the threat to stir up talk and rumours in the community, which even I had to admit would have been inconvenient. About once a year this would come up, subtle threats would give way to blatant ones, until finally I would have to counterattack, usually by blackmail or bribery. Once I was forced to ask Holmes to produce evidence that he was still too highly regarded, despite having been purportedly retired for over a decade, for any official to believe her low gossip. The letter that reached her, and particularly the address from which it had been written, silenced her for eighteen months. The entire campaign reached its head when I proposed to accompany Holmes to the Continent for six weeks. She would very likely have succeeded in, if not preventing my going, at least delaying me inconveniently. By that time, however, I had traced her bank account, and I had no further trouble from her before my twenty-first birthday.

So much for my mother's only sister. I shall leave her here, frustrated and unnamed, and hope she does not intrude further on my narrative.

❊ 2 ❊

The Sorcerer's Apprentice

One came hither, to the school of the bees, to be taught the
preoccupations of all-powerful nature . . . and the lesson of
ardent and disinterested work; and another lesson too . . . to
enjoy the almost unspeakable delights of those immaculate
days that revolved on themselves in the fields of space,
forming merely a transparent globe, as void of
memory as the happiness without alloy.

THREE MONTHS AFTER my fifteenth birthday Sherlock
Holmes entered my life, to become my foremost friend, tutor,
substitute father, and eventually confidant. Never a week passed
when I did not spend at least one day in his house, and often I would
be there three or four days running when I was helping him with
some experiment or project. Looking back, I can admit to myself
that even with my parents I had never been so happy, and not even
with my father, who had been a most brilliant man, had my mind
found so comfortable a fit, so smooth a mesh. By our second meeting
we had dropped "Mr." and "Miss." After some years we came to end
the other's sentences, even to answer an unasked question—but I get
ahead of myself.

In those first weeks of spring I was like some tropical seed upon which was poured water and warmth. I blossomed, my body under the care of Mrs. Hudson and my mind under the care of this odd man, who had left behind the thrill of the chase in London and come to the quietest of country homes to raise bees, write his books, and, perhaps, to meet me. I do not know what fates put us less than ten miles from each other. I do know that I have never, in all my travels, met a mind like Holmes'. Nor has he, he says, met my equal. Had I not found him, had my aunt's authority been uncontested, I could easily have become twisted like her. I am fairly certain that my own influence on Holmes was also not inconsiderable. He was stagnating—yes, even he—and would probably have bored or drugged himself into an early death. My presence, my—I will say it—my love, gave him a purpose in life from that first day.

If Holmes slid into the niche my father had occupied, then I suppose one could say that dear Mrs. Hudson became my new mother. Not, of course, that there was anything between the two of them other than the strictest housekeeper-employer relationship, tempered by a long-standing camaraderie. Nonetheless, mother she was and I a daughter to her. She had a son in Australia who wrote dutifully every month, but I was her only daughter. She fed me until my frame filled out (I never did become voluptuous, but my shape was quite fashionable for the twenties.) and I went up another two inches that first year, one and one-half the second year, to a total of one inch short of six feet. I became comfortable with my height eventually, but for years I was incredibly clumsy and a real hazard around knickknacks. It was not until I went away to Oxford that Holmes arranged for lessons in an Oriental form of manual defence (most unladylike: at first only the teacher would work with me!), which brought my various limbs under control. Mrs. Hudson, needless to say, would have preferred ballet lessons.

Mrs. Hudson's presence in the house made possible my visits to the solitary man who lived there, but she was considerably more than a mere nod to propriety. From her I learnt to garden, to sew on a button, to cook a simple meal. She also taught me that being womanly was not necessarily incompatible with being a mind. It was she, rather than my aunt, who taught me the workings of the female body (in words other than the anatomy textbooks I had previously depended upon, which concealed and obfuscated rather than clarified). It was she who took me to the London dressmakers and hairdressers so that when I came home from Oxford on my eighteenth birthday I could inflict on Holmes a case of apoplexy with my appearance. I was very glad for the presence of Dr. Watson on that occasion. Had I killed Holmes with my dressing up I should surely have thrown myself into the Isis by the end of term.

Which brings me to Watson, a sweet bumbly man whom I came to call, to his immense pleasure, Uncle John. I was quite prepared to detest him. How could anyone work so long with Holmes and learn so little? I thought. How could an apparently intelligent man so consistently fail to grasp the point? How *could* he be so *stupid?* my teenaged mind railed at him. Worst of all, he made it appear that Holmes, *my* Holmes, kept him near for one of two purposes: to carry a revolver (though Holmes himself was a crack shot) or to act dense and make the detective appear even more brilliant by contrast. What did Holmes see in this, this buffoon? Oh, yes, I was ready to hate him, to destroy him with my scathing tongue. Only it didn't work out that way.

I arrived unannounced at Holmes' door one day in early September. The first storm of autumn had knocked out the telephone exchange in the village, so I could not ring ahead to say that I was coming, as I usually did. The road was a muddy mess, so rather than use the bicycle I had bought (with Mrs. Hudson's loan account, of course) I put on my high boots and set off across the downs. The sun came out as I walked the sodden hills, and the heat soared. As a result I left my muddy boots outside the door and let myself in through the kitchen, spattered with mud and dripping with sweat from the humidity and the wrong clothing.

Mrs. Hudson was not in the kitchen, a bit odd for that early in the day, but I heard low voices from the main room. Not Holmes, another man, rural tones heavily overlaid with London. A neighbour, perhaps, or a house guest.

"Good morning, Mrs. Hudson," I called out softly, figuring that Holmes was still asleep. He often was in the mornings, as he kept odd hours—sleep was a concern of the body and of convenience, he declared, not of the clock. I went into the scullery and pumped water into the sink to wash my sweaty face and dirty hands and arms, but when my fingers groped for the towel they found the rail empty. As I patted about in blind irritation I heard a movement in the scullery doorway and the missing towel was pressed into my hand. I seized it and put my face into it.

"Thank you, Mrs. Hudson," I said into the cloth. "I heard you talking with someone. Is this a bad time to come?" When no answer came I looked up and saw a portly, moustachioed figure in the doorway, smiling radiantly. Even without my spectacles I knew instantly who it was and concealed my wariness. "Dr. Watson, I perceive?" I dried my hands and we shook. He held on to mine for a moment, beaming into my face.

"He was right. You are lovely."

This confused me to no end. Who on earth was "he"? Surely not Holmes. And "lovely"? Stinking of sweat, in mismatched wool stockings with holes in both toes, hair straggling and one leg mud to the knee—lovely?

I extricated my hand, found my glasses on the sideboard, put them on, and his round face came into focus. He was looking at me with such complete, unaffected pleasure that I simply could not think what to do, so I just stood there. Stupidly.

"Miss Russell, I am so very happy to meet you at last. I will speak quickly because I think Holmes is about to arise. I wanted to thank you, from the bottom of my heart, for what you have done for my friend in the last few months. Had I read it in a casebook I would not have believed it, but I see and believe."

"You see what?" I said. Stupidly. Like a buffoon.

"I'm sure you knew that he was ill, though not perhaps how ill. I watched him and despaired, for I knew that at that rate he would not see a second summer, possibly not even the new year. But since May he has put on half a stone, his heartbeat is strong, his colour good, and Mrs. Hudson says he sleeps—irregularly, as always, but he sleeps. He says he has even given up the cocaine to which he was rapidly becoming addicted—given it up. I believe him. And I thank you, with all my soul, for you have done what my skills could not, and brought back my truest friend from the grave."

I stood there struck dumb with confusion. Holmes, ill? He had looked thin and grey when we first met, but dying? A sardonic voice from the next room made us both start guiltily.

"Oh come now, Watson, don't frighten the child with your exaggerated worries." Holmes came to the doorway in his mouse-coloured robe. "'From the grave' indeed. Overworked, perhaps, but one foot in the grave, hardly. I admit that Russell has helped me relax, and God knows I eat more when she is here, but it is little more than that. I'll not have you worrying the child that she's in any way responsible for me, do you hear, Watson?"

The face that turned towards me was so stricken with guilt that I felt the last of my wish to dislike him dissolve, and I began to laugh.

"But, I only wished to thank her—"

"Very well, you've thanked her. Now let us have our tea while Mrs. Hudson finds some breakfast for us. Death and resurrection," he snorted. "Ridiculous!"

I enjoyed that day, although at times it gave me the feeling of opening a book halfway through and trying to reconstruct what had gone before. Previously unknown characters meandered in and out of the conversation, place-names referred in shorthand to whole adventures, and, overall, the long years of a constructed relationship stood before me, an intricate edifice previously unseen. It was the sort of situation in which a third party, namely myself, could have easily felt awkward and outdistanced, but oddly enough I did not. I think it was because I was so very secure in my knowledge of the building Holmes and I had already begun. Even in the few weeks I had known him we had come far, and I no longer had any fear of Watson and what he represented. Watson, for his part, never feared or resented me. Before that day I would have scornfully said he was too dim-witted to see me as a threat. By the afternoon I knew that it was because his heart was too large to exclude anything concerning Holmes.

The day went quickly, and I enjoyed being an addition to the trio of old friends, Holmes, Watson, and Mrs. Hudson. When Watson went off after supper to gather his things for the evening train to London, I sat down beside Holmes, feeling a vague need to apologise to somebody.

"I suppose you know I was prepared to hate him," I said finally.

"Oh yes."

"I can see why you kept him near you. He's so . . . good, somehow. Naïve, yes, and he doesn't seem terribly bright, but when I think of all the ugliness and evil and pain he's known . . . It's polished him, hasn't it? Purified him."

"Polished is a good image. Seeing myself reflected in Watson's eyes was useful when contemplating a case that was giving me problems. He taught me a great deal about how humans function, what drives them. He keeps me humble, does Watson." He caught my dubious look. "At any rate, as humble as I can be."

THUS MY LIFE began again, in that summer of 1915. I was to spend the first years of the war under Holmes' tutelage, although it was some time before I became aware that I was not just visiting a friend, that I was actually being taught by Holmes, that I was receiving, not casual lessons in a variety of odd and entertaining areas, but careful instruction by a professional in his area of considerable expertise. I did not think of myself as a detective; I was a student of theology, and I was to spend my life in exploration, not of the darker crannies of human misbehaviour, but of the heights of human speculation concerning the nature of the Divine. That the two were not unrelated did not occur to me for years.

My apprenticeship began, on my part, without any conscious recognition of that state. I thought it was the same with Holmes, that he began by humouring this odd neighbour for lack of anything more demanding at hand, and ended up with a fully trained detective, until some years later I recalled that odd statement he had made in his garden on our very first day: "Twenty years ago," he had muttered. "Even ten. But here? Now?" I did ask him, but of course he said that he had seen it within the first minutes. However, Holmes has always thought of himself as omniscient, so I cannot trust him on it.

On the face of things it would have been extremely unlikely for a proper gentleman such as Holmes to take on a young woman as pupil, much less apprentice her to his arcane trade. Twenty years before, with Victoria on the throne, an alliance such as Holmes and I forged— close, underchaperoned, and not even rendered safe by the bonds of blood—would have been unthinkable. Even ten years before, under Edward, ripples of shock would have run through the rural community and made our lives difficult.

This was, however, 1915, and if the better classes clasped to themselves a semblance of the old order, it did little more than obscure the chaos beneath their feet. During the war the very fabric of English society was picked apart and rewoven. Necessity dictated that women work outside the home, be it their own or that of their employers, and so women put on men's boots and took control of trams and breweries, factories and fields. Upper-class women signed on for long stretches nursing in the mud and gore of France or, for a lark, put on smocks and gaiters and became Land Girls during the harvest. The harsh demands of king and country and the constant anxieties over the fighting men reduced the rules of chaperonage to a minimum; people simply had no energy to spare for the proprieties.

Mrs. Hudson's presence in the cottage made my long hours with Holmes possible. My parents being dead and my aunt caring little for my actions, as long as they did not intrude on hers: that too made it possible. Rural life conspired as well, for rural society, though rigid, recognises a true gentleman when it sees one, and the farmers trusted Holmes in a way that town-dwellers would never have done. There may have been gossip, but I rarely heard of it.

Looking back, I think that the largest barrier to our association was Holmes himself, that inborn part of him that spoke the language of social customs, and particularly that portion of his makeup that saw women as some tribe of foreign and not-entirely-trustworthy exotics. Again, events conspired. Holmes was, after all, unconventional if not outright bohemian in his acquaintances and in his business dealings. His friendships ran the social spectrum, from the younger son of a duke through the staid and conventional Dr. Watson to a Whitechapel pawnbroker, and his profession brought him into contact with kings, and sewer-men, and ladies of uncertain virtue. He did not even consider lesser criminal activities any bar to social and professional relationships, as his ongoing fellowship with some of the shadier Irregulars of his Baker Street days would illustrate. Even Mrs. Hudson had originally come into his purview through a murder case (that written up by Dr. Watson as "Gloria Scott").

Perhaps, too, there is some truth in the immutability of first impressions. I know that from that first day he tended to treat me more as a lad than as a girl and seemed in fact to solve any discomfort my sex might cause him by simply ignoring it: I was Russell, not some female, and if necessity required our spending time alone together, even spending the night without escort, then that is what we would do. First and foremost a pragmatist, he had no time for the interference of unnecessary standards.

As with Watson before me, we met by accident, and I too became a habit. My attitudes, my choice of clothing, even the shape of my body combined to protect him from having to acknowledge my nature. By the time I grew into womanhood, I was a part of his life, and it was too late for him to change.

In those early days, though, I had no inkling of what was to be. I simply adopted the habit of dropping by his cottage every few days on my walks, and we would talk. Or, he would show me an experiment he was working on, and we would both see that I lacked the background to comprehend fully the problem, so he would load me with books and I would take them home, returning when I had finished. Sometimes I would arrive to find him at his desk, pawing through stacks of notes and scribbles, and he would gratefully break off to read me what he had been writing. Questions would follow, and more books.

We spent much time touring the countryside, in sun, rain, or snow, following footprints, comparing samples of mud, noting how the type of soil affected the quality and longevity of a footprint or hoofmark. Every neighbour within ten miles was visited by us at least once, as we studied the hands of the dairy farmer and the woodsman, comparing their calluses and the musculature in their arms and, if they allowed it, their backs. We were a common sight on the roads, the tall, thin, grey man with his cloth cap beside the lanky blonde-plaited girl, heads together, deep in conversation or bent over some object. The farmers waved to us cheerily from their fields, and even the residents of the manor house hooted their horn as they flew past in their Rolls.

In the autumn Holmes began to devise puzzles for me. As the rain fell and the short hours of daylight cut into our time of walking the downs, as men died in the trenches in Europe and zeppelins dropped bombs on London, we played games. Chess was one of them, of course, but there were others as well, exercises in detecting and analysing material. He began by giving me descriptions of some of his cases and asking me to solve them from his collected facts. Once, the case was not from his files but compiled from newspapers, a murder investigation currently under way in London. I found that one frustrating, as the facts presented were never complete or carefully enough gathered to be workable, but the man I chose as the best candidate for guilty party was eventually charged and confessed, so it turned out all right.

One day I came to his farm on a prearranged visit, to find a note pinned to the back door, which said merely:

R,
Find me.
—H.

I knew immediately that a random search was not what he had in mind, so I took the note to Mrs. Hudson, who shook her head as if at the play of children.

"Do you know what this is about?" I asked her.

"No, I don't. If I ever understand that man, I'll retire in glory. I'm down on my knees this morning, cleaning the floor, when up he comes and says can I have Will take his new shoes to the village today, there's a nail coming loose. So Will gets ready to go, and is there any sign of Mr. Holmes or his shoes? None. I'll never understand him."

I stood and figuratively scratched my head for a few minutes before I realised that I had stumbled on his clue. I went out the door and found, of course, large numbers of footprints. However, it had rained the day before, and the soft ground around the cottage was relatively clear. I found a set of prints with a tiny scuff at the inside corner of the right heel, where the protruding nail dug a small hole at each step. They led me down to a part of the flower beds where I knew Holmes grew herbs for various potions and experiments. Here I found the shoes, but no Holmes. No footprints led off across the lawn. I puzzled at this for a few minutes until I noticed that some of the full seed pods had been recently cut off. I turned to the house, gave the shoes to a puzzled Mrs. Hudson, and found Holmes where I knew he would be, up in his laboratory, bent over the poppy seed pods, wearing carpet slippers. He looked up as I came in.

"No guesses?"

"No guesses."

"Good. Then let me show you how opium is derived."

The training with Holmes served to sharpen my eyes and my mind, but it did little for the examinations I should have to pass to qualify for Oxford. Women were not at that time admitted to the University proper, but the women's colleges were good, and I was free to attend lectures elsewhere. At first I had been disappointed that I would not be accepted at sixteen, due to wartime problems, my age, interest, and, it must be admitted, my sex. However, the time with Holmes was proving so engrossing, I hardly noticed the change in plans.

The examinations would be a problem if I continued this way, though, and I cast about for someone to fill in the large gaps in my education. I was most fortunate here, because I found a retired schoolmistress in the village who was willing to guide my reading. God bless Miss Sim and all like her, who gave me a love for English literature, force-fed me with poetry, and gently badgered me into a basic knowledge of the humanities. I owed my qualifying marks on the exams to her.

I was due to enter my college at Oxford in the autumn of 1917. I had been with Holmes for two years, and by the spring of 1917 could follow a footprint ten miles across country, tell a London accountant from a Bath schoolmaster by their clothing, give the physical description of an individual based on his shoe, disguise myself well enough to deceive Mrs. Hudson, and recognise the ashes from the 112 most common brands of cigarettes and cigars. In addition, I could recite whole passages of the Greek and Latin classics, the Bible, and Shakespeare, describe the major archaeological sites in the Middle East, and, thanks to Mrs. Hudson, tell a phlox from a petunia.

And yet, beneath it all, underneath the games and the challenges, in the very air we all breathed in those days, lay death, death and horror and the growing awareness that life would never be the same, for anyone. While I grew and flexed the muscles of my mind, the bodies of strong young men were being poured ruthlessly into the 500-mile gutter that was the Western Front, an entire generation of men sub-jected to the grinding, body-rotting, mind-shattering impossibility of battle in thigh-deep mud and drifts of searing gas, under machine-gun fire and through tangles of wire.

Life was not normal during those years. Everyone did abnormal amounts of unusual work, children in the fields, women in the facto-ries and behind the wheels. Everyone knew someone who had been killed, or blinded, or crippled. In one of the neighbouring villages the men had enlisted en masse in a "pals regiment." Their position was overrun in October of 1916, and after the war there was not a single whole man in the village between the ages of fourteen and forty-six.

I was young enough to adapt to this schizophrenic life, flexible enough to find nothing inordinately strange in spending my morning at the nearby makeshift hospital, fetching bandages for blistering skin, trying not to gag on the putrid smell of gangrenous flesh, and wonder-ing which man would not be there the next time, and then the after-noon with Holmes over Bunsen burner or microscope, and finally the evening at my desk deciphering a Greek text. It was a mad time, and looked at objectively was probably the worst possible situation for me, but somehow the madness around me and the turmoil I carried within myself acted as counterweights, and I survived in the centre.

I occasionally wondered that it did not seem to trouble Holmes more, watching his country being flayed alive on the fields of Somme and Ypres while he sat in Sussex, raising bees and carrying on abstruse experiments and long conversations with me. He did perform an advi-sory function at times, that I knew. Strange figures would appear at odd hours, closet themselves with him for much of the day, and skulk away into the night. Twice he went to London for week-long training courses, although when he reappeared from the second with a thin cut down the side of his face and a racking cough that lingered for months, I did wonder what kind of training it was. When I asked him he looked embarrassed and refused to tell me. I did not hear the an-swer for years.

Eventually the strain of it began to tell on me, and the momentum of normality faltered. For what, I began to wonder, did a University degree count? For that matter, what was the point of training to hunt down a criminal, even a murderer, when half a million Tommies were bleeding into the soil of Europe, when every man setting foot on a troop ship knew he held barely even odds of returning to England unmaimed?

The bitter hopelessness of it surged over me one bleak day in early 1917, when I sat on the bed of a young soldier and read him a letter from his wife, and a short time later watched him drown in the fluids from his blistered lungs. Most seventeen-year-old girls would have crept home and cried. I stormed into Holmes' cottage and vented my rage, threatening the beakers and instruments as I strode wildly up and down before the apprehensive detective.

"For God's sake, what are we doing here?" I shouted. "Can you think of nothing that we could do? Surely they must need spies or translators or something, but here we sit playing games and—" This went on for some time. When I began to run down, Holmes silently stood up and went to ask Mrs. Hudson to make some tea. He carried it back up himself, poured us each a cup, and sat down.

"What was behind that?" he asked calmly. I dropped into the other chair, suddenly exhausted, and told him. He drank his tea.

"You think we are doing nothing here, then. No, do not back down from your position, you are quite right. In the short view, with some minor exceptions, we are sitting this war out. We are leaving it to the buffoons in power and the faithful sloggers who march off to die. And afterwards, Russell? Are you able to take the long view, and envisage what will take place when this insanity comes to an end? There are two possibilities, are there not? One is, we will lose. That even if the Americans do come in, we will run out of food and warm bodies to funnel into the trenches before the Germans do, and this small island will be overrun. The other possibility, one which I admit looks remote at present, is that we will succeed in pushing them back. What then will happen? The government will turn its face to rebuilding, the people who survive will limp home, and on the surface all will be happiness and prosperity. And beneath the surface there will be an unparalleled growth of the criminal class, feeding off the carrion and thriving under the inattentive eyes of authority. If we win this war, Russell, people with my skills—our skills—will be needed."

"And if we don't win?"

"If we lose? Can you imagine that a person skilled at assuming rôles and noticing details would not be of some use in an occupied Britain?"

There was little to say to that. I subsided and returned to my books with dogged determination, an attitude that persisted for the following year, until I was given the opportunity to do something concrete for the war effort.

When the time came I chose two main areas of study to read at Oxford: chemistry and theology, the workings of the physical universe and the deepest stuff of the human mind.

THAT LAST SPRING and summer of undiluted Holmes was a time of great intensity. As the Allies, strengthened now by the economic aid and, eventually, armed entrance of the United States, slowly made headway, my tutorials with Holmes became increasingly strenuous and often left us both feeling drained. Our chemical experiments became ever more sophisticated, and the challenges and tests he devised for me sometimes took me days to resolve. I had grown to relish the quick, proud smile that very occasionally followed a noteworthy success, and I knew that these examinations I was passing with flying colours.

As summer drew to a close the examinations began to taper off, to be replaced by long conversations. Although massive bloodshed was being committed across the Channel, although the air throbbed and glass rattled for days on end with the July bombardment of the Somme, although I know I must have spent great numbers of hours in the emergency medical station, what I recall most about that summer of 1917 is how beautiful the sky was. The summer seemed mostly sky, sky and the hillsides on which we spent hours talking, talking. I had bought a lovely little chess set of ivory, inlaid wood, and leather to carry in my pocket, and we played games without number under the hot sky. He no longer had to handicap himself severely in order to work for his victories. I still have that set, and when I open it I can smell the ghost of the hay that was being cut in a field below us, the day I beat him evenly for the first time.

One warm, still evening just after dusk we walked back from an outing on the other side of Eastbourne. We were strolling towards the cottage from the Channel side, and as we neared the small fenced orchard that housed his hives Holmes stopped dead and stood with his head tipped to one side. After a moment he gave a little grunt and strode rapidly across the turf to the orchard gate. I followed, and once among the trees I could hear the noise that his experienced ears had caught at the greater distance: a high, passionate sound, a tiny, endless cry of unmistakable rage coming from the hive in front of us. Holmes stood staring down at the otherwise peaceful white box, and clicked his tongue in exasperation.

"What is it?" I asked. "What's that noise they're making?"

"That is the sound of an angry queen. This hive has already swarmed twice, but it seems determined to swarm itself into exhaustion. The new queen had her nuptial flight last week, and she is now anxious to murder her rivals in their beds. Normally the workers would encourage her, but either they know she is going to lead another swarm, or they are somehow driving her to do so. In either case, they are keeping her from doing away with the unborn queens. They cover the royal cells with thick layers of wax, you see, so she cannot reach the princesses and they can't chew their way out to answer her challenge. The noise is the queens, born and imprisoned, raging at each other through the prison walls."

"What would happen if one of the unhatched queens escaped from her cell?"

"The first queen has the advantage, and would almost certainly kill it."

"Even though she is going to abandon the hive anyway?"

"The lust for murder is not a rational thing. In queens, it is an instinctual response."

I went up to Oxford a few weeks later. Both Holmes and Mrs. Hudson went on the train with me, to deliver me to my new home. We walked by the Cherwell and down to the Isis to feed the ill-tempered swans, and back by way of Mercury's fountain and the silent, brooding bell named Tom to the station. I embraced Mrs. Hudson and turned to Holmes.

"Thank you," was all I could come up with.

"Learn something here," he said. "Find some teachers and learn something" was all he could say, and we shook hands and walked off to our separate lives.

THE OXFORD UNIVERSITY I came up to in 1917 was a shadow of her normal, self-assured self, its population a tenth of that in 1914 before the war, a number lower even than in the years following the Black Death. The blue-coated wounded, wan and trembling beneath their tanned skins, outnumbered the black-robed academics, and several of the colleges, including my own, had been given over to housing them for the duration.

I expected great things of this University, many of which it gave me in abundance. I did find teachers, as Holmes had ordered, even before the remnant of male dons trickled back from France, having left parts of themselves behind. I found men and women who were not intimidated by my proud, rough-cut mind, who challenged and fought me and were not above reducing me sharply to size when criticism was due, and a couple of them were even better than Holmes at the delivery of a brief and devastating remark. Both for better and for worse, one received considerably more of their attentions during the war years than after the young men returned. I found that I did not miss Holmes as much as I had feared, and the intense pleasure of being away from my aunt went quite far to balance the irritation of the chaperonage rules (permission required for any outing, two women in any mixed party, mixed parties in cafés only between two o'clock and five-thirty in the afternoon, and then only with permission, etc., etc.). Many girls found these rules infuriating; I found them less so, but perhaps that was only because I was more agile at climbing the walls or scrambling between hansom roof and upper window in the wee hours.

One thing I had not expected to find at University was fun. After all, Oxford was a small town composed of dirty, cold stone buildings filled with wounded soldiers. There were few male undergraduates, few male dons under the age of retirement, few men, period, who were not Blighty returns, fragile and preoccupied and often in pain. Food was scarce and uninteresting, heating was inadequate, the war was a constant presence, volunteer work intruded on our time, and to top it off, half the University societies and organizations were in abeyance, up to and including the dramatic society, OUDS.

Oddly enough, it was this last gap in the Oxford landscape that opened the door of *communitas* for me, and almost immediately I arrived. I was in my rooms on the first morning, investigating on all fours the possibility of repairing a bookshelf that had just collapsed under the combined weight of four tea chests of books, when there came a knock on my door.

"Come in," I called.

"I say," a voice began, and then changed from enquiry to concern. "I say, are you all right?"

I shoved my spectacles back onto my nose and dashed the hair out of my face with the back of my hand, and caught my first sight of Lady Veronica Beaconsfield, all plump five feet one inch of her, wrapped in an incredibly gaudy green-and-yellow silk dressing gown that did nothing for her complexion.

"All right? Of course. Oh, the books. No, they didn't fall on me; I lay on them. I don't suppose you have such a thing as a screwdriver?"

"No, I don't believe I do."

"Ah well, the porter may. Were you looking for someone?"

"You."

"Then you have found her."

"Petruchio," she said, and seemed to pause in expectation. I sat back on my heels amongst the strewn volumes for a moment.

"Come on, and kiss me Kate?" I offered. "What, sweeting, all amort?"

She clapped her hands together and squealed at the ceiling. "I knew it! The voice, the height, and she even knows the words. Can you do it à la vaudeville?"

"I, er—"

"Of course we can't use real food in your scene where you throw it at the servants, not with all the shortages, it wouldn't be nice."

"May I ask . . . ?"

"Oh, sorry, how stupid of me. Veronica Beaconsfield. Call me Ronnie."

"Mary Russell."

"Yes, I know. Tonight then, Mary, nine o'clock, my rooms. First performance in two weeks."

"But I—" I protested. But she was away.

I was simply the latest to discover the impossibility of refusing to co-operate in one of Ronnie Beaconsfield's schemes. I was in her rooms that night with a dozen others, and three weeks later we performed *The Taming of the Shrew* for the entertainment of the Men of Somerville, as we called them, and I doubt that staid college of women had ever heard such an uproar before, or since. We gained several male converts to our society that night, and I was soon excused the rôle of Petruchio.

I was not, however, excused from participation in this amateur dramatic society, for it was soon discovered that I had a certain skill in make-up and even disguise, although I never let slip the name of Sherlock Holmes. I cannot now recall the process by which I, shy bluestocking intellectual Mary Russell, came to be the centre of the year's elaborate prank, but some weeks later in the madness of the summer term I was to find myself disguised as an Indian nobleman (Indian, for the turban to cover my hair) eating with the undergraduates of Baliol College. The breath of risk made it all the more delicious, for we should all have been sent down, or at the very least rusticated for the term, had we been caught out.

The career of Ratnakar Sanji in Oxford lasted for nearly the entire month of May. He was seen in three of the men's colleges; he spoke briefly (in bad English) in the Union; he attended a sherry party with the aesthetes of Christ Church (where he demonstrated exquisite manners) and a football game with the hearties of Brasenose (where he appeared to down a large quantity of beer and contributed two previously unknown verses to one of the rowdier songs); he even received a brief mention in one of the undergraduate newspapers, under the heading "Rajput Nobleman's Son Remarks on Oxford." The truth inevitably trickled out, and I only escaped the proctor's bulldogs by moments. Miss Mary Russell walked demurely away from the pub's back entrance, leaving Ratnakar Sanji in the dustbin behind the door. The proctors and the college authorities conducted a thorough search for the malefactors, and several of the young men who had been seen dining or at functions with Sanji received stern warnings, but scandal was averted, largely because no one ever found the woman who rumour said was involved. Of course the women's colleges received their close scrutiny. Ronnie was called in, as one of the most likely due to temperament, but when I followed her in the door—quiet and bookish, loping along at Ronnie's heels like a lugubrious wolfhound—they discounted my height and the fact that I wore spectacles similar to Sanji's, and excused me irritably from the interrogation.

The conspiracy left me with two legacies, neither of which had been in my original expectations of University life: a coterie of lasting friends (Nothing binds like shared danger, however spurious.) and a distinct taste for the freedom that comes with assuming another's identity.

All of which is not to say that I gave up work entirely. I revelled in the lectures and discussions. I took to the Bodleian Library as to a lover and, particularly before Sanji's career began in May, would sit long hours in Bodley's arms, to emerge, blinking and dazed with the smell and feel of all those books. The chemistry laboratories were a revelation in modernity, compared to Holmes' equipment, at any rate. I blessed the war that had taken over the college rooms I might normally have been given, for the modernised quarters I found myself in had electrical lights, occasionally operating central heating radiators, and even—miracle of miracles—running water piped in for each resident. The hand-basin in the corner was an immense luxury (Even the young lords in Christchurch depended on the legs of the scouts for their supply of hot water.) and enabled me to set up a small laboratory in my sitting room. The gas ring, meant for heating cocoa, I converted into a Bunsen burner.

Between the joys of work and the demands of a burgeoning social life I found little time for sleep. At the end of the term in December I crept home, emptied by the passion of my first weeks in academia. Fortunately the conductor remembered my presence and woke me in time to change trains.

I turned eighteen on the second of January 1918. I arrived at Holmes' door with my hair elaborately piled on my head, wearing a dark-green velvet gown and my mother's diamond earrings. When Mrs. Hudson opened the door I was glad to see that she, Holmes, and Dr. Watson were also in formal dress, so we all glittered regally in that somewhat worn setting. When Watson had revived Holmes from the apoplectic seizure my appearance had caused, we ate and we drank champagne, and Mrs. Hudson produced a birthday cake with candles, and they sang to me and gave me presents. From Mrs. Hudson came a pair of silver hair combs. Watson produced an intricate little portable writing set, complete with pad, pen, and inkwell, that folded into a tooled leather case. The small box Holmes put before me contained a simple, delicate brooch made of silver set with tiny pearls.

"Holmes, it's beautiful."

"It belonged to my grandmother. Can you open it?"

I searched for a clasp, my vision and dexterity hindered somewhat by the amount of champagne I had drunk. Finally he stretched out his fingers and manipulated two of the pearls, and it popped open in my hand. Inside was a miniature portrait of a young woman, with light hair but a clear gaze I recognised immediately as that of Holmes.

"Her brother, the French artist Vernet, painted it on her eighteenth birthday," said Holmes. "Her hair was a colour very similar to yours, even when she was old."

The portrait wavered in front of my eyes and tears spilt down my cheeks.

"Thank you. Thank you everybody," I choked out and dissolved into maudlin sobs, and Mrs. Hudson had to put me to bed in the guest room.

I woke once during the night, disorientated by the strange room and the remnants of alcohol in my bloodstream. I thought I had heard soft footsteps outside my door, but when I listened, there was only the quiet tick of the clock on the other side of the wall.

I RETURNED TO Oxford the following week-end, to a winter term that was much the same as the autumn weeks had been, only more so. My main passions were becoming theoretical mathematics and the complexities of Rabbinic Judaism, two topics that are dissimilar only on the surface. Again the dear old Bodleian opened its arms and pages to me, again I was dragged along in Ronnie Beaconsfield's wake (*Twelfth Night* this time, and also a campaign to improve the conditions for cart horses plying the streets of the city). Ratnakar Sanji was conceived in the term's final weeks, to be born in May following the spring holiday, and again I simply did without sleep, and occasionally meals. Again I emerged at the end of term, lethargic and spent.

The lodgings house was looked after by a couple named Thomas, two old dears who retained their thick Oxfordshire country accents. Mr. Thomas helped me carry my things to the cab waiting on the street as I was leaving for home. He grunted at the weight of one case, laden with books, and I hurried to help him with it. He brushed off his hands, looked at the case critically, then at me.

"Now, Miss, not to be forward, but I hope you'll not be spending the whole of the holiday at your desk. You came here with roses in your cheeks, and there's not a hint of them there now. Get yourself some fresh air, now, y'hear? Your brain'll work better when you come back if you do."

I was surprised, as this was the longest speech I had ever heard him deliver, but assured him that I intended to spend many hours in the open air. At the train station I caught a glance of myself in a mirror and could see what he meant. I had not realised how drawn I was looking, and the purple smudges under my eyes troubled me.

The next morning the alien sounds of silence and bird song woke me early. I pulled on my oldest work clothes and a pair of new boots, added heavy gloves and a woolly hat against the chill March morning, and went to find Patrick. Patrick Mason was a large, slow-moving, phlegmatic Sussex farmer of fifty-two with hands like something grown from the earth and a nose that changed direction three times. He had managed the farm since before my parents had married, had in fact run with my mother as a child (he three years older) through the fields he now tended, had, I think, been more than half in love with her all his life. Certainly he worshipped her as his Lady. When his wife died and left him to finish raising their six children, only his salary as manager made it possible to keep the family intact. The day his youngest reached eighteen, Patrick divided his land and came to live on the farm I now owned. In most ways this was more his land than mine, an attitude both of us held and considered only right, and his loyalty to his adoptive home was absolute, if he was unwilling to suffer any nonsense from the legal owner.

Up until now my sporadic attempts to help out with the myriad farmyard tasks had been met with the same polite disbelief with which the peasants at Versailles must have greeted Marie Antoinette's milk-maid fantasies. I was the owner, and if I wanted to push matters he could not actually stop me from dirtying my hands, but other than the seasonal necessity of the wartime harvest (which obviously pained him) My Lady's Daughter was taken to be above such things. He ran the farm to his liking, I lived there and occasionally wandered down from the main house to chat, but neither he nor I would have thought of giving me a say in how things were run. This morning that was about to change.

I trudged down the hill to the main barn, my breath smoking around my ears in the clear, weak winter sunshine, and called his name. The voice that answered led me through to the back, where I found him mucking out a stall.

"Morning, Patrick."

"Welcome back, Miss Mary." I had long ago forbidden greater formality, and he in turn refused greater familiarity, so the compromise was Miss and my first name.

"Thank you, it's good to be back. Patrick, I need your help."

"Surely, Miss Mary. Can it wait until I've finished this?"

"Oh, I don't want to interrupt. I want you to give me something to do."

"Something to do?" He looked puzzled.

"Yes. Patrick, I've spent the last six months sitting in a chair with a book in my hands, and if I don't get back to using my muscles, they'll forget how to function altogether. I need you to tell me what needs doing around here. Where can I start? Shall I finish that stall for you?"

Patrick hurriedly held the muck-rake out of my reach and blocked my entrance to the stall.

"No, Miss, I'll finish this. What is it you'd like to do?"

"Whatever needs doing," I said in no uncertain terms, to let him know I meant business.

"Well . . ." His eyes looked about desperately and lit on a broom. "Do you want to sweep? The wood shavings in the workshop want clearing up."

"Right." I seized the big broom, and ten minutes later he came into the workshop to find me furiously raising a cloud of dust and wood particles that settled softly onto every surface.

"Miss Mary, oh, well, that's too fast. I mean, do you think you could get the stuff out the door before you fling it in the air?"

"What do you mean? Oh, I see, here, I'll just sweep it off of there."

I took the broom and made a wild sweep along the workbench, and an edge of the unwieldy head sent a tray of tools flying. Patrick picked up a chipped chisel and looked at me as if I had attacked his son.

"Have you never used a broom before?"

"Well, not often."

"Perhaps you should carry firewood, then."

I hauled barrow-cart after barrow-cart of split logs up to the house, saw that we needed kindling as well, and had just started using the double-bitted axe to split some logs on a big stone next to the back door when Patrick ran up and prevented me from cutting off my hand. He showed me the cutting block and the proper little hand axe and carefully demonstrated how not to use them. Two hours after I had walked down the hill I had a small pile of wood and a very trembly set of muscles to show for my work.

The road to Holmes' cottage seemed to have lengthened since last I rode that way, or perhaps it was only the odd sensation of nervousness in the pit of my stomach. It was the same, but I was different, and I wondered for the first time if I was going to be able to carry it off, if I could join these two utterly disparate sides of my life. I pushed the bicycle harder than my out-of-condition legs cared for, but when I came over the last rise and saw the familiar cottage across the fields, faint smoke rising from the kitchen chimney, I began to relax, and when I opened the door and breathed in the essence of the place, I was home, safe.

"Mrs. Hudson?" I called, but the kitchen was empty. Market day, I thought, so I went to the stairs and started upwards. "Holmes?"

"That you, Russell?" he said, sounding mildly surprised, though I had written the week before to say what day I would be home. "Good. I was just glancing through those experiments on blood typology we were doing before you left in January. I believe I've discovered what the problem was. Here: Look at your notes. Now look at the slide I've put in the microscope. . . ."

Good old Holmes, as effusive and demonstrative as ever. Obediently, I sat before the eyepieces of his machine, and it was as if I'd never been away. Life slid back into place, and I did not doubt again.

On the third week of my holiday I went to the cottage on a Wednesday, Mrs. Hudson's usual day in town. Holmes and I had planned a rather smelly chemical reaction for that day, but as I let myself in the kitchen door I heard voices from the sitting room.

"Russell?" his voice called.

"Yes, Holmes." I walked to the door and was surprised to see Holmes at the fire beside an elegantly dressed woman with a vaguely familiar face. I automatically began to reconstruct mentally the surroundings where I had seen her, but Holmes interrupted the process.

"Do come in, Russell. We were waiting for you. This is Mrs. Barker. You will remember, she and her husband live in the manor house. They bought it the year before you came here. Mrs. Barker, this is the young lady I was mentioning—yes, she is a young lady inside that costume. Now that she is here, would you please review the problem for us? Russell, pour yourself a cup of tea and sit down."

It was the partnership's first case.

✣ 3 ✣

Mistress of the Hounds

At the smell of the smoke, they imagine that this is not the
attack of an enemy . . . but that it is a force or a natural
catastrophe whereto they do well to submit.

IT WAS, I suppose, inevitable that Holmes and I would collaborate eventually on one of his cases. Although ostensibly retired, he would, as I said, occasionally show all the signs of his former life: strange visitors, erratic hours, a refusal to eat, long periods at the pipe, and endless hours producing peculiar noises from his violin. Twice I had come to the cottage unannounced and found him gone. I did not enquire into his affairs, as I knew that he accepted only the most unusual or delicate of cases these days, leaving the investigation of more conventional crimes to the various police agencies (who had come to adopt his methods over the years).

I was immediately curious as to what Holmes might see in this case. Although Mrs. Barker was a neighbour, and a wealthy one, that would

hardly keep him from referring her to the local police if he thought
her problem was of the common or garden variety, yet far from rebuff-
ing her, I could see that he was more than a bit interested. Mrs. Barker,
however, seemed puzzled at his vague manner, and as he spent the better part of the interview slouched down in his chair with his fingers
steepled, staring at the ceiling, she talked at me. I knew him well
enough to see that this apparent lack of interest was actually the opposite, the first stirrings of mental excitement. I listened carefully to
her story.

"You may know," she began, "that my husband and I bought the
manor house four years ago. We had been living in America before the
war, but Richard—my husband—had always wanted to come home.
He was very fortunate with several of his investments, and we came to
England in 1913 to look for a house. We saw the manor house here,
fell in love with its possibilities, and bought it just before the war
started. Of course, with all the shortages and the men off in Europe it
has been slow work doing the renovations, but one wing is now quite
livable.

"At any rate, about a year ago my husband became ill for a few
days. At first it seemed nothing serious, merely an upset stomach, but
it progressed until he was curled up in his bed, bathed in sweat, and
groaning horribly. The doctors could find no cause, and I could see
they were beginning to despair, when the fever finally broke and he
went to sleep. In a week he had fully recovered, or so we thought.

"Since then he has had ten episodes similar to the first, though
none as bad. Each one begins with a chill sweat, and proceeds through
cramps and delirium, and finally a pitch of fever and a deep sleep. On
the first night he cannot bear to have me with him, but a few days later
he is restored to himself, until the next time. The doctors were baffled,
and suggested poison, but we always eat the same foods. I watch it being cooked. It is not poison but an illness.

"Now, I know what you're thinking, Mr. Holmes." Holmes raised
an eyebrow at this statement. "You're wondering why I'm asking you

about a medical problem. Mr. Holmes, I have come to believe it is not a medical problem. We have consulted specialists here and on the Continent. We even made an appointment with Dr. Freud, thinking it might be of mental origin. They all throw up their hands, with the exception of Dr. Freud, who seemed to think that it was the physical manifestation of my husband's guilt over marrying a woman twenty years younger than himself. I ask you, have you ever heard such twaddle?" she asked indignantly. We seriously shook our heads in sympathy.

Holmes spoke from the depths of his chair.

"Mrs. Barker, please tell us why you do not believe your husband's illness to be simply a medical problem."

"Mr. Holmes, Miss Russell, I will not insult you by making you swear that what I next say goes no further than this room. I decided before I came here that you would have to know, and that your discretion in the matter was a certain thing. My husband is an advisor to the government of England, Mr. Holmes. He does not inform me of the details of his work, but I could hardly miss such activities when they are under my nose. It is also the reason why the telephone line runs such a distance from the village exchange. Your own telephone, Mr. Holmes, is available because the Prime Minister needs to be able to reach my husband at any time. Everyone assumes the line comes this way because we were willing to spend the money for it, I know, but it was not our idea, I assure you."

"Mrs. Barker, the fact that your husband is a government advisor and the fact that he periodically becomes ill are not necessarily related."

"Perhaps not, but I have noticed a very odd thing. My husband's illnesses always correspond with a particular weather phenomenon: It is always during a period of considerable clarity, never during fog or rain. It came to my attention six weeks ago, in the first week of March, I believe it was, following that long period of rain and snow we had. It finally cleared, and was a sparkling clear night, and my husband became ill for the first time in more than two months. That was when I realised, looking back, that it had always been so."

"Mrs. Barker, when you consulted the European doctors, did your husband become ill during that time? How long were you there, and what were the weather conditions?"

"We were there for seven weeks, with a number of clear nights, and his health was fine."

"I think this is not all you have to tell us, Mrs. Barker," said Holmes. "Pray finish your story."

The lady sighed deeply, and I was astonished to notice that her beautifully manicured hands were trembling.

"You are correct, Mr. Holmes. There are two other things. The first is this: He became ill again two weeks ago, one month after I began to wonder about the coincidence of the air's clarity. The night his illness began he asked me to leave him alone, as usual. I left his sickroom and went outside for some air. I walked around the gardens for a time, until it was quite late, and when I turned back towards the house I happened to look up at my husband's room. I saw a light, winking on and off from the roof over his room."

"And you think it might be your husband, secretly passing on government secrets to the Kaiser," Holmes interrupted with an impatient edge to his voice.

Mrs. Barker's face went dead white and she swayed in her chair. I leapt to my feet and held her upright while Holmes went for the brandy. She never fainted completely, and the spirits revived her, but she was still pale and shaken when we sat back down in our chairs.

"Mr. Holmes, how could you have known that?"

"My good lady, you told me yourself." Seeing her bewilderment, he said with exaggerated patience, "You told me that his illnesses correspond with clear nights when signals can be seen for miles and you told me that he is invariably alone at those times. In addition, I have seen his distinctly Germanic features in the car. Your emotions make it obvious that you are torn between finding the truth and discovering that your husband is a traitor. If you suspected someone else you would not be so upset. Now, tell us about your household."

She took a shaky sip of brandy and continued.

"We have five full-time servants who live in the house. The others are day help from the village. There is Terrence Howell, my husband's man, and Sylvia Jacobs, my maid; Sally and Ronald Woods, the cook and chief gardener; and lastly Ron Athens, who keeps the stable and the two cars. Terrence has been with my husband for years; Sylvia I hired eight years ago; the others came when we opened the house."

Holmes sat staring off at a corner for some minutes, then leapt suddenly to his feet.

"Madam, if you would be so good as to go home now, I think it very likely that a couple of your neighbours may be around to your door later this afternoon. Shall we say, around three o'clock? An unexpected visit, you understand?"

The lady rose, clutching her bag.

"Thank you, Mr. Holmes, I hope—" She looked down. "If my fears are correct, I have married a traitor. If I am wrong, I am myself guilty of traitorous thoughts against my husband. There is no win here, only duty."

Holmes touched her hand and she looked up at him. He smiled with extraordinary kindness into her eyes.

"Madam, there is no treachery in the truth. There may be pain, but to face honestly all possible conclusions formed by a set of facts is the noblest route possible for a human being." Holmes could be surprisingly empathetic at times, and his words now had a gentling effect on the lady. She smiled wanly, patted his hand, and left.

Holmes and I proceeded with our odoriferous experiment and at two o'clock left the cottage, leaving the windows and doors full open, to walk to the manor house. We approached it casually, from cross-country rather than along the road, and studied the setting as we walked up the hill towards it.

The three-storey house dominated the area, built as it was atop one of the tallest hills. Moreover, at one end was a tall, square tower that had all the earmarks of a folly added on to imitate some spurious Norman original. It served to unbalance the rest of the building, which apart from the excrescence had a comfortable, sturdy appearance. I said as much to Holmes.

"Yes, the builder may have had some desire to view the sea," he replied. "I believe that a close examination of the topographical maps would show a correlation between that tower and the gap in the hills over there."

"They do."

"Ah, so that was where you went while I was lacing on my boots."

"To look at your maps, yes. I don't know this part of the downs as well as you do, so I thought I would take a glance at how the land lies."

"I think we may assume that the upper rooms in the tower are those of Richard Barker. Put on a casual, happen-to-be-in-the-neighbourhood face, now, Russell, here's the gentleman himself."

He raised his voice, calling "Hello, the house!"

His hail had two immediate and astonishing results. The old gentleman shot from his sunlit chair, turned his back to us and waved his hands in the air, shouting unintelligibly. Holmes and I looked at each other curiously, but the reason for his extraordinary behaviour was apparent in another instant, as a pack of what looked like forty dogs came baying and scrabbling across the terrace towards us. The multi-coloured sea parted around the old gentleman, ignoring his frantic waves entirely. Holmes and I stepped slightly apart and readied the heavy walking sticks we always carried for such occasions, but the canine mob was not out for blood and simply encircled us, baying, yapping, and barking madly. The old man came up, his mouth moving, but his presence made absolutely no impact. However, another man came running around the corner of the house, followed shortly by a third, and waded into the sea, seizing scruffs, tails, and fistfuls of fur. Their voices gradually prevailed, and order was slowly restored. Having

done their jobs, the dogs sat and stood merrily awaiting further fun,
tongues lolling, tails wagging. At this point Mrs. Barker came from the
house, and the dogs and her husband all turned to her.

"My dear," said he in a thin voice, "something really must be done
about these dogs."

She looked sternly at the dogs and spoke to them.

"Shame on you. Is this how you act when neighbours come to visit?
You should know better than that."

The effect of her words on the crowd was instantaneous. Jaws
snapped shut, heads went down, tails were tucked in. Looking totally
abashed and glancing at us guiltily, the dogs tiptoed silently away. There
were only seventeen of them, I noticed, ranging from two tiny Yorkshire
terriers to a massive wolfhound who could easily have weighed eleven
stone. Mrs. Barker stood with her hands on her hips as the last of them
disappeared into the shrubbery, then turned to us, shaking her head.

"I am very sorry for that. We have so few visitors, I'm afraid they
become overly excited."

"Let dogs delight to bark and bite, for God hath made them so,"
Holmes commented politely, if unexpectedly. "We ought not to have
come here unannounced, for their sakes if not yours. My name is
Holmes; this is Mary Russell. We were out for a walk and wished for a
closer view of your handsome home. We'll not bother you further."

"No, no," said Mrs. Barker before her husband could speak. "You
must come in for refreshment. A glass of sherry, or is it not too early
for tea? Tea it is, then. We are neighbours, I believe. I've seen you from
the road. I am Mrs. Barker; this is my husband." She turned to the
other two men. "Thank you, Ron, they'll be quiet now. Terrence,
could you please tell Mrs. Woods that we will take tea now, and there
will be four. We'll be in the conservatory in a few minutes. Thank
you."

"That's very kind of you, Mrs. Barker. I am sure Miss Russell is as in
need of refreshment as I am after our walk." He turned to the older
man, who had stood watching his wife affectionately as she dealt with

dogs, guests, and men. "Mr. Barker, this is a most interesting building. Portland stone, is it not? From the early eighteenth century? And when was the folly added?"

The obvious interest Holmes had in the structure led to a deep conversation concerning cracking foundations, wood beetles, leaded windows, the cost of coal, and the drawbacks of the British tradesman. After a hearty tea we were offered a tour, and Holmes, the amateur architectural enthusiast, talked his way into the tower as well. We climbed up the narrow, open wooden steps while Mr. Barker rode in the tiny lift he had installed. He met us at the top.

"I've always wanted an ivory tower." He smiled. "It was the main reason I bought the place, this tower. The lift was an extravagance, but I have problems with climbing the stairs. These are my rooms here. I'd like you to see my view."

The view was indeed panoramic, a northerly outlook up to the beginnings of the dark weald. Having admired it and the rooms, we set off again for the stairs, but before we reached them Holmes abruptly turned and made for a ladder leaning against a wall at the end of the hallway.

"I do hope you don't mind, Mr. Barker, but I must see the top of this magnificent tower. I'll just be an instant, Russell. Note this clever trapdoor here." His voice faded and echoed as his feet disappeared.

"But it's not safe up there, Mr. Holmes," Mr. Barker protested. He turned to me. "I can't think why that door is unlocked. I told Ron to fix a padlock to it. I was up there three years ago, and I didn't like the look of it at all."

"He'll be quite careful, Mr. Barker, and I'm sure he'll be just a moment. Ah, see, here he comes now." Holmes' long legs reappeared down the ladder, and his eyes seemed darker as he turned happily towards us.

"Thank you, Mr. Barker, you have a most interesting tower. Now, tell me about the primitive art you have in your hall downstairs. New Guinean, isn't it? The Sepik River, I believe?"

Mr. Barker was successfully distracted and walked slowly down the stairs on Holmes' arm, talking about his travels in the wilder places of the world. By the time we left an hour later, we had admired several magnificent African bronzes, an Australian aboriginal didgeridoo, three Esquimaux carved walrus tusks, and an exquisite golden figure from Incan Peru. The Barkers saw us to the door and we said good-bye, but suddenly Holmes pushed back past them.

"I must thank the cook personally for that superb tea she produced. Do you think she would give Miss Russell the recipe for those little pink cakes? The kitchen is down here, I believe?"

I answered the Barkers' startled looks with an expressive shrug, to tell them that I was not to be held responsible for his behavioural oddities, and ducked down the hallway after him. I found him shaking the hand of a bewildered little woman with grey hair and ruddy cheeks, thanking her profusely. Another woman, younger and prettier, had been sitting at the table with a cup of tea.

"Thank you, Mrs. Woods is it? Miss Russell and I so appreciated your revivifying tea, it helped restore us after those dreadful dogs set upon us. Amazing number of them—do you have to care for them? Oh, good, yes, it is a better task for a man. Still, they must eat a lot, and I suppose you have to prepare their food?"

Mrs. Woods had responded to his banter with an oddly girlish giggle.

"Oh yes, sir, they fairly keep the town butcher in business. This morning it took all three of us to carry the order from the butcher's—there must've been twenty pounds of bones alone."

"Dogs eat a lot of bones, don't they?" I wondered what this was all leading up to, but it appeared that he had what he was after.

"Well, thank you again, Mrs. Woods, and don't forget that Miss Russell wants that recipe."

She waved us merrily out the kitchen door. The dogs were there, lying about on a struggling patch of much-dug-up lawn, and ignored us completely. We circled the house and strode off down the road.

"Holmes, what was that about the cakes? You know I don't know a thing about baking. Or do you think the poisonous things are the cause of Mr. Barker's illness?"

"Merely a ruse, Russell. Is it not nice of the government to arrange this telephone line for the use of the Barkers and myself? To say nothing of the birds." The line overhead was dotted with singing black bodies, and a pointillist line of white defined one edge of the road. I looked at the face of my companion and read satisfaction and not a little mischief.

"I'm sorry, Holmes, but what are we looking for? Did you see something on the roof?"

"Oh, Russell, it is I who should apologise. Of course, you did not see the roof. Had you, you would have found this," he said, holding out a tiny splinter of black wood, "and half a dozen cigarette ends, which we shall analyse when we get back to the cottage."

I examined the tiny sliver of wood, but it said nothing. "May I have a hint, please, Holmes?"

"Russell, I am most disappointed. It is really quite simple."

"Elementary, in fact?"

"Precisely. Consider, then, the following: a chip of treated wood atop an unused tower; market day; bones; Sepik River art; an absence of poison; and the woods that the road cuts through up ahead."

I stopped dead, my mind working furiously while Holmes leant on his stick and watched with interest. A chip of wood . . . someone on the tower . . . we knew that, why should . . . market day . . . a set market day . . . with bones to feed the dogs while the telephone line that lay along the road—I looked up, affronted.

"Are you telling me the butler did it?"

"I'm afraid it does happen. Shall we search the woods for the débris?"

It took us about ten minutes to find a small clearing strewn with bones. The butcher had been contributing to the dogs' diet for some months, judging by the age of some of the dry brown knuckle-bones.

"Do you feel like a spot of climbing, Russell? Or shall I?"

"If I might borrow your belt for safety, I should be happy to." We examined the nearby telephone poles until Holmes gave a low exclamation.

"This one, Russell." I went over to where he stood and saw the unmistakable signs of frequent, and recent, climbing spikes.

"I saw no sign of spikes or climbing on his shoes, did you?" I asked as I bent to unlace my own heavy boots.

"No, but I am certain that a search through his room would give us a pair with suggestive scuffs and scratches."

"Right, I'm ready. Catch me if I fall." Leaning back against the circle of our combined belts I planted my bare feet firmly onto the rough wood and began slowly to inch my way up: step, step, shift the belt; step, step, shift. I made the top without mishap, hooked myself into greater security, and set to an examination of the wires that were attached to the pole. The marks were clear.

"There are signs of a line being tapped in here," I called down to Holmes. "Someone has been here within the last few days, from the lack of dust at the contact point. Shall we come back with a fingerprint kit?" I climbed down and returned to Holmes his belt. He looked dubiously at the bent buckle. "Perhaps a stronger climbing tether would be advised," I added.

"I think, if the weather holds, we will be able to catch the fingers themselves in action, if not tonight, then certainly tomorrow. Remind me to telephone our good hostess when we get back, to thank her and to enquire as to her husband's state of health."

The sun was low when we walked into the cottage, where the air was sweeter now than it had been at midday. Holmes went off to the laboratory with the cigarette ends while I found the cold food Mrs. Hudson had left for us and made coffee. We ate hunched over microscopes, though our greasy fingerprints on the slides helped not at all. Finally, Holmes sat back.

"The cigarettes are from a small tobacconist in Portsmouth. I trust the police there could make a few enquiries for us. First, however, Mrs. Barker."

The telephone was answered by the lady herself. Holmes thanked her again for her hospitality, and I could tell by his subtle reaction to her words that she was not alone.

"Mrs. Barker, I wanted to thank your husband as well. Is he there? No? Oh, I am sorry to hear that, but you know, he didn't seem well this afternoon. Tell me, does your husband smoke cigarettes? No, I thought not. Oh, it's nothing. Mrs. Barker, listen to me. I believe your husband will be fine, do you understand? Just fine. Yes. Good night, Madam, and thank you again."

His eyes positively glowed as he hung up.

"It's tonight then, Holmes?"

"So it appears. Mr. Barker has retreated to his room, to the gentle ministrations of his manservant. Why don't you have a rest, Russell? I will make a telephone call to the people in charge of this sort of thing, but I am certain we have at least two hours before anything will happen."

I did as he suggested, and despite my excitement I drifted off to the mutter of his voice in the next room. I was awakened some time later by wheels in the drive and came down to find Holmes in the sitting room with two men.

"Good, Russell, get yourself ready. Your warmest coat, now, we may be some time. Russell, this is Mr. Jones and Mr. Smith, who have come from London for our little affair. Gentlemen, Miss Russell, my right hand. Shall we go?" Holmes shouldered a small knapsack and shoved his cloth cap on his head, and we crunched off down the drive.

The manor house was three miles away by road, and we walked silently along the grass verge. Where the trees came up we left the road, following the woods down to the base of the main gardens. There we stood together and whispered quietly. A slight breeze had come up, covering our noises and carrying our scent away from the noses of the pack that inhabited the house.

"We can see the top of the tower from here, I believe. Your colleagues should be in place by now at the hill gap and the sea?"

"Yes, Mr. Holmes. We agreed to be settled in by eleven o'clock. It's ten past now. We're ready."

The lights went off one by one in the house above us, and we entered that particular state of boredom and excitement that accompanies a long wait. And long it was. At one o'clock I bent to whisper in Holmes' ear.

"Surely it was not so late when Mrs. Barker saw the lights from the garden? Perhaps it will not be tonight."

Holmes sat silent and unseen beside me, tense with thought.

"Russell, do your eyes pick up anything from that tower?"

I looked so hard at the black tower rising against the black night that my eyes began to quiver. I looked away slightly, and my eyes caught the faintest of changes in the air above the darkness. I let out a soft exclamation, and Holmes was up at once.

"Quick, Russell, up in the tree. Here we sit, blind as moles, while he's so far back from the edge we can't see him. Up, Russell. What do you see?"

As I climbed in the dark I watched the tower, and fifteen feet up the beam suddenly appeared—an intermittent flash from the back corner of the folly, pointing over our heads at the low hills and the sea beyond.

"It's there!" I scrambled down the branches, losing flesh. "He's up there with a light—" but they were already off up the hill, their hand torches waving wildly in the darkness. I went after them, plunging across flower beds and around a fountain, and suddenly ahead of me the night exploded. Seventeen throats opened at the invaders, yaps and bays and blood-chilling snarls split the air, and the shouts of men, and then a tinkle of glass. I heard Holmes shouting to his companions, dogs began to yelp and howl, two voices coughed and cursed, a larger breakage of glass, and the sound of a door flung open. Electrical lights began to go on in the house, and I could see dogs fleeing in every direction. The first whiff of stink made me hold my breath until I got inside the door. Inside was all lights now, the main kitchen switches all on, the tower next to me blazing with light. I ran in that direction, hearing heavy feet above me on the stairs. They and the voices faded suddenly, and I pictured them on the roof.

A sudden thought occurred to me. There had been a good twenty seconds between the first alarm of the dogs and the time Holmes hit the steps. What if—? On the first-floor landing I ducked silently under the open stairway and waited, just in case. Suddenly a noise came from above, hushed, silent footsteps, hurrying down. I put my hand ready between the treads, caught sight of an unfamiliar shoe, and, praying it did not belong to Smith, Jones, or Barker, grabbed at it. A scream and a crashing fall that continued down the next flight of stairs were followed by shouts and steps from above. I unfolded myself slowly from my hiding place and went to see what I had done.

I stood at the top of the flight, looking down at the crumpled figure of Terrence Howell and feeling my stomach wanting to rise up out of my throat. Then Holmes stood beside me, and I turned to him, and his arm went around my shoulders as the two men pushed past us. I was shaking.

"Oh God, Holmes, I killed him. I didn't think he'd fall that hard, oh God, how could I have done it?" I could feel the texture of the shoe leather impressed on my fingertips and see the tumble of limbs glimpsed through the steps. A voice came up to us.

"Ring for a doctor, would you please, Mrs. Barker? He's got a bad bang on his head and a few broken bones, but he's alive."

Sweet, sweet relief flooded in, and my head suddenly felt light.

"I need to sit down for a minute, Holmes."

He pushed me onto the top step and shoved my head down to my knees. His rucksack plopped down next to me, and I vaguely saw him pull a little bottle out of it. There was the pop of a small cork, and the concentrated reek of the morning's experiment exploded into my nasal passages. I jerked back, and my head smacked hard onto the stone wall. Tears came to my eyes and my vision swam. When it cleared I saw Holmes, a stricken expression on his face.

"Are you all right, Russell?"

I felt my head delicately.

"Yes, no thanks to your smelling salts, Holmes. I can't see much point in reviving someone quite so dramatically, though it does make a fine weapon against a pack of dogs." Relief edged into his eyes, and his normal sardonic expression reappeared.

"When you're up to it, Russell, we should see to Mr. Barker."

I reached for his hand and pulled myself up, and we walked slowly up to the old man's room. A fug of sweat and illness met us at his door, and the light revealed the pale, wet skin and unfocussed eyes of high fever.

"You sponge his face for a bit, Russell, until Mrs. Barker comes. I'm going to see what I can find in Howell's room. Ah, there you are, Mrs. Barker. Your husband needs you. Come, Russell." He swept past her anxious questions.

"What are we looking for?" I asked in his wake.

"A packet of powder or a bottle of liquid, one or the other. I'll start with the wardrobe, you take the bathroom." The bedroom was soon filled with mutters and flying articles of clothing, and the bathroom was awash with odours as I opened one after another of the multitude of scents, after-shave lotions, and bath soaps I found in the drawers. My poor nose was a bit numb, but I eventually found a bottle that did not smell right. I took it into the next room, where Holmes stood calf-deep in clothing, upended drawers, and bedclothes.

"Have you found anything, Holmes?"

"Cigarettes from Fraser's of Portsmouth, boots with scratches over the arches. What have you there?"

"I don't know, I can't smell a thing anymore. Does this smell like *Eau d'Arabe* to you?" A quick sniff and he waded out of the room, the bottle held high.

"You've found it, Russell. Now to figure how much to give him." He went to the stairs and poked his head over. "I say, Jones, is he awake yet?"

"Not a chance. It'll be hours."

"Ah well," he said to me, "we'll just have to experiment. Mrs. Barker." She looked up as we came into the room, wet cloth in her hand. "Mrs. Barker, have you a small spoon? Yes, that will do. Russell, you pour, your hands are steady. Two drops to begin with. We'll repeat it every twenty minutes until we see some results. Just slip it in between his teeth, that's right. Will he take some water? Good. Now we wait."

"Mr. Holmes, what was that?"

"It was the antidote to the poison which is affecting your husband, Madam. It is sure to be quite concentrated, and I don't want to harm him by giving too much, too fast. He will have to take it for the rest of his life, but with it he will never be ill like this again."

"But, I told you he's not being poisoned. I should be ill too, if he were."

"Oh no, he's not received any poison for over a year. He receives the antidote regularly, as do you, without harm. You told me that his manservant had been with him for many years. Did that include his time in New Guinea?"

"Yes, I believe so. Why do you ask?"

"Madam, one of my hobbies is poisons. There is a small number of very rare poisons that, once administered, reside permanently in the nervous system. They are never got rid of, but can be effectively blocked by the regular ingestion of the antidote. One of these poisons is popular with a tribe in the Sepik River area of New Guinea. It is manufactured from a very odd variety of shellfish native to the area. In an interesting serendipity, the antidote comes from a plant which is also found only in that area. Obviously, while your husband was there, his servant conducted his own research on the side. I suppose he will tell us eventually why he chose to turn traitor, but turn traitor he did, and made use of the poison last year. Your husband made telephone calls generally on market day, did he not?"

"Why, yes, how did you know? The Woodses were always driven to town by Ron, and I would either walk or go for a drive. And Howell—"

"Howell would take the dogs for a walk, would he not?"

"Why, yes. How—"

"They would go down to the woods; he would climb up to the telephone line and listen in on your husband's conversations while the dogs gnawed bones. On the next clear night he would fail to administer the antidote, cloister himself up with his master, and slip up to the roof to signal the results of his spying to a confederate on the coast. Ah, I think it is beginning to work already."

Two dazed eyes looked out of a pale face and fastened onto those of Mrs. Barker.

"My dear," he whispered, "what are these people doing here?"

"Russell," Holmes said quietly, "I believe we should see if we can help with moving Mr. Howell and leave these two good people. Mrs. Barker, I suggest that you guard this bottle most carefully until it can be analysed and duplicated. Good evening."

We found the ambulance attendants working their way awkwardly down the narrow steps. At the front door Jones waited to let them out. A familiar cacophony came from the other side. Holmes reached into his rucksack for the small bottle, but I laid a hand on his arm.

"Let me try first," I said. I cleared my throat, drew myself up to my full height (over six feet in those boots), and opened the door to face the pack. I put my hands on my hips and glared at them.

"Shame on you!" Seventeen jaws slowly shut, thirty-four eyes were glued to my face. "Shame on you, all of you! Is this any way to treat agents of His Majesty? Whatever are you thinking?" Seventeen faces looked at each other, at me, at the men in the doorway. The wolfhound was the first to turn tail and skulk away into the dark, the Yorkie with the blue bow the last, but they all went.

"Russell, there are unexplored depths to you," murmured Holmes at my elbow. "Remind me to call you whenever there is a savage beast to be overcome."

We saw the traitorous butler and his guards off through the gates and walked off down the dark road beneath the telephone line, and talked of various matters all the way home.

❦ 4 ❧

A Case of My Own

What is petty and vile is better than that which is not at all.

THE BARKER PROBLEM was the first time Holmes and I collab-
orated on a case (if one can consider it a collaboration when
one person leads and the other follows instructions). The remaining
days of the spring holiday went by uneventfully, and I returned to Oxford much invigorated by my hard labour under Patrick's eye and by
having bagged my first felon. (I ought perhaps to mention that the
night's work resulted in the capture of an even dozen of German spies,
that Mr. Barker recovered his health, and that Mrs. Barker was quite
generous in her payment for services rendered.)

When I returned to my lodgings house Mr. Thomas seemed to approve of my appearance, and I know that I returned to maths, theological enquiry, and the career of Ratnakar Sanji with renewed

enthusiasm. I made it a point also to take exercise more often, walking into the hills surrounding the city (with a book in hand, of course) and did not find myself quite so exhausted when the year ended in June.

That spring and summer of 1918 was a time of intense emotions and momentous events for the country as well as for one female undergraduate. The Kaiser had begun his final, massive push, and the pinched and hungry faces around me began to look grim as well. We did not sleep well, behind our blackout curtains. And then, miraculously, the German offensive began to falter, while at the same time the Allied forces were taking on a constant flow of American transfusions, men and supplies. Even the huge and deadly May air raid on London did not change the increasing awareness that the German army was bleeding to death into the soil, and that after so many years of mere dogged existence, there was now a glimmer of future in the air.

I strode home in midsummer eighteen and a half years old, strong and adult and with the world at my feet. That summer I began to take an active interest in the running of my farm, and began to ask Patrick the first questions about farming equipment and our plans for the postwar future.

I found that in my absence Holmes had changed. It took a while to see that perhaps he was a bit taken aback by this young woman who had suddenly emerged from gangly, precocious, adolescent Mary Russell. Not that I was outwardly very different—I had filled out, but mostly in bone and muscle, not curves, and I still wore the same clothes and braided my hair in two long plaits. It was in my attitude and how I moved, and how I met him eye to eye (in conversation, but nearly so in stature). I was beginning to feel my strength and explore it, and I think it made him feel old. I know that I first noticed caution in him that summer, when he went around a cliff rather than launch himself down it. That is not to say that he became a doddery old man—far from it. He was just a bit thoughtful at times, and I would catch him looking at me pensively after I had done some exuberant thing or other.

We went to London a number of times that summer to see her limited wartime offerings, and I saw him move differently there, as if the very air changed him, making his muscles go taut and his joints loosen. London was his home as the downs never would be, and he returned relaxed and renewed to his experiments and his writing. If the summer before I went up to Oxford was one of sun and chess games under the open sky, my first summer home had a tinge of bitter in the sweet, as I realised for the first time that even Holmes was limited by mortality.

That awareness was at the time peripheral, however. Bitterness is an aftertaste that comes when the sweetness has had time to fade, and there was much that was sweet about that summer. Sweetest of all were the two cases that came our way.

I say two, although the first was hardly a case, more of a lark. It began one morning in July when I walked down to Patrick's house with an article I had read concerning a new mulching technique developed in America, and found him slamming furiously about in his kitchen. Taking the hot kettle from his hand before he injured himself, I poured it over the leaves and asked him what was the matter.

"Oh, Miss Mary, it's nothing really. Just that Tillie Whiteneck, down the inn? She was robbed last night." The Monk's Tun, on the road between Eastbourne and Lewes, was popular with locals and holiday trippers. And with Patrick.

"Robbed? Was she hurt?"

"No, everyone was asleep." Burglary, then. "They forced the back door and took her cash box and some of the food. Real quiet about it—nobody knew until Tillie came down to start the stove in the morning and found the back door open. She had a lot in the box, too, more than usual. There were a couple big parties, and she was too busy to take the money down to the bank."

I commiserated, gave him the article, and walked back to the main house, thinking. I put a telephone call through to Holmes, and while Mrs. Hudson went to fetch him I sat at the desk and watched Patrick move across the yard between the barns, his shoulders set in anger and depression. When Holmes came on the line I came to the point.

"Holmes, didn't you tell me a few weeks ago that there has been a series of burglaries from inns and public houses in Eastbourne?"

"I hardly think two qualifies as a series, Russell. You are interrupting a delicate haemoglobin experiment, you know."

"Now it's three," I said, ignoring his protest. "Patrick's lady-friend at the Tun had her cash box taken last night."

"My dear Russell, I am retired. I am no longer required to retrieve missing pencil boxes or track down errant husbands."

"Whoever took it just happened to choose a time when the box was much fuller than it normally is," I persisted. "It is not a comfortable feeling, knowing that the thief may be in the area. Besides," I added, sensing a faint waver down the telephone line, "Patrick's a friend." It was the wrong card to play.

"I am so pleased for you that you can count your farm manager as a friend, Russell, but that does not justify dragging me into this little affaire. I believe I heard a rumour that Sussex now has a constabulary force. Perhaps you would be so good as to let them be about their work and let me be about mine."

"You don't mind if I look into it, do you?"

"Good heavens, Russell, if time hangs so heavy on your hands and you've run out of bandages to wrap, by all means thrust your nose into this momentous crime, this upsurge of depravity on our very doorsteps. I only suggest that you not annoy the constabulary more than you have to."

The line went dead. In irritation I hung up my earpiece and went to get out my bicycle.

I was hot and dusty when I reached the inn, not a very prepossessing figure, and I had practically to tug the sleeve of the village constable before I was allowed a glimpse of the scene of the crime. I positively itched to look more closely, but the good PC Rogers, proud of his outré little crime, had the better part of the downstairs roped off awaiting his inspector, and he would not hear of trespass. Even the owner and her workers and guests were forced to edge through the room behind a wall of potted palms, which were already suffering from the attentions of steamer trunks and Gladstone bags.

"I promise you," I begged, "I won't disturb anything. I just want to look at the carpet."

"Can't do it, Miss Russell. Orders were to let no one through."

"Which means, of course," snapped a voice from the violently waving palms, "that I cannot have any food from my kitchen, so I lose not only my cash box, but today's income as well. Oh, hello, you're Patrick's Miss Russell, aren't you? Here to look at our crime?"

"Trying to," I admitted.

"Oh, for heaven's sake, Jammy, let her—Oh all right, all right: 'Constable Rogers,' let her have a peep. She's a bright girl, and she's here, which is more than I can say for this inspector of yours."

"Yes, Rogers, do let her have a peep," drawled a voice from the door. "I'll stand bail that she won't disturb anything."

"Mr. Holmes!" said the startled police constable, reaching for his helmet and then, changing his mind, straightening his shoulders instead.

"Holmes!" I exclaimed. "I thought you were busy."

"By the time you let me go the blood had clotted beyond all recognition," he said dismissively. He ignored the expressions on the faces around us that his statement had brought, and waved a hand at the young constable.

"Let her in, Rogers." Meekly, the uniformed man went to drop the rope for me.

Torn between fury and mortification I stalked forward to the beginning of the runner carpet and, wrapping myself in every shred of dignity I could muster, bent to examine it. The carpet was new this season, had been brushed the night before, and did not take long to reveal its secrets. With my cheek nearly touching the fibers to take advantage of the angle of the light, I spoke to Holmes.

"This is from a medium-sized man's boot with a pointed toe and a worn heel on the left foot. The pile of the carpet has lifted off more of an impression than the bare floor. There are also tiny bits of gravel, dark grey and black, or—?"

Holmes materialised at my knee and held out the glass I had neglected to bring. Through its lens the three bits of stone came into focus.

"Dark gravel with tar on it, and an overall haze of oil. And down here—is that a bit of reddish soil, rubbed off on the edge of the carpet?"

Holmes took the heavy glass from my hand and retraced my steps on his hands and knees. He made no comment, just handed the glass back to me and gestured that I should continue. He was turning this into an all-too-public viva voce exam.

"Where does red soil come up?" I asked. "There's a patch where the road dips, south of the village, I remember, and two or three along the river. And wasn't there some near the Barkers' house?"

"Not so red, I think," said Holmes. "And I believe a strong lens might reveal that this has a more claylike texture." He volunteered nothing more. Fine, I thought, be that way. I turned to Constable Rogers, who was looking uncomfortable.

"The council has been surfacing a number of the roads recently, hasn't it? Would you happen to know where the crews have been working in the last week or so?"

He shifted, looked to Holmes for advice, and apparently received it, because he looked back at me and answered. "There's a patch about six miles north, and the mill road they did last week. And a section just east of Warner's place. Nothing closer since last month."

"Thank you, that narrows it down a bit. Now, Mrs. Whiteneck, if I might have a word?" I took Patrick's friend to one side and asked her for a list of the names and addresses of her employees, and told her that as soon as the police inspector had been, he would allow her to use her kitchen. She looked much relieved.

"Did Patrick say the thief took food, too?" I asked her.

"That he did: four beautiful hams I had just taken from the smoke-house; lovely, fat things they were. And three bottles of the best whisky. Set me back a bit, they did, and heaven knows how I'll replace them, what with the shortages and the rationing. Here, you're sure he'll let me use the kitchen?"

"I'm sure he will. Even if he's struck by a fit of mad efficiency he'll only want to leave that part of the carpet and the doors for a finger-print expert, but that may be hoping for too much. I will let you know what I've found."

Outside the Monk's Tun the sun was fully up and the narrow village lane was hot and bright. I spared a moment's thought for the work crew I was supposed to be in and pushed it away. I felt Holmes at my elbow.

"I'd like to take a look at your topographical maps, if I may," I said. This in itself was an admission of failure, that I did not hold the details of the Ordnance Survey for my own district firmly to mind, but he did not comment.

"All the resources of the firm are yours to command," he said. This proved to include one of the automobiles his neighbour ran as the rural taxi service, which was standing next to the inn. We got in and returned to Holmes' cottage.

I greeted Mrs. Hudson and went through the sitting room to the cabinet where Holmes kept his vast collection of maps. I found the ones I needed and spread them out on the worktable and made notes of the five places that I knew had red clay surfacing from the chalky soil of the downs. Holmes had busied himself with some other project, but when he walked past the table to fetch a book he casually laid a fingertip first at one place on the map, then another, reminding me of two more occurrences.

"Thank you," I said to his back. "In all but one of the places where the red soil is found, the map shows an outcropping of rock. Two of those correspond both with—Are you at all interested in this,

Holmes?" He did not look up from his book but waved his hand in a gesture I took to mean "continue," so I did. "There are only two places where we find a combination of red soil, recent road work, and employees of the Tun. One is north two miles on the Heathfield road, and the other is west, down near the river." I waited for a response, received none, and went to the telephone. Apparently I was to be in charge of this investigation, although, I suspected, with a hawk-eyed critic at my shoulder. As I waited to be connected it occurred to me that I had not heard the taxi leave and indeed, when I glanced out the window, there it was in the drive, the man behind the wheel settled back with a book. I was briefly annoyed at Holmes, not so much because of his easy anticipation of our needs as because I had not thought to have the automobile wait.

The exchange connected me with the Monk's Tun.

"Mrs. Whiteneck? Mary Russell here. Has the inspector arrived yet? He did? Oh, did he? PC Rogers must have been disappointed. Yes. Still, you have your kitchen back. Look, Mrs. Whiteneck, could you tell me which of your employees are at the inn today, and the hours they'll be working? Yes. Yes. Fine, thanks, then. Yes, I'll be in touch." I rang off.

"Inspector Mitchell came, took a look, gave PC Rogers a dressing-down for wasting his time, and left," I said to the room at large, received back the response I expected, which was none, and sat looking at the list of names. They included Jenny Wharton, a maid at the inn who lived on the north road and worked today until eight o'clock, and Tony Sylvester, a new barkeep, who would be away from his home near the river until well after seven.

Now what?

I could not very well arrive at their respective houses and search them in their absence. Were I to stumble innocently across the cache of stolen goods, though, that might be a different matter. However, I could scarcely claim that I just happened to see the box under a bed up in the first-storey bedroom or smell the ham in—Wait now, smelling four hams, that might be . . . What if . . . ?

"Holmes, do you suppose—Oh, never mind." I took down the telephone again and asked for another number. Holmes turned a page in his book.

"Mrs. Barker, good morning. This is Mary Russell. How are you? And your husband? Good, I'm glad. Yes, we were quite fortunate, weren't we? I say, Mrs. Barker, of your dogs, do you have one that's good at tracking? Yes, you know, following a scent. You do? Would you mind lending him to me for a little while? No, no, I'll come up and get him. He'll ride in an automobile, won't he? Good, I'll be there in a bit, then. Thank you."

I put up the receiver. "Holmes, do you mind if I use the car that is waiting so obviously in the drive?"

"But of course," he said, and put his book back on the shelf.

We rode to the inn, where I borrowed a clean tea towel and rubbed it into one of the remaining hams, then went back up the road to the Barkers' house. The ravening hordes descended on the car, causing the driver to swerve and curse under his breath as the dogs leapt and bit at the wheels and carried on as if they were about to eat us alive, tyres and all. I opened the door into their midst, and when I stepped out the entire pack went instantly silent and began to study the sky and sniff at the tussocks of grass growing along the drive, and to drift away unobtrusively. Mrs. Barker came out with a collar and lead in her hand, looked surprised at the tame mob, and went over to a bush to retrieve a very sorry-looking specimen with long ears, patchy fur, and an undercarriage that brushed the ground. She led him back to us and handed me the lead.

"This is Justinian," she said, and added, "They're all named after emperors."

"I see. Well, we shall have the emperor in before nightfall, I expect. Come, Justinian." He ambled along at the end of the lead, climbed laboriously into the car, and proceeded to give Holmes' boots a thorough bath with his tongue.

I directed the driver first to the road that led north and had him let us out to wander the roads. Justinian sniffed industriously but gave no response to the hammy tea towel. After a while we got back into the car and drove on to the mill road, beyond which lived Tony Sylvester. Again Holmes and I walked the verge while Justinian snuffled in the weeds and anointed them. We walked on, and on, a parade of dog, humans, and automobile, and I had quite enough time to regret bitterly that I had ever involved myself in this farce. Holmes said nothing. He did not have to.

"Another half mile," I said between clenched teeth, "and we assume either that the man was not on foot, or that the imperial nose is not what it was. Come on, Justinian." I took the cloth and waved it under his nose. "Find! Find!"

He paused in his delicate examination of a flattened toad at the side of the road to savour the hammy cloth, his eyes lowered pensively. He stood for a moment, thinking deep thoughts inside his unkempt head, sat down to scratch a flea in his left ear, stood up, sneezed vigorously, and set off firmly down the road. We followed, more quickly now, and in a few minutes he dove off onto a thin track, under a fence, and into a field. Holmes signaled the car to wait where it was, and we clambered over in Justinian's wake.

"I hope this is not the field with the bull in it," I muttered.

"There is a path, so it is doubtful. Hello, what is this?"

It was a ten-shilling note, crushed into a patch of soft soil by a bovine hoof. Holmes carefully extricated it and placed it in my hand.

"Not the most professional job in the world, would you say, Russell? He couldn't even wait to get home to gloat over his booty."

"I did not take up this investigation for its intense mental stimulation," I snapped. "I only wished to help out a friend."

"One cannot be too demanding, I suppose. Still, I may be home in time to resume the haemoglobin experiment. Ah yes, I believe we—I believe you have found Mr. Sylvester's house."

The faint path went through another fence and dwindled away at a small stone farmhouse that had a faintly desolate air. There was no sign of life, no answers to our calls. Justinian tugged us along to a little smokehouse that stood apart, gently emitting curls of fragrant smoke. He went up to it and stood, nose to the crack, whining irritably. I opened the door, and in the dark, smoke-filled interior saw three whole hams and part of a fourth. I took my knife from my pocket and cut off a large piece, tossing it to the ground in front of Justinian.

"Clever dog." I patted him and snatched my hand back when he snarled at me. "Stupid dog, I'm not about to give it to you and then take it away."

"Where will you look for the cash box, Russell?"

"It's bound to be someplace inconvenient, such as in the rafters of this smokehouse or down the pit in the privy. Nothing that requires a great deal of imagination or intellect: I admit it was a nice touch to hide the hams in an active smokehouse, but I'd have thought that an indication of sound criminal instinct rather than brains; even an urban investigator might think it odd to find the remains of a pig blessed with two pairs of hams but neither trotters nor bacon."

"Yes," he sighed. "My life has been plagued by criminals with instinct and no sense; I shall leave this one to you. You search, while I walk back and bring the driver. Shall I open the house for you before I go?" he asked politely, holding out his ring of picklocks.

"Yes, please."

The inn's box was not in the smokehouse rafters, nor down the odoriferous pit. Nor did I find it dangling in the well or, moving inside, under the man's bed or on the attic rafters or even under a loose floorboard. The driver outside was deeply entrenched in a cheap novel, happy enough to wait, but it was getting late. Holmes and I met in the tiny kitchen over the dirty dishes. Sylvester had eaten beans for supper the night before, and the pan stood on the sideboard, well crusted over. The remainder of the fourth ham was on a plate in the cupboard. The flies were enjoying it.

"He wasn't too clever in the taking of it, but he has hidden it well," I said.

"Yes, has he not? What time did Mrs. Whiteneck say he was re-lieved? That's right, seven o'clock. It's six-thirty now, so the car must go. May I suggest we send him off with a note to our good constable, whose presence might be of some service at about, shall we say, seven-thirty?"

"Perhaps slightly later. It will take Sylvester at least twenty minutes to bicycle back here from the inn. It wouldn't do to have him over-taken by the police on his way home."

"You are right, Russell, make it seven-forty-five. Good. I'll give a note to the driver and have him take it to Constable Rogers."

"Have him take Justinian back, too. Let him go home in glory."

The car turned around in the front of the house and departed, and Holmes disappeared into one of the outhouses and returned with a rusty chisel and hammer, with which he approached the open door.

"What are you doing, Holmes?" I asked. He stopped.

"I beg your pardon, Russell, I was forgetting myself. Old habits die hard. I shall just return these to their place."

"Wait, Holmes, I was only asking."

"Ah. Well, I have occasionally taken advantage of the fact that a person who sees a clear danger to something he or she values tends to reach immediately for that object. You undoubtedly have another plan. Forgive me for interfering."

"No, no, that's fine. You go right ahead, Holmes." I stood watching while he deftly locked the kitchen door with his picklocks, then de-stroyed the lock in a shower of splinters with the hammer and chisel. He went to return the tools, and I stepped into the kitchen to liberate four stale bread rolls from a parcel on the table and then returned to the smokehouse to help myself to a few slices of one of Mrs. White-neck's purloined hams that had not already fed half the houseflies in Sussex. I do not normally eat pork, but decided that this time I might make an exception. I brushed a dirty smear from the greasy surface, sliced the ham onto the rolls, and looked thoughtfully at my hand, then at the ham, then at the floor.

"Holmes!" I called.

"Found something, Russell?"

"Is senility contagious, Holmes? Because if so, we've both got it."

"Beg your pardon?"

"This ham has been put down in a patch of red clay soil, and a foot has deposited red clay soil onto the floor of the smokehouse. Don't you think it might be a good idea to investigate further that outcropping of red clay soil? Here's a sandwich; sorry there's no beer to go with it."

"Just a moment." Holmes walked back through the broken door and, after several heavy thuds and the crash of breaking glass, returned with a large bottle of Bass ale and two glasses, which he rinsed off under the pump. "Shall we go?"

We carried our picnic up the slope that lay near the house and found the red clay lying at the side of an upthrust cliff of tumbled boulders. It was now after seven o'clock, and it would take some time to scramble over the rocks and look for possible hiding places. An examination of the soil showed several mates to the print we had seen on the inn's carpet. Red smudges led up the cliff. I took a bite of my sandwich and grimaced at the bread.

"I propose we let him bring the box down for us, Holmes. I should like to enjoy this ham and have something to drink."

"It is a very nice ham, despite the second smoking. Perhaps Mrs. Whiteneck could be persuaded to part with some, in lieu of payment. I believe, Russell, that if we take up a position among those shrubs there, it will afford us both cover and an excellent view of house and hillside."

That is precisely what we did. Holmes opened the bottle and we refreshed ourselves. Soon our quarry appeared, pedalling rapidly down the road and into his gate. From there it went rather like a well-constructed fall of dominoes, set off by the splintered lock on the back door. We munched and drank and peered through the leaves at the sight of Sylvester standing shocked at his door, disappearing inside, where he found all the signs of a violent search, then bursting outside again and hurtling up the hill towards us. His face was red and sweat-ing as he scrambled up the rocks, and I winced as he slid hard and bashed his shin. At the halfway point he lay down and reached far back behind two large rocks, and we could see his entire body relax as his hand encountered the box.

"Come, now," murmured Holmes, "bring it down like a good boy, and save us a climb. Ah, good, I thought you might like to play with it again."

Sylvester, hugging the metal box awkwardly to his chest, worked his way slowly down the rocks. He nearly fell once, and I held my breath in anticipation of broken bones and scattered money, but he re-covered with no more than a torn knee and made it safely to the bot-tom. His face was eager and gloating as he trotted off to his house, cradling the heavy box in his arms. Holmes and I finished the beer and followed him.

"Russell, I believe this is the point at which your reinforcements come into play. I shall wait here while you go up the road and bring PC Rogers—quietly!"

"Holmes, the Barkers' dogs may listen to me, but PC Rogers does not. I think if there is any fetching and commanding to be done, you had best do it."

"Hum. You may be right. However, if you remain here you must under no circumstances approach Mr. Sylvester. If he leaves, then fol-low, at a very discreet distance. Cornered rats bite, Russell: no heroics, please."

I assured him that I had no intention of taking on the man single-handed, and we separated. I took up a position behind the smoke-house, where I could see if he made a dash for the river, and picked up a handful of stones to practise my juggling. I had managed to work my way up to keeping five stones in the air when something invisible and inaudible to me set off another series of rapid events.

The first indication was a scrabble and thump from within the house. The kitchen door crashed open and a young thief with black hair and a frightened face exploded out, trailing currency notes like autumn leaves. Shouts and the pounding of heavy feet came from the front of the house, but Sylvester was fast and had a considerable lead. He flew past me, accelerating, and without thinking I plucked one of my remaining stones from the air and sent it spinning after him. It took him on the back of his leg and must have numbed it for an instant, because the knee collapsed and he tumbled heavily onto the ground. I reached down to snatch up another rock, but Holmes and Rogers came up then, and it was unnecessary.

W E DINED THAT night at Mrs. Whiteneck's inn. Holmes had the ham, and I enjoyed mutton with mint sauce, and we helped ourselves from bowls of tiny potatoes and glazed carrots and a variety of other delicacies from the good earth of the Sussex countryside. Mrs. Whiteneck herself served us with an unfussy competence and withdrew.

Some time passed before I sat back and sighed happily.

"Thank you, Holmes. That was fun."

"You find even such rustic and unadorned sleuthing satisfying?"

"I do. Did. I cannot see spending my life pursuing such activities, but as a romp through the countryside on a summer's day, it was most pleasurable. Don't you agree?"

"As an exercise, Russell, you conducted the investigation in a most professional manner."

"Why, thank you, Holmes." I was ridiculously pleased.

"By the way, where did you learn to throw like that?"

"My father thought all young ladies should be able to throw and to run. He was not amused by cultivated awkwardness. He was a great lover of sports, and was trying to introduce cricket into San Francisco the summer before . . . the accident. I was to be his bowler."

"Formidable," my companion murmured.

"So he thought. It is a useful skill, you must admit. One can always find chunks of débris to heave at wrong-doers."

"*Quod erat demonstrandum.* However, Russell . . ." He fixed me with a cold eye, and I braced myself for some devastating criticism, but what he said was, "Now, Russell: concerning that haemoglobin experiment . . ."

Book Two

INTERNSHIP

The Senator's Daughter

❦

The Vagrant Gipsy Life

Seize her, imprison her, take her away.

THE MONK'S TUN case was, as I said, but a lark, the sort of non-case that even a dyed-in-the-wool romantic like Watson would have been hard put to whip into a thrilling narrative. The police would surely have caught Sylvester before long, and truly, thirty guineas and four hams, even in those days of chronic food shortages, were hardly the stuff of *Times* headlines.

Nonetheless, across all the tumultuous events of the intervening years that one case stands out in my mind, for the simple reason that it marked the first time Holmes had granted me free rein to make decisions and take action. Of course, even then I realised that, had the case been of any earthly significance whatsoever, I should have been kept firmly in my auxiliary role. Despite that, the glow of secret satisfaction it gave me lasted with a curious tenacity. A small thing, perhaps, but mine own.

Five weeks later, however, a case came upon us that put the Monk's Tun affair into its proper, childish perspective. The kidnapping of the American senator's daughter was no lark, but a matter of international import, dramatic, intense, a classic Holmes case such as I had not yet observed, much less been involved with, and certainly not as a central protagonist. The case brought into sharp focus the purpose surrounding my years of desultory training, brought forcibly home the entire raison d'être of the person Sherlock Holmes had created of himself, and moreover, brought me up against the dark side of the life Holmes led.

That single case bound us together in ways my apprenticeship never had, rather as the survivors of a natural disaster find themselves inextricably linked for the rest of their days. It made me both more certain of myself and, paradoxically, more cautious now that I had witnessed at first hand the potentially calamitous results of my unconsidered acts. It changed Holmes, too, to see before him the living result of his years of half-frivolous, half-deliberate training. I believe it brought him up sharply, to be confronted with the fact that he had created a not inconsiderable force, that what had begun as a chance meeting had given birth to me. His reappraisal of what I had become, his judgement of my abilities under fire, as it were, profoundly influenced the decisions he was to make four months later when the heavens opened on our heads.

And yet, I very nearly missed the case altogether. Even today my spine crawls cold at the thought of December without the mutual knowledge of the preceding August, for the groundwork of trust laid down during our time in Wales made December's partnership possible. Had I missed the Simpson case, had Holmes simply disappeared into the thin summer air (as he had done with numerous other cases) and not allowed me to participate, God alone knows what we would have done when December's cold hit us, unprepared and unsupported.

TOWARD NOON ON a blistering hot day in the middle of August our haying crew reached the end of the last field and dispersed, in heavy-footed exhaustion, for our homes. This year the easy camaraderie and rude high spirits of the Land Girls had been cooled by the presence of a man amongst the crew, a silent, rigid, shell-shocked young man—a boy, really, but for the trenches—who did no great work himself and who started at every sudden noise, but who served to keep us at our work by his mere distressing presence. Thanks to him we finished early, just before midday on the eighteenth. I trudged home, silently inhaled a vast meal in Patrick's kitchen, and, wanting only to collapse between my clean sheets for twenty hours, instead took myself to the bathroom and stripped off my filthy Land Girl's smock, sluiced off my skin's crust of dust and chaff cemented there by sweat, and, feeling physically tired but glowing with strength and well-being and marvelling in the sense of freedom following a hard job well done, I mounted my bicycle and, hair streaming damply behind me, rode off to see Holmes.

Cycling slowly up the lane to the cottage, my ears were caught by a remarkable sound, distorted by the stone walls on either side. Music, but no music I had before heard, emanating from Holmes' house, a gay, dancing tune, instantly invigorating and utterly unexpected. I stood more firmly on the pedals, rode around the house to the kitchen door, and let myself in, and when I followed the sound through to the sitting room, for an instant I failed to recognise the dark-skinned, black-haired man with the violin tucked under a chin scruffy with two days of stubble. The briefest flash of apprehension passed across the familiar face, followed rapidly by a gleam of gold from his left incisor as this exotic ruffian gave me a rakish grin. I was not fooled. I had seen his original reaction to my unexpected appearance in his doorway, and my guard went instantly up.

"Holmes," I said. "Don't tell me, the rector needs a gipsy fiddler for the village fête."

"Hello, Russell," he said with studied casualness. "This is an unanticipated pleasure. I am so glad you happened to stop by, it saves me from having to write. I wanted to ask you to keep track of the plant experiment. Just for a few days, and there's nothing terribly—"

"Holmes, what is going on?" He was entirely too innocent.

" 'Going on'? Nothing is 'going on.' I find I must be away for a few days, is all."

"You have a case."

"Oh, come now, Russell—"

"Why don't you want me to know about it? And don't give me some nonsense about governmental secrets."

"It is secret. I cannot tell you about it. Later, perhaps. But I truly do need you to—"

"Jigger the plants, Holmes," I said angrily. "The experiment is of no importance whatsoever."

"Russell!" he said, offended. "I only leave them because I have been asked by someone I cannot refuse."

"Holmes," I said warningly, "this is Russell you're talking to, not Watson, not Mrs. Hudson. I'm not in the least bit intimidated by you. I want to know why you were planning to sneak out without telling me."

" 'Sneak out'! Russell, I said I was glad you happened by."

"Holmes, I'm not blind. You're in full disguise except for your shoes, and there's a packed bag in the corner. I repeat: What is going on?"

"Russell, I am very sorry, but I cannot include you in this case."

"Why not, Holmes?" I was becoming really very angry. So was he.

"Because, damn it, it may be dangerous!"

I stood staring across the room at him, and my voice when it came was, I was pleased to note, very quiet and even.

"My dear Holmes, I am going to pretend you did not say that. I am going to walk in your garden and admire the flowers for approximately ten minutes. When I come back in we will begin this conversation anew, and unless you wish to divorce yourself from me entirely, the idea of protecting little Mary Russell will never enter your head." I walked out, closing the door gently, and went to talk with Will and the two cats. I pulled some weeds, heard the violin start up again, this time a more classical melody, and in ten minutes I went back through the door.

"Good afternoon, Holmes. That's a natty outfit you're wearing. I should not have thought to wear an orange tie with a shirt that particular shade of red, but it is certainly distinctive. So, where are we going?"

Holmes looked at me through half-shut eyes. I stood blandly in the doorway, arms folded. Finally he snorted and thrust his violin into its disreputable case.

"Very well, Russell. I may be mad, but we shall give it a try. Have you been following the papers, the Simpson kidnapping case?"

"I saw something a few days ago. I've been helping Patrick with the hay."

"Obviously. Take a look at these while I put your persona together."

He handed me a pile of back issues of *The Times*, then disappeared upstairs into the laboratory.

I sorted them by date. The first, dated the tenth of August, was a small item from a back page, circled by Holmes. It concerned the American Senator Jonathan Simpson, leaving to go on holiday with his family, a wife and their six-year-old daughter, to Wales.

The next article was three days later, the central headline on the first page of the news. It read:

SENATOR'S DAUGHTER KIDNAPPED
HUGE RANSOM SOUGHT

A carefully typed ransom note had been received by the Simpsons, saying simply that she was being held, that Simpson had one week to raise £20,000, and that if he went to the police the child would die. The article did not explain how the newspaper had received the information, or how Simpson was to keep the police out after it had been on the front page. The newsworthiness of the case gradually dwindled, and today's paper, five days after the heavily leaded kidnap headlines, held a grainy photograph of two haggard-looking people on a back page: the parents.

I went and perched my shoulder against the door of the laboratory as Holmes measured and poured and stirred.

"Who called you in?"

"Apparently Mrs. Simpson insisted."

"You don't sound pleased."

He slammed down a pipette, which of course shattered.

"How could I be pleased? Half of Wales has trudged the hillside into mud, the trail is a week old, there are no prints, nobody saw anyone, the parents are hysterical, and since nobody has any idea of what to do, they decide to humour the woman and bring in old Holmes. Old Holmes the miracle worker." He stared sourly at his finger as I fastened a plaster to it.

"Reading that drivel of Watson's, a person would never know I'd had any real failures, the kind that grind away and keep one from sleeping. Russell, I know these cases, I know the feel of how they begin, and this has all the marks. It stinks of failure, and I don't want to be anywhere near Wales when they find that child's body."

"Refuse the case, then."

"I can't. There's always a chance they overlooked something, that these suspicious old eyes might see something." He gave a sharp bark of cynical laughter. "Now, there's a morsel for Watson's notes: Sherlock Holmes trusting in luck. Sit down, Russell, and let me put this muck on your face."

It was horrid, warm and black and slimy like something the dog left behind, and had to go up my nose, in my ears, and around my mouth, but I sat.

"We will be a pair of gipsies. I've arranged for a caravan in Cardiff, where we'll see the Simpsons and then make our way north. I had planned to hire a driver, but since you've been practising on Patrick's team, you can do it. I don't suppose you've picked up any useful skills at Oxford, such as telling fortunes?"

"The girl downstairs from me there is a fiend for Tarot. I could probably imitate the jargon. And there's the juggling."

"There was a deck in the cupboard—Sit still! I told Scotland Yard I'd be in Cardiff tomorrow."

"I thought the ransom note said they had one week? What can you expect to do in two days?"

"You overlooked the agony columns in the papers," he scolded. "The deadline was as much a pro forma demand as the insistence that the police be kept out of it. Nobody takes such demands seriously, least of all kidnappers. We have until the thirtieth of August. Senator Simpson is trying to raise the money, but it will come near to breaking him," he added in a distracted voice, and smeared the repulsive goop onto my eyelids. "A senator, even a powerful one like Simpson, is not always a rich man."

"We're going to Wales. You think the child is still there?"

"It is a very remote area, no one heard an automobile after dark, and the police had every road blocked by six o'clock in the morning. The roadblocks are still up, but Scotland Yard, the Welsh police, and the American staff all think she's in London. They're busy at that end, and they've thrown us Wales as a sop to get the Simpsons out from under their feet. It does mean that we'll have a relatively free hand once we're there. Yes, I think she is still in Wales; not only that, I think she's within twenty miles of the place from which she disappeared. I said sit still!" he growled. He was rubbing the sludge into my ear, so I could not see his face.

"A cool character, if that's the case," I offered, not meaning the child.

"Cool, as you say. And careful: The notes are on cheap, common paper, in common envelopes, typed on the second most common kind of typewriter, three or four years old, and mailed in busy post offices across London. No fingerprints. The spelling, choice of words, and punctuation are consistently atrocious. The layout on the page is precise, the typist indents exactly five spaces at the beginning of each paragraph, and the pressure on the keys indicates some familiarity with typing. Other than the window dressing of illiteracy, the messages are clear and not overly violent, as these things go."

"Window dressing?"

"Window dressing," he said firmly. "There is a mind behind this, Russell, not some casual, uneducated lout." In his face and in his voice a total abhorrence of the crime itself fought a losing battle with his constitutional relish for the chase. I said nothing, and he continued to coat my hands and arms past the elbow with the awful stuff. "That is why we will take no risks, assume no weaknesses on their part. Our disguise is assumed the instant we step outside of that door over there, and not let down for a moment. If you cannot sustain it, you'd best say so now, because one slip could mean the child's life. To say nothing of the political complications that will result if we allow a valued and somewhat reluctant Ally's representative to lose his child while on our soil." His voice was almost mild, but when he looked into my eyes I nearly quailed before him. This was no game of putting on Ratnakar Sanji's turban and a music-hall accent, where the greatest risk was being sent down; the penalty for failure in this rôle could be a child's life. Could even be our own lives. It would have been easy, then, to excuse myself from the case, but—if not now, I asked myself, when? If I refused now, would I ever find the necessary combination of courage and opportunity again? I swallowed, and nodded. He turned and put the beaker on the table, where it would sit, undisturbed, to greet our weary eyes when we returned.

"There," he said. "Let us hope it doesn't stop up the plumbing again. Go have your bath and rinse this through your hair."

I took the bottle of black, viscous dye across the corridor to the bathroom, and some time later stood looking in the mirror at a raven-haired young woman with skin the colour of milky coffee and a pair of exotic blue eyes, dressed in a multitude of voluminous skirts from Holmes' trunks, draped with colourful scarves and a hotchpotch of heavy yellow gold and bright, cheap trinkets at my neck and wrists. I put on my spectacles to study my reflection in the glass, decided that my standard ones were too scholarly and exchanged them for a pair with heavier gold rims and lightly tinted lenses. The effect was incongruous, but oddly appropriate—a modern variation on the conspicuous wealth I already wore. I stepped back to practise a seductive, flashing smile, but only succeeded in making myself giggle.

"Fortunately, it is Mrs. Hudson's day off," was all Holmes said when I swirled into the sitting room. "Sit down, and we shall see what you can do with these cards."

We left after dark to meet the last train going east. I telephoned from the cottage to let my aunt know that I had decided to spend a few days with my friend Lady Veronica in Berkshire, her grandmother had just died and she needed the assistance of her friends, not to expect me back for a week, and I rang off in the midst of her queries and protests. I should have to deal with her anger when I returned, but at least she was not about to complicate matters by calling in the police over her missing niece.

At the station we climbed down from the wheezing omnibus and took our multiple parcels over to the ticket window. I slipped my spectacles from my nose into my pocket, lest the familiar Seaford agent think to look twice at me, but even half-blind there was no mistaking the expression of dislike on his face, held in by the thin rein of his office manners.

"Yes, sir?" he said coldly.

"First class to Bristol," Holmes muttered.

"First class? I'm sorry, there won't be anything suitable. You'll find the second class quite comfortable this time of night."

"Naow, s'got to be first class. 'S me daughter's birfday, she wants a first class."

The agent looked at me, and I smiled shyly at him (which was, I thought, a bit like schoolgirl braids on a lady of the evening, but it seemed to soften him).

"Well, perhaps, it being night we might be able to find something. You'll have to stay in your compartment, though. No wandering about, bothering the other passengers."

Holmes drew himself up and glared blackly at the man.

"If they'll not be bothering us, we'll not be bothering them. How much is it?"

Scandalised eyes looked away as we climbed colourfully aboard with our various bags and parcels (I imagined letters going off in the morning post to the editorial page of *The Times*, but as we were busy for the next few days I do not know if they actually appeared.), and we had a compartment to ourselves for the trip. I opened the case file Holmes handed me, but the long day's work under the hot sun and the tension conspired against me. Holmes woke me at Bristol, where we found rooms in a sleazy hotel near the station and slept until morning.

The remainder of the trip to Cardiff was decidedly less luxurious than the first part, and Holmes had to help me off the train, as my leg had fallen asleep with the weight of the bags and the woman wedged in beside me. When I could walk, he put his whiskered face against my ear and spoke in a low voice.

"Now, Russell, we shall see what you can do on your own. We have an appointment with the Simpsons in the office of Chief Inspector Connor at half-twelve. It would not be the best of ideas to go in through the front door, as I told you, so we are going to be arrested. Kindly don't manhandle your persecutor too badly. His bones are old."

He picked up the two smallest bags and walked away, leaving me to deal with the remaining four. I followed him to the exit, past a uniformed constable watching the crowd—and us, closely no doubt. The crush at the door grew thick, and Holmes stopped suddenly to avoid stepping on a child. I bumped into him and dropped a parcel, and as I struggled to retrieve it it was kicked away by various feet, beginning with a pair of garish gipsy boots. By dint of elbows and shoulders I followed the parcel, and as I reached down to pick it up something suddenly slammed me against the wall, where I collapsed in a heap of skirts and baggage. A voice snarled loudly above my head.

"Aw for God's sake, can you not 'ang on t'yer bags? I shoulda brought your brother; at least he can stand up straight." A hard hand seized my arm and jerked me upright, but when it let go too soon I stumbled into a group of elegantly dressed men. Gloved hands kept me from falling, but all movement through the doors had come to an abrupt halt.

"Damn you, girl, you're worse than your mother for falling into the arms of strange men. Get over here and pick up your things," he yelled and, hauling me out of the supporting hands of my rescuers, shoved me hard towards the bags. Tears had come into my eyes with the pain of the wall's initial impact, and now I groped blindly for the handles and strings. A murmur of properly accented voices protested my mistreatment, but none moved to stop my "father."

"But Da', they was only tryin' to help me—"

I saw his hand coming towards me and moved with it, but it still connected with a crack. I cowered against the wall with my arms over my head and cried out piteously when his shoe kicked the valise beneath me.

Finally a police whistle rang out.

"Stop you that, man," cried the Welsh voice of authority. "There's shameful, there is, hurting a child."

"She's no child, and she needs some sense beat into her."

"That you will not, man. No," he shouted, and grabbed Holmes' upraised arm. "We'll not be having that. There's to the station with the both of you; we shall see if that cools your tempers." He looked at me more closely and then turned to the group of men. "Perhaps you gentlemen might care to check your pockets, see if there might be anything missing?"

To my relief there was nothing, although I would not have put it past Holmes to add that bit of verisimilitude to the proceedings. The constable made good his threat anyway, and as my voice joined with Holmes' in vociferous abuse we were bundled into the back of a police van and taken away. Once inside the wagon we did not look at each other. I sniffed occasionally. It concealed the smile that kept creeping onto my lips.

At the station a PC seized Holmes' handcuffed arm and led him roughly away. My own young constable and the matronly sort he handed me over to both seemed undecided as to whether I was an innocent victim or a worse scoundrel than my father, and it required an enormous amount of effort and a tedious amount of time before I could make myself sufficient of a nuisance to be granted my request, which was a brief interview with Chief Inspector Connor. Finally, I stood outside the door that held his name on a brass plaque. The tight-lipped, over-corseted matron hissed at me to stay where I was and went to speak with a secretary. Matron glared at me, secretary raked me with scandalised eyes, but I did not care. I was there, and it was only twenty past twelve.

To my dismay, however, the secretary decided to stand firm. She shook her head, waved her hand at the closed door, and was very obviously refusing me access to the man inside. I dug out a pen and a scrap of paper from my capacious pockets and, after a moment's thought, wrote on it the name of the child whose fate brought us here. I folded it three times and walked over to hold it out deferentially to the secretary.

"I'm terribly sorry, Miss," I said. "I shouldn't think of bothering the chief inspector if I weren't absolutely certain that he would want to see me. Please, just give this to him. If he does not wish to see me after that, I shall go away quietly."

She looked at the folded scrap, but perhaps the uplifted syntax got through to her, because she took my note and went resolutely through the door. Voices from inside cut off short, then came hers in tones of apology, and then an abrupt and stifled exclamation was all the warning I had before a florid, middle-aged man with thinning red hair and an ill-fitting tweed suit stormed out of the doorway, growling magnificently in the rumble and roll of his Welsh origins.

"If the Pharaoh in Egypt had been so plagued by Moses as I have been by all the troublemakers of the world he would have delivered the children of Israel in his own carriage to the very gates of Jericho. Now look you here, Miss," he pinned me down with a pair of tired, brilliant blue eyes, "there's pitiful, there is, the sly ways of your sort, coming by here and—"

I leant into the gale of his speech and contributed two low, forceful words of my own.

"Sherlock Holmes," I pronounced. His head snapped up as if I had slapped him. He took a step back and ran his eyes over me, and I was amused to see him think that even a man famous throughout the world for his skill at disguise was not likely to be the person before him. His eyes narrowed.

"And how are you knowing about—" He stopped, glanced at the startled woman in the doorway, went back to close his door, and then led me away into a smaller, shabbier office than the one I had caught a glimpse of—an interview room, with three doors. He closed the door behind us.

"You will explain yourself," he ordered.

"With pleasure," I said sweetly. "Would you mind awfully if I were to sit down?"

For the first time he actually looked at me, drawn up short by the thick Oxford drawl emerging from the gipsy girl, and I reflected upon the extraordinary effect gained by speech that is incongruous with one's appearance. He gestured to a chair, and I took possession of it. I sat. I waited. He sat.

"Thank you," I said. "There is a certain Romany gentleman being held in your cells—my 'father.' That is actually Sherlock Holmes. I understand that he did not wish it known that he was being called in on the Simpson case, so we chose to arrive for the appointment through the back door, shall we say, rather than the front. Your officers were very polite," I hastened to reassure him, not altogether truthfully.

"Jesus God," he swore under his breath. "Sherlock Holmes in the lockup. Donaldson!" he bellowed. A door opened behind me. "I want here the gipsy they arrested by the train station. You will bring him, yourself."

Heavy silence descended, until Connor abruptly recalled the two Americans in his office and scrambled away. His voice vibrated through the intervening space for several minutes. He then came out of his office and spoke in a low voice to his secretary.

"We will drink tea, Miss Carter, biscuits, whatever. A tray in to the Simpsons, if you please. And by here, three teas. Yes, three."

He came back into the interview room, lowered himself cautiously into the chair across from me, and folded his hands together on top of the table.

"Nah," he said, "there's funny there is. Why was I not told . . ." He stopped, and with an effort shook the Welsh from his tongue and put on English like a uniform. "That is to say, I did not know that there would be someone accompanying him."

"He himself did not know it until yesterday. My name is Mary Russell. I shall be his assistant on the case."

His mouth slid out of control, but he was saved from further conversation on the matter by the arrival of Donaldson and Holmes. The latter was still in handcuffs, but his eyes sparkled with amusement, and he was patently enjoying himself despite the bruise darkening the ridge of his already dusky cheek and the puffiness to the left side of his mouth. Connor looked at him aghast.

"Donaldson, what does this mean? What has happened to his face? And take those cuffs from his hands."

Holmes cut in with his roughened voice.

"Naow, cap'n, there bain't no problem. They was just doin' their job, like."

Connor looked hard at Holmes, then glanced at his sergeant.

"Mister Donaldson, you will go down into the cells and you will tell the men with the ready fists that I will have no more of that thing. I do not care what the man before me permitted or encouraged; there will be no more of it. There's bad, that is, Donaldson. Go, you."

Miss Carter came in as the sergeant slunk out and put a tray with three cups and a plate of cakes on the table, keeping her eyes to herself but positively radiating curiosity. Evidently we were not Connor's normal variety of tea guests.

The door closed behind her, and Holmes came to sit in the chair next to mine.

"You are quite to time, Russell. I trust I did not harm you?"

"A few bruises, nothing more. You managed to miss my spectacles. And you?"

"As I said, there were no problems. Chief Inspector Connor, I take it you have met Miss Russell?"

"She . . . introduced herself. As your 'assistant.' I ask you, Mr. Holmes, is this truly necessary?"

There were multiple layers insinuated into his question but, innocent that I was, I did not immediately read them . . . until I saw the way Holmes was just looking at the man, and suddenly I felt myself flush scarlet head to toe. I stood up.

"Holmes, I think you would be better off alone on this case, after all. I shall return home—"

"You will sit down." With that note in his voice, I sat. I did not look at Chief Inspector Connor.

"Miss Russell is my assistant, Chief Inspector. On this case as on others." That was all he said, but Connor sat back in his chair, cleared his throat, and shot me a brief glance that was all the apology I would have, considering that nothing had actually been said aloud.

"Your assistant. Fine."

"That is correct. Her presence makes no difference with the arrangements, however. Are the Simpsons here?"

"In the next room. I thought you and I might have a word, before."

"Quite. We shall leave the city immediately we have seen them. I assume that the roadblocks are still up but that your men are away from the area, as I specified."

"As you asked," Connor agreed, though the resentment in his voice said clearly that he had been forced to follow direct orders from above and was none too happy about it.

Holmes looked up sharply, then settled back deliberately into his chair, his long fingers laced across his stained waistcoat and a thin smile on his lips. "Perhaps we need clarify this matter, Chief Inspector. I 'asked' for nothing. I certainly did not 'ask' that this case be wished upon me. You people approached me, and I only accepted after it had been agreed by all parties that my orders take priority in regards to those few square miles of Welsh countryside. Call them requests if you like, but do not treat them as such. Furthermore, I wish to make clear that Miss Russell here is my official representative, that if she appears without me, any message or 'request' is to be honoured, immediately and without cavil. Are we quite in agreement, Chief Inspector?"

"Nah, Mr. Holmes," Connor began to bluster, the Welsh rhythm creeping back into his throat, "I can hardly think—"

"That is eminently clear, young man. Were you to pause for thought you might realise that a simple 'yes' or 'no' would suffice. If you agree, then we shall speak with the Simpsons and get on with the job. If your answer is 'no,' then you may give Miss Russell back her bags, and I in return will hand you back your case. The decision is entirely yours. Personally I should be glad to get back to my experiments and sleep in my own bed. Which shall it be?"

Cold grey eyes locked with brilliant blue ones, and after a long minute, blue wavered.

"Have no choice, do I? That woman'd have my head." He shoved back from the table, and we followed the disgruntled chief inspector through the room's third door and into his office.

The two people who looked up at our entrance wore catastrophe on their aristocratic faces, that stretched appearance of human beings who have passed the threshold of terror and exhaustion and can feel only a stunned apprehension of what will come next. Both of them were grey, unkempt, and fragile. The man did not stand when we came in, only looked past us at Connor. The tea on the desk was untouched.

"Senator, Mrs. Simpson, may I introduce Mr. Sherlock Holmes and his assistant, Miss Mary Russell."

The senator reared back like the chief mourner at a funeral confronted by a tasteless joke, and Holmes stepped forward quickly.

"I must apologise for my singular appearance," he said in his most plummy Oxbridgian. "I thought it best for the sake of your daughter's safety that I not be seen entering the station, and came in, as it were, through the servant's entrance. I assure you that Miss Russell's disguise is every bit as sham as the gold tooth I am wearing." Simpson's feathers went down, and he rose to shake Holmes' hand. Mrs. Simpson, I noticed, seemed blind to what Holmes and I looked like: From the moment Connor spoke his name her haunted eyes had latched onto Holmes like a drowning woman staring at a floating spar and followed his every move as he shifted a chair around to sit directly in front of them. I sat to one side, and Connor went around to take up his normal chair behind the desk, separated by it from the amateur and unconventional happenings before him.

"Now," said Holmes briskly, "to business. I have read your statements, seen the photographs, reviewed the physical evidence. There is little purpose served in forcing you to go through it all yet again. Perhaps I might merely state the sequence as I understand it, and you will please correct me if I stray." He then went over the information gained from the file and the newspapers: the decision to strike off into the hills of Wales with only a tent, the train to Cardiff and the car up into the hinterland, two days of peace, and the third day waking to find the child vanished from her sleeping roll.

"Did I miss anything?" The two Americans looked at each other, shook their heads. "Very well, I have only two questions. First, why did you come here?"

"I'm afraid I . . . insisted," said Mrs. Simpson. Her fingers were twisting furiously at a delicate lace handkerchief in her lap. "Johnny hasn't had so much as a day off in nearly two years, and I told him . . . I told him that if he didn't take a vacation, I was going to take Jessie and go home." Her voice broke and in an instant Holmes was before her, with that compassion and understanding for a soul in trouble that was so characteristic of him, yet which for some reason always took one by surprise. This time he went so far as to seize her hand, in order to force her to meet his gaze.

"Mrs. Simpson, listen to me. This was not an accident," he said forcibly. "Your daughter was not kidnapped because she just happened to be on that hill at the wrong time. I know kidnappers. Had she not been taken here in Wales, it would have been while out with her nurse at the park, or from her bedroom at home. This was a deliberate, carefully planned crime. It was not your fault."

She, of course, broke down completely, and it took copious supplies of handkerchiefs and a judicious application of brandy before we could return to the point.

"But why here?" Holmes persisted. "How far in advance did you plan it, and who knew?"

The senator answered. "Because we wanted to get as far from civilisation as we could. London—well, I know I'm not being diplomatic, but London's a god-awful place: The air stinks; you can't ever see stars, even with the blackout; it's always noisy; and you never know when the bombs won't start up again. Wales seemed about as far from that as a person could get. I arranged for a week off, oh, it must have been the end of May we started planning it, just after that last big bombing raid."

"Did anyone suggest this area to you?"

"Don't think so. My wife's family came originally from Aberystwyth, so we knew the country in a general sort of way. It's hilly like Colorado, where I grew up, no real mountains of course, but we thought it'd be nice to walk into the hills and tent for a few days. Nothing strenuous because Jessie was—because Jessie's so small. Just someplace quiet and out of the way."

"And the arrangements—the equipment, transportation—an automobile dropped you, did it not? and you arranged for it to meet you after five days—notifying the police and newspapers. Who did all that?"

"My personal assistant. He's English. I believe his brother knew where to hire the tent and whatnot, but you'd have to ask him for the details."

"I have that information for you, Mr. Holmes," growled Connor from his desk. "You'll have it before you leave."

"Thank you, Chief Inspector. Now, Senator, that last day. You went for a walk, bought sausages and bread from a farmhouse, cooked and ate them at five o'clock, stayed inside the tent reading after that because it began to rain. You were asleep by eleven and woke at four o'clock to find your daughter missing."

"She didn't go!" Mrs. Simpson broke in. "Jessica didn't go out of the tent by herself. The dark frightens her; she wouldn't go outside even for the horses. I know she loved those ponies that wander around wild, but she wouldn't follow them off, not my Jessie."

Holmes looked directly into her shell-shocked features.

"That brings me to my second question. How did you feel when you woke up the following morning?"

"Feel?" The senator looked at Holmes with incredulity, and I admit that for an instant I too thought the question mad. "How the hell do you think we felt? Waking up to find no sign of our daughter."

Holmes halted him with a pacifying hand.

"That's not what I meant. Naturally you felt panic and disorientation, but physically? How did you feel physically?"

"Perfectly normal, I guess. I don't remember." He looked at his wife.

"I remember. I felt ill. Thickheaded. The air outside felt so good, it was like breathing champagne." The great lost eyes stared at Holmes. "Were we drugged?"

"I think there's a very good chance. Chief Inspector, was anything done on the sausages?"

"Analysed, of course. Nothing there in the two that were left, or in the other food. The old couple on the farm seemed harmless. It's in the report as well."

For another half-hour Holmes continued to question both the inspector and the Simpsons, with little result. No known enemies, they'd seen no strangers the day before, the ransom money was being brought in from America, a loan from his father. At the end of it Mr. Simpson was pale and his wife shaking. Holmes thanked them.

"I deeply regret having put you through this painful ordeal. At this point in an investigation one never knows which small detail will be of vital importance. Russell, have you any questions?"

"Just one, about the child herself. I'd like to know how you think she's taking it, Mrs. Simpson. How do you think she's reacting to having been spirited away by what may well be complete strangers?" I was afraid my question would break her, but oddly enough it did not. She sat upright and looked straight at me for the first time.

"Jessica is a very self-contained, determined child. She is highly intelligent and does not panic easily. To tell you the truth, assuming she is being treated well, she is probably less upset than her mother is." A ghost of a smile flickered across her bare face. There were no more questions.

Connor saw them out and returned with a thick, bound folder.

"Here's the full report, everything we've found, copies of the prints, interviews with the locals, everything. Most of it you've seen already. I imagine you'll want to take it with you, not stop to read it now."

"Yes, I want to be away as soon as possible. Where's the caravan?"

"The north end of town, on the road to Caerphilly. Stables run by Gwilhem Andrewes. He's not what you might call a friend of the police, and I wouldn't trust him with my back turned, but he's what you wanted. Shall I have a car take you?"

"No, I don't think that would be appropriate treatment for a pair of gipsies, do you? And you'll have to have a talk with Miss Carter and Sergeant Donaldson. We do not want the whole police force to know that Senator Simpson spent an hour with two arrested gipsies, do we? No, I think we'll just carry on as if you've let us off with a warning, if you'd be so good as to arrange my release. You know where we'll be; if you need to talk with me, have one of your constables stop me. No one will think twice of a copper rousting a gipsy. But, if he needs to arrest me, have him do it gently. I do promise not to beat up my daughter in railway stations anymore." Connor hesitated, then forced a laugh. Perhaps only the circumstances had rendered him humourless.

We rose to take our leave. Connor rose with us, and after a small hesitation, came around the desk and held out his hand to Holmes.

"There's sorry I am, Mr. Holmes, for what you found here in my building. I am newly come here, but I say that in explanation, not in excuse." Holmes took the hand and shook it.

"I found good men here, Mr. Connor. Young men, it is true, but I think from the look of you they will age quickly."

"They will that, Mr. Holmes. Now, I'll be wishing you Godspeed, and a good hunting to you. And to you, Miss Russell."

We were soon out on the street, carrying three bags apiece, working our way up to the outskirts of town, where we soon located Andrewes Stables. Holmes left me in the office and went to find the owner. I cooled my heels by juggling for half an hour, desperate for something to read (though strictly speaking I should be barely literate) until I heard voices outside the door, and in came a shifty, greasy character followed by the marginally less disreputable figure of Holmes, smelling strongly of whisky and flashing his gold tooth. Andrewes leered at me until Holmes distracted him by holding money under his nose.

"Well, then, Mr. Andrewes, that's settled. I thanks you for holdin' my brother's wagon for me. Here's what I owes you. Come, Mary, the wagon's out in the yard."

"Just a minute, Mr. Todd, you're a shilling short here."

"Ah, terrible sorry, I must a dropped it." He laboriously counted out three pennies, a ha'penny, and six farthings. "There it is, now we're quit. Get the bags, girl," he snarled.

"Yes, Da'." I meekly followed him, laden with the four largest bags again, through the muck-slimed yard to the gipsy caravan standing in the back. A rough-coated, heavy-legged horse was being introduced between the traces. I deposited my load and went around to help with the process, blessing Patrick's tutoring as I did so, and found that though the arrangement of the harness was different from that of a plough or a hay cart, it was logical and quickly mastered. I climbed up beside Holmes on the hard wooden seat. He handed me the reins, his face a blank. I glanced at the two men standing nearby, arranged the thick straps in my hands, and slapped them hard across the broad back in front of me. The horse obligingly leant forward, and we pulled out onto the road north, on the trail of Jessica Simpson.

❧ 6 ❧

A Child Gone from Her Bed

Let her be restored . . . and they will receive her with
extraordinary, pathetic welcome. . . . The strange
hymn of rejoicing.

O N THE VERY outskirts of the town Holmes had me pull over
and apply the brake.

"We need to do a thorough check on this equipment, I fear," he
said. "The last time I hired one of these the wheel fell off. It would not
be convenient this time. You strip the horse down, take a look under
the traces, and I think you'll find a few sores. Currycomb, rags for
padding, and ointment for the sores are in the calico bag." He disappeared beneath the caravan, and while I brushed and treated the puzzled horse, he tightened bolts and applied grease to dry axles. With the
horse back in harness, I went around to see if I might be of help and
found his long legs protruding from the back.

"Need a hand?" I called.

"No point in both of us looking like mechanics. I'm nearly finished." A minute passed, silent on my part, grunts and low impreca-
tions on his.

"Holmes, there's something I must ask you."

"Not just now, Russell."

"I need to know. Is my presence . . . an embarrassment?"

"Don't be absurd."

"I mean it, Holmes. Inspector Connor today all but accused
you . . . me . . . I just need to know if my presence is inconvenient."

"My dear Russell, I hope you don't flatter yourself that because you
talked me into bringing you on this delightful outing, that means I am
incapable of refusing you. To my considerable—Oh blast! Give me a
rag, would you? Thank you. To my considerable surprise, Russell, you
have proven a competent assistant and, furthermore, hold some promise for becoming an invaluable one. It is, I can even say, a new and occasionally remarkable experience to work with a person who inspires,
not by vacuum, but by actual contribution. Hand me the large span-
ner." His next remarks were punctuated by grunts. "Connor is a fool.
What he and his ilk choose to believe is no concern of mine, and thus
far it has not seemed to harm you. You cannot help being a female,
and I should be something of a fool as well were I to discount your tal-
ents merely because of their housing."

"I see. I think."

"Besides," he added, his voice muffled now by the undercarriage, "a
renowned bachelor such as myself, you probably would be more of an
embarrassment were you a boy."

There really was no possible response to that statement. In a few
minutes, filthy as a miner, Holmes emerged, cleansed himself as well as
he was able, and we set off up the road again.

We wobbled along north in the colourful, remarkably uncomfortable little caravan, walking up the hills whenever the sway of the high
wooden seat and the jolts to the base of the spine became too much,
which was most of the time. Holmes peppered me with information,

badgered me mercilessly into my rôle, criticised and corrected my walk and speech and attitude, forced Welsh vocabulary and grammar down my throat, and pontificated between times on the Welsh countryside and its inhabitants. Were it not for the constant awareness of a frightened child's life and the fraying thread that held it, the outing would have been great sport.

Up through Glamorgan we walked and rode and walked again, into Gwent and then Powys, turning west now into the hilly greensward that curled up towards the Brecon Beacons, all hill farm and bracken fern, terraces and slag heaps and sheep. The shepherds eyed us with mistrust as we rumbled past, although their thin, black, sharp-eyed, suspicious dogs, lying with bellies pressed to the ground, as alert as so many pessimistic evangelists to snatch back a straying charge, spared us not a glance. As we passed through the villages and hamlets children ran shrieking to the road, and then stood in silent wonder staring up at our red, green, and gold splendour, their fingers in their mouths and their bare feet spattered with mud.

Wherever we went, we performed. While the children watched, I juggled, pulled colourful scarves from their colourless pockets and ha'pennies from dirty ears, and when we had the attention of their mothers, Holmes would come out of the pub wiping his mouth with the back of his hand and pull out his fiddle. I told the fortunes of women who had none, read the cracked lines on their hard palms and whispered vague hints of dark strangers and unexpected wealth, and gave them stronger predictions of healthy children who would support them in their old age. In the evenings when the men were present their wives looked daggers at me, but when their ears were caught by "me Da's" ready tongue, and when they saw that we were moving on for the night, they forgave me their husbands' glances and remarks.

On the second day we passed the police roadblock, receiving only cursory abuse since we were going into the area being guarded, not coming out. On the third day we passed the Simpsons' camping site, went on a mile, and pulled off into a side track. I cooked our tea, and when Holmes remarked merely that he hadn't thought it possible to make tinned beans taste undercooked, I took it that my cooking was improving.

When the pans were clean we lit the oil lamp and closed the door against the sweet dusk, and went again through all the papers Connor had given us—the photographs and the typed notes, the interviews with the parents, statements from witnesses on the mountain and from the senator's staff in London, a glossy photograph of Jessica taken the previous spring, grinning gap-toothed in a studio with its painted backdrop of a blooming arbour of roses. Page after page of the material, and all of it served only to underline the total lack of solid evidence, and the family's coming financial emasculation, and the brutal, staring fact that all too often kidnappers who receive their money give only a dead body in return, a corpse who can tell no tales.

Holmes smoked three pipes and climbed silently into his bunk. I closed the file on the happy face and shut down the lamp, and lay awake in the darkness long after the breathing above me slowed into an even rhythm. Finally, towards the end of the short summer's night, I dropped off into sleep, and then the Dream came and tore at me with its claws of blame and terror and abandonment, the massive, shambling, monstrous inevitability of my personal hell, but this time, before its climax, just short of the final moment of exquisite horror, a sharp voice dragged me back, and I surfaced with a shuddering gasp into the simple quiet of the gipsy caravan.

"Russell? Russell, are you all right?"

I sat up, and his hand fell away.

"No. Yes, I'm all right, Holmes." I breathed into my hands and tried to steady myself. "Sorry I woke you. It was just a bad dream, worry about the child, I guess. It takes me that way, sometimes. Nothing to be concerned about."

He moved over to the tiny table, scratched a match into life, and lit a candle. I turned my face away from him.

"Can I get you anything? A drink? Something hot?"

His concern raked at me.

"No! No, thank you, Holmes, I'll be fine in a minute. Go back to bed."

He stood with his back to the light, and I felt his eyes on me. I stood up abruptly and went for my spectacles and coat.

"I'll get some fresh air. Go back to sleep," I repeated fiercely, and stumbled from the caravan.

Twenty minutes down the road my steps finally slowed; ten minutes after that I stopped and went to sit on a dark shape that turned out to be a low wall. The stars were out, a relatively uncommon thing in this rainy corner of a rainy country, and the air was clean and smelt of bracken and grass and horse. I pulled great draughts of it into me and thought of Mrs. Simpson, who had called it breathing champagne. I wondered if Jessica Simpson were breathing it now.

The Dream gradually receded. Nightmare and memory, it had begun with the death of my family, a vivid re-creation that haunted and hounded me and made my nights into purgatory. Tonight, though, I had Holmes to thank for interrupting it, and its aftermath was considerably lessened. After an hour, cold through, I walked back through the first light of dawn to the wagon, and to bed and a brief sleep.

In the morning neither of us mentioned the night's occurrences. I cooked porridge for breakfast, flavoured with light flecks of ash and so lumpy Mrs. Hudson would have considered it suitable only for the chickens. We then walked up towards the described campsite, taking a roundabout route and a spade to justify our presence.

The site was unattended when we arrived. The tent was still standing, slack-roped and flabby-sided, with a blackened circle and two rusting pans to one side where Mrs. Simpson had cooked her meals. The area smelt of old, wet ashes, and had the forlorn look of a child's toy left out in the rain. I shuddered at the image.

I went up to the tent door and looked in at the jumble of bedrolls and knapsacks and clothing, all abandoned in the scramble to locate the child and now compulsively preserved in situ by police custom.

Holmes walked around to the back of the tent, his eyes on the tram-pled, rain-soaked ground.

"How long have we?" I asked him.

"Connor arranged for the constable on guard to be called away un-til nine o'clock. A bit under two hours. Ah."

At his expression of satisfaction I let the canvas flap fall and picked my way around to the tent's back wall, where I was met by the singular vision of an ageing gipsy stretched full out between the guy ropes with a powerful magnifying glass in his hand, prodding delicately at the tent's lower seam with his fountain pen. The pen disappeared into the interior of the tent. I turned and went back inside, and when the bed-ding had been pulled away I saw what Holmes had discovered: a tiny slit just at seam line, the edges pushed inward and the threads at both ends of the cut slightly strained.

"You expected that?" I asked.

"Didn't you?" I was tempted to make a face at him through the canvas, but refrained; he'd have known.

"A tube, for sleeping gas?"

"Right you be, Mary Todd," he said, and the pen retreated. I stood up, head bent beneath the soggy canvas roof, and looked at the corner where Jessica Simpson had slept. According to her parents, the only things missing from her knapsack or the tent had been her shoes. No pullover, no stockings, not even her beloved doll. Just the shoes.

The doll was still there, feet up beneath the tangle of upturned bed-ding, and I pulled out the much-loved figure, straightened her crum-pled dress, and brushed a tangle of yarn hair from her wide painted eyes. The once-red lips smiled at me enigmatically.

"Why don't you tell me what you saw that night, eh?" I addressed her. "It would save us a great deal of trouble."

"What was that?" asked Holmes' voice from a distance.

"Nothing. Would there be any objection if we took the doll with us, do you think?"

"I shouldn't think so. They only left these things here for us to see; they have their photographs."

I pushed the doll into my skirt pocket, took a last look around, and went outside. Holmes stood, back to the tent and fists on his hips, looking down the valley.

"Getting the lie of the land?" I asked.

"If you were kidnapping a child, Russell, how would you get her away?"

I chewed my lip for a few minutes and contemplated the bracken-covered hillsides.

"Personally, I should use an automobile, but no one seems to have heard one that night, and it's a goodly hike to anywhere with three and a half stone of child on one's back, even for a strong man." I studied the hill and saw the trails that wandered over and around it. "Of course. The horses. No one would notice one more set of prints with all these here. They came in on horseback, didn't they?"

"It's a sad state of affairs when, being confronted by a hillside, the modern girl thinks of an automobile. That was slow, Mary Todd. Overlooking the obvious. Theological training is proving as destructive to the reasoning abilities as I had feared."

I cringed away and whined at him.

"Aw, Da', it waren't me fault. I war lookin' a't'evidence."

"Harden your *t* more," he corrected absently. "So, which way?"

"Not towards the road; there'd be too much chance of being seen."

"Down the valley then, or over the hill?" he considered aloud.

"A pity we weren't here a week ago; there might have been something to see."

"If wishes were horses . . ."

"Detectives would ride," I finished. "I should go further away from the nearest village, I think, along the hill or over it."

"We have an hour before the guard is back. Let us see what there is to find. I'll go up the hill; you take the base of it."

We zigzagged along and up the hill in increasingly wide arcs out from the tent. Half an hour went by with nothing but aching backs and stiff necks to show for our scrutiny. Forty-five minutes, and I began to listen nervously for the Welsh equivalent of "Oy, what's this then?" from the campsite behind us. The two of us reached the furthest points in our arcs and turned back toward the middle. Something caught my eye—but it was nothing, just a gleam of bare stone where a hoof had scraped a rock. I went on, then turned back for a second look. Would an unshod hoof actually scrape into stone? On the whole I thought not.

"Hol—Uh, Da'!" I called. His head came up, and he started across the hillside at a long-legged trot, the spade bouncing on his shoulder. When he came up he was barely winded. I pointed and he dropped down with his glass to look more closely.

"Well done indeed. That excuses your lapse earlier," he said magnanimously. "Let us see how far this might take us." We continued in the direction we had come, walking slowly on either side of the clear path cut by generations of hoofs. An hour later we passed the limits of the police search.

Holmes and I spotted the white patch at the same moment. It was a small handkerchief, nearly trampled into the mud. Holmes worked it out of the soil and held it outspread. In one corner was an embroidered *J.*

"Was this an accident?" I wondered aloud. "Could she have been awake enough to drop it deliberately? Might a six-year-old do that? I shouldn't have thought so."

We continued, and in a few minutes my doubts were stilled, for to one side of the path a narrow strip of blue ribbon hung limply from a patch of bracken. I held it up triumphantly.

"That's my girl, Jessie. Your hair ribbon."

We walked on, but there were no further signs. Eventually the path split, one going up and over the hill, the other dropping down towards some trees. We stood looking at the two offerings expectantly, but no ribbons or signals caught our eyes.

"I'll take the uphill again."

"Wait. Down near those trees, is the ground scuffed up?" We went down, and there, in a little hollow, were indeed signs of some flurry of activity. Holmes walked around it carefully, and then bent down quickly, reaching for something invisible to me twenty feet away. He continued his scrutiny, picked up another object, and finally allowed me to approach.

"She jumped off the horse," he said, running his fingertips back and forth an inch above the trampled ground. "She had bare feet, although they had taken her shoes; they had not bothered to put them on her. Her hands were not tied. Here," he said stabbing a finger at a clod of turf, "you see the short parallel lines? Her toes. And here, the longer lines that draw together? Her fingers made those as she gathered herself off the ground and sprinted towards those bushes." Once he had pointed out the signs I could see them, clear despite the intervening rains. He rose and followed the marks left by hoofs and heels. "She made it this far before they caught her, by her night dress, which popped a button," he held out the object he had picked up earlier, "and by her hair, which was of course loose from having the ribbon removed." He held up several mud-crusted strands of auburn hair.

"Dear God," I groaned, "I hope they didn't hurt her when they caught her."

"There's nothing on the ground that tells one way or the other," he said absently. "What was the moon doing on the twelfth of August?"

I was quite certain he did not need me to tell him, but I thought for a moment, and answered. "Three-quarters full, and it had stopped raining. She may have been able to see well enough to tell when the path split, or perhaps she was trying to make it to the trees. In either case, we know where she's come. Quite a child, our Miss Simpson. But I doubt there will be any further signs."

"It is unlikely, but let us be thorough."

We followed the horse trail for another hour, but there were no more signs or marks of shod hoofs. At the next trail fork we stopped.

"Back to the caravan, Mary, my girl. A bite of lunch, and the gipsies will resume their itinerant musicale."

We got back to the wagon to find company, in the form of a large constable with a very dark expression on his face.

"And what might the two of you have been doing on this hillside?" he demanded.

"Doin'? We been stayin' the night, I'd a thought that obvious," retorted Holmes, and walked past him to store the spade in its niche.

"And where have you been gone to all mornin'?"

"Out diggin' for truffles." He jerked his thumb at the implement.

"What?"

"Truffles. Little roots, very expensive in the shops. The Lords and Ladies like 'em in their food. Find 'em sometimes in the hills."

"Truffles, yes, but they use pigs to find them, not spades."

"Don't need pigs if you've got the gift. My daughter here, she's got the gift of sight."

"You don't say." He looked at me with skepticism, and I smiled at him shyly. "And did this daughter of yours with the gift of truffles find any?"

"Naow, not today."

"Good. Then you'll not mind moving on. Within the hour."

"Want m'dinner first," said Holmes sulkily, though it was closer to teatime than the noon hour.

"Dinner, then. But gone in two hours, you'll be, or it's in a cell you'll find yourselves. Two hours."

He stalked off over the hill, and I sat down and giggled in relief. "Truffles? For God's sake, *are* there truffles in Wales?"

"I suppose so. See if you can find some food while I dig out the maps."

Holmes' maps were of the extremely large-scale topographical sort, showing the kinds of vegetation, the rights-of-way, and small black squares indicating houses. He folded the table up out of the way and chose a series of maps from a shallow drawer beneath my bunk. I handed him a sandwich and a tin mug of beer, and we walked across the paper floor-covering in our stockinged feet.

"This is our route," he pointed out. "The campsite, here, and the trail going away, roughly along this contour line." The tip of his brown finger followed the contour of the hill, dropped down into the hollow on the next map, and stopped at the Y junction on the edge of the third. "From here, where? She had to be inside, Russell, before light. In a building, or a vehicle."

"But not . . . under the ground?"

"I think not. Had they intended to kill her, surely they would have done so when she tried to escape, to save themselves further trouble. I saw no indication of blood there."

"Holmes!" I protested in dismay.

"What is it, Russell?"

"Oh, nothing. You just sound so . . . callous."

"You prefer a surgeon who weeps at the thought of the pain he is about to inflict? I should have thought you had learnt that lesson by now, Russell. Allowing the emotions to involve themselves in an investigation can only interfere with the surgeon's hand. Now, assuming the child was taken as early as midnight, and it is light by five o'clock; without an automobile, that would place the limits they could have ridden approximately here," and he drew a semicircle, using as its center the Y where the trail had disappeared. "Within this area; a place where a telephone is to hand; a large enough village for the delivery of *The Times* out of London to go unremarked. You won't overlook the significance of the agony column?"

"Of course not," I hastened to reassure him.

He reached back onto his sheaf of maps, withdrew half a dozen of the very largest scale, and fitted them together. We puzzled over the lines of streams and roads, footpaths and houses. I absently wiped a smear of pickle from the map and brushed off some crumbs, and thought aloud.

"There are only four small villages in that direction. Five, if we count this furthest, though it would have forced them to ride very fast. All are near enough to the road, they might have a telephone line. These two villages seem rather more scattered than the others, which might give whatever house they're in more privacy. I can't see that we'll make them all by tomorrow."

"No."

"We have only six more days before the ransom is to be paid."

"I am aware of that," he said testily. "Get the horse in the traces."

We were away before the constable returned, but it was nearly dark before we came to the first village. Holmes trudged off to the pub, which looked to be on the ground floor of someone's home, while I cared for the horse and tried to concentrate my brain on conversation with the children who inevitably appeared at our arrival. I had found that there was usually one who took responsibility for communicating with this strange visitor. In this case the representative was a dirty girl of about ten. The others kept up a running commentary, or perhaps a simultaneous translation in a Welsh that was too fast and colloquial for me to grasp. I ignored them all and proceeded with my tasks.

"Are you a gipsy then, lady?"

"What do you think?" I grunted.

"My Dad says yes."

"Your Dad is wrong." Shocked silence met the heresy. After a minute she plucked up her nerve again.

"If it's not a gipsy you are, then what?"

"A Romany."

"A Romany? There's foolish, there is! They carried spears and they're all dead."

"That's a Roman. I'm Romany. Want to give this to the horse?" A small boy took the oats from me. "Is there anyone in town who'd like to sell me a couple of suppers?" My crowd silently consulted, then:

"Maddie, run you by there and ask your Mam. Go now, you." The tiny girl, torn between the desire to keep watch and the undeniable honour of providing service, reluctantly took herself down the road and disappeared into the pub.

"Have you no pan?" asked a small person of one sex or another.

"I don't like to cook," I said regally, and shocked silence, deeper than before, descended. If the other was heresy, I could be burnt for this. "Is there a telephone in town?" I asked the spokesman.

"Telephone?"

"Yes, telephone, you know, the thing you pick up and shout down? It's too dark to see any wires. Is there one in town?" The puzzled faces showed me this was the wrong village. A child piped up.

"My Da' used one once, he did, when the Grand' died and he had to tell his brother by Caerphilly."

"Where did he go to use it?"

An eloquent shrug in the light of the lamps. Oh, well.

"What for do you need a telephone machine?"

"To call my stockbroker." I continued before they could ask for a definition, "You don't get many strangers through here, do you?"

"Oh, many there are. Why, only at Midsummer's, an autocar filled with English came here and stopped, and drank a glass at Maddie's mam's."

"Just coming through don't count," I asserted loftily. "I mean comin' in and eatin' and drinkin' here and stoppin' for a time. Don't get many of them, do you?"

I could see from their faces that they didn't have any convenient group of strangers to offer me, and sighed internally. Tomorrow, perhaps. Meanwhile—"Well, I'm here, but we're not stopping long. If you want to run home and tell your people, we'll have a show for you to watch in an hour. Unless my Da' finds the beer here too good," I added. "I tell fortunes too. Run along now."

The supper was good and plentiful, the take from the fiddling and cards poor. Before dawn the next morning we jingled off down the road.

The next village had telephone wires but few isolated buildings. Neither my small informant nor the pub inhabitants could be gently prodded into revealing any recent influx of strangers. We moved on after midday, not pausing to perform.

Our next choice started out promising. Telephone lines, several widely scattered buildings, and even a response to questions about strangers caused my pulse to quicken. However, by teatime the leads had petered out, and the strangers were two old English ladies who had come to live here six years before.

We had to backtrack to reach the road to the other villages, and as dusk closed in on us I was thoroughly sick of the hard, jolting seat and the imperturbable brown rump ahead of me. We lit the wagon's side lamps and climbed down with a lantern to lead the horse. I spoke to Holmes in a low voice.

"Could the kidnappers be locals? I know it looks like outsiders, but what if it was just a couple of locals?"

"Who spotted an American senator and thought up a gas gun and letters in *The Times* on the spur of the moment?" he drawled sarcastically. "Use the wits God gave you, Mary Todd. Locals are almost certainly involved but are not alone."

We crept wearily into village number four, where for the first time we were not greeted by a company of children. "Too late for the little ones, I suppose," Holmes grunted, and looked at the small stone pub with loathing.

"What I would give for a decent claret," he sighed, and went off to do his duty for his king.

I settled the horse, found and heated a tin of beans over the caravan's tiny fire, and slumped at the minuscule wooden table with the Tarot deck, sourly reading my fortune: The cards gave me the Hanged Man, the enigmatic Fool, and the Tower with its air of utter disaster. Holmes was a long time in the pub, and I was beginning to consider moving over to my bunk, travel-stained clothing and all, when I heard his voice come suddenly loud into what passed for the village's high street.

"—my fiddle, and I'll play you a dancin' tune, the merriest of tunes that ever you'll hear." I jerked upright, all thought of sleepiness snatched from me and the beans turning instantly to bricks in my stomach. The caravan's door flew open and in came me old Da', several sheets to the wind. He tripped as he negotiated the narrow steps, and fell forward into my lap.

"Ah, me own sweet girlie," he continued loudly, struggling to right himself. "Have you seen what I done with the fiddle?" He reached past me to retrieve it from the shelf and whispered fiercely in my ear. "On your toes, Russell: a two-storey white house half a mile north, plane tree in front and another at the back. Hired in late June, five men living there, perhaps a sixth coming and going. Curse it!" he bellowed, "I told you to fix the bloody string," and continued as he bent over the instrument, "I'll make a distraction at the front of the house in fifty minutes. You make your way—carefully, mind you—around to the back and see what you can without getting too close. Black your skin and take your revolver, but use it only to save your life. Watch for a guard, or dogs. If you're seen, that's the end of it. Can you do it?"

"Yes, I think so, but—"

"Me sweet Mary," he bawled drunkenly in my ear, "you're all tired out, ain't you? Off t'bed wi' you naow, don't wait up for me."

"But Da', some supper—"

"Nah, Mary, wouldn't want to be spoiling all this lovely beer with food, would I? Off to dreamland now, Mary," and he slammed heavily at the door. His fiddle skittered into life and, heart-pounding and hands fumbling, I made myself ready: trousers pulled on beneath my dark skirts, a length of brown silk rope around my waist, tiny binoculars, a pencil-sized torch. The gun. A smear of black from the dirty lamp-glass onto my face and hands. A final glance around before shutting down the lamps, and the rag doll caught my eye, slumped disconsolately on the shelf. On sudden impulse—for luck?—I pushed her into a pocket and slipped out silently into the shadows, away from the pub, to make my way down to the big square house that sat well off the road, the one with no neighbours.

I crept up the road with infinite care but met no one and was soon squatting down among some bushes across from the house, studying it through my binoculars. The rooms on the ground floor were lit behind thin but effective curtains, and other than the voices coming from, I thought, the corner room on the far side, there was no way of knowing what the house concealed. Upstairs the front was dark.

After ten minutes the only sign of life had been a tall man crossing the room in front of the lamp, and coming back again a minute later. There were no indications of outside watchmen or dogs, and I continued up the road, scuttled across at a crouch, and worked my way back to a ramshackle outhouse, which smelt of coal and paraffin. The house's thin curtains allowed lamplight to escape so that the ground around the house was illuminated for night-adapted eyes; ten more minutes in that spot, and nothing moved, other than a fitful breeze.

I fell back from the outhouse and picked my painstaking way through an overgrown vegetable garden, over a fence in need of mending, behind a second outhouse (this one smelling faintly of petrol) and its attached chicken coop, under the branches of a small orchard where the plums rotted underfoot, and up to a third shed whose diminutive size and location would have declared its function even if its aroma had not. It also gave me a full view of the back of the house and its yard.

There was a light on in a room upstairs. From the arrangement of windows I decided there were probably two rooms on this side, with perhaps a small windowless lumber-room between them, and it was the room on the right, away from the tree, that was lit. To my distinct pleasure the house's general decrepitude came to a climax in the curtains of this room, which were either torn or simply not adequately closed, because a shaft of yellow lamplight fell across the sill. If I could get high enough I might see into that room, and I very much wanted to know what lay inside.

I looked around. Somewhere there was sure to be a hill, but in the darkness all I could tell was that it did not tower up immediately behind the house. I looked speculatively at the building beside me. It might give enough height, and the slates looked strong enough to hold my weight. I glanced around for something to step up on, to lessen the scrabbling noises, remembered a discarded bucket among the weeds in the orchard, and went to retrieve it. The bottom had a hole in it, but the sides were sound, and upturned with a board across it the makeshift step enabled me to reach the privy's ridge. I gained the tiny roof and had just begun to congratulate myself on the minimum of noise I had made when the back door was flung open and a very large man with a terrifying bright lamp in his hand was revealed on the steps.

Holmes' training held. The mad urge to leap off and dash into the covering darkness washed through me, leaving little more than a set of absolutely rigid muscles and a desire to mould myself into the cracks of the roof slates, but before the man was halfway across the yard my mind had notified me that although he was coming towards me, he had nothing in his other hand, and nothing on his mind other than a visit to the room beneath me. I clung there in an agony of trepidation lest the slates creak, mixed with an almost unconquerable urge to hilarity, but when he finally took himself back inside the house (Seven minutes had passed, an eternity!), the amusement faded and left me feeling queasy.

Two other things came to me, slowly. The room he came from had been the kitchen, and, much more important, there had been no reaction to his presence in the yard. Nor, I decided, had he expected there to be one. Therefore, no dog, no guard.

Probably.

The sky was lightening with the moonrise, and as I stood slowly upright I felt as exposed as an elephant on a cricket pitch, and all for naught: The angle was wrong. All my binoculars showed me was the top of the door frame on the other side of the room. I let myself silently off the building, carried the bucket and board back to their resting places, and stood looking at the window, thinking.

Without a guard, there was nothing to keep me from that tree behind the house. From its thick, leafy, concealing, and comparatively safe branches I should have a choice of viewpoints into that lighted room, and although the ground around it and the first dozen feet of trunk were exposed, it was certainly safer than stumbling about the gravel yard waiting for someone else to come outside and step on me.

However, I had first to rid myself of encumbrances. Just beyond the drive a low shape rose, which proved to be a poorly maintained privet hedge, vastly overgrown but easily breached. I deposited my boots and the several skirts behind it, tucked the doll into the back waistband of my trousers and thrust the other belongings into various pockets, and crept across the drive to the wall of the house. Just under eight minutes until Holmes appeared with his diversion, and I spent two of them with my ear against the kitchen window before I was satisfied that all the activity—a card game, by the sound of it—was in the opposite end of the house.

The tree's first branches were too far overhead to jump for, and a straight climb would make too much noise. I unwound the rope from my waist (Always carry a length of rope; it's the most useful thing in the world.) and tossed it at a branch that faced away from the house. On the second try it looped over, and I walked it up the trunk. The crackles and creaks this made sounded like shouts in the night, but when no reaction came I gathered the rope up onto the branch and monkeyed myself up the tree for a view through the curtain.

And the fates were with me, because she was there.

At first all I could see was a bed and rumpled bedclothes, and my heart sank, but when I worked my way out to the precarious end of the limb and looked again I saw against the pillow a small head with auburn brown hair gathered into a rough plait. Jessica Simpson's hair, Jessica Simpson's face.

Half of my task was fulfilled: We now knew she was here. The other half, vastly the more important, was to explore ways to get her out. Unfortunately, there was no nice thick branch leading directly to her window, a fact that even my constipated friend could not have overlooked in the choice of the prisoner's room. However, the tree was much closer to the other room, the dark one. (There came a sudden and unexpected sound from the direction of the town—men's voices raised in a song, a first inkling of the kind of diversion Holmes had in mind.) I clambered over to the dark side and saw that one of the branches did indeed nearly brush the house. Suggestive. But once to the house, I considered, what then? There was no convenient ledge connecting the two windows; the guttering was too far overhead; and I did not much care for the vision of Holmes dangling like a spider from a rope wrapped around the chimney pots. No, it would probably mean a surreptitious entrance through the dark room.

Five men, and the possibility of a sixth. Four were playing cards—four voices, I corrected myself, and one wild card for certain. Downstairs? Or in with the child? Or, in the dark room? It hardly mattered tonight, but tomorrow, when we returned—

It was then that the idea hit me, a mad flash of derring-do that I immediately squelched, shocked at myself. This isn't a game, Russell, I told myself in disgust. Do what you were told, then go back to the caravan.

But the thought had lodged itself like a thorn, and I could not help picking at it while I squatted motionless and attentive in the tree, my eyes open and my mind worrying at this crazy thought, examining it, turning it around, pushing it away, finding it persistent and unwilling to be discarded.

What if I did not wait for Holmes to effect the rescue tomorrow?

Madness. To take a child's life into my own absurdly inexperienced hands—I shook my head as if to discourage an irritating fly and settled myself more firmly into my post of observer. My assigned post. My vital and agreed-to post. The chorus of voices was growing, soaring in almost-audible song, outside the village now and starting up the road.

In a minute now the men inside would hear . . . I shifted, to keep a closer eye on the lit room.

In a moment the niggling idea had returned, stronger, surer. How else could we do it, if not through the dark window with a distraction out in front? There was no point in a direct show of force; a hostage with a gun to her head is even more a hostage than when in a quiet room in bed. And how could Holmes hope to reach her but across these narrow branches? Holmes, approaching sixty and becoming just the least bit hesitant about risking his bones, would have to balance his greater weight and height on the same branch—and in the few days left us before the deadline (How terribly appropriate that word sounded.), while the five men inside were becoming increasingly wrought up, to say nothing of being on their guards for a second unusual happenstance such as the one that was fast approaching on the road.

Madness. Lunacy. I couldn't possibly carry it off, couldn't even carry *her* off, out the window, across the branch, down the tree and away, not if she fought me, which she would. Even a "self-contained, intelligent" child might well panic at being snatched from her bed by a strange woman with lampblack smeared on her face and carried off a second time into the night.

My mind veered wildly between obedient caution and reckless insanity, between a sensible preparation for future action and the hard knowledge that we might never have the chance to use it, between carrying out Holmes' direct orders and seizing what even common sense told me might be the only chance offered us, and I wished to God that Holmes might miraculously appear beneath my feet and take the choice from me.

They were Christmas carols, I decided with the portion of my mind that was not paralysed with indecision. Somehow me Da' had raised a drunken mob in this tiny place, had summoned thick voices in song, and was driving them down the lane with the goad of his mad fiddle— a magnificent Welsh chorus, singing Christmas carols, in English, in an infinitesimal Welsh village, on a warm August night. Suddenly nothing seemed impossible, and as if the thought had loosed the house from stasis there was movement within.

A shadow moved across the slice of yellow light before me. I hung precariously out and was rewarded by the sight of a man's back. He was in shirtsleeves and a waistcoat, with a dark knitted cap that covered his head down to his wide shoulders, and he was standing at the open door next to the head of Jessica's bed. He leant out into the hallway, paused (Was that a man's voice, shouting something unintelligible above the growing tumult?), opened the door wider, and went through it.

Had it not been for the vision of the broad back going through the door, I should never have done it, never have moved towards the dark window. Even as I moved, even as I looped the silk rope over an over-head branch with muscles and mind freed so blessedly (insanely!) from indecision, a small part still offered to be sensible, made a bargain with the fates that were controlling this night that, if the window did not unlatch, I should withdraw in an instant.

A thump and a series of raucous guffaws reached my ears above the song, and I stepped with one foot from the branch to the window, bal-anced in a triangle of rope, branch, and sill, took out my pocket knife and (*A-here we come a-wassailing among the leaves so green . . .*) fumbled open its thinnest blade, slid it up between the window frames, and in a brief eternity felt more than heard the latch snick open. I waited, but there was no reaction from within, so I reached down (*A-here we come a-wand'ring so fair to be seen . . .*) and eased the lower window up with barely a squeak. I stepped down onto the bare floorboards, taut for at-tack, but none came; the room was empty, and I let go a deep and shaky breath and moved quickly across to (*Love and joy come to you . . .*) the door. The hallway and stairs were empty, voices raised downstairs both inside and out, the door to the corner room slightly ajar. I pulled the doll from the waistband of my trousers and stepped into the horribly bright hallway.

(*And to you your Wassail, too, and God bless . . .*)

"Jessica!" I whispered. "Don't be frightened. There's someone here to see you." I held the doll in front of me, pushed the door open, and looked down into a very serious six-year-old face. Jessica pushed herself slowly up onto her elbows, studying my black-smeared but evidently unthreatening visage, and waited.

"Jessie, your mama and papa sent me to bring you home. We have to go right now, or those men will stop us."

"I can't," she whispered.

Oh God, I thought, what now?

"Why not?"

Wordlessly she sat up and pulled the covers back from her foot, revealing a metal cuff and a chain fastened to the leg of the bed.

"I tried to get away, so they put this on me."

The riot outside was coming to a climax, with a crash and the tinkle of breaking glass, followed by furious shouts and a rush of drunken laughter. In an instant they would remember, and we had to be away before then. I had to risk a noise.

"Just a minute, honey. Here, you take the doll."

Her arms went tightly around the beloved object, and I knelt to examine the chain. It was new and strong, fastened at one end to her ankle cuff—which was padded, I was glad to see—by a sturdy padlock, and at the other end to the leg of the bed, held by a bolt the size of my little finger, which seemed to have been welded to its nut. The bed was a cheap one, but the wooden leg was a good three inches thick, glued and fitted into place. I could see only one option, given the time, and could only hope that I didn't break every bone in my foot.

I hoisted up the end of the bed, balanced my weight on my left leg, drew back my right foot, and then straightened it out explosively. The angle was awkward and the jar of it did, I later found, crack one bone, but it was a small price to pay, because the bed now had only three legs. She was free. Careless of noise now, I lowered the bed to the floor, scooped up child, chain, and the stub of the bed leg, and tossed her over my shoulder like a sack of potatoes.

The key was in the lock, so I obligingly turned it as I went out and then pocketed it. Heavy boots sounded on the stairs as I ducked into the dark room. I closed the door, shot out the window, and had a bad moment when I stood balanced precariously between sill and limb and tried to close the window. I nearly dropped her, but she made no sound, just clung to my shirt with one hand and to her doll with the other. I caught up the end of the rope that I'd left hanging there and with it to support me, eased the window down with my aching foot, then half-walked, half-swung up the branch, and had just gained the trunk when the pounding came on Jessica's door. Shouts followed. I tossed the rope up into a branch so its trailing end might not give us away and prepared to drop. "Hang on really tight, Jessie," I hissed, and with her arms and legs wrapped around me we scrambled and fell down the tree, took five huge bounds to the privet hedge, and burst through, losing skin in several directions, and I just had time to place a hand across her lips when the back door slammed open.

This time the man who came out had a weapon in his hand, a massive shotgun. I pressed my fingers more firmly into the warm face and saw him walk out into the yard, under the tree that had held us ten seconds earlier, and look up at the lighted window. He shouted into the house, "She's not come out, Owen. The window's tight shut." I could not make out the answer from within, drowned out as it was by the angry shouts in the road, but the man walked towards us a few feet and peered up into the tree. The child and I breathed at each other and listened to each other's heart beat wildly, but she made no noise, and I did not move a hair for fear of rattling the chain or causing my spectacles to flash in the light from the kitchen. The man walked around for two or three minutes until a voice called at him from the house (It was quieter, I realized.) and he went inside. Immediately the door closed I snatched up child and boots, swung Jessica around piggyback, and trotted down the rough verge in my bare feet.

"You're doing fine, Jessica, just stay quiet and we'll have you out of here. Those men out in front are our friends, though they may not know it yet. We've got to hide very quietly for a little while until the police can get here, and then you'll see your parents. All right?"

I could feel her nod against my neck. I could also feel the rag doll, squashed between us. I moved rapidly ahead of the noisy mob (which was indeed beginning to break up), holding the chain and bed leg securely so as not to rattle. I kept to the blackest shadows, but when I looked back, against the glow from the house I saw an arm wave in wild salute from the midst of the carolers. Holmes had seen us; the rest was up to him.

I stopped at the caravan just long enough to gather blankets and food, and took the child back along the road and up a dimly seen hill. My eyes had been in the dark long enough to distinguish vague shapes, and I stopped under a tree and let her slide to the ground. Keeping one hand in light contact with her shoulder I eased my spine, then turned to sit up against the trunk, pulling her, unresisting and unresponsive, onto my lap, blankets around us both.

The relief was overwhelming, and I could only sit, shivering with reaction and with the drying sweat that had soaked my clothes. I was struck by the sudden vision of the expressions on those men's faces when they managed to open the door, and began to giggle. Jessica stiffened, and I forced the incipient hysteria down, took a deep breath, and another, and murmured into her ear.

"You're safe now, Jessica, completely safe. Those men cannot find you now. We're just going to wait here for a while until the police come for them, and then your parents will come to take you home. Let's wrap this rug around you so you don't get cold. Are you hungry?" I felt her head shake side to side. "Right. Now, we'll have to stop talking and be still, as still as baby deer in the woods, all right, Jessica? I'll stay with you, and your doll is here now. By the way, my name is Mary."

She greeted this with silence, and I pulled the rugs around us, put my back against the tree, and waited. The thin body in my arms slowly relaxed, gradually went loose, and eventually, to my amazement, dropped off to sleep. I listened to the last sounds of the beery men returning home, and after half an hour several cars came swiftly up the road. Distant yells, two shots (the child twitched in her sleep), and then silence. An hour later came the sound of solitary footsteps on the road, and the light of a lantern through the trees.

"Russell?"

"Here, Holmes." I took the hand torch from the basket of food and flashed it. He climbed the hill and stood looking down at us. I could not read his expression.

"Holmes, I'm sorry if I—" I began, but the simple and immediate plea for understanding was not to be, for Jessica woke at my voice and cried out at the sight of Holmes in the lamplight, and I moved quickly to reassure her.

"No, Jessie, this is a friend; he's my friend and your mother's friend, and he's the friend who made all that noise so I could take you from the house. His name is Mr. Holmes, and he doesn't always look so funny; he's dressed up, like I am." This soothing prattle took the worst of the tension from her body. I bundled the rugs together and handed them to Holmes and walked down the hill with the child in my arms.

We took her to the caravan, lit a fire, and dressed her in one of my woollen shirts, which flapped around her ankles. The publican's wife produced a hot, thick mutton stew, which we wolfed and the child picked at. Holmes then put the kettle of water on the little stove, and when it was warm he washed and examined my sore foot, wrapped it securely to stop the bone ends from their tedious creaking, and finally used the rest of the water to make a pot of coffee and shave the bristle from his cheeks. Jessica watched his every move. When his face was clean he sat down and showed the child how his gold tooth came out, which was the cause for serious consideration. He then brought his ring of picklocks from his pocket and spread it on the table for her to examine, and asked if she wished him to take the chain from her leg. She cringed away from him and tucked as much of herself as she could get into my lap.

"Jessica," I said, "nobody's going to touch you if you don't want. If you like, I can take it off you, but you'll have to sit on the table—I can't do it with you on my lap." There was no response. We waited a while, and then Holmes shrugged and reached for the picklocks. She stirred, and then slowly pushed her foot towards him. Without comment he got to work and, touching her as little as possible, within two minutes had the shackles on the floor. She gave him a long, grave look, which he returned, and then gathered herself up against me again and put her thumb into her mouth.

We sat, and dozed and waited, until finally there came another car on the road, which braked to a halt just outside the caravan. Holmes opened the door to the Simpsons, and Jessie flew into her mother's arms and glued her arms and legs around her as if she would never come free, and Mr. Simpson put an arm around both of them and led them to the car, and I found it hard to see properly, and Holmes blew his nose loudly.

❋ 7 ❋

Words with Miss Simpson

. . . directing all things without giving an order, receiving
obedience but not recognition.

THE END OF a case is always long, tedious, and anticlimactic, and since this is my story I choose to save myself from having to describe the next hours of weariness and physical letdown and questions and the ugliness of confronting those men. Suffice it to say that the night ended and I crawled into my hard bunk for a few hours of collapse before a fist on the caravan door brought me into the day. Cup after cup of black coffee did not help the soggy thickness in my bones and brain, and it was with considerable sour satisfaction that later that afternoon I watched the last of the cars drive off down the narrow track. I rubbed my tired eyes and propped up my sore foot and thought vaguely of a bath but found I could not summon the energy to do anything except sit on the wagon's back step and watch the horse graze.

It must have been nearly an hour later that I became aware of Holmes, sitting on a stump and tossing his jackknife repeatedly into the tree next to him.

"Holmes?"

"Yes, Russell."

"Is it always so grey and awful at the end of a case?"

He didn't answer me for a minute, then rose abruptly and stood looking down the road towards the house with the plane trees. When he looked around at me there was a painful smile on his lips.

"Not always. Just usually."

"Hence the cocaine."

"Hence, as you say, the cocaine."

I hobbled into the caravan for more coffee and brought the luke-warm cup back into the last rays of the evening sun. The oily slick on top was slightly nauseous, and I abruptly tipped it out, watched it soak into the trampled grass, and spoke in a rush of words I had not intended to say.

"Holmes, I don't think I can sleep here tonight. I know it's late and we should barely get on the road before we had to stop, but would you mind awfully if we didn't stay here until morning? I really don't think I can bear it." My voice came out a bit shaky at the end, but I looked up to see Holmes with a genuine smile in his eyes.

"Mary, me girlie, you took the very words from me mouth. If you'll get the nag in place, I'll have these things stowed away in a minute."

It was considerably more than a minute, but the sun was still above the hills when we turned the painted wagon around and faced back up the road we had come down the day before. I began to breathe more easily, and after a couple of miles Holmes put his back against the caravan's painted door and let out a sigh.

"Holmes? Do you think they'll catch the person behind this?"

"It's possible but not, I think, likely. He's been very cautious. He was not seen—he has certainly never been here, he'd never have overlooked the tree branch, or the curtains. These five were hired and paid anonymously, had no address or telephone number, no means of contacting him other than the newspaper, and received their orders from postboxes all over London: The ones I saw were all from the same typewriter, which will soon be lying on the bottom of the Thames. The Yard may have luck with tracing the money, but something tells me they won't. However, sooner or later he'll put his head up again, and perhaps we'll see him then. Russell? Come, Russell, don't fall off under the wheels, I beg you. Hand me those reins and go to sleep. No, go on. I've been driving horses since before you were born. Get on wi'ya, Mary." So I got on.

I woke up many hours later in stillness and heard the little caravan's back door open. Boots thumped gently onto the wooden floorboards, outer clothing rustled, and Holmes climbed into his bunk. I turned over and went back to sleep.

It was a blessing that we were saddled with the caravan and horse and were forced to make our way slowly to Cardiff. If we had gone off by car and plunged immediately into official business and then whisked ourselves back home by train, it would have left me, and perhaps even Holmes, gasping and stunned. As it was, two long days of plodding travel forced us to put the case into its proper place. We rode and walked, Holmes alternated between pipe and gentle, lyrical violin pieces. We talked, but not of the case, or of what I had taken upon myself to do.

Leaving the horse and caravan with Andrewes, we piled our assorted bags into a cab and were driven to the best hotel that the driver thought might accept us. It did. The baths were sheer sybaritic pleasure, deep and hot, and four rinses later I was again blonde, with a definite tan colour remaining on my skin. I stood in front of the mirror, tying my necktie, when two taps came at the door.

"Russell?"

"Come in, Holmes, I'm nearly ready."

He let himself in, and I saw that he too remained slightly brown, though the grey had reappeared around his ears. He sat down to wait as I pinned up my still-damp hair, and it occurred to me that he was probably the only person I knew who could simply sit nearby and watch me without one or the other of us needing to make conversation. I finished and picked up my room key.

"Shall we go?"

The Simpsons, as might have been expected, were grateful and fragile. Mrs. Simpson kept touching her daughter gently as if to reassure herself of the child's presence. Mr. Simpson looked rested and apologised for having to rush about—his words—instead of talking, as he was needed urgently in London. In the midst of it sat Jessica. She and I greeted each other solemnly. I noticed the faint shadow of a fading bruise on her cheekbone that I hadn't seen in the dark. I asked after her doll, and she replied seriously that she was quite well, thank you, and would I like to see her hotel room? I excused myself and followed Jessica down the hallway. (The Simpsons' suite and hotel were considerably more upstage than ours.)

We sat on the bed and talked to the stuffed person, and I was introduced to a bear, two rabbits, and a jointed wooden puppet. She showed me a few books, and we spoke of literature.

"I can read them," she informed me, with the barest trace of self-satisfaction.

"I can see that."

"Miss Russell, could you read when you were six?" Oddly enough there was no overtone of pride here, just a request for information.

"Yes, I believe I could."

"I thought so." She nodded her head in prim satisfaction and smoothed the skirt of the rag doll.

"What is your doll's name?"

I was surprised at her reaction to this simple question. Her hands went still, and she concentrated on the battered face in her lap, biting her lip. Her voice when she answered was quiet.

"Her name used to be Elizabeth."

"Used to be? What is her name now?" I could see that this was important but failed to grasp just how.

"Mary." She spoke in a whisper, and after a few seconds her eyes came up to mine. Light dawned.

"Mary, is it? My name?"

"Yes, Miss Russell."

It was my turn now to look down and study my hands. Hero worship was not one of the topics Holmes had thought fit to tutor me in, and my voice was not quite steady when I spoke.

"Jessica, would you do something for me?"

"Yes, Miss Russell." No hesitation. I could ask her to throw herself from the window for me, her voice said, and she would do it. Gladly.

"Would you call me Mary?"

"But Mama said—"

"I know, mothers like good manners in their children, and that is important. But just between the two of us, I should like it very much if you were to call me Mary. I never—" There was something blocking my throat and I swallowed, hard. "I never had a sister, Jessica. I had a brother, but he died. My mother and father died, too, so I don't have much of a family anymore. Would you like to be my sister, Jessica?"

The amazed adoration in her eyes was too much. I pulled her to me so I did not have to look at it. Her hair smelt musky-sweet, like chamomile. I held her, and she began to cry, weeping oddly like a woman rather than a young child, while I rocked us both gently in silence. In a few minutes she drew a shuddering breath and stopped.

"Better?"

She nodded her head against my chest. I smoothed her hair.

"That's what tears are for, you know, to wash away the fear and cool the hate."

As I suspected, that last word triggered a reaction. She drew back and looked at me, her eyes blazing.

"I do hate them. Mama says I don't, but I do. I hate them. If I had a gun I'd kill them all."

"Do you think you really would?"

She thought for a moment, and her shoulders slumped. "Maybe not. But I'd want to."

"Yes. They are hateful men, who did something horrid to you and hurt your parents. I'm glad you wouldn't shoot them, because I shouldn't want you to go to gaol, but you go ahead and hate them. No one should ever do what they did. They stole you and hit you and tied you up like a dog. I hate them too."

Her jaw dropped at so much raw emotion aired.

"Yes, I do, and you know what I hate them for most? I hate them for taking away your happiness. You don't trust people now, do you? Not like you did a few weeks ago. A six-year-old girl oughtn't to be frightened of people." The child needed help, but I was quite certain that her parents would greet the suggestion of psychiatric treatment with the standard mixture of horror and embarrassment. She would, for the present, have to settle for me. Physician, heal thyself, I thought sourly.

"Mary?"

"Yes, Jessica?"

"You took me away from those men. You and Mr. Holmes."

"We helped the police get you back, yes," I said carefully and not entirely truthfully, and wondered what was on her mind. I did not wonder for long.

"Well, sometimes when I wake up, I think I'm still in that bed. It's like . . . I can hear the chain rattle when I move. And even during the day, sometimes I think I'm dreaming, and that when I wake up I'll be in bed, with one of those men sitting in the chair with his mask on. I mean, I know I'm back with Mama and Papa, but I feel like I'm not. Do you know what I'm talking about?" she asked without much hope.

The experiential reality of the residual effects of a traumatic experience, I thought, in the precise Germanic tones of Dr. Leah Ginzberg, M.D., Ph.D., and then went on almost automatically as she would have, with a push for more truth.

"Oh yes, I do know that feeling, Jessica. I know it very, very well.

And it gets all tied up with lots of other feelings, doesn't it? Like feeling maybe it was somehow your fault, that if you'd tried just a little harder you could have gotten away." She gaped at me as if I were conjuring half-crowns from the air. "Like even being angry at your mother and father for not rescuing you sooner." Both of those hit home, like charges at the base of a dam, and the pent-up waters came gushing out in an intense monotone.

"I almost got away, but I slipped and fell and he caught me, and then I thought maybe if I didn't eat anything they'd have to let me go, but I was so hungry, even if it meant I had to—had to use the pot, and then I couldn't get the chain off my leg, and then there was always someone there, and after all those days went by and nobody came, I thought maybe, maybe . . . well, that Mama'd gone away home to America and Papa wouldn't want me back." This last came out in a tiny whisper, and she picked at the hem of her skirt.

"Do you talk to your Mama about it?"

"I tried to yesterday, but it made her cry. I don't like to see Mama cry."

"No," I agreed, and felt a flicker of anger at the woman's lack of control. "She's been upset, Jessie, but she'll be much better in a few days. Try again then, or talk to your father."

"I'll try," she said uncertainly. I put my hands on her shoulders and made her look at me.

"Do you trust me, Jessie?"

"Yes."

"I mean really trust me? A lot of grown-ups say things that aren't exactly true because they want to make you feel better, but will you believe me when I say I won't do that to you? Ever?"

"Yes."

"Then listen to me, Jessica Simpson. I know you've heard this before from other people, but now you're hearing it from me, your sister, Mary, and it's the truth. You did everything you possibly could, and you did it perfectly. You left your handkerchief and your hair ribbon for us to find—"

"Like Hansel and Gretel," she inserted.

"Exactly, a trail through the woods. You tried to get away, even though they hurt you for it, and then when they had you in a place where you could do nothing, you waited, you kept strong, and you didn't do anything that might make them want to hurt you. You waited for us. Even though it was boring and scary and very, very lonely, you waited. And when I came you acted like the intelligent person you are, and you kept quiet and let me carry you away over those skinny branches, and you were absolutely quiet, even when I squashed your arm coming down the tree."

"It didn't hurt much."

"You were brave, you were intelligent, you were patient. And as you say, it isn't really over yet, and you're going to have to be brave and intelligent and patient for a while longer, and wait for the anger and the fear to settle down. They will." (And the nightmares? my mind whispered.) "Not right away, and they'll never go away completely, but they'll fade. Do you believe me?"

"Yes. But I'm still very angry."

"Good. Be angry. It's right to be angry when someone hurts you for no reason. But do you think you can try not to be too afraid?"

"To be angry and—happy?" The incongruity obviously appealed to her. She savoured it for a moment and jumped to her feet. "I'm going to be angry and happy." She ran out of the room. I followed, carrying Mary doll, and entered the sitting room as she was declaring her new philosophy of life to her bewildered mother. I caught Holmes' eye, and he rose. Mrs. Simpson made as if to stop him.

"Oh, can't you stay for tea, Mr. Holmes? Miss Russell?"

"I am sorry, Madam, but we have to go to the police station and then catch the seven o'clock train. We must be gone."

Jessica hugged me, hard. I dropped down to her level and gave her the doll.

"Can you write yet, Jessie?"

"A little."

"Well, perhaps your mother might help you write me a letter sometimes. I'd love to hear from you. And remember to stay happy with your anger. Good-bye, sister Jessie."

"Good-bye, sister Mary." She whispered it so her mother shouldn't hear, and giggled.

W E T O O K O U R leave of an uncomfortable Chief Inspector Connor, who arranged a car to Bristol so we might catch an earlier train and be off his turf all the sooner. Again we had a compartment to ourselves, though we were no longer more disreputable than our bags. Bristol turned to fields outside our window, and Holmes reached for his pipe and tobacco pouch. Normality tugged at me, becoming more firm with each accelerating clack of the iron wheels, but there was something to be set aright between Holmes and myself before we went further.

"Holmes, you did not wish to let me join you in this case," I said. He grunted in agreement. "Do you now regret that you did so?" He knew immediately what I was talking about and did not pretend otherwise. However, he did not look at me, but took his pipe out of his mouth and examined the bowl closely, retrieved his little tool, and fussed with the tobacco for a moment before answering.

"I was indeed filled with a singular lack of enthusiasm at the prospect. I admit that. However, I hope you understand that this was not due to any doubts concerning your abilities. I work alone. I always have. Even when Watson was with me, he functioned purely as another pair of hands, not in anything resembling true partnership. You, however—I have seen for some time that you are not the type to be content to follow directions. My hesitation was not out of fear that you might put a foot disastrously wrong, but that I might cause you to do so by misdirection and my longstanding disinclination to work in harness with another. As it happened, by hesitating to give you even the responsibility for creating the necessary diversion, I paradoxically presented you with an opportunity for independently solving the case."

"I'm sorry, Holmes, but as I was—"

"For God's sake, Russell," he interrupted impatiently, "don't apologise. I know the circumstances; you made the correct decision. You should have been quite wrong, in fact, had you let the opportunity slip through your fingers. I admit that I was severely taken aback when I saw you running down the road with the child on your back. It was something Watson could never have done, even discounting his bad leg. Watson's great strength has always been his utter, dogged dependability. His attempts at independent action tend to blow up in my face, so I have never encouraged them, but I allowed you to come in with me on this case because the step had to be taken at some time, and it was best done while I was immediately to hand at every moment. Or so I thought, not knowing that the first time I let you out of my sight you would take it into your head to perform an appallingly dangerous stunt like—" He stopped and turned again to his pipe, which seemed to be giving him considerable difficulty. When it was finally belching smoke to his satisfaction, he looked at me, and in his eye was what I can only describe as a rueful twinkle. "It was, in fact, precisely what I myself might have done, given the circumstances."

In an instant twenty pounds were lifted from my shoulders and five years added to my posture. Although the compliment was distinctly backhanded, I felt ridiculously pleased, though I hid the satisfied smile on my lips by looking out the window. After a few dozen telegraph posts my thoughts turned back to other concerns, to the child in the hotel and the struggle she faced. Holmes read my mind.

"What did you say to the child, to cheer her so? She seemed a different person when we left."

"Did she? Good." The poles flipped rhythmically past, and the steady beat of the wheels called hypnotically, and because he was Holmes I finally answered him.

"I told her some things that someone told me, when my family died. I hope they do her some good."

I sat and watched our reflections in the darkening window, and Holmes smoked his pipe, and we spoke no more until we came to Seaford.

HOLMES' ASSESSMENT OF the case had been quite right, of course. The men in Wales had been paid—well paid—for their work and had received their orders anonymously, from a hoarse voice in London and through the post. All had been meticulously planned. They had been instructed in every detail, from the hiring of the house and the purchase of clothing in Cardiff to the construction of the gas-gun, the route to take away from the tent, how to word messages in the agony column, the wearing of masks around the child (which had been a relief to me, knowing that murder was not intended)—all this within the space of a few weeks, and all without any trace of the link with London. When the men were taken, all threads snapped, and we were left with five talkative men, some untraceable money, and the knowledge that the puppet-master behind the deed had walked away scot-free.

Book Three

PARTNERSHIP

The Game's Afoot

❧

❋ 8 ❋

We Have a Case

The ambushes laid by a hastening twilight . . .
the cold menace of winter.

THREE TERMS GO to make up the Oxford calendar, each with its own very distinct flavour. The year begins with Michaelmas term and the autumn closing in, when minds and bodies that have ranged free during the summer are bent again to the life of academe. Days grow short, the sky disappears, the stones and bricks of the city become black in the rain, and the mind turns inward to discipline.

In Hilary term winter seems eternal, with the barest hint of lengthening days and the first sprouts of new life, but with the return in May for Trinity term the sap rises strong with the sun, and all one's energies are set to flower in the end-of-the-year examinations.

Of the terms, my favourite is that of Michaelmas, when the mind is put back into harness and the wet leaves of autumn lie thick in the streets.

I find I cannot look back on that Michaelmas term of 1918 as an isolated thing, separate from the storms that followed. I know I was filled with tremendous joy as I began seriously to flex my muscles in the realm of the mind. The first year had set my feet underneath me, and I was now ready to build. I was no longer intoxicated by long hours in the Bodleian, though my spirit still soared at the smell of the books. I began serious work with my tutors, and I remember two or three occasions when their looks of respect and interest pleased me as much as a "well done, Russell" from Holmes. The world's intrusions were few, although the vision of the High on the day the guns of Europe stopped will remain with me to my dying day, with the black gowns swarming the streets and the mortarboards flung into the air, the shouting and the kissing and the wild clamour of the long-stilled bells, and the fervent and reverent minute of silence.

I can hardly call the adventure that began at the end of that term a "case," for the only clients were ourselves, the only possible payment our lives. It burst upon us like a storm, it beat at us and flung us about and threatened our lives, our sanity, and the surprisingly fragile thing that existed between Holmes and myself.

For me it began, appropriately enough, on a filthy, bitterly wet night in December. I was quite fed up with Oxford and all the tricks she played, not the least of which was her infamously gruesome climate, in this case snow followed by great downpours of near-sleet, buckets of icy rain that drenched the thickest of wool coats and turned normal shoes into sodden leather sacks. I was dressed for the weather, but even so my high hiking boots and shiny so-called waterproof had let in a miserable amount of weather on the walk from the Bodleian to the lodgings house. I was sick of the weather, tired of Oxford, irritated by the demands of my tutors, prickly from being cooped up inside, hungry, tired, and generally ill-tempered.

One thing alone kept me from total bleak despair, and that was the awareness that this was a temporary state. I hugged to myself the knowledge that tomorrow I should be far away from it all, that tomorrow evening at this hour I should be seated before an immense stone fireplace with a glass of something warming in one hand and a large and expertly prepared meal about to find its way to the table, with good company, good music, good cheer. To say nothing of Veronica Beaconsfield's darkly good-looking older brother, home on Christmas leave.

Best of all—oh joy, oh bliss—no Christmas with my aunt: I was going to Ronnie's country house in Berkshire for two weeks, beginning tomorrow. Indeed I might have been there already, for I had intended to leave with her three days ago, but for the unreasonable and unexpected demand for a final, late essay from one of my more capricious and demanding tutors.

But it was now over: The essay had been presented and the three points that had been raised in the presentation had been beaten into place by six hours in Bodley; the essay and its annotations I had left (damp, but legible) at the tutor's college. I was free now of responsibility. The tiny glow of what tomorrow meant protected me from the worst of the cold and, as it warmed and grew, even nudged me into a dash of mordant humour.

I felt very like the proverbial drowned rat when I reached the lodgings house. Stopping in the portico I peeled off several outer layers and left them on a nail, dripping morosely onto the stones. I could then dig an almost dry handkerchief from a pocket to clean my spectacles while I let myself into the porter's lodge.

"Good afternoon, Mr. Thomas."

"Evening is more like it, Miss Russell. Real nice out, I see."

"Oh, it's a perfectly lovely evening for a stroll, Mr. Thomas. Why don't you take the Missus out for a picnic on a punt? Oh, I like that. Did Mrs. Thomas do it?" I put on my glasses, which promptly fogged up, and peered at the tiny Christmas tree that stood bravely on one end of the long counter.

"That she did. Looks pretty, don't it? Oh yes, there's a couple things in your box. Let me get them for you." The old man turned to the series of pigeonholes behind him, which were arranged by the location of each person's rooms. The top, third row, far left box was for my own top floor, far back room. "Here they are. One from the late post, the other from an old, er, elderly woman. She was by, asking for you."

The post was the weekly letter from Mrs. Hudson, which invariably arrived on a Tuesday. Holmes wrote rarely, though I occasionally received a spate of cryptic telegrams, and Dr. Watson (now Uncle John) wrote from time to time as well. I looked at the other offering.

"A lady? What did she want?"

"I don't rightly know, Miss. She said she needed to talk to you, and when I said you weren't in until later, she left that note for you."

I took up the indicated envelope curiously. It was a cheap one, such as can be bought at any news agent's or the railway station, bulky and grubby, with my name written on it in a precise copperplate script.

"This is your writing, isn't it, Mr. Thomas?"

"Yes, Miss. It was blank when she handed it to me, so I put your name on it."

Carefully avoiding the smudged thumbprint on one corner, I opened it with Mr. Thomas's letter opener and took out its tightly folded contents. With difficulty, as it seemed to be glued damply together, I undid it. To my astonishment the contents were no more than an advertisement for a window manufacturer on the Banbury Road, such as I had seen posted up at various places around town. This specimen had the remnants of paste on the back, but as it was still damp it was not permanently attached to itself. A partial bootprint in one corner and the mark of a large dog's paw in the centre indicated that it had lain in the street before being inserted in the envelope. I turned it over, wondering what it meant. Mr. Thomas was watching me, obviously itching to ask the same thing, but too polite to pry. I held it up to the light on his desk. There were no pinpricks, no design.

"A very strange sort of a message, Miss Russell."

"Yes, isn't it? I have a rather eccentric aunt who occasionally tracks me down. I suppose it was she. I'm sorry if she bothered you. How was she looking?"

"Well, Miss, I would never have taken her as a relative of yours. Black hair like that and ugly as—Beg your pardon, Miss, but she should really have a doctor do something about that great ugly mole on her chin."

"When was she here?"

"About three hours ago. I offered to let her stay here and wait for you, and gave her a cuppa tea, but when I went to lock up the back, she said she'd go, and she was gone when I got back. If she returns, shall I bring her up?"

"I think not, Mr. Thomas. Send someone for me and I'll come down." The way from my rooms to the gate house was enclosed, so I wouldn't get wet again. However, I did not want a stranger admitted straightaway. My eyes went to the pigeonhole from which he had taken my letters. Very curious. Who was this who wanted to know where my room was, and more important, why?

I thanked Mr. Thomas and went past him into the hallway that led to the wing my rooms were in. I sat on the bottom step to remove my boots—I think, though I cannot be sure, that I only removed them because they were so uncomfortable, and I did not wish to make more of a mess for Mrs. Thomas to deal with. Whatever the motive, conscious or no, I continued up the stairs in stockinged feet, without even the rustle of the waterproof to betray my presence.

The building was silent, oppressively so. The rain on the landing windows was the loudest sound. And to think I had often, coming up these stairs, shuddered fastidiously at the quantity of noise a number of women living together can produce. Veronica's rooms here, the doors shut as they rarely were, her presence so strong I could almost hear the wild party she'd had in that room a week earlier. Jane De-laField's rooms here, quiet and religious and cocoa-drinking Jane with the unforeseeable gift of limericks, followed always by a blush. And Catharine, whose attractive brother had the odd passion for, what was it, roses? No, iris. And all of them gone now, back in the bosoms of their families, warm and secure, while Mary Russell, cold and lonely, went up the cold draughty stairs to her rooms.

At the top of the stairs I turned towards the back of the building and pulled my key from my pocket. As I reached for the knob my mind was so filled with dolorous thoughts as to have forgotten the odd episode of Mr. Thomas's ugly woman, and so I very nearly overlooked the marks on my door. The key was inches from the lock when I froze, feeling something like an automobile engine must when it is moving forward and is suddenly thrown into reverse gear. There was a black and greasy smudge on my shiny brass doorknob. There were tiny, fresh scratches on the inside of my keyhole. There was light coming from under the door . . .

I shook myself. Come, Russell, don't be absurd. Mrs. Thomas often set a light burning at dark for me and laid a coal fire in the grate. There was nothing to be concerned about. I was on edge still, from the vile weather and the delay of my escape to Berkshire, my nerves were raw from the tutorial I had been through, nothing more. Nothing but an ordinary room on the other side of the door, as I could even see when I bent down and looked, through the keyhole and, feeling ever more ridiculous, under the door.

I reached again with my key, but my antennae were well and truly quivering now, and I drew back and looked around me, for confirmation of one attitude or the other, but no omens presented themselves. However, looking down the corridor, I was aware of a vague feeling that I had indeed seen something, some tiny thing. I went slowly back down towards the stairway and saw, on the sill of the window that had been built to illuminate the landing, a smear of mud, two ivy leaves, and a scattering of raindrops.

How did those get in? How did that smear of soil escape Mrs. Thomas's vigilant cleaning rag?

No, Russell. Your imagination is going berserk. It must have been Mrs. Thomas herself, opening the window to let out a moth and letting in the drops and the leaves and . . . No? The crew that had trimmed the ivy so inadequately last spring, returned to finish the job? But why should they have the window open . . .

I took hold of myself firmly and strode down the hall to my door, and there I stood for several minutes, the key in my hand, and I could not bring myself to use it. More than anything I wished I had the revolver that Holmes had insisted I take, but it sat in my chest of drawers, as useless as if it had been in China.

The truth of the matter was that Holmes had enemies, many of them. He had explained this to me a number of times, drilled me on the precautions I had to take, forced me to acknowledge that I too could become a target for vengeance-seeking acquaintances. I thought it highly unlikely, but I had also to admit that it was not impossible. And right now, all the suspicions Holmes had so laboriously implanted in me wondered if tonight, in my lodgings house, on this wet night in Oxford, someone's animosity against Holmes had not spilled over onto me.

I was sorely tempted to go back downstairs and have Mr. Thomas ring the police, but I found the thought of the Oxford constabulary walking through here with their big shoes and heavy manner little comfort. They might frighten off an evildoer temporarily, but I could not imagine myself sleeping any better after they had gone.

Discounting the police, then, I had two choices. I could use my key after all and confront whomever I found inside my rooms, but that was an action my association with Holmes made me loath to carry out. The other was to approach my rooms by another means than the door. Unfortunately, the only other entrance was through the windows that looked out onto a stone courtyard twenty-five feet below. In the summer I had once climbed the ivy in the nonalcoholic exhilaration of a long midsummer's dusk, but it had been warm and light then, with nothing more dangerous at the end of the climb than a fall forward through an open window. I did know that the vines would hold my weight, but would my fingers?

"Oh for God's sake, Russell, it's only twenty-five feet. Oxford is making you lazy, sitting on your backside in the library all day. You're afraid of the cold? You'll warm up again. There's really no other choice, now is there? Get on with it." My father's American drawl often surfaced when I spoke to myself, as did his irritating tendency to be right.

I went silently back down the hallway, down one flight of stairs, up that hallway, and down the stairs at the far end. These led into the building's inner quad rather than out onto the street. I removed my wool stockings and jacket and left them with my boots and book bag in a dark corner. My glasses I buttoned carefully into a shirt pocket and, taking a deep breath, let myself quietly out into the wicked hands of the storm.

The temperature had dropped further since I had been out on the street, and I stood in wool clothing that might have been gauze when faced with a downpour that was perhaps three degrees from freezing. It took my breath away as the icy wave drove over me, plastering my shirt against my shrivelled breasts and encasing my legs in a thick layer of frigid wool. I pulled myself up into the greasy ivy with fingers that already had trouble moving and thrust into the branches with unfeeling toes. I really ought to get Mr. Thomas to call the police, I thought, but my body had taken over and numbly continued the climb.

I reached the second layer of dark windows and could see the lighted squares of my own just above my head. With renewed caution I reached for the next handhold, only to find that my hand had not loosed from the previous hold. From then on I had to consciously think the muscles of my hands open and, more important, shut on the vine. Slowly, slowly I pulled myself up beside the first of my windows and peered in the inevitable crack between the scant curtains. Nothing there, only the room fire blazing merrily. Cursing gently to myself

I forced my fingers to carry me across to the other window. The ivy was thinner here, and once, when my hand did not completely close, I nearly fell to the stones below, but my other hand kept hold, and the wind hid my noises. I made it to the second cheerily lit rectangle and dangled myself like a sodden monkey to peer into the narrow curtain-crack.

This time I was successful. Even without my spectacles I could see the old woman Mr. Thomas had described, sitting before the fire, bent over a book, her stockinged feet propped upon the rail. I fumbled with the sensationless protuberances on my hand and managed to pop the button from my shirt pocket, lay hands on my spectacles, nearly dropping them to destruction twice, and finally draped them crookedly across my nose. Even from the side she was extraordinarily ugly, with a black mole that resembled a large insect crawling across her chin. I pulled back, trying to think. I should have to do something quickly, as my hands were on the verge of becoming completely useless.

A stream of liquid ice was running down the back of my shirt and streaming off my bare foot. My brain was sluggish with the penetrating cold, but something stuck in my mind about this old woman. What was it? I rested one foot on the mossy stone sill, leant precariously forward, and studied the figure. The ear, was it? And then suddenly it all fell together in a neat pattern. I wedged my poor frozen fingers under the edge of the window and pulled. The old woman looked up from her book, then rose and came to open the window more fully. I looked up at "her" bitterly.

"Damn you, Holmes, what the hell are you doing here? And for God's sake help me in this window before you have to scrape me up off the pavement."

Soon I stood shivering and dripping on my carpet, and awkwardly dried my spectacles on the curtain so I wouldn't have to squint to see Holmes. He stood there in his dingy old lady's dress, that horrid mole on his face, looking not in the least apologetic for the trouble he had put me to.

"Damn it, Holmes, your flair for the dramatic entrance could have broken my neck, and if I avoid pneumonia it'll be no thanks to the last few minutes. Turn your back; I must get out of these clothes." He obediently turned a chair to a blank wall, one with no reflecting object, I noticed, and I peeled off my clothes clumsily in front of the hot little fire, put on the long grey robe I had left folded over the stool that morning, and got a towel for my hair.

"All right, you may turn around now." I pushed the sodden clothing into a corner until I could deal with them later. Holmes and I were close, but I didn't care to wave my underclothing about in front of his nose. There are limits to friendship.

I went to the night table for my comb and, pulling a stool in front of the fire, I began to undo my wet braids to steam in the heat. My fingers, toes, and nose were fiery with returning sensation. The shivering had subsided somewhat, but I could not suppress the occasional hard shudder. Holmes frowned.

"Have you any brandy?" he asked in a low voice.

"You know I don't drink the stuff."

"That is not what I asked," he said, all patience and condescension. "I asked if you had any. I want some brandy."

"Then you'll have to ask my neighbour for some."

"I doubt that the young lady would appreciate a figure like myself at her door, somehow."

"It doesn't matter, she's home in Kent for the holidays anyway."

"Then I shall just have to assume that she gave her permission." He let himself out into the hallway, then put his head back in the door. "By the way, don't touch that machine on the desk. It's a bomb."

I sat eyeing the tangle of wires with the black box in its centre until he returned with my neighbour's bottle and two of her magnificent glasses. He poured generously and handed me a glass, and poured a smaller amount for himself.

"Not a very nice brandy, but it will taste better in these glasses. Drink it," he ordered.

I dutifully took a large mouthful and swallowed. It made me cough but calmed my shudders, and by the time I finished it I was aware of a warm glow spreading out to my very fingertips.

"I suppose you know that alcohol is not the optimum treatment for hypothermia?" I accused him, somewhat truculently. I was really most annoyed at the whole charade, and the melodramatic touch of the bomb was tiresome.

"Had you been in danger of that I would not have given you brandy. However, I can see that it has made you feel better, so finish combing out your hair and then sit in a comfortable chair. We have a long conversation ahead of us. Ah, how forgetful I am in my old age." He went over to the old lady's shopping basket and drew out a parcel that I immediately recognised as Mrs. Hudson's handiwork. My attitude lightened immediately.

"What a life-giving surprise. Bless Mrs. Hudson. However, I cannot eat sitting across from a dirty old woman with an insect crawling up her chin. And if you leave fleas in my rooms, I shan't forgive you easily."

"It's clean dirt," he assured me and peeled off the gruesome mole. He stood up and removed the skirt and loose overshirt, moving stiffly, and sat down again as Sherlock Holmes, more or less.

"My appetite thanks you."

I finished towelling my wet hair and reached greedily for one of Mrs. Hudson's inimitable meat pies. I did keep bread and cheese for informal meals, but even two days old, as this one seemed to be, it was much superior even to the Stilton that lay festering nobly in my stocking drawer.

I emerged from the feast some time later to find Holmes watching me with a curious expression on his face, which disappeared instantly, replaced by his customary slightly superior gaze.

"I was hungry," I declared unnecessarily, somewhat defensive. "I had a murderous tutorial, for which I skipped lunch, and then worked in the Bodleian all afternoon. I don't remember if I had breakfast. I may have done."

"What so engrossed you this time?"

"Actually, I was doing some work that might interest you. My maths tutor and I were working with some problems in theory, involving base eight, when we came across some mathematical exercises developed by an old acquaintance of yours."

"I assume you speak of Professor Moriarty?" His voice was as cold as the ivy outside my window, but I refused to be subdued.

"Exactly. I spent the day hunting down some articles he published. I was interested in the mind and the personality as well as the mathematics."

"What impression did you have of the man?"

" 'The subtlest of all the beasts in the garden' comes to mind. His cold-blooded, ruthless use of logic and language struck me as somehow reptilian, although that may be unkind to snakes. I believe that had I not known the identity of the writer, the words alone would have succeeded in raising my hackles."

"Being a good mammal yourself apparently, rather than a cold-blooded thinking machine such as your teacher is known to be," he said drily.

"Ah," I said, speaking lightly with the freedom of the brandy's glow, "but *I* have never called you cold-blooded, now have I, my dear Holmes?"

He sat very still for a moment and then cleared his throat. "No, you have not. Have you finished with Mrs. Hudson's picnic?"

"Yes, thank you." I allowed him to pack away the remnants. His movements seemed terribly stiff, but as he hated to have his ailments noted, I said nothing. He had probably taken a chill in his old woman's clothes, and his rheumatism was acting up. "If you would just put it over there, I will enjoy it greatly for lunch tomorrow."

"No, I am sorry, but I shall have to put it back in my shopping basket. We may need it tomorrow."

"Holmes, I don't much like the sound of that. I have an engagement for tomorrow. I am going to Berkshire. I have already put it off for three days, and I have no intention of further delaying it because of some demand of yours."

"You have no choice, Russell. We must be away from here, before they find us."

"Who? Holmes, what is going on? Don't tell me you suggest we go out again into that." I waved my hand at the window, where the damp, splashing drops told of rain halfway to being snow. "I'm not even dry from the first time. And what is that thing you've brought—is it really a bomb? Why did you bring it here? Talk to me, Holmes!"

"Very well, to be succinct: We shall go out, but not yet; the bomb was here, attached to your door when I arrived; and 'what's going on' is nothing less than attempted murder."

I stared at him aghast. The tangled object on the desk seemed to writhe gently in the edges of my vision, and I felt cold fingers running up my spine. When I had my breath back I spoke again and was pleased to find that my voice was almost firm.

"Who wishes to kill me? And how did you know about it?" I did not think it necessary to ask why.

"Well done, Russell. A quick mind is worthless unless you can control the emotions with it as well. Tell me first, why did you come up the ivy, rather than through the door? You did not have your revolver and could hardly have expected to leap in the window and overpower your intruder." His dry voice was marginally too casual, but I could not see why this was so important to him.

"Information. I needed to know what awaited me before making a decision. Had I found an armed reception party I'd have gone down and had Mr. Thomas telephone for the police. Am I correct in assuming that you left the black smudge on the doorknob for me to find?"

"I did."

"And the mud and leaves on the opposite window ledge?"

"The mud was there before I came. One leaf I added, as assurance that you should notice."

"Why the charade, Holmes? Why risk my bones coming up the wall?"

He looked straight at me and his voice was dead, flat serious.

"Because, my dear child, I needed to be absolutely certain that despite being tired, cold, and hungry, you would pick up the small hints and act correctly."

"The business of the note in my pigeonhole was hardly a 'small hint.' A bit heavy-handed for you. Why didn't you ask Mrs. Hudson which room I was in? She has been to my rooms before." There was something here I was just not seeing.

"I have not seen Mrs. Hudson for some days."

"But—the food?"

"Old Will brought it to me. You may have seen that he's more than just the gardener," he added with apparent irrelevance.

"I surmised that some time ago, yes. But why have you been away—?" I stopped, and my eyes narrowed as various facts merged and his stiffness came back to me. "My God, you're hurt. They tried to kill you first, didn't they? Where are you injured? How badly?"

"Some distinctly uncomfortable abrasions along my back, is all. I'm afraid I may have to ask you to change the dressings at some point, but not immediately. The person who set the bomb thinks I'm dying, fortunately. Some poor tramp was run over just after they took me to the hospital, and he's there still, with bandages about his head and my name on his chart. And, I might add, a constable at his side at all times."

"Was anyone else hurt? Mrs. Hudson?"

"Mrs. Hudson is fine, although half the glass in the south wall is out. The house is miserable in this weather so she's off to that friend of hers in Lewes until repairs are made. No, the bomb was not actually in the house; they set it in one of the beehives, of all places. He, or they, must have laid it the night before, expecting it to catch me on my morning rounds. Perhaps he used a radio transmitter to trigger it, or else motion at the adjoining hives was enough. In any case, I can only be grateful that it did not go up in my face."

"Who, Holmes? Who?"

"There are three names that come to mind, although the humourous touch of using the hive is of a level I should not have credited to any of the three. There are four bombers I have put away in the past. One is dead. One has been out for five years, though I had heard that he had settled down and become a strong family man. The second was let out eighteen months ago and has apparently remained in the London area. The third escaped from Princetown last July. Any one of the three could have been responsible for my bomb, which was professionally laid and left very little intact evidence. Yours, however, is a different matter. A thing like that is as individual as a fingerprint. Not being entirely up to date on bombs myself, however, I need an expert to read this particular fingerprint. We shall take it with us when we go."

"Where are we going?" I asked with considerable patience, I thought, considering the havoc I could see this was going to wreak on my plans for a lovely holiday.

"To the great cesspool, of course."

"Why London?"

"Mycroft, my dear child, my brother Mycroft. He possesses the knowledge of Scotland Yard without the obsessional reticence of that good body, which tends to hoard information like a dragon its gold. Mycroft can, with a single telephone call, tell me the precise locations of our three possibilities, and who is the most likely author of your mechanism here. Assuming my attempted murderer still believes me to be in hospital, he would not connect you with Mycroft, as the two of you have never so much as met. We will be safe with him for a day or two, and we shall see what trail turns up. The scent in Sussex is, I fear, very cold. I did come up here as quickly as I could, but I was not in time to catch him at his work. I am sorry about that. You see before you a distinctly inferior version of Sherlock Holmes, old, rusty, and easily laid out."

"By a bomb that nearly killed you." His long, expressive fingers waved away my proffered excuse. "Do we go now?"

"I think not. He already knows the bomb did not go off. He will no doubt assume that you will be on full guard tonight—that you have not called the police already tells him that. He will bide his time to-night, and tomorrow either lay another bomb for you, or if, as I sus-pect, he is intelligent and flexible enough, he will be creative and use a sniper's rifle or a runaway motorcar, should you be so foolish as to provide a target. However, you will not. We will be on the streets be-fore light, but not earlier. You may rest until then."

"Thank you." I tore my eyes from the bomb. "First, your back. How much gauze will I need?"

"A considerable quantity, I should think. Do you have it?"

"One of the girls down the hall is a hypochondriac with a nurse mother. If you can do your lock trick on her door as well as you did on that of my other neighbour we should be well supplied."

"Ah, that reminds me, Russell. An early birthday present."

Holmes held out a small, narrow package wrapped in shiny paper. "Open it now."

I undid the wrappings with great curiosity, for Holmes did not nor-mally give gifts. I opened the dark velvet jeweller's box and found in-side a shiny new set of picklocks, a younger version of his own.

"Holmes, ever the romantic. Mrs. Hudson would be pleased." He chuckled and stood up cautiously. "Shall we try them out?"

Some time later we were back in front of my fire, richer by several square yards of gauze, a huge roll of sticking plaster, and a quart bottle of antiseptic. I poured him a large brandy, and when he took off his shirt I could see that I was going to need most of that gauze. I refilled his glass and stood assessing the job.

"We ought to let Watson do this."

"If he were standing here I would. Get on with it." He swallowed this second brandy neat, so I poured him a third, picked up the scissors, and paused.

"Personally I have found that the mind handles pain best if it is given a counterirritant to distract it. Aha, I have just the thing. Holmes, tell me about the case of the King of Bohemia, and Irene Adler." Holmes was seldom beaten, but that woman had done it, with an ease and a flair that I knew still rankled. Her photograph stood on his bookshelf, as a reminder of his failure, and telling me about it would very possibly distract him from his back.

At first he refused, but as I continued snipping and pulling off bits of sticking plaster, bandage, and skin, he began speaking through clenched teeth. "It began one night, in the spring of 1888, March I think, when the King of Bohemia came to my door to ask for some—dear God, Russell, leave me a bit of skin, would you?—some assistance. It seems he had been involved with a woman, a totally unsuitable woman from the point of view of a royal marriage, an opera singer. Unfortunately for him she loved him, and refused to return a photograph she possessed of the two of them in a position of obvious affection. This photograph he wanted back, and he hired me to retrieve it."

The narrative wound on as I doused and snipped and peeled, pausing often as his jaws clamped down and beads of sweat came to his brow. I finished before his account had ended, but he continued as I took his bloodstained shirt to the basin in the corner. With the end of the story, the final description of how she saw through Holmes' disguises and with her new husband eluded both detective and monarch, he swallowed the last of the brandy and sat staring into the fire, breathing heavily.

I arranged the shirt in front of the coals to dry and turned to the exhausted man next to me.

"You need to lie down and sleep. Take my bed—no, I'll not hear protest. You need to be on your stomach for a while, and you cannot sleep in a chair in that position. No, I refuse to accept gallant stupidity in place of rational necessity. Go."

"Defeated again. I surrender." With a wan imitation of his sardonic smile he stood and followed me. I pulled aside the bedclothes, and he slowly lowered himself forward into my bed. I gently pulled the blankets up over his naked shoulders.

"Sleep well."

"You will need to wear a young man's clothing tomorrow. I trust you have some," he said around the pillow.

"Of course."

"Take a small knapsack with a few things in it. We will buy clothing if we are to be gone very long."

"I will pack it tonight."

"And write a note to Mr. Thomas, telling him you've been called away for a few days, that you understand Mr. Holmes has been in an accident. He is in my employ; he'll understand."

"In your—You are a devious man. Go to sleep."

I wrote the note, including a request to ring Veronica Beaconsfield, telling her not to meet my train, and sat before the fire to braid my hair, which was dry at last. (The one drawback to long hair is washing it in the winter.) I studied the flickering coals as my hands slowly bound one-half of the fluffy cloud into a long plait that reached past my waist and tied a cord around the end. I had started on the other side when his voice came again from the dark corner, low and slurred with drink and sleep.

"I asked Mrs. Hudson once why she thought you wore your hair so long. She said it was a vestige of femininity."

My hands went still. This was the first time in our acquaintance that he had commented on my appearance, other than to disparage it. Watson would never have believed it possible. I smiled down at the fire and continued the plait.

"Yes, she would think that, I suppose."

"Is it true?"

"I think not. I find short hair too much fuss, always needing combing and cutting. Long hair is much easier, oddly enough."

There was no answer, but soon a gentle snore reached my ears. I took a spare blanket from the shelf and pulled it around me on the chair. My spectacles I laid on the little table next to me, the room retreated into fuzziness, and I slept.

I awoke once, some hours later, stiff and uncertain of my surroundings. The fire had burnt down, but I could see a figure seated at the window, wrapped in a blanket looking out at the night. I sat up and reached for my spectacles.

"Holmes? Is it—?"

The figure turned quickly toward me and held up a finger.

"No, hush, child, go back to sleep. I'm only thinking, as best I can without lighting my pipe. Go back to sleep for a while. I'll wake you when it's time."

I laid my spectacles back onto the table, reached over to throw more coal on the fire, and settled myself again into the chair. As I drifted back into sleep, I experienced one of those odd and memorable dream-moments that lodge in the mind and, with hindsight, seem precognitive of events that follow. A phrase presented itself to my mind, with such stark clarity that it might have been in print before my eyes. It was a remembered phrase, from the speculative or philosophical introductory chapter in Holmes' book on bee-keeping. He had written, "A hive of bees should be viewed, not as a single species, but as a triumvirate of related types, mutually exclusive in function but utterly and inextricably interdependent upon each other. A single bee separated from its sisters and brothers will die, even if given the ideal food and care. A single bee cannot survive apart from the hive."

The surprise of the statement half woke me, or I seemed to half wake, and when I looked over at Holmes I had the oddest impression that there was a drop of rain on his cheek.

Impossible, of course. I am now quite convinced that it was a dream, although the visual impression was vivid, if blurred through myopia. I mention it, not as historical truth, but as an indication of the complex state of my unconscious mind at the time . . . and, as I mentioned, because of the events it foreshadowed.

❧ 9 ❧

The Game, Afoot

We must disentangle, therefore, what now is obscure.

"WAKE, RUSSELL," SAID a voice in my ear. "The game's afoot!" The room was dark but for the flame of the Bunsen burner, and the air smelt of coffee.

"Cry 'God for Harry! England and Saint George!'" I muttered grumpily to complete Henry's speech. Once more unto the breach, and all that.

"Indeed. But I fear that the game after whom the greyhounds strain is us. Up, now, drink your coffee. It may be some long time before your next hot drink. And your clothing—everything warm you own, while I return our borrowed goods to your neighbour. Perhaps," he added, "you might purchase another bottle of this ghastly brandy before your near neighbour returns. No light, now, we must be invisible."

By the time he returned I was dressed as a young man and held my heaviest boots in my hands.

"I shall put these on at the outer door. Mr. Thomas has excellent hearing."

"You know the building better than I, Russell, but I had thought to leave from the other end. Your corner here will be under observation from the street."

I sipped gingerly at the steaming coffee while I thought, and grimaced at the taste.

"Couldn't you have washed out the beaker before you made coffee in it? It tastes like the sulphur I was using yesterday. It's a good thing I wasn't experimenting with arsenic."

"I smelt it first. A little sulphur is good for the blood."

"Spoils the coffee."

"Don't drink it then. Come, Russell, stop dawdling."

I gulped half the scalding drink and poured the rest into the hand-basin.

"There is another way," I suggested thoughtfully, "one that avoids both the street and the back alleyway, and I doubt that anyone who hasn't studied a medieval map of the area would know about it. It debouches into an absolutely foul yard," I added.

"That sounds ideal. Do not neglect to bring your revolver, Russell. It may be needed, and it does us no good in your drawer with that disgusting cheese."

"My lovely Stilton; it's almost ripe, too. I do hope Mr. Thomas enjoys it."

"Any riper and it will eat through the woodwork and drop into the room below."

"You envy me my educated tastes."

"That I will not honour with a response. Get out the door, Russell."

We crept noiselessly through passages and hallways, into an attic where I used my new picklocks on the connecting door, and into a kind of priest's hole that had lain undisturbed for 250 years until the previous summer, when the fiancé of one of my housemates found a reference in a letter in the bowels of the Bodleian, searched it out, and landed a readership for his efforts. At one point we took to the dangerously slick roof, two inches of snow over ice. Finally Holmes hissed at me.

"Are you lost, Russell? We've been nearly twenty minutes in this labyrinth. Time is of the essence, I trust you understand."

"I do. Our other possible route involved hanging by our hands and swinging between the buildings. While I know that physical discomfort is nothing in your eyes, I should prefer to wait until later in the day to have your back opened up, if you don't mind." The strain of responsibility was sharpening my tongue, and I bit back further words to concentrate on the route.

We eventually reached the noxious yard and stood before its pristine white surface, which obscured decades of horse droppings, kitchen slops, and other unmentionables. In the summer it rivalled my Stilton for olfactory potency.

We huddled in the door's recess, and I spoke to Holmes in a whisper.

"As you see, other than this doorway and two others, neither of which could conceal anyone, the yard itself is secure. I see two possible problems: one, that there may be watchers in the street outside the gate, and two, that when they find me gone they may search the area and find two sets of footprints. If you prefer, we could take to the roofs again."

"Really, Russell, you do disappoint me, allowing yourself to be limited by the obvious options. There is no more time for scaling the heights. They will soon know that you have escaped them; giving them your footprints will do no harm. We will not give them mine. If there are watchers, use your gun."

I swallowed, put my hand in my pocket, and strode off firmly into the open yard, grateful for the heavy nails on my boots. I looked back to see Holmes mincing within my footsteps, his skirt drawn up to reveal the trousers below. Were it not for the threat hanging over us, I would have given out with a girlish giggle at the sight, but I refrained. I passed the gates with the revolver in my hand, but there was no human there, only a scurry in the dustbins.

We followed this singular method of travel up the alleyway to the main road, where the few early travellers had already turned the snow to mire. Here we could walk abreast, Holmes as a hobbling old lady, myself as a gawky farm boy. His dingy black skirt and cape of yesterday had been reversed to an equally dingy blue, and the mole on his chin had disappeared, to be replaced by a mouthful of rotten teeth. Not an improvement from my point of view, but few eyes would look past the mouth to the face beyond—what face there was between scarves and hat.

"Don't stride so, Russell!" Holmes whispered fiercely. "Throw your boots out in front of you as you walk and let your elbows stick out a bit. It would help if you let your mouth hang open stupidly, and for God's sake take off your glasses, at least until we get out of town. I won't allow you to walk into anything. Do you think you could persuade your nose to drip a bit, just for the effect?"

Soon I was slouching along blindly in the bleak dawn light, stumbling occasionally while appearing to support my aged mother. By the time it was fully light we stood on the Banbury Road going north out of town.

"North, away from London? This is going to be a long day."

"It's safer. See if you can persuade that wagon to take us a few miles."

I clumped off obediently into the road to intercept the farmer returning from town with an empty wagon and glad for thruppence, to "save me old mum a walk to Bamb'ry to see her newest grandchild."

He was a talkative man and jabbered away the whole time as his horse meandered about the road. It saved us from having to construct a story for him, though by the time he left us in Banbury I was most weary of smiling stupidly out from under my hat brim and trying not to squint. As his wagon pulled away I turned to Holmes.

"Next time we do this, I will play the deaf old woman and you can laugh at rude jests for an hour."

Holmes cackled merrily and shuffled off down the road.

I T WAS A long day's work that brought us to London, two cold and hungry travellers who kept moving largely through force of habit. We went north and west out of Oxford to reach London to the southeast, and covered a weary number of miles in circling widely across the countryside in order to enter the city from the south, for the Oxford road was the natural target of watchers. From Banbury to Broughton Poggs, Hungerford to Guildford, touching Kent and Greenwich we came; on foot, farm wagons, horse buses, and motorcars we bought, begged, and—once—stole rides to bring ourselves to the great city of London, to which all roads lead, eventually. I could tell by Holmes' silence that his back was paining him, but there was nothing to do but buy him a bottle of brandy and press on. With Mycroft we would find the assistance we needed.

The snow started up again late in the afternoon, but not severely enough to stop the flow of vehicles. It was half past seven when we numbly stepped from a public omnibus onto Pall Mall, a hundred yards from the doors of the Diogenes Club, of which Mycroft Holmes was a founder and prime member.

Holmes fished out a pencil stub and a grubby, twice-used envelope from a pocket. By the light of the lamp overhead the ends of his fingers looked blue where they stuck out from his fingerless gloves, and he wrote slowly and awkwardly. His thin lips appeared purple in his pale face, despite the shawl pulled up tight to hide his day's stubble.

"Take this to the front of the Club. They won't let you in, I shouldn't think, but they will take this to Mycroft if you tell them it's from his cousin. Have you a half crown if they're hesitant? Good. I will stay here. And, Russell, perhaps you should put your glasses on."

I pushed myself into a heavy trot, the boots which had kept me so dry during the day now seeming to weigh approximately two stone each. The man at the entrance to the Club was indeed reticent about taking my disreputable-looking message to a member, but I persisted and within a minute found myself being escorted into the warm air inside. My glasses promptly fogged up, and when a voice rumbled from before me, "I am Mycroft Holmes. Where is my brother?" I could only thrust out a hand in the general direction of the speaker. It was seized and shaken firmly by what felt like a pillow of warm, raw bread dough. I peered over my glasses at his enormous figure.

"He waits outside, sir. If it is convenient, he needs—we need—a roof for the night and a hot meal. Also," I added in a low voice, "a doctor might be of some use."

"Yes, I knew he was injured. Mrs. Hudson telephoned me with a very graphic account, and would have turned me out to bring Dr. Watson to Sussex had I not convinced her that our presence would not be a kindness, and that the doctors in Sussex were quite adequate. In the end she agreed not to inform the good doctor until Sherlock seemed strong enough for visitors. I admit I was surprised to hear from my friends at Scotland Yard that he had disappeared from the hospital. Are the wounds so light, then?"

"Not light. I'm certain they are very painful, but his life is not in danger, if he avoids infection, that is. He needs rest, food, and quiet."

"And he stands in the cold." He raised his voice and called for his coat, and we plunged back into the snowy street outside. My spectacles cleared quickly, and I looked down towards the next streetlamp.

"I left him there," I said, and pointed.

The man next to me was every bit as large as his grip had indicated but surprisingly quick on his feet, and he was first to reach the rumpled figure in dark blue and help it rise from an upturned crate.

"Good evening, Mycroft," said Holmes. "I apologise for intruding on your quiet reading with my little problem, but unfortunately it appears that someone is attempting to exterminate Miss Russell and myself. I thought you might be willing to be of assistance."

"Sherlock, you're a fool not to have called me in earlier. I could have saved you what was obviously a strenuous day's work. And you know that I am always interested in these cases of yours—apart from those requiring excessively physical activity, of course. Come, let us cross over to my rooms."

My glasses rendered me blind again as we entered the building across from the Club, so I removed them and stumbled heavily up the stairs behind the brothers. Once inside, the curtains drawn tight, I dropped my laden knapsack to the floor, remembering belatedly the explosive device it contained, and collapsed into a chair before the fire. I was vaguely aware of Mycroft Holmes sending for some food and pressing hot drinks into our hands, but the warmth and the lack of movement were such sheer bliss that I was not interested in anything else.

I must have drifted off to sleep there, for I awoke with a start some time later with Holmes' hand on my shoulder and voice in my ear.

"I won't permit you to spend two nights running perched in a chair, Russell. Come and have some food with us."

I stood up sheepishly and put on the tiresome spectacles. "May I wash first?" I asked to a point halfway between Holmes and his brother.

"Of course," exclaimed Mycroft Holmes. He ushered me down a hall to a small room with a daybed. "This will be yours while you are here, and the bath and such are through here. I borrowed a few things from a neighbour, if you would like to shed your present attire." He looked a bit embarrassed at the inescapable intimacy of this offer, but I thanked him warmly, and he looked relieved. He was quite obviously no more accustomed to having to take the needs of a female into account than Holmes had been before I walked into him on the downs.

"Just one thing," I added hesitantly, and saw the anxiety come back to his corpulent face. "Your brother's injuries—he really should not be allowed to spend the night in a chair. If he would be better in here . . . ?"

His face cleared. "No, worry not, Miss Russell. I have sufficient space for the both of you," and he left me for his imminent food.

I washed quickly and dressed in a thick blue robe I found hanging in the wardrobe. My hair I left pinned up on my head, escaping tendrils and all. My feet went gratefully into a pair of slightly too small carpet slippers, and I went to join the brothers at the table.

When I walked into the room, Mycroft immediately scraped back his chair, stood up, and went to pull out a chair for me. Holmes (returned now to his normal self, white teeth and all) watched him for a moment, looked at me, laid his serviette on the table, and slowly stood, smiling curiously. I was seated, Mycroft took his seat, and Holmes sat, a peculiar twist to the corner of his lips. Reminders of my femininity always took him by surprise. However, I could not hold him to blame, for they took me by surprise as well.

The roast capon was delicious, the breads fresh, the wine sparkled on the tongue. We spoke of inconsequentials and finished with a platter of cheese, among which I was pleased to find a piece of old Stilton. Mycroft and I shared it, leaving the cheddar to Holmes. It was a most satisfying meal. I said as much as I pushed back my plate.

"A full stomach, a slightly tipsy brain, and the knowledge of a safe place to sleep. What more could a person ask? Thank you, Mr. Holmes." We adjourned to the fire, and Mycroft poured out three large brandies. I looked at my glass and wished for bed, and sighed quietly.

"Will you see a doctor tonight, Holmes?"

"I will not see a doctor, no. It must not be known that we are here."

"What of the Club, and the cook? They must know, surely."

"The Club is discreet," said Mycroft, "and I told the cook that I was exceedingly hungry."

"So, no doctor. Even Watson?"

"Especially Watson."

I sighed again. "I suppose this is another of your tests of my abilities at basic first-aid, or some such. Very well, bring on the gauze."

Mycroft went off to find the necessaries, and Holmes removed his jacket and began to undo his buttons.

"How may I distract you this time?" I asked sympathetically. "The story of Moriarty and the Reichenbach Falls, perhaps?"

"I need no distraction, Russell," he said curtly. "I believe I have already told you that a mind which cannot control its body's emotional reactions is no mind worth having."

"As surely you should know, Holmes," I responded tartly. "Perhaps you could turn your mind to closing the physical reaction of those holes in your back. This shirt is beyond salvation."

The gauze that met my eyes was stained brown, and underneath it the skin was a mass of purple bruises and scabs. However, all but the worst of the wounds were intact, and only one, puckered by several sutures, was angry and red.

"I think there may be some bit of débris left in this one," I said. I looked over at Mycroft, who had perched fastidiously in a corner during the work. "Can you bring me something for a hot poultice?"

For the next half hour I held heated poultices to Holmes' side as he and Mycroft reviewed the known facts of the two attempts. Holmes had me insert my part of the story as he lit a pipe with unsteady hands.

"And the bomb?" asked Mycroft at the end of it.

"In Russell's haversack."

Mycroft retrieved it and sat with it on the table in front of him, lifting up wires and gently prodding connexions. "I will have a friend look at this tomorrow, but it does look similar to the one you took from the Western Street bank attempt some years ago."

"And yet, you know, I had placed that man, Dickson his name was, on the bottom of the list of possibilities. In the five years since he was released, Inspector Lestrade informed me, he was married, had two children, made a success of himself at his father-in-law's music shop, and worships his family. An unlikely candidate."

As Holmes talked an unpleasant suspicion began to unfurl itself in my mind. When his voice stopped I blurted it out.

"Holmes, you said that Mrs. Hudson was out of the way, but do you think we should ask Watson to move into an hotel for two or three days, or go visit a relative, until we know what's going on?"

The thin back went rigid beneath my hands, and he jerked, cursed, and turned more slowly to me, aghast. "My God, Russell, how could I—Mycroft, you're on the telephone. You talk to him, Russell. Do not let him know where you are, or that I am with you. You know his number? Good. Oh, if anything has happened to him through my utter and absolute, boneheaded stupidity . . ."

I held the telephone to my ear and waited to be connected. Watson usually retired early, and it was after eleven o'clock. Holmes gnawed on his thumb as he waited, watching my face. Finally the connexion was made and the sleepy voice came up on the line.

"Hmmmph?"

"Watson, dear Uncle John, is that you? Mary here, I must—no, I am fine. Listen Uncle, I—no, Holmes is well, or was well, when I spoke with him last. Listen to me, Uncle John, you must listen to me. Are you listening? Good, yes, I am sorry that it is so late, I know I woke you, but you must leave your house, tonight, as soon as possible. Yes, I know it is late, but surely there is an hotel that would take you in, even at this hour? The what? Yes, good. Now you must take some things and go now. What? No, I have no time for explanations, but there have been two bombs set, one for Holmes and one for me, and— yes. No. No, mine did not go off, and Holmes had only minor injuries, but Uncle John, you may be in great danger and must leave your house at once. Now. Yes, Mrs. Hudson is safe and sound. No, Holmes is not with me, I don't know exactly where he is." I turned my back carefully so I could not see Holmes, and thus preserve an iota of the truth. "He told me to ring you. No, I am not in Oxford, I'm at the house of a friend. Now please go; I will call you at the hotel when I've heard something from Holmes. And Uncle, you must not mention this call to anyone, do you understand? No one must think that Holmes is anywhere but safely at home. You are not terribly good at dissimulation, I know, but it is terribly important. You know what the newspapers would do if they heard of it. Go to your hotel, stay there, talk to no one, until I call. Please? Ah, thank you. My mind will rest easier. You won't delay, will you? Good. Good-bye."

I rang off and looked at Holmes. "Mrs. Hudson?" I asked.

"No need to disturb her at this hour. The morning is soon enough."

The tension subsided in the room, and the weariness crept back into my bones. I lightly fastened the dressings over Holmes' back, picked up my glass, and lifted it to the two brothers.

"Gentlemen, I bid you good night. I trust our plans may wait until morning for their formulation?"

"When brains are fresher," said Holmes, as if quoting someone whose opinions he considered suspect—Oscar Wilde perhaps. "Good night, Russell."

"I trust, Holmes, that you will allow your body some rest tonight."

He reached for his pipe.

"Russell, there are times when the infirmities of the body may be used as a means of concentrating the mind. I should be something of a fool were I not to take advantage of that phenomenon."

This from a man who could not even sit back in a chair. I unclenched my jaw and spoke with deliberate cruelty.

"No doubt that marvellous concentration explains why you neglected to include Watson in your calculations." I regretted it as soon as the words were said, but I could not very well take them back. "Get some sleep, for God's sake, Holmes."

"I say again, good night, Russell," he bit off, struck a match with a violence that must have hurt his back, and applied it to the bowl. I looked at Mycroft, who shrugged minutely, threw my hands in the air, and went to bed.

It was very late, or very early, when the smell of tobacco no longer drifted under my door.

❧ 10 ❧

The Problem of the Empty House

The massacre of the males . . .

I WAS AWAKENED by the shout of a street hawker in the grey morning, and as I lay there summoning the energy to find my watch, the gentle clatter of cup meeting saucer in the next room evoked certain possibilities. I dressed quickly in crumpled trousers and shirt from my knapsack and made my way to the sitting room.

"I hear I have not missed breakfast entirely," I said as I entered, and stopped dead as I saw the third figure at the table. "Uncle John! But how . . . ?"

Holmes vacated a chair and took his cup over to the window, where the curtains were still tightly drawn. He moved with care and looked his age and more, but there was no pain in his face, and his shaven chin and combed hair bespoke a degree of back movement that would have been difficult the previous day.

"I fear my long-time chronicler has taken a few of my lessons to heart, Russell. We have been run to earth." His expression was of amusement and chagrin laid over something darker, worry, perhaps. He grimaced as Watson chuckled and buttered his toast.

"Elementary, my dear Holmes," he said, and Holmes snorted. "Where would Mary be, if you were both in danger, but with you, and where would you go but to your brother's? Have some tea, Mary," he offered, and looked at me over his glasses. "Though I should like an apology for your telling me an untruth." He did not sound hurt, only resigned, and it occurred to me that Holmes was well accustomed to deceiving this man, because he was, as I had said, not gifted with the ability to lie, and thus quite simply could not be trusted to act a part. For the first time I became aware of how that knowledge must have pained him, how saddened he must have been over the years at his failure, as he would have seen it, his inability to serve his friend save by unwittingly being manipulated by Holmes' cleverer mind. And when I continued the pattern, he only looked a mild reproach at me and beheaded a second egg. I sat down in the chair Holmes had left and put a hand on his.

"I am sorry, Uncle John. Really very sorry. I was afraid for you, and afraid that if you came here they'd follow you. I wanted to keep you out of it."

He harrumphed in embarrassment and patted my hand awkwardly, pink to his bushy grey eyebrows.

"Quite all right, my dear, quite all right. I do understand. Just remember that I've been watching out for myself for a long time now, I'm hardly a babe in the woods."

And perhaps also, my mind continued, it was an unkind way to remind him that he had been displaced from Holmes' side by an active younger person—a female at that. I was struck anew by the size of this man's heart.

"I know that, Uncle John. I should have thought it out more carefully. But you—how did you get here? And when did you shave off your moustache?" Very recently, from the looks of the skin.

Holmes spoke from his position by the curtains, sounding for all the world like a parent both proud and exasperated at a child's clever but inconvenient new trick.

"Put on your alter ego, Watson," he ordered.

Watson obligingly put down his spoon and went to the door, where he struggled into a much-repaired great-coat cut for a man considerably taller than he, a warped bowler, knit wool gloves out at the fingers in three places, and a knit scarf with a distinctly loving-hands-at-home air about it.

"They belong to the doorman at the hotel," he explained proudly. "It was just like old times, Holmes, really it was. I left the hotel by the kitchen entrance, through three restaurants and Victoria Station, took two trams, a horse bus, and a cab. It took me half an hour to walk the last quarter mile, watching for loiterers from every doorway. I do not think even Holmes himself could have followed me without my seeing," he winked at me.

"But, why, Uncle John? I told you that I'd ring you."

The old man drew himself up proudly. "I am a doctor, and I have a friend who is injured. It was my duty to come."

Holmes muttered something from the window, where one of his long fingers pulled back one edge of the thick draperies. Watson did not hear it, but to me it sounded like, "Goodness and mercy shall plague me all the days of my life." I had once thought him to be nearly illiterate when it came to Scripture, but he was ever full of surprises, although he did tend to change quotes to suit the circumstances.

"Watson, why should I let you do further damage to my epidermis, what little Russell has left for me? It has already entertained two doctors and a number of nurses at my local hospital. Are you so needy of patients?"

"You will allow me to examine your injuries because I will not leave until I have done so," Watson said with asperity. Holmes glared at him furiously, and at Mycroft and myself as we began to laugh. He jerked his hand from the drapes.

"Very well, Watson, let us get it over with. I have work to do." Watson went with Mycroft to wash his hands, taking with him the black doctor's bag he had openly carried through the streets. I looked at Holmes despairingly. He closed his eyes and nodded, then gestured to the window. "At the end of the street," he said and went off after Watson.

I put one eye to the edge of the fabric and looked cautiously out. The snow had melted into yellow-grey drifts along the walls, and far down the street there sat a blind man selling pencils. Business was almost nonexistent at that hour, but I watched for several minutes, half hearing the raised voices in the next room. I was just about to turn away when a child came up to the well-swaddled figure and dropped something into the cup, receiving a pencil in return. I watched thoughtfully as the child ran off. A very ragged schoolboy, that one. The black figure reached into the cup, as if to feel the coin, but it had looked to me like a folded square of paper. We were discovered.

Mycroft came into the room then and poured himself a cup of tea dregs. There was a rustle outside the door, and I tensed, but he calmly said, "The morning news." He went to bring it in from his mat. Just then Watson's voice came from the next room asking for something, so he handed me the paper and went off. I unfolded it, and my breath stopped. A headline on the front page read:

BOMBER KILLED BY OWN DEVICE

WATSON, HOLMES TARGETS?

A large bomb exploded shortly after midnight this morning at the home of Dr. John Watson, famous biographer of Mr. Sherlock Holmes, apparently killing the man who was in the act of setting it. Dr. Watson was evidently not at home, and his whereabouts are currently unknown. The house was badly damaged. The resultant fire was quickly brought under control, and there were no other injuries. A spokesman for New Scotland Yard told this paper that the man killed has been identified as Mr. John Dickson, of Reading. Mr. Dickson was convicted of the 1908 bombing attempt on the Empire Bank on Western Street, Southampton. Mr. Holmes gave key evidence against him during the trial.

Unconfirmed reports of an earlier bomb at the isolated Sussex farm of Mr. Holmes have reached this newspaper, and one reliable source states that the detective was seriously injured in the blast. There will be further details in our later edition.

I reread the short article, little more than a notice, with a feeling of drunken unreality. I quite literally could not comprehend the words before me, partly due to shock, but more because it simply made no sense. I felt as if my brain were moving through tar. My hands laid the paper down on top of the débris of teacups and eggshells and then folded themselves into my lap. I am not certain how long it was before I heard Mycroft speak sharply over my shoulder.

"Miss Russell, what is the matter? Shall I send for more tea?"

I unfolded one hand and laid a finger across the newsprint, and when he had read it he lowered himself into a sturdy chair. I looked over at him and saw Holmes' glittering, intense eyes sunk into a fleshy, pale face, and knew he was thinking as furiously and as fruitlessly as I.

"That is most provocative," he said at last. "We were barely in time, were we not?"

"In time for what?" Holmes came into the room fastening his cuffs, his voice edged. Mycroft handed him the paper, and a sibilant whistle escaped him as he read it. When Watson entered, Holmes turned to him.

"It seems, my old friend, that we owe a considerable and deeply felt thanks to Russell."

Watson read about his near escape and collapsed into the chair Holmes pushed into the back of his knees.

"A whisky for the man, Mycroft," but the big man was already at the cabinet pouring. Watson held it unseeingly. Suddenly he stood up, reaching for his black bag.

"I must go home."

"You must do nothing of the sort," retorted Holmes, and took the bag from his hand.

"But the landlady, my papers." His voice drifted off.

"The article states that no one was hurt," Holmes said reasonably. "Your papers will wait, and you can contact the neighbours and the police later. Right now you will go to bed. You have been up all night and you have had a bad shock. Finish your drink." Watson, through long habit of obedience to the voice of his friend, tipped the liquor down his throat and stood looking dazed. Mycroft took his elbow and led him off to the bed that Holmes had occupied for such a short while the night before.

Holmes lit his pipe, and its slight sough joined the mutter of the traffic below and the indistinct voices from the bedroom down the hall. We were silent, although I fancy the sound of our thinking was almost audible. Holmes frowned at a point on the wall, I fiddled with a piece of string I had found in my pocket and frowned, and Mycroft, when he appeared, sat in the chair between us at the fire, and frowned.

My fingers turned the string into a cat's cradle and made various intricate shapes until I dropped a connexion and held only a tangle of string. I broke the silence.

"Very well, gentlemen, I admit I am baffled. Can either of you tell me why, if Watson was followed here, Dickson would persist in setting the bomb? Surely he couldn't have cared about the house itself, or Watson's papers?"

"It is indeed a pretty problem, is it not, Mycroft?"

"It changes the picture considerably, does it not, Sherlock?"

"Dickson was not operating alone—"

"And he was not in charge of the operation—"

"Or if he was, his subordinates were extremely ineffective," Holmes added.

"Because he was not informed that his target had left an hour before—"

"But was that deliberate or an oversight?"

"I suppose a group of criminals can overlook essential organisational—"

"For pity's sake, Mycroft, it's not the government."

"True, a certain degree of competence is required for survival as a criminal."

"Odd, though; I should not have thought Dickson likely to be clumsy."

"Oh, not suicide, surely? After a series of revenge killings?"

"None of us are dead," Holmes reminded him.

"Yet," I muttered, but they ignored me.

"Yes, that is provocative, is it not? Let us keep that in mind."

"If he was employed—" Holmes began.

"I suppose Lestrade will examine his bank accounts?" Mycroft asked doubtfully.

"—and it was not just a whim among some of my old acquaintances—"

"Unlikely."

"—to band together to obliterate me and everyone close to me—"

"I suppose I should have been next," Mycroft mused.

"—then it does make me wonder, rather, about Dickson's death."

"Accident and suicide are unlikely. Could a bomber's boss bomb a bomber?"

"Pull yourself together, Mycroft," Holmes ordered sternly.

"It is a valid question," his brother protested.

"It is," Holmes relented. "Can some of your people look at it, before the Yard?"

"Perhaps not before, but certainly simultaneously."

"Though there will not be much evidence left, if it was tampered with."

"And why? Dissatisfaction with the man's inefficiency?"

"Or wishing to save a final payment?"

"Makes it difficult to hire help in the future," Mycroft noted practically.

"And I shouldn't have thought money was a problem, here."

"Miss Russell's bomb is of the highest quality," agreed Mycroft.

"It is most irritating that Dickson is no longer available," Holmes grumbled.

"Which may be why he was removed."

"But he did not manage to kill us," Holmes protested.

"Anger at his failure, and determination to use alternate methods?"

"That's encouraging," I tried, "no more bombs," but Holmes ploughed on.

"You're probably right. Still, I should have liked to speak with him."

"I blame myself. I ought to have put a man to watch immediately, but—"

"You had no reason to assume he would arrive so quickly."

"No, not after his gap of—"

"—a full day," supplied Holmes blandly.

"—a full day," said Mycroft, not looking at me.

"If only I had been able to reach Russell's place earlier. . . ."

I had had enough of this verbal tennis match, so I walked out onto the court and sliced through the net.

"You did not reach 'Russell's place' because Sunday's attempt to blow you into many untidy bits left you unconscious until dusk on Monday." Holmes looked at me, Mycroft Holmes looked at his brother, and I looked at the string in my hands complacently, like Madame Defarge at her knitting.

"I did not say I was unconscious," Holmes said accusingly.

"No, and you tried to make me think the bomb went off Monday night. You forget, however, that I have had some experience of the progressive appearance of cuts and bruises, and the wounds on that back of yours were a good forty-eight hours old when I first saw them, not twenty-four. On Monday I was in my rooms until three o'clock, and you did not get in touch with me. Mrs. Thomas laid a fire, presumably at her customary time. Therefore you were still non compos mentis until at least five o'clock. At eight o'clock, however, when I returned, I found Mr. Thomas unnecessarily repairing a light fixture in the hallway outside my door, and as you now tell me he is in your employ, it becomes evident that at some point between five and eight you telephoned him and ordered him to watch my rooms until I returned. And probably after that, as well, knowing you.

"On Tuesday I expect that you would have had Mr. Thomas keep me from my rooms, had you not been determined to make your way up yourself, despite a concussed brain and a raw back. I assume that you intended to arrive somewhat earlier than you did, and Mr. Thomas went off his guard, as he had been told that his services would after that time no longer be required. What held you up, that you did not arrive until six-thirty?"

"Six twenty-two. A positively diabolical series of happenstances. Lestrade was late for our meeting, the matron hid my clothes, the tramp was brought in, and I had to seize the opportunity to arrange a sleight-of-body with the hospital staff, and then when I arrived at the cottage it was swarming with police and I had to wait for them to amble off for their tea before I could get what I needed from the house and see what they'd left at the hive—thank God for Will, I'd never have managed without him. And I missed a train and there were no taxis at the rank in Oxford—positively diabolical, as I said."

"Why didn't you just telephone from the hospital? Or send a telegram?"

"I did send a telegram, to Thomas, from a station so small I doubt more than six trains stop there in a year. And when I finally made Oxford I telephoned to him and told him not to mention anything to you, that the little problem had been taken care of."

"But, Holmes, what made you come? Did you have any cause to think I was in danger? Or was it just your generally suspicious mind?" He was looking very uncomfortable, and not because of his back. "Did you have any reason—?"

"No!" My last word made him shout, made us all aware of the glaring inconsistency of his actions. "No, it was a fixation visited upon an abused brain. Reason demanded I stay on the scene of the crime, with perhaps a telephone call to put you on your guard, but I . . . to tell you the truth, I found it impossible to retain a logical train of thought. It was the most peculiar side-effect of concussion I've ever experienced. At dawn on Tuesday all I could think of was reaching your door by dusk, and when I found I was able to walk—I walked."

"How odd," I said, and meant it. I would not have thought his affection for me would be allowed to interfere with the investigation of a case, shaken brain or no. And as for his obvious reluctance to trust me with the necessary actions—lying in wait for an attack, using my gun if necessary—that hurt. Particularly as he had not been altogether successful himself. I opened my mouth to confront him with it but managed to hold my tongue in time. Besides, in all honesty I had to admit that he was right.

"Very odd," I repeated, "but I am glad of it. Had you not interfered, I should almost certainly have walked in the door, as the only indications of tampering were two tiny scratches on the keyhole and one small leaf and a spot of mud on a window that was across a dim passageway from where I would stand to insert my key."

He let slip a brief flash of relief before an impassive reply. "You'd have noticed it."

"I might have. But would I have thought enough of it to climb up the outside ivy, on a night like that? I doubt it. At any rate, you came, you saw, you disconnected. Incidentally, did you come up the ivy too, with your back like that? Or did you manage to disarm the bomb from outside the door?"

Holmes met his brother's eyes and shook his head pityingly. "Her much learning hath made her mad," he said, and turned back to me. "Russell, you must remember the alternatives. Alternatives, Russell."

I puzzled for a minute, then admitted defeat.

"The ladder, Russell. There was a ladder on the other side of the courtyard. You must have seen it every day for the last few weeks."

Both Holmes and his brother started laughing at the chagrin on my face.

"All right, I missed that one entirely. You came up the ladder, disconnected the bomb, put the ladder away, and came back through the hall, leaving one leaf and an unidentifiable greasy thumbprint. But Holmes, you couldn't have missed Dickson by much. It must have been a near thing."

"I imagine we passed each other in the street, but the only faces I saw were hunched up against the rain."

"It shows that Dickson, or his boss, was well acquainted with my circumstances. He knew which were my rooms. He knew that Mrs. Thomas would be in the rooms and waited until she left, which I suppose he could see from the street below. He went up the outside ivy in the dark, carrying the bomb, went in the window, picked my lock, set the thing . . ." I thought of something to ask Mycroft. "Could he have left through the door after the bomb was set?"

"Certainly. It was triggered by a one-way toggle. He mounted it with the door standing open, and closing the door armed it."

"Then he went out the window and made his escape, all of that in little over an hour. A formidable man, Mr. Dickson."

"And yet, thirty hours later he makes a fatal mistake and dies in blowing up an empty house," Holmes said thoughtfully.

"Your young lady has brought up another point worthy of consideration," Mycroft Holmes said. "That is the fact of Dickson's familiarity with her habits. The same could surely be said of his—their—awareness of your own movements."

"That I check my hives before retiring? Surely most beekeepers do so?"

"But you yourself state that to be your habit, in your book?"

"I do, yes, but had it not been then, it would have been in the morning."

"I cannot see that it would have made much difference," agreed Mycroft.

"I suppose I ought to purchase a dog," said Holmes unhappily.

"However, no published account that I know of includes Miss Russell."

"Our collaboration is no doubt common knowledge in the village."

"So, this opponent has read your book, knows the village, knows Oxford."

"Lestrade must be made aware of these facts," said Holmes.

"There is also the matter of the use of children as messengers."

"An uncomfortable similarity with my Irregulars, you feel?"

"I do. You said, though Watson forgot today, that they are invisible."

"I dislike the idea of a murderer employing children," said Holmes darkly.

"It is, I agree, bad for their morals, and interferes with their sleep."

"And their schooling," added Holmes sententiously.

"But who?" I broke in desperately. "Who is it? Surely there cannot be all that many of your enemies who hate you enough to kill off not only you but your friends as well, who have the money to hire bombers and watchers, and who have the wits to put all this conspiracy together?"

"I sat up until the wee hours contemplating precisely that question, Russell, with absolutely no results. Oh, there are any number of people who fit the first category, and a fair handful of those would have the financial means, but that third characteristic leaves me, to borrow your word, baffled. In all my varied acquaintance I cannot call to mind one who fits with what we know of the mastermind behind these attacks."

"There is a mastermind, you would say?" I asked.

"Well, a mind, certainly. Intelligent, painstaking, at the least moderately wealthy, and absolutely ruthless."

"Sounds like Moriarty," I said jokingly, but he took it seriously. "Yes, remarkably like him."

"Oh, Holmes, you can't mean—"

"No, no," he hastened to add. "Watson's account was accurate enough; the man is dead. No, this feels very like another Moriarty, come on us unawares. I think the time has come for me to renew my contacts with the criminal world in this fair city." His eyes gleamed at the prospect, and my heart sank.

"Today? Surely your brother here—"

"Mycroft moves in circles rather more exalted than those I have in mind. His is the realm of espionage and political backstabbing, with only a peripheral interest in the world of retired bombers and hungry street urchins. No, I must go and ask questions of certain friends."

"I shall join you."

"That you most definitely will not. Don't look at me like that, Russell. I am not protecting your gentle virtue, although I admit that there are sights to be seen underground in London that might give even your eyes pause. It is a job for a specific old man, a man already known to be an occasional visitor to the dregs of London society. A companion would cause comment, and tongues would not flap so freely."

"But your back?"

"Is very well, thank you."

"What did Watson say?" I persisted.

"That it was healing more quickly than I deserved," he said in tones that said very clearly that the matter was closed. I gave in.

"You wish me to remain here today?"

"That will not be necessary, as long as you are not followed. In fact, it is probably best if you are not here, and if they are aware of that. How shall we—ah, yes," he breathed, with the satisfied air of genius operating. "Yes, that will do nicely. Where did we stash the box of make-up last time, Mycroft?"

His brother heaved his weight from the relieved chair and padded off. Holmes squinted at me.

"Russell, if I have learnt nothing by seven o'clock, there will be little point in persisting, and it is an Italian night at Covent Garden. Shall we agree to meet there, at seven-forty-five? After that, depending on what the day's results are, we can decide to come back here or to go home for our Christmas preparations." This last I took as a symbol for carefree frivolity rather than any actual possibility. The previous year we had both spent Christmas Day dissecting a poisoned ram. "You will, I trust, have a greater than normal caution during the day, stay in crowds, double back occasionally, that sort of thing? And you will keep your revolver close to hand?" I reassured him that I would do my best to make our rendezvous that evening, and he gave me specific instructions both for shedding the disguise in which I would make my escape, and for getting to Covent Garden.

Mycroft came in carrying a bulky carpetbag, which he set down in front of Holmes, and looking vaguely worried.

"You will take luncheon before you go, please, Sherlock. Do not drag Miss Russell out into the cold again without allowing her to eat first, I beg you."

It was barely two hours since the breakfast things had been cleared away, but Holmes answered his brother soothingly.

"But of course. The preparations alone will take an hour. Order some lunch, while I make a start."

"But first," I said, "the telephone." I made Holmes speak with Mrs. Hudson. It was a long conversation, cut off once by the exchange and threatened twice more, but in the end she agreed to stay where she was for a few days, and not approach the cottage or the hospital. My own conversation with Veronica Beaconsfield was briefer and even less amicable; lies to friends are usually less successful than lies to strangers or villains, and I did not think she believed in my sudden emergency. I returned saddened to the meal that arrived while Holmes was making his disguise.

Sherlock Holmes had invented his profession, and it fit him like a glove. We watched in admiration that verged on awe as his love of challenge, his flair for the dramatic, his precise attention to detail, and his vulpine intelligence were called into play and transformed his thin face by putty and paint into that of his brother. It would not stand up to close supervision, but from a few yards the likeness was superb. He removed the putty pads to speak, and I hurriedly swallowed the last of my lunch.

"Fortunately, if uselessly, Watson has sacrificed his moustache for his own masquerade, or we should have to glue some hair under your nose, Russell. Mycroft, would you kindly go and lift the trousers and coat worn by our friend from his bed, and also find us some suitable padding and a large quantity of sticking plaster?" Under his hands I felt the putty fill out my cheeks, hair was added to my eyebrows, lines and creases painted on. He eyed me critically. "Don't move your face too much. Now, I'll tear up some of these blankets while you tape yourself to reduce your height. Take off your shirt, Russell," he said absently, and so matter-of-fact was his command that I had my hand on my shirt-collar when Mycroft cleared his throat gently behind us.

"Is that really necessary, Sherlock? Perhaps the sticking plaster could be put on over her clothing?"

"What?" Holmes looked up from his bundles and scraps and realised what had just happened. "Oh, yes, I suppose so." He looked slightly flustered. "Come here, then."

Layers of padding gave me Watson's outline; his hat, scarf, and gloves left only my made-up face exposed; and his spectacles were close enough to mine in appearance to allow me to retain my own, a great blessing.

Holmes added similar padding to himself, and we stood resembling two obese Egyptian mummies risen from our rest. He worked himself carefully into his brother's clothing and gave his make-up a final adjustment.

"Now to review our plan—Ah, Watson, you're just in time."

"Holmes? Is that you? Where are my trousers? What are you doing?" Watson's puzzled, sleepy voice brought home the absurdity of this entire venture, and I started to giggle. Holmes/Mycroft looked askance, but the real Mycroft joined in, and soon even Holmes was smiling half-willingly.

"My dear Watson, we are making our escape. The enemy followed you here, I'm afraid, or were here already. If they followed you, they may not yet realise that I am at liberty, and assume that only Russell is here. There are too many 'ifs' here for my pleasure, but there's no helping that. Yet. I will leave here now, dressed as my brother. Russell will leave in twenty minutes, dressed as you, Watson. I shall turn to the right out the door, as my disguise is the more realistic. Russell will turn left, so they will see her clearly only from a distance. Twenty minutes after she leaves, the two of you shall depart, together, hatless, and stroll slowly down the street to the right. You will both have revolvers, but I believe they will be more interested in catching up with us than they will in committing double murder in broad daylight. You go with Mycroft, Watson, and you will be quite safe. We will meet up when we may."

He put Mycroft's hat onto his head, where it slid down to his eyebrows. Imperiously ignoring our smiles, he put multiple layers of sticking plaster inside the brim and returned it to his head. Mycroft's thick scarf went around his neck, leather gloves puffed up his hands. Holmes' own eyes looked out from Mycroft's face. "Seven-forty-five, then, Russell, at the theatre. You know what to do. And for God's sake, be careful."

"Holmes?" It was Watson, very, very tentative. "Old friend, are you going to be all right? The pain, I mean. Do you want something? I have a bottle of morphia in my bag. . . ." He trailed off uncomfortably.

Holmes looked astonished, then began to laugh uncontrollably, until his make-up threatened to flake off.

"After all the times—" he spluttered. "*You* offer *me* morphine. My dear Watson, you do have a talent for reducing things to their proper perspective." He softened and raised one mocking eyebrow. "You know I never indulge when I'm on a case, Watson." He slipped the putty forms into his cheeks and was gone.

His passage down the street sent a small, ragged boy away from the blind beggar's side and out of sight. It was soon my turn. I turned to thank Mycroft and shook his hand, then leaned forward impulsively and kissed his cheek. He turned scarlet. Watson returned my embrace with avuncular affection, and I let myself out into the hallway, black medical bag in hand, the revolver a comforting weight in my pocket.

As the outside door latched behind me I was aware of eyes on me, Watson and Mycroft Holmes watching from the window above, but other, hostile eyes also, from the street behind me at the very least. It took considerable control to hold myself to Watson's ponderous and limping gait rather than dash off down the street, but I plodded on through the slush, for all the world an old, retired doctor on his way home. Following Holmes' precise instructions, I hailed a cab, then changed my mind. I walked west, as if towards Green Park, then hailed another. I turned it away too, and a street later finally got warily into the third. I gave the driver Watson's address, in a gruff voice, but when we had rounded Park Lane I redirected him. At the building Holmes had told me to go to, I paid the driver generously, went inside, checked my medical bag (which was empty) with the attendant, climbed to the third floor—watching the stairs below me—and through the tearoom on that floor to a passageway, a further set of stairs, and at last a door marked Storage Room. The key Holmes had given me let me in. I flicked the electrical light switch on, closed the well-fitting door, spat out the mouthful of noxious putty, leant against the door, and gave way to a fit of mild hysterics.

EVENTUALLY IT RAN its course. I got somewhat shakily to my feet, curiosity coming to the fore. The Storage Room was one of Holmes' bolt-holes, his handful of small, almost inaccessible hide-aways in unlikely places across London, from Whitechapel to White-hall. Watson had mentioned them in several of his stories, and Holmes had made passing reference to one or another of them in conversations with me, but I had never actually been inside one.

It was, I found, little more than its name implied, a windowless, stuffy, oddly shaped room providing the most basic necessities of life and a remarkably elaborate amount of equipment for changing identities. Three metal dressmaker's racks bulging with clothes took up a quarter of the floor space, and an enormous dressing table littered with tubes, pencils, and pots and overhung by a wall-sized mirror surrounded by small electrical light bulbs took up another quarter. The kitchen consisted of a stained hand-basin, a minuscule geyser, a gas ring, and two pots. There was one chair, at the desk, a piece that looked to my half-educated eyes like a particularly beautiful Chippendale that had spent part of its recent life as a painter's stool, judging from the varicoloured splashes across the seat and back. The only other furniture was a long sofa, taking up more than its quarter of the room and looking as if it had been hauled up from beneath a bridge somewhere, and a garish Chinese screen behind the "kitchen." Behind the screen, as I might have suspected, was a water closet, gleaming new and, I soon discovered, remarkably silent.

As I nosed about I began to shed my numerous layers of disguise. The outer clothing I folded neatly to return to Watson, the mummy layers I shoved, plaster and all, into a bin of what I took to be rags behind the sofa, and the make-up joined the stains in the hand-basin. My own shirt was hopelessly stuck together by the tape that Holmes had strapped on to change the set of my shoulders, but after a bit of rummaging about in the clothes racks (where I found an evening suit and tweed plus-fours cheek-by-jowl with a linen chasuble, the brocade tunic and trousers of a maharajah, and a stunning scarlet evening dress) I came up with a comfortable embroidered cotton dressing gown and put it on in lieu of the shirt, which followed the mummy strips into the bin.

In the kitchen I found a canister of tea leaves, a pot, and some tins of milk, so I made tea, poured myself a cup (superb bone china, no saucer) and carried it to the dressing table. As I sipped it and sat poking through the objects in and on the table, I was struck by the extraordinary fact of the room's existence. What kind of a man would keep an entire drawer full of moustaches and beards? I thought. Or a shelf of wigs—a bushy redhead, a slicked-down black hairpiece, a woman's blonde curls—arranged on stands to resemble eerily a row of heads on pikes? Could Holmes actually, honestly consider wearing that evening gown, high-necked though it was? Or the—was it a sari? How many normal men had hair ribbons trailing from their chest of drawers, a collection of well-padded female undergarments, three pair of false eyelashes, two dozen old-school and club ties, and a macabre cigar box filled with sets of false teeth? And even if one overlooked the reason for its existence, *how* did he manage it? How had he brought that sofa up here without inviting comment, and the mirror? Granted, it was a large and busy building, but did no one notice the occasional unexpected noise from a supply room, the sound of running water at night, the comings and goings of odd characters—some of them very odd indeed? What did Holmes do if, I wondered, while disguised as one of his more unsavoury characters, he were accosted and explanation of his presence demanded of him? The possibilities for comedy of the burlesque variety were greatly appealing, and several vignettes worthy of the lower classes of stage went through my mind. And, my mind continued, who had plumbed in the sink and WC? Who paid for the gas, the electricity, for heaven's sake?

The more I thought about it, the curiouser it became. What kind of human being would need a refuge capable of sustaining life in a siege? For the plentiful if desultory tins of food, the two travelling rugs tossed over the sofa, three tins of pipe tobacco, a pound of coffee, and the copious reading material—staid medical journals, philosophical tomes, novels with lurid covers, and brittle newspapers ancient enough to qualify as archaeology—all testified that the room's purpose was to make possible a prolonged captivity. It was quite patently not a refuge for comfort or convenience; at his height, Holmes would find the sofa a dismal night's sleep. And it was also clearly no holiday retreat; the threadbare line down the center of the carpet bespoke hours spent measuring its half a dozen paces of clear space.

No, there was no question in my mind: Either my friend and mentor was quite mad, a man willing to go to considerable difficulty and expense to satisfy a bizarre and romantic fantasy of paranoia, or else the life of my rustic beekeeping companion with the odd skills was extraordinarily more demanding, even dangerous, than I had fully realised.

Somehow I could not think him mad.

There was no doubt that the room had been recently occupied: The tea leaves were relatively fresh, the dust had not settled much onto the desk or teapot, the air, though stuffy, was not stifling and smelt faintly of tobacco. I shook my head. Even I had not suspected how very active his career still was.

I wondered, not for the first time that day, nor for the last, what he was doing and how he was holding up.

Which brought me around to wonder what I was going to do. I could, of course, stay here until it was time to meet Holmes, and at the thought of explosive devices and flexible and imaginative would-be murderers, the bolt-hole's canister of tea, tins of beans, and lurid novels (to say nothing of the revolver I had brought and the other one I had found in the kettle) seemed both tempting and eminently sensible.

Still, there was Holmes in the streets, and Mycroft and Watson bolting for cover, and to sit in a hole with the bedclothes over my head seemed disloyal, cowardly even. Illogical, but true. There might well be nothing I could do, but my own self-respect demanded that I not be completely intimidated by this unknown assailant. Of course, had I known then how very flexible and imaginative our foe actually was, I should probably have stayed well hidden, but as it was I decided defiantly to see what I could do about depleting the number of high-denomination notes that lay in my handbag on top of the gun, and went to assemble an appropriate wardrobe.

By the end of four years of war, standards of dress had become markedly less demanding, and even the upper levels of society were occasionally seen in clothing that before 1914 would have been given to the maid or the church's next jumble sale. Still, it took me some time to find myself clothes among Holmes' collection. In the end I uncovered a tweed skirt that I might tuck up to current length, and a blouse that did not look like something handed down from the butcher's wife. Stockings and suspenders I found aplenty, but I nearly gave up altogether on the shoes. Holmes' feet were larger than mine, and his selection of women's shoes somewhat limited. I held up a pair of scarlet satin sandals with four-inch heels and tried to imagine Holmes in them. My imagination failed. (But if not Holmes, then who? I put them down abruptly, shocked at myself. Keep your mind on the business at hand, please, Russell.) I picked up a pair of dowdy black shoes with a strap across the instep and low Cuban heels and found that I could at least walk in them.

I switched on the row of lights and sat down with the pots and sticks to change my face (How many young women had been taught the subtleties of make-up by a man? I reflected idly.), added a long string of pearls (real) and small earrings (fake), wrapped my head in a piece of cloth from the scarf drawer (which had, judging from the shape, once been the lining of a coat), and finally stood away from the desk to look at myself.

Amazing. Nothing fit me, nothing matched, and my feet hurt already, yet I would easily pass for a Young Thing out for a day in Town. I darkened the rims of my spectacles with some odd brown fingernail enamel and decided reluctantly that I should have to leave them off for much of the day, as any other vain young myopic would do. I gathered up Watson's clothes, turned off the lights, took a deep breath, and, with my hand inside my bag, opened the door.

No bombs went off, no bullets flew, no rough hands grabbed at me. I closed the door behind me and went off to spend the money I had borrowed so shamelessly from the Holmes brothers.

✳ 11 ✳

Another Problem: The Mutilated Four-Wheeler

Ever and anon, from a sudden wave that shall be more
transparent than others, there leaps forth a fact that in an
instant confounds all we imagined we knew.

MY FIRST TASK was to make a move towards reuniting Watson with his trousers, but as I made my way back through the tearoom and the store's many levels, it occurred to me that Holmes' bolt-hole was ideally situated, that I could easily spend the day without having to set foot on the street, for this was one of the two stores in London (I shall not mention which, as the Storage Room may still be in use.) that touted itself as catering for needs from cradle to grave. It could certainly afford me protection, nourishment, and entertainment for a single day.

With that happy thought I deposited the bundle of Watson's salvaged clothing into his black bag and left it checked, mailed the receipt to Mycroft at his club, and set off on the unfamiliar but surprisingly agreeable task of spending money. Late that afternoon, my Storage Room reach-me-downs long since vanished into the rubbish bin, my hair sculpted, my fingernails buffed and gleaming beyond all recognition, my legs encased in sheer silk stockings that were actually long enough, and my feet in heeled shoes that didn't pinch, I decided that, all things considered, the occasional dose of pampering could be great fun.

I took a light and leisurely tea, assembled my multitude of parcels (which they offered to deliver, and I refused), and was escorted to the door. Here I ran into a problem. Holmes had insisted that I follow the same routine as the morning's, except to take the fourth cab, but here stood the uniformed doorman, and the first cab. I put on my spectacles, gave him a huge tip, and shook my head.

Fifteen minutes later the third cab arrived. It was getting very dark, and at that hour few cabs were free. This one looked enticingly warm, and my new evening clothes were not. Surely Holmes had not meant to be inflexible, had he? I looked through the door at the bored driver, stepped back, and waved him on. He looked highly irritated, which matched my mood precisely. I peered down the street in wan hope, studiously ignoring the doorman, when up before me pulled a very old and very battered cab drawn by one very old and battered horse.

"Cab, Miss?" said the voice from the moving anachronism.

I cursed Holmes under my breath. It looked very cold in there compared to the others, but it was a cab, or it had been thirty years before: a London growler. I told the driver where I wanted to go, saw my purchases piled inside, and got in. The doorman looked after me as if I were stark raving mad. Which I was.

I did not know London at all well then, though I had studied the maps a bit, so it took me a while to realise that we were going in the wrong direction. Not completely wrong, just very roundabout. My first thought was that the driver was pulling a swindle in order to charge me more for the ride. I had opened my mouth to call out when I froze with a terrible thought. Perhaps I had been followed. Perhaps this driver was an ally of the blind pencil seller. First I was frightened, but then I was furious. I fought the remnants of a window down and craned my neck out to see him.

"Oy, driver, where are you taking me? This isn't the way to Covent Garden."

"Yes, Miss, this is the faster way, away from the heavy traffic, Miss," the voice whined obsequiously.

"All right, you, now look. I have a revolver, and I will shoot you if you do not stop immediately."

"Now, Miss, you doesn't want to be doing that, now," he snivelled.

"I'm feeling more like it every moment. Stop this cab, now!"

"But I can't do that, Miss, I really cannot."

"Why not?"

The shaggy head leaned over the side, and I stared up at him. "Because we'll miss the curtain if I do," said Holmes.

"You! You utter bastard," I growled. The gun shook in my hand, and Holmes, seeing it, drew his head back quickly. "Look, you, that's the second time you've played your bloody tricks on me in three days." I caught the startled look of a passerby and lowered my voice. "If you do it again and I have a gun in my hand, I won't be responsible, d'you hear? As sure as my mother's name is Mary McCarthy, I'll not be responsible for my temper."

I sat back in the swaying cab and caught my breath. Several minutes later a thin voice drifted down to me.

"Yes, Miss."

Some distance from the theatre he pulled the ancient cab into a dark spot adjoining one of London's innumerable small and hidden parks. The growler sagged sideways with his weight, and in a moment the door fell open. He eyed me.

"Your mother's name was not Mary McCarthy," he said accusingly.

"No, it was Judith Klein. Just don't scare me again, please. I've been walking around frightened and blind since I left your brother's rooms, and I'm tired."

"Apologies, Russell. My twisted sense of humour has had me in trouble before this. Pax?"

"Pax." We clasped hands firmly. He stepped up into the cab. "Russell, this time it is you who must turn your back. I can hardly go into the theatre looking like the driver of a four-wheeler." I hastily departed out the other side.

Coat and hat, stick and proper evening coat, hair combed, moustache applied, he alighted from the cab. A small man wandered up, whistling softly.

"Good evening, Billy."

"Evenin', Mr. . . . Evenin', sir." He touched his hat to me.

"Don't break your neck over the boxes inside, Billy. And there's a rug under the seat if you need it. Just keep your eyes open."

"That I will, sir. Have a good evenin', sir, Miss."

I was so preoccupied that I did not notice when Holmes tucked my arm in his.

"Holmes, how on earth did you find me?"

"Well, I cannot claim it was entirely a coincidence, as I thought it possible you would fall victim to the charms of the place and be there all day. Also, both the doorman and the attendant to whom you gave Watson's bag were watching and swore you hadn't yet left when I asked an hour ago. That was a slip, incidentally, Russell. You ought to have abandoned the trousers."

"So I see. Sorry. What did you find today?"

"Do you know, I found absolutely nothing. Not a rumour, not a word, nary a breath of someone moving against that old scoundrel Holmes. I must be losing my touch."

"Perhaps there was nothing?"

"Perhaps. It is a most piquant problem, I must admit. I am intrigued."

"I am cold. So, what are we going to do now?"

"We shall listen to the voices of angels and of men, my child, set to the music of Verdi and Puccini."

"And after that?"

"After that we shall dine."

"And then?"

"I fear we shall skulk back to my brother's rooms and hide behind his drapes."

"Oh. How is your back?"

"Damn my back, I do wish you would stop harping on the accursed thing. If you must know, I had it serviced again this afternoon by a retired surgeon who does a good line in illegal operations and patching up gunshot wounds. He found very little to do on it, told me to go away, and I find the topic tiresome."

I was pleased to hear his mood so improved.

The evening that followed was a lovely, sparkling interval, set off in my mind by what went before and what came after as a jewel set into mud. I fell asleep twice and woke with my hat in Holmes' ear, but he seemed not to notice. In fact, so carried away was he by the music that I believe he forgot I was there, forgot where he was, forgot to breathe, even, at certain passages. I have never been a great lover of the operatic voice, but that night—I cannot tell you what we saw, unfortunately—even I could begin to see the point. (Incidentally, I feel that this is one place where I must contradict the record of Holmes' late biographer and protest that I never, ever witnessed Holmes "gently waving his fingers about in time to the music," as Watson once wrote. The good doctor, on the other hand, was wont earnestly to perform this activity of the musically obtuse, particularly when he was tipsy.)

We drank champagne at the intermission and took to a quiet corner lest he be recognised. Holmes could be charming when he so desired, but that evening he positively scintillated, during the intermission with stories about the primary cast members, and over supper later talking about his conversations with the lamas in Tibet, his most recent monographs on varieties of lipstick and the peculiarities of modern tyre marks, the changes occasioned by the disappearance of castrati from the music world, and the analysis of some changes in rhythm in one of the arias we had just heard. I was quite dazzled by this rarely seen Holmes, a distinguished-looking, sophisticated bon vivant without a care in the world (who could also spend hours in a grey, biting mood, write precise monographs on the science of detection, and paint blobs on the backs of bees to track them across the Sussex Downs).

"Holmes," I asked as we stepped into the street, "I realise the question sounds sophomoric, but do you find that there are aspects of yourself with which you feel most comfortable? I only ask out of curiosity; you needn't feel obliged to answer." He offered me his arm and, formally, I took it.

"'Who am I?' you mean." He smiled at the question and gave what was at first glance a most oblique answer. "Do you know what a fugue is?"

"Are you changing the subject?"

"No."

I thought in silence for some distance before his answer arranged itself sensibly in my mind. "I see. Two discrete sections of a fugue may not appear related, unless the listener has received the entire work, at which time the music's internal logic makes clear the relationship."

"A conversation with you is most invigorating, Russell. That might have taken twenty frustrating minutes with Watson. Hello, what is this?" He pulled me to a halt in the shadow of the building we had just rounded, and we gazed across to the area where the cab and Billy had been left, seeing with sinking hearts the flicker of naphtha flares and the distinctive milling outline of many constabulary helmets and capes. Loud voices called to one another, and as we watched, an ambulance pulled swiftly away. Holmes slumped against the building, stunned. "Billy?" he whispered hoarsely. "How could they track us? Russell, am I losing my grip? I have never come across a mind that could do this. Even Moriarty." He shook his head as if to clear it. "I must see the evidence before those oafs obliterate it."

"Wait, Holmes. This could be a trap. There may be someone waiting with an airgun or a rifle."

Holmes studied the scene before us through narrowed eyes and shook his head again, slowly. "We were excellent targets a number of times this evening. With all these police here it would be a great risk for him. No, we will go. I only hope that someone with a bit of sense is in charge here."

I followed his vigorous stride as best I could in my heeled shoes, and as I came up behind him I saw a small, wiry man of about thirty-five thrust out his hand and greet Holmes.

"Mr. Holmes, good to see you up and about. I wondered if you might not make an appearance. I figured you must be behind this somewhere."

"What precisely is 'this,' Inspector?"

"Well, as you can see, Mr. Holmes, the cab—May I help you, Miss?" This last was to me.

"Ah, Russell, I should like to introduce you to an old friend of mine. This is Inspector Lestrade, of Scotland Yard. His father was a colleague of mine on a number of cases. Lestrade, this is my . . ." A quick smile touched his lips. "My associate, Miss Mary Russell."

Lestrade stared at the two of us for a moment, then to my dismay burst into raucous laughter. Was this to be the reaction of every policeman we met?

"Oh, Mr. Holmes, always the comedian, you were. I forgot your little jokes for a minute."

Holmes drew himself up to his full height and glared at the man in icy hauteur.

"Have you ever known me to jest about my profession, Lestrade? Ever?" The last word cracked through the cold air like a shot, and Lestrade's humour was cut off in an instant. The remnant of the smile made his face sour and slightly ratlike, and he glanced at me quickly and cleared his throat.

"Ah, yes, well, Mr. Holmes, I presume you'd like to see what they left of your cab. One of the men recognised Billy from the old days and thought to give me a ring on it. He'll get a promotion out of tonight's work, I don't doubt. And don't worry about your man—he'll be all right in a day or two, I imagine. It looked like a clout on the head followed by a bit of chloroform. He was already coming around when they took him off."

"Thank you for that, Inspector. Have you already gone over the cab?" His voice held little hope.

"No, no, we haven't touched it. Looked inside, that's all. I told you the man'd get a promotion. Quick-thinking, he is." I noticed one of the uniformed men nearby fiddling needlessly with the horse's reins, his head tilted slightly in our direction. I nudged Holmes and addressed Lestrade.

"Inspector, that I believe is the individual over there?" The man started and moved away guiltily, busying himself elsewhere. Lestrade and Holmes followed my eyes.

"Why yes, how did you guess?"

Holmes interrupted. "I believe you will find, Lestrade, that Miss Russell never guesses. She may occasionally reach tentative hypotheses without absolute proof, but she does not guess."

"I am glad," I added, "that the gentleman is working his way back up to his former position of responsibility. Men with his background can be a valuable model for younger members of the force." I had Lestrade's full attention now.

"Do you know him then, Miss?"

"As far as I know I've never seen him before tonight." Holmes allowed his eyes to wander off to the cab, his face inscrutable.

"Then how—?"

"Oh, but it is too obvious. An older man in a low position can either have got there by being, shall we say, of limited mental resource, which according to you he is not, or by backsliding. It could not have been a criminal act that pushed him down the ladder, or he would not still be in uniform. Which personality flaw it is can readily be ascertained by the broken veins in his face, while the deep furrows around his mouth indicate either pain or sorrow in recent years. I should suspect, as his body seems unimpaired, that the latter is to blame, which would explain the abuse of alcohol, and that in turn accounts for the demotion in rank. However, his general competency and the fact that you mention the possibility of promotion tell me that he has passed through the crisis, and will now serve as an example to the men around him." I gave the flabbergasted Lestrade my most innocent of smiles. "It's really quite elementary, Inspector."

The little man gaped and burst out laughing again. "Yes, sir, Mr. Holmes, I do see what you mean. I don't know how you've done it, but it could have been you saying that. You're absolutely right, Miss. His wife and daughter were killed four years ago, and he took to drinking, even at work. We kept him on at a desk job where he'd do no one any harm, and a year ago he pulled himself together. He'll be back up there in no time, I think. Come now, I'll get a lamp so we can look at your cab." He went off shouting for a light.

"Russell, that last line was a bit overly dramatic, don't you think?" Holmes murmured at my side.

"A good apprentice learns all from her master, sir," I answered demurely.

"Then let us go and see what is to be learnt from this old horse cab. I greatly desire news of this person who plagues us and continually attacks my friends. I hope that the case will at last provide us with a thread to grasp."

The cab stood cordoned off in a circle of flares, its shabby exterior even more obvious now than it had been by the streetlamps.

"This is where we found your man," Lestrade said, pointing. "We tried to keep off the ground right there, but we had to get him up and out of there. He was lying on his side, curled up on that old suit with a rug tucked around him."

"What?" The suit was Holmes' cabbie outfit; the rug was from the cab.

"Yes, wrapped up and snoozin' like a baby he was."

Holmes handed his hat, coat, and stick to Lestrade and took a small, powerful magnifying lens out of his pocket. Down on the ground he looked for all the world like some great lanky hound, casting about for a scent. Finally he gave a low exclamation and produced a small envelope from another pocket. Scraping gently at various tiny smudges on the paving stones, he sat back on his haunches with an air of triumph, careless of the beating his back had taken.

"What do you make of this, Russell?" he asked, sketching a vague circle.

I walked over to peer at the marks. "Two pairs of feet? One has been in the mud today, the other—is that oil?"

"Yes, Russell, but there will be a third somewhere. At the door to the cab? No? Well, perhaps inside." And so saying, he opened the door. "Lestrade, your men will go over the whole cab for fingerprints, I take it?"

"Yes, sir. I've sent for an expert; he should be here before too long. New man, but seems good. MacReedy, his name is."

"Oh yes, Ronald MacReedy. Interesting article of his, comparing whorls with the personality traits of habitual criminals, didn't you think?"

"I, er, didn't happen to see it, Mr. Holmes."

"Pity. Still, never too late. Russell, I take it these were all your things?"

I looked in past his shoulder at the wreckage. All that was left of my lovely and exorbitantly expensive clothes were the dress and cloak I was wearing and numerous scraps of coloured fabric. Small shreds of blue wool, green silk, and white linen littered the inside of the cab, alternating with torn bits of the boxes, twine, and paper they had been in. I picked up a short bit of string for something to fiddle with. The tufted leather seat had been deeply and methodically slashed from one end to another, with the exception of approximately a foot on one end of the front seat cushion. Horsehair stuffing had sifted over everything.

Holmes got to work with his glass by the light Lestrade held for him. Envelopes were filled, notes made, questions asked. The finger-print man arrived and set to. A brazier had appeared from somewhere, and the uniformed police were standing around it, warming their hands. The night was very late, and the cold, though not bitter, was penetrating. Impatient grumbles and glances were beginning to drift our way. There was no room for me in the cab, so I left and went to stand by the fire with the police constables.

I smiled up at the big one next to me. "I wanted to tell you how glad I am of your presence here, all of you. Someone seems to bear Mr. Holmes considerable ill will, and he is—well, his body is not quite so fast as it once was. I feel considerably better with some of the force's best on hand. Particularly you, Mr.—?" I leaned toward the older con-stable, a question on my face.

"Fowler, Miss. Tom Fowler."

"Mr. Fowler, particularly with you. Mr. Holmes found your fast ac-tion most impressive." I smiled sweetly around the fire. "Thank you, all of you, for your vigilance and attention to duty."

I went back to the cab then, and though there were numerous glances, they were directed into the dark night, and there were no more grumbles. When Lestrade was called away to attend to some matter, I held the lamp for Holmes.

"So you think I am slowing down, do you?" he said, amused.

"Your mind, I think not. I said that to encourage the troops, who were getting careless with having to stand about to no purpose. I exag-gerated, perhaps, but they will be attentive now."

"I told you, I do not think we shall be attacked."

"And I am beginning to suspect that this opponent of yours knows you well enough to take your thoughts into account when planning his actions."

"Slow as I am, Russell, that idea had come to me. Now." He sat back. "Your turn. I need you to go through and tell me if there are any scraps that are not from your things. It will take some time, so I will send over that tall young PC to help you, and another to find some hot drink. I shall go and examine the neighbourhood."

"Take someone with you, Holmes, please."

"After your performance out there they'll be tripping over each other in their eagerness to protect my doddering old frame."

It took some time to sift through the cab's contents, but eventually, with the help of young PC Mitchell, I had a large pile of paper and fabric scraps heaped outside, and three thin envelopes in my hand. We climbed out of the cab and stood stretching the cricks out of our spines, drinking mugs of hot, sweet tea until Holmes reappeared with his eager bodyguards.

"Thank you, gentlemen, you have been most dutiful. Go and have some tea, now. Off you go, there's a good fellow," he said, giving the most persistent constable a pat between the shoulder blades that shoved him off towards the tea station. "Russell, what have you found?"

"One button, with a scrap of brown tweed attached, cut recently from its garment by a sharp instrument. Another thick smudge of light brown clay. And one blonde hair, not my own, considerably shorter. Plus a great deal of dust and rubbed-about dirt and débris, indicating that the cab has not been cleaned in some time."

"It has also not been used in some time, Russell, so your three finds are undoubtedly worthy of our attention."

"And you, Holmes, what have you found?"

"Several things of interest, but I need to smoke a pipe over them, perhaps two, before I have anything to say."

"Will we be here long, Holmes?"

"Another hour, perhaps. Why?"

"I have been drinking champagne, then coffee, now tea. I cannot last another hour without doing something about it." I was determined not to be embarrassed about the problem.

"Of course." He looked around at the noticeable dearth of female company. "Have the older man—Fowler—show you the . . . facilities . . . in the park. Take a lamp with you."

With dignity I summoned the man and explained the mission, and he led me off through the park along its soft gravel paths. We talked inconsequentially of children and green areas, and he stood outside as I entered the little building. I finished and went to wash my hands, placing the lamp on the shelf that stood above the basin. I reached for the tap and saw there a smear of light brown clay. I took the lamp to look more closely, unwilling to believe.

"Mr. Fowler," I called sharply.

"Miss?"

"Go and get Mr. Holmes."

"Miss? Is something wrong?"

"No, something is not wrong, for a change. Just get him."

"But I shouldn't . . ."

"I'll be safe. Just go!"

After a moment's hesitation, his heavy footsteps went off quickly into the night. I heard his voice calling out loudly, answering shouts, and the thud of several running men returning up the path. Holmes stood at the door of the Ladies', looking in uncertainly.

"Russell?"

"Holmes, could the man we're looking for be a woman?"

❋ 12 ❋

Flight

She eludes us on every side; she repudiates most of our rules
and breaks our standards to pieces.

USSELL, YOU HAVE struck the very question upon which I proposed to meditate with my pipe. You have also saved me from the worst sin a detective can commit: overlooking the obvious. Show me what you have found." His eyes gleamed fiercely in the lamplight. More lamps were sent for, and soon the little stone building blazed with light. Fowler was consulted and confirmed that the building had been cleaned about eight o'clock on what was now the previous night. I stood back with Lestrade, watching Holmes as he worked, tensely examining every scrap of evidence, muttering to himself continually, and occasionally snapping out instructions.

"Boots again, the small boots, square heels, not new. A bicycle rider I see. Lestrade, have you had the Men's blocked off, and the street outside? Good. She went here, here she stood. Hah! Another blonde hair; yes, too long for a man in this day, I think, and quite straight. Mark these envelopes please, Russell. Mud on her heels, traces in the sink, yes, and the tap. But no fingerprints on the mud. Gloves?" Holmes looked up absently at his reflection in the mirror, whistling softly through his teeth. "Why should she have mud on her gloves, and wash them? A perplexing question. Another light over here, Lestrade, and have the photographer take another set of the cab, would you, after MacReedy has finished? Yes, as I thought, right-handed. Washed, shook the water from her hands, or rather her gloves, and to the door. Off the footprints, man! Heaven help us. To the street, then . . . no! Not to the street, back on the path, here it is, and here." He straightened up, winced, frowned vacantly up the bare branches overhead while we watched in silence. "But that makes no sense, unless—Lestrade, I shall need your laboratory to-night, and I want this entire park cordoned off—nobody, nobody at all to set foot here until I've seen it by daylight. Will it rain tonight, Russell?"

"I don't know London, but it does not feel like rain. It's certainly too warm to snow."

"No, I think we may risk it. Bring those envelopes, Russell. We have much to do before morning."

Truth to tell it was Holmes who had much to do, as there was but one microscope and he refused to say what he was looking for. I labelled a few slides, my eyes heavy despite strong coffee, and the next thing I knew it was morning, Holmes was standing at the window tapping his pipe on his teeth, and I was nearly crippled from being asleep with my head on the desk for several hours. My spine cracked loudly as I sat back in the chair, and Holmes turned.

"Ah, Russell," he said lightly, "do you always make such a habit of sleeping in chairs? I doubt your aunt would approve. Mrs. Hudson definitely would not."

I rubbed my eyes and glared at his ever-tidy person bitterly. "I take it that your revolting good humour means that something from last night's exercise has pleased you?"

"On the contrary, my dear Russell, it has displeased me considerably. Vague suspicions flit about my mind, and not one of them pleases me." His manner had grown distant and hard as he gazed unseeingly at the slides sprawled out on the workbench. He looked back at me with his steely eyes, then relaxed into a smile. "I shall tell you about it on our way to the park."

"Oh, Holmes, be reasonable. You may be presentable, if a bit idiosyncratic in topper and tails, but how can I go out like this?" He took in my rumpled gown, my town stockings and impractical shoes, and nodded. "I'll ask if there's a matron who can help us." Before he could move, there was a knock at the door.

"Come in."

A tense young PC with an untamed cowlick stood in the doorway.

"Mr. Holmes, Inspector Lestrade asked me to tell you that there's a parcel for the young lady at the front desk, but—"

Holmes exploded out of the room, giving lie to any rumours of slowness, pain, or rheumatism. I could hear his voice shouting "Don't touch that parcel, don't touch it, get a bomb disposal man first, don't touch it, did you catch the person who brought it, Lestrade . . ."

His voice faded as I followed him down the hall to the stairs, the young policeman jabbering away at my side.

"I was going to say, but he left, the package is with the bomb squad now, and Inspector Lestrade would like Mr. Holmes present at the questioning of the young man who brought it in. He didn't give me a chance to finish, sir." This last to Lestrade, who had intercepted Holmes in his precipitous flight. We could see the men at work downstairs, one with a stethoscope to the paper-wrapped parcel on the desk. We watched tensely, and I became aware of the unaccustomed silence. Traffic had been diverted. Holmes turned to the inspector.

"You have the man who brought it?"

"Yes, he's here. He says a man stopped him in the street an hour ago, offering two sovereigns to deliver this package. Small blond man in a heavy coat, said it was for a friend who needed it this morning but he couldn't take it himself. Gave him a sovereign then, and took his address to send the second after he'd confirmed delivery."

"Which will never arrive."

"The boy expects it to. Not too bright, this one. Not even sure he knows what a sovereign's worth, just likes the shine."

We had watched the two men work this whole time, their strain palpable as they gently snipped twine, cut away paper, and uncovered the contents, which had the appearance of folded clothing. Gently, slowly, the package was disassembled. In the end there lay draped over the police desk one silk shirt, a soft wool jacket, matching trousers, two angora stockings, and a pair of shoes. A folded note fell out of this last set of items and fluttered to the floor.

"Use your gloves on that," called Holmes.

The puzzled but relieved bomb man brought the note to Lestrade in a pair of surgical tweezers. He read it, handed it to Holmes, and Holmes read it aloud in a voice that slowed and climbed in dismay and disbelief.

"Dear Miss Russell [he read],
Knowing his limitations, I expect your companion will neglect to provide you with suitable clothing this morning. Please accept these with my compliments. You will find them quite comfortable.
—An admirer"

Holmes blinked several times and hurled the note at Lestrade. "Give this to your print man," he snarled. "Give the clothes to the laboratory, check them for foreign objects, corrosive powder, everything. Find out where they came from. And, for the love of God, can someone please provide Miss Russell with 'suitable clothing' so this case will not come to a complete standstill?" As he turned away in a cold fury I heard him breathe, "This becomes intolerable."

A variety of clothing appeared, part uniform, part civilian, all un-comfortable. We set off for the park in a police automobile, Lestrade in front with the driver, Holmes beside me, silent and remote and star-ing out the window while his long fingers beat a rhythm on his knee. He did not divulge his laboratory findings. At the park he dashed up and down the paths for a very few minutes, nodding to himself, then bundled us brusquely back into the car. He turned a deaf ear to Lestrade's questions, and we rode in silence back to New Scotland Yard to make our way to Lestrade's office, where we were left alone. Holmes went over to Lestrade's desk, opened a drawer, took out a packet of cigarettes, removed one, lit it with a vesta, and went to the window, where he stood with his back to me, staring unseeing out onto the busy Embankment and the river traffic beyond, smoke curl-ing through the dirty glass. He smoked the cigarette to the end with-out speaking, then walked back to the desk and pressed the stub with great deliberation into the ashtray.

"I must go out," he said curtly. "I refuse to take any of these heavy-footed friends of yours with me. They will send the wildlife scurrying for cover. While I am away, draw up a list of necessities and give it to the matron. Clothing for two or three days, nothing formal. Men's or women's, as you like. You'd best add a few things for me as well—you know my sizes. It will save me some time. I shall be back in a couple of hours."

I stood up angrily. "Holmes, you can't do this to me. You've told me nothing, you've consulted me not at all, just pushed me here and there and run roughshod over any plans I might have had and kept me in the dark as if I were Watson, and now you propose to go off and leave me with a shopping list." He was already moving toward the door, and I followed him across the room, arguing.

"First you call me your associate, and then you start treating me like a maid. Even an apprentice deserves better than that. I'd like to know—"

I had just come up to the window when a sound like a meaty palm slapping a table came from just outside the wall, followed a second later by a more familiar report. Holmes reacted instantly and dove across the room at me just as the window imploded in a shower of flying razor-sharp glass and a second slap came from the opposite wall. We both came up in a crouch, and Holmes seized my shoulder.

"Are you hit?"

"My God, was that—"

"Russell, are you all right?" he demanded furiously.

"Yes, I think so. Do you—" but he was sprinting low towards the door as it opened and an inspector in mufti looked in open-mouthed. Holmes gathered him up, and they pounded off down the stairs in pursuit. I steeled myself to creep around to the broken window and edge one eye over the lower corner. A steam launch was making its rapid way downriver, but there was also a mother with a pram stopped on the bridge, turned to look at a retreating taxi-cab, her shoulders in an attitude of surprise. Inside of a minute Holmes and the others had swept up to her, and she was soon surrounded by gesticulating men pointing east over the river and south across the bridge. I saw Holmes look unerringly up to where I stood in the window, turn to say something to the tweedy inspector, and then set his shoulders resolutely and walk, hatless and head down, back to the Yard.

With typical police efficiency and priorities, Lestrade's office was filled with people measuring angles and retrieving bullets from the brickwork, none of whom had a dustpan or a means of blocking the icy air from the window. I retreated into the next office but one, a room with no window. As soon as Holmes appeared I knew there would be no arguing with him, although I intended to try. "I think you'd best change that order to clothing for several days, Russell," were his first words. "Stay away from windows, don't eat or drink anything you're not absolutely certain is safe, and keep your revolver with you."

"Don't take sweets from strangers, you mean?" I said sarcastically, but he would not anger.

"Precisely. I shall return in two or three hours. Be ready to leave when I get back."

"Holmes, you must at least—"

"Russell," he interrupted, and came over to grasp my shoulders, "I am very sorry, but time is of the utmost urgency. You were going to say that I must tell you what is happening, and I shall. You wish to be consulted; I intend to do so. In fact, I intend to place a fair percentage of the decisions to be made into your increasingly competent hands. But not just at this moment, Russell. Please, be satisfied with that." And he shifted his hands to both sides of my head, bent forward, and brushed his lips gently across my brow. I sat down abruptly, felled by this thunderbolt, until long after he had gone . . . which, I realized belatedly, was precisely why he had done it.

HOLMES' AIR OF illicit excitement told me that he was extremely unlikely to be back from his haunts in two or three hours. Irritated, I scribbled the lists for the young policewoman, gave her the last of my money, and turned my back on the windowless office. I was jumpy at every window I passed, but I wanted to take a closer look at the parcel of clothing that had arrived for me that morning, which I had only seen from a distance. I made my way to the laboratories, where I disturbed a gentleman in an unnecessarily professional white coat standing at a bench with a shoe in one hand. He turned at my entrance, and when I saw what he held, I was stunned speechless. The shoe was my own.

This pair of shoes now inhabiting the laboratory bench had disappeared from my rooms some time during the autumn, in one of those puzzling incidents that happen and are finally dismissed with a shrug. I had worn them the second week of October, and two weeks later when I went to look for them, they were not there. It troubled me, but frankly more because I took it as a sign of severe absentmindedness than anything sinister. I had obviously left them somewhere. And here they were.

I was relieved to see that the clothes were not familiar to me, although very much to my taste. They were all new, ready-made from a large shop in Liverpool, unremarkable, though not inexpensive. Thus far the examiners had found nothing but clothing—not so much as a stray shirt pin.

The note that had accompanied the parcel lay in a steel tray across the bench, and I walked around to take a look at it. It was grey with fingerprint powder, but even if the sender had been careless, the paper was too rough to retain prints. I picked it up, read it with grudging amusement, noted casually the characteristics of the type, and started to lay it back down, and then I froze in disbelief. Yes, that's one too many shocks in the last few days, my brain commented analytically. I fumbled for a stool and after some time became aware of the technician's alarm. I told him what I had seen. I told Lestrade the same thing when he appeared. Some time later I found myself in the windowless room with the policewoman who had returned from shopping saying how she'd been careful to watch each item taken down and wrapped, and I made polite noises of (I suppose) gratitude and then sat there for a long while with my brain steaming furiously away.

By the time Holmes blew in, hair awry and a wild light in his eyes, I had recovered enough to be examining the woman's purchases. I drew back sharply as he entered and dropped a boot.

"Good God, Holmes, where have you been to pick up such a stench? Down on the docks, obviously, and from your feet I should venture to say you'd been in the sewers, but what is that horrid sweet smell?"

"Opium, my dear protected child. It clawed its way into my hair and clothes, though I was not partaking. I had to be certain I was not being followed."

"Holmes, we must talk, but I cannot breathe in your presence.

There is a fine, if austere, set of shower baths in the prisoners' section. Take these clothes, but don't let them touch the thing you have on."

"No time, Russell. We must fly."

"Absolutely not." My news was vital, but it would wait, and this would not.

"What did you say?" he said dangerously. Sherlock Holmes was not accustomed to outright refusals, not even from me.

"I know you well enough, Holmes, to suspect that we are about to embark on a long and arduous journey. If it is a choice between expiring slowly from your fumes or being blown to pieces, I choose the latter. Gladly."

Holmes glowered at me for some seconds, saw that I was on this issue inflexible, and with a curse worthy of the docks snatched the proffered clothes and hurled himself out the door, furiously demanding directions from the poor constable stationed outside.

When he burst in again I was ready for travel, a booted young man. No doubt, I thought, the newness of the clothes would quickly fade in Holmes' company.

"Very well, Russell, I am clean. Come."

"There's a cup of tea and a sandwich for you while I look to your back."

"For God's sake, woman, we must be on the docks in thirty-five minutes! We've no time for a tea party."

I sat calmly, my hands in my lap. I noticed with interest that his cheekbones became slightly purple when he was severely perturbed, and his eyes bulged slightly. He was positively quivering when he threw off his coat, and one button of his misused shirt skittered across the floor. I put it into a pocket and picked up the gauze while he gulped his tea. I worked quickly on the nearly healed wound, and we were on the street within five minutes.

We dove into the back of a sleek automobile that idled at the kerb and squealed away. The driver looked more like a ruffian than he did the owner of such a machine, but I had no say in the matter. I waited for Holmes to stop his silent fuming, which was not until we were south of Tower Bridge.

"Look here, Russell," he began, "I won't have you—" but I cut him off immediately by the simple expedient of thrusting a finger into his face. (Looking back I am deeply embarrassed at the effrontery of a girl not yet nineteen pointing her finger at a man nearly three times her age, and her teacher to boot, but at the time it seemed appropriate.)

"*You* look here, Holmes. I cannot force you to confide in me, but I will not be bullied. You are not my nanny, I am not your charge to be protected and coddled. You have not given me any cause to believe that you were dissatisfied with my ability at deduction and reasoning. You admit that I am an adult—you called me 'woman' not ten minutes ago—and as a thinking adult partner I have the right to make my own decisions. I saw you come in filthy and tired, having not eaten, I was sure, since last evening, and I exercised my right to protect the partnership by putting a halt to your stupidity. Yes, stupidity. You believe yourself to be without the limitations of mere mortals, I know, but the mind, even your mind, my dear Holmes, is subject to the body's weakness. No food or drink and filth on an open wound puts the partnership—puts me!—at an unnecessary risk. And *that* is something I won't have."

I had forgotten the driver, who proved an appreciative audience to this dramatic declaration. He burst into laughter and pounded on the wheel as he slid through the narrow street, dodging horses, walls, and vehicles. "Right good job, Miss," he guffawed, "make him wash his socks at night, too, whyn't ya?" At last here I had the grace to blush.

The driver was still grinning, and even Holmes had softened when we reached our destination, a dank and filthy wharf somewhere down near Greenwich. The river was greasy and black in the early twilight, high and very cold looking, its calmer reaches one undulating mat of flotsam. The swollen body of a dog rocked gently against a pier. The area was deserted, though voices and machinery noises drifted from the next row of buildings.

"Thank you, young man," said Holmes quietly, and "Come, Russell." We walked carefully down the planks to a gate of peeling corrugated iron, which slid open with an eerie silence and closed again after us. The man on the gate followed us down to the end of the wharf, where lay a nondescript small ship, a boat, really. A man standing on the deck hailed us in a low voice and came down the gangway to take our valises.

"Good day, Mr. Holmes. Welcome aboard, sir."

"I am very glad to be aboard, captain, very glad indeed. This is my"—He cocked an eyebrow at me—"my partner, Miss Russell. Russell, Captain Jones here runs one of the fastest boats on the river and has agreed to take us out to sea for a while."

"To sea? Oh, Holmes, I don't think—"

"Russell, we will talk shortly. Jones, shall we be away?"

"Aye, sir, the sooner the better. If you'd like to go below, my boy Brian will be with you in a minute to show you your quarters." The child appeared as we made our way down the narrow passage, opened a door, ducked his head shyly, and went to help his father cast off.

A narrow set of stairs led down to a surprisingly spacious cabin, a lounge of sorts with a tiny kitchen/galley at one side and soft chairs and a sofa bolted to the floor. A corridor opened off the forward side, and doors led to two small bedrooms with a lavatory and bath, between them. Those are not the proper technical terms, I am aware, but the whole area so obviously was intended for the comfort of non-sailors, the lay terms are perhaps more accurate. We settled ourselves on two chairs as the engine noise deepened, and watched London slip by outside the windows. I leant forward.

"Now, Holmes, there is something I must tell you—"

"First some brandy."

"Your plying me with that stuff becomes tedious," I said crossly.

"Prevents seasickness, Russell."

"I don't get seasick."

"Miss Russell, I believe you are becoming quite dissolute with the shady associations of the last few days. That, if my ears do not deceive me, was an untruth. You were about to tell me on deck that you did not wish to go to sea because it made you feel ill, were you not?"

"Oh, very well, I admit I don't like going to sea. Give me the brandy." I took two large and explosive mouthfuls, to Holmes' disapproving grimace, and banged the glass on the table. "Now, Holmes—"

"Yes, Russell, you wish to hear the results of today's opium dens and—"

"Holmes," I nearly shouted. "Would you listen to me?"

"Of course, Russell. I am happy to listen to you, I merely thought—"

"The shoes, Holmes, those shoes that arrived in the parcel? They were mine, my own shoes, taken from my rooms at Oxford. They disappeared some time between the twelfth and the thirtieth of October."

A half minute of silence fell between us.

"Good Lord," he said at last. "How extraordinary. I am most grateful to you, Russell, I should have missed that entirely." He was so obviously disturbed that any faint malicious glee I might have had at my second piece of news withered away.

"There is more. I think, in fact, that you might like to finish that drink first, Holmes, because that note, that was in the shoes? I examined it very, very closely, Holmes, and I believe it was typed on the same machine as the notes concerning Jessica Simpson's ransom."

There was no softening the blow. The bare facts were awful enough, but the implications inherent in *my* having to tell *him* were, for him, truly terrible: twice now in little more than two days I had rescued him from a major error. The first might have been excused, though it nearly cost Watson his life; this one had been in his hands, under his nose, at the very time he had been searching for just such a clue. It changed the investigation, and he had missed it. He stood up abruptly and turned his back to me at the window.

"Holmes, I—"

One warning finger was raised, and I bit back the words that would only have made matters worse: Holmes, four days ago you were concussed and bleeding. Holmes, you've had less than a dozen hours' sleep in the last eighty. Holmes, you were exhausted and furious when you saw the note, and you would have called to mind the characteristic missing serif on the *a* and the off-centre, tipsy *l* and the high M, you'd have consciously remembered seeing them, if not today, then tomorrow, or the next day, Holmes. However, I said nothing, because he would hear only: Holmes, you're slipping.

We were well clear of London's fringes by the time I saw the back of his neck relax into an attitude of straightforward contemplation of data. I heaved a silent sigh of relief and settled myself to a study of the opposite windows.

Ten minutes later he came back and sat down with his pipe. He paused with the match alight in his hand.

"You are quite certain, I take it?"

"Yes." I began to recite the characteristics I had noted, but he cut me off.

"That is not necessary, Russell. I have great faith in your eyes." He puffed up a small cloud and shook out the match. "And your brain," he added. "Well done. It does mean we now have something resembling a motive."

"Revenge for thwarting Jessica's kidnapping?"

"That, and the knowledge that we are waiting to pounce on any similar attempt in the future. Anyone familiar with Watson's literary fabrications will be certain that Sherlock Holmes always gets his man. Or, in this case, woman." I was pleased to hear the customary ironic humour, and no more, in his voice. "It is, however, intriguing that I could find no indication of an up-and-coming gang of criminals with a female head."

I gratefully shelved the uncomfortable topic and asked for the results of the last eighteen hours. He looked mildly surprised.

"Eighteen hours? Surely I kept you abreast of my thoughts last night?"

"Your mutterings in the park were completely unintelligible, and if you spoke to me in the laboratory before dawn, I did not hear it."

"Odd, I thought I was quite garrulous. Well then, to the park, or rather to the remnants of a once-noble four-wheeler, which at first glance appears to be the least interesting of the night's works. There were two large men there, and one, so I thought, smaller, lighter man wearing boots with distinctive square heels. The two large men came up behind Billy as he was standing talking to someone, though I should have thought him too wary. At any rate, they disposed of Billy with a cosh, and chloroform was applied by Small Boots. The destruction of your clothing was carried out by the two big men while the smaller stayed with Billy and kept the chloroform dripping onto his face. When they had finished, Small Boots climbed in and applied the knife methodically to the seat, at which time the fibres of the other fabric pieces became embedded in the cuts, despite the extreme sharpness of the blade. It was, incidentally, a short-handled, double-edged knife, the blade being about six inches in length and relatively narrow."

"Nasty weapon. A flick-knife?"

"Probably. The circumstances of the cab destruction troubled me. Did you see anything amiss?"

"The slashes seemed odd. They're so precise, all the same height and direction, but they stop before the end of the seat. It was almost as if they were searching for something under the leather. There was no sign that a hand had pushed into the cuts, was there?"

"There was not. And of equal interest is the question, why was it given over to Small Boots, the boss, to do those final cuts? I am missing something there, Russell. I desire to study the photographs. Perhaps that will refresh my memory."

"And when will that be?" A look of grim humour flickered across his face.

"That, Russell, is up to you. No, let me explain that in its logical place, at the end. I dislike having to leap about in the narration of evidence, as you well know.

"To continue: Left in the cab were one button, complete with a well-defined thumbprint of a large man, one blonde hair, and a number of smudges of light brown mud on the floor and the seats. We shall return to that last item in a moment.

"As you were sifting through the wreckage of your wardrobe, I was tracking. The mud was quite clearly followed: It had come across the park on the soft gravel pathway. Or so it seemed at first. Of the big boots there was no sign, which was singular. It was not until you found the same mud in the Ladies' that I discovered the truth: that the three had not come across the park, but rather had come around the side of the park on the hard, well-travelled paved path. The two big boots had returned that way, but Small Boots, walking *backwards*, had crossed on the soft central path, entered the Ladies', backwards, washed and walked, still backwards, to the same point where they had entered the park. The three then boarded a vehicle of some kind and drove away."

"And you needed to see the prints by daylight to be certain that the set running down the middle was indeed backwards?"

"Precisely. You have seen my monograph on footprints, *Forty-Seven Methods of Concealing One's Trail*? No? In it I mention that I have used various means of reversing footprints and, as you saw Tuesday morning, hiding one inside the other, but there seem to be flaws detectable to the careful eye. Another article I am working on is concerned with the innate differences between the male and female footprint. Have I shown that to you? No, of course, you've been away. I have found that no matter what kind of shoe is on the foot, the lie of the toes and the way the heel hits the ground differ between the sexes. I took the idea from a conversation we once had. At night, I suspected. After your find, and after I had seen the footprints by day, I knew. This is a woman, five and a half feet tall, and slim—less than eight stone. She may be blonde—"

"Just may be?"

"Just may be," he repeated. "She is intelligent, well-read, and has a particularly grotesque and creative sense of humour."

"The note, you mean?"

"I was aware of it before that arrived. You know my monograph on London soils?"

"*Notes on Some Distinctive Characteristics*—" I began.

"That one, yes. I have not demanded of you an expertise in the study of London, but as you know, I spent most of my life there before I retired. I breathed her air, I trod her ground, and I knew her like—as a husband knows his wife." I did not react to the simile, despite the Hebraic overtones to the verb, "know." "Some of her soils I can identify by eye, others need a microscope. The soil I found in the cab and on the washbasin was a not-uncommon variety. My own lodgings in Baker Street were built on top of such a soil, but it crops up in several places, each distinguishable one from the other only by very close examination under a strong lens."

"And the mud on Small Boots came from Baker Street."

"How did you know?" he said with a smile.

"Lucky guess," I answered drily. He raised an eyebrow.

"Low jokes do not suit you, Russell."

"Sorry. But what does the fact that she chose to walk through Baker Street before going to the park have to do with it?"

"You tell me," he demanded, in a thin echo from a spring day long, long ago.

Obediently I set to reviewing the entire episode, running my mind over the facts like a tongue over teeth, searching for a gap in the smooth, hard surfaces. The mud, which was on the path, in the cab, on the seats (On the seats? my mind whispered), and in the Ladies' (grotesque and creative sense of humour) on the floor, in the washbasin (the basin? That means—)

"It was on her hand, the mud. Her left hand, and the right boot." I stopped, disbelieving, and looked at Holmes. His grey eyes were positively dancing. "She replenished the mud, to keep the path obvious. This whole episode—it was deliberately staged. She wants you to know that she was there, and she put the Baker Street mud on her shoe to thumb her nose at you. She even washed her hands of it in the Ladies' to leave you that datum, if you hadn't already worked out that he was a she. I can't believe it—no one could be mad enough to mock you like that. What kind of game is she playing?"

"A decidedly unpleasant sort of a game, with three bombs and a death thus far, but I agree, the style of humour is a match with the clothing parcel and the exploding beehive. One is forced to wonder . . ." he mused, and his voice drifted away.

"Yes?" I encouraged.

"Nothing, Russell. Merely speculation without data, a fruitless exercise at the best of times. I was reflecting that the only truly superior mind I have encountered among the criminal classes was Moriarty, which ill equips me for the possibility of subtlety in our current foe. Were I quite certain of, for example, the intent of the marksman who shot at us in Lestrade's office, or of Dickson's efforts, or even . . . Yes, I suppose . . ." He drifted off again.

"Holmes, do I understand you aright? That the actions against us were not actually intended to be deadly?"

"Oh, deadly, certainly, though perhaps not merely deadly. But yes, you understand me. I mistrust a series of failures when the author otherwise gives signs of great competence. Accidents are not unknown, but I dislike coincidences, and I deny out of hand the existence of a guardian angel. Yes," he said thoughtfully, and I winced as I heard his next phrase coming, "it is quite a pretty problem."

"Quite a three-piper, eh Holmes?" I said in hearty jocularity. He could be the most irritating individual.

"No, no, not yet. Nicotinic mediation serves to clarify the known facts, not pull them out of thin air. I do not feel we have all the facts."

"Very well, but surely you can speculate in generalities. If she didn't wish to kill us, what are her intentions?"

"I did not say she does not intend to kill us, just possibly not yet. If for the sake of hypothesis we assume that what has occurred over the course of the last few days is more or less what she had in mind, then we are left with three possible inferences: one, that she does not want us all actually dead at this moment; two, that she wishes us to be fully aware of an intelligent, dedicated, resourceful, and implacable enemy breathing almost literally down our collars; and three, that she wants us either to go to ground or leave England."

"And isn't that what we're doing?"

"Indeed," he said complacently.

"I—" I stopped, shut my mouth, waited.

"Her actions tell me that it is what she wants me to do. She knows me well enough to assume that I will perceive her intent and refuse to cooperate. Therefore I shall do what she wants."

I decided finally that the brandy was to blame for the dullness of my logical faculties, for though I was certain there was a basic fallacy in his reasoning, I could not put my finger on precisely the juncture. I shook my head and plunged on.

"Why not just disappear for a few days? It is really necessary to . . ."

"Take flight?" he supplied. "Beat a hasty retreat? Run away? You're quite right. This morning I should have agreed that a few days' retreat to Mycroft's flat or one of my bolt-holes was sufficient for regrouping." (I shuddered here at the thought of being confined with Holmes in the Storage Room for any length of time.) "But today's events have proven me wrong. Not the clothing parcel—that was a clever joke. Even the shoes, though sinister, could be got around. But—that bullet. It nearly hit you. I believe it was meant to," he said, and although he did not look at me, the control in his voice and the small twitch in the right side of his mouth spoke volumes of the rage and apprehension this threat set off in him. To cover his gaffe he rose in a jerk and began to stride up and down, his hands behind him as if tucked beneath the tails of a frock coat, the smouldering pipe he still gripped endangering his clothing. Words tumbled out of him as he paced, spoken in his high voice as if berating himself.

"I begin to feel like a piece of driftwood tumbling about between waves and sand, snatched up and tossed from one place to another. It is a most disconcerting feeling. Were I alone I might almost be tempted to let myself be tumbled, just to see where I washed up. That, however, is not an option.

"What then are the options? Offensive—an all-out attack? On what? Beating a mist with a cricket bat. Defence? How does one defend against a mirror-image? She has read Watson's tales, and my bee book, the monographs on soil and footprints—not available to the general public—and God knows what else. A woman! She has turned my own words against me, caused me considerable mental and physical distress, kept me off my balance for five whole days, chased and harried me across my home territory until I am forced to go to ground—to sea. Do you know—" he broke off, and whirled around to shake an outraged pipe stem at me, "this . . . person has even penetrated into one of my bolt-holes! Yes, today, there were signs. . . . I still cannot believe that a woman can have done this, deducing my deductions, plotting my moves for me, and all the time giving the impression that to her it is a deadly but effortless and highly amusing game. Even Moriarty did not go so far, and he was a master without parallel. The mind, capable of such *coups de maître. Maîtresse.*" He stopped, and straightened his shoulders with a jerk as if to settle his clothing back into place.

"A most gratifying challenging opponent, this," he said in a calmer voice, and lit his pipe, which had gone out. When it was going again he continued in a completely different vein.

"Russell, I have been considering your words of this morning. I do occasionally take the thoughts of others into account, you know. Particularly yours. I have to admit that you were completely justified in your protest. You are an adult, and by your very nature I was quite wrong to treat you as if you were Watson. I apologise."

I was, as one might imagine, completely flabbergasted, and highly suspicious, but he went on as if discussing the weather.

"Today while I was on my distressingly fruitless quest for information through the human sewers of fair London town, it occurred to me that the matter of your future has come to a head. This peculiar . . . present situation has forced it, but it should have come sooner or later. The question I am faced with is, what does one do with a student who has passed every examination laid before her? Eventually she must be removed from *in statu pupularis* and allowed to assume the rights and responsibilities of maturity. In your case every paper I've set you, every test, up to the viva voce question of the mud on our opponent's footwear, has come up an alpha.

"I have, then, a limited number of options. Considering the gravity of this particular case, I feel I should be justified in removing you from the firing line as I did Watson, until I can clear it up. No, do not interrupt. Much to my displeasure, I find I cannot bring myself to attempt that. For one thing, the logistics of keeping you under control are too daunting.

"It has been on my mind since Wales that an apprentice kept from her journeyman's papers will spoil. Faced with this, what for lack of a better term I shall call a case, I have two choices: I can maintain your 'apprenticeship' (as you yourself called it), or I can grant you your Mastery. Having never been one for half-measures, I see no point in delaying the inevitable. Therefore . . ." He stopped, took his pipe from his mouth, looked into the bowl, put it back into his mouth, reached for the pouch in his pocket, and I very nearly screamed at him with the tension of being torn between "Thank God, here it comes, at last!" and "Oh, God, here it comes, he's sending me away."

He opened the tobacco pouch and dug from it a small, much-folded scrap of onionskin, dropped it in front of me, went to the ashtray clipped to the table, and began to scrape the dottle from his pipe while I unfolded the paper. On it, in five lines of minute, cramped, antique, and graphologically cryptic script, were written:

Egypt—Alexandria—Sayeed Abu Bahadr
Greece—Thessaloniki—Thomas Catalepo
Italy—Ravenna—Fr. Domenico

Palestine—Jaffa—Ali & Mahmoud Hazr
Morocco—Rabat—Peter Thomas

Each of the personal names was followed by a series of numbers that looked like a radio frequency. I looked up, but Holmes was at the window again, his unrevealing back to me.

"I have said before this time that I regard it as stupidity rather than courage to overlook a danger that presses as close as this one has. Even my critics will not accuse me of stupidity, else I should not have reached my present age after a lifetime of the rough-and-tumble. I remember vividly, as if it were last week rather than two and a half decades ago, sitting in Watson's chair and admitting to him that London was too hot for my safety. The current state of affairs is . . . remarkably similar.

"The admission then caused me some shame. But, that was half a lifetime ago, and since then I have learnt, slowly, and painfully, that time and distance can prove a powerful weapon. It is not one that comes naturally to my hand, I admit. I much prefer direct attack, complete immersion, and a quick finish. However, there is much to be said for the occasional, judicious, prodigious expenditure of time."

"What sort of time are you thinking of here, Holmes?" I asked warily. His most famous hiatus had lasted three years; that would certainly drive a cart and horses through my University degree.

"Not terribly long. Enough to instill doubts in our opponent—Was she wrong after all? Did I just choose to vanish? Where on earth am I?—and to allow Mycroft and the elephantine Scotland Yard to sweep up the data and begin to sift it over. By the time we return" (we! I snatched at) "the momentum will have been taken from her. She will be furious, and careless, with the knowledge that we have removed ourselves from her rules, that we have opted out of the traditional and expected program of threat, challenge, response, and counterattack.

"For better or for worse, you are in this case." My brief surge of triumph was quickly submerged in a backwash of conflicting questions and feelings: Was he fleeing because he was saddled with me? And what on earth did he have in mind? Tibet? "What is more, you are in it as, God help us, my partner, or as near to such a creature as I am ever likely to see. Given the circumstances, I have no choice: I have to trust you."

I could think of no sensible response to this, so I blurted out the first thing that came to mind.

"What should you have done if I had walked through my lodgings door the other night?"

"Hmmm. I wonder. Perhaps unfortunately, that question does not pertain. Here we stand; I can no other. And as a means of noting the fact of your accession to the lofty rights and privileges of partnership, I shall grant you a boon: I shall allow you to make the next decision. Where shall we go to keep from harm's way for a bit? Do you know, Russell," he said in a voice that verged on playful, "I don't believe I've had a holiday in twenty-five years."

In the past seventy-two hours I had seen a bomb on my door and the results of another on Holmes' back, spent thirteen hard, tense hours slogging towards London, waved a gun at Holmes, seen my first major attempt at high fashion reduced to shreds, been ill-fed, under-slept, half-frozen, and shot at, witnessed Holmes in more perturbation than ever before, and now this wild swing from matter-of-fact confidences to near-teasing merriment. It was all a bit much.

I looked down at the paper in my hand, two inches of nearly transparent onionskin and its five lines of writing.

"Are these our only options?" I asked.

"By no means. Captain Jones is quite willing to steam around in circles if we ask him, or to head for South America or to the northern lights. There are few limits, although if you wish to try breaking the bank at Monte Carlo I shall have to arrange a discreet transfer of funds. Just avoid the United Kingdom or New York for six or eight weeks."

"Two months! Holmes, I can't be away for two months, I'll be sent down if I miss that much time. And my aunt will have the army out. And Mrs. Hudson, and Watson . . ."

"Mrs. Hudson will embark tomorrow on a cruise."

"A cruise! Mrs. Hudson?"

"To visit her family in Australia, I believe. And you need not concern yourself with Dr. Watson, either; his greatest danger will be gout from high living, where Mycroft has him secreted. Your college and tutors will grant you an exeat, while you attend to your urgent family business. Your aunt will be told that you are away."

"Good Lord. If Mycroft can tame her, he's a valuable ally indeed." I could feel my objections beginning to waver.

"Well?"

"Who are these people?" I asked. Holmes plucked the paper from my hand.

"This is Mycroft's writing," he said by way of explanation.

"And Mycroft has . . . tasks that need doing in these places?"

"Precisely. His words were, if we choose to remove ourselves from the field of combat whilst the scouts assess the enemy's position, we may as well be of some use to His Majesty, and might care for a change of scenery under auspices." Holmes' eyes were filled with mischief and amusement, and I could see that he had already laid our case to one side. He waved the paper gently in front of my nose. "It has been my experience," he added, "that Mycroft's assignments tend to offer quite extraordinary amounts of entertainment."

I acquiesced, took the paper from his fingers, spread it out on the table in front of me, and pointed to the fourth line.

"Yisroel."

"What?"

"Palestine, Israel, Zion, the Holy Land. I desire to walk through Jerusalem."

Holmes nodded slowly, bemused. "I think I can honestly say, that particular destination should not have been my first choice. Greece, yes. Morocco, perhaps. Even Egypt, but Palestine? Very well, the choice is yours, and I am certain our foe will never guess that as my destination. To Palestine it is."

B Y MIDNIGHT WE were off the coast of France and, with no signs of anyone in our wake and strict radio silence maintained, the tight knot that had held me since Tuesday evening was beginning to loosen. Captain Jones came into our cabin, a barrel-shaped and lugubrious individual with thinning, once-red hair, distinguishable from the four crew members under his command by the state of his fingernails, which were slightly blacker than theirs, and the straight-spined, confident air of one who caters to royalty. The boy was a smaller version of his father, and all, including the child, had been chosen by Mycroft from wherever he was holed up with Watson.

"Good evening, Jones," said Holmes. "Brandy? Or whisky?"

"No thank you, sir. I don't drink when I'm out to sea. Asking for problems, it is, sir. I just came down to ask if you'd decided on our course."

"Palestine, Jones."

"Palestine, sir?"

"Palestine. You know—Israel, Zion, the Holy Land. It is on your charts, I assume?"

"Of course, sir. It's just that, well, if you've not been there recently, you'll not find it the easiest place to move around in, so to speak. There has been a war on, you know," he offered in a mild understatement.

"I am aware of that, Jones. London will have to be notified, and they shall make all the necessary arrangements."

"Very good, sir. Shall I set course tonight, then?"

"The morning is just as well, Jones, there is no hurry. Is there, Russell?"

I opened my eyes. "None at all," I confirmed, and closed them again.

"In the morning it is, then, sir, Miss." His footsteps faded up the stairs.

Holmes stood silently, and I felt his gaze on me.

"Russell?"

"Mmm."

"There's nothing more that needs doing tonight. Go to bed. Or shall I cover you with a blanket again?"

"No, no, I shall go. Good night, Holmes."

"Good night, Russell."

I AWOKE WHEN the engines changed their sounds in the early grey light of dawn. Passing through the cabin for a glass of water I saw the silhouette of Holmes, curled in a chair staring out at the sea, knees to chin, pipe in hand. I said nothing as I went back to bed, and I do not think he noticed me. I slept all that day, and when I awoke it was a summer's evening.

It was not actually summer, of course, and we were to have rain during the weeks that followed, but we had sun enough that Holmes and I could spend hours darkening our skins up on the deck. To think of London huddled under its blanket of sleet and thick yellow fogs as we sweated and dozed was like imagining another world, and I often found myself hoping fervently that our attempted murderer was caught in the worst of it, with bronchitis. And chilblains.

The days passed quickly. To my surprise Holmes did not seem to chafe under the enforced rest but appeared relaxed and cheerful. We spent hours devising complex mind games, and he taught me the subtleties of codes and ciphers. We took apart and rebuilt the ship's spare radio, and began an experiment on the point at which various heated substances will self-ignite, but as it made the captain exceedingly nervous, we moved on to picking pockets. Christmas came and went, with flaming pudding and crackers with paper crowns and carols about iron-hard ground and snowy footprints, and after dinner Holmes came onto the upper deck with a chess set.

We had not played more than a handful of games since I had gone up to Oxford, and we quickly set to rediscovering the other's gambits and style. I had improved in the last eighteen months, and he no longer had to spot me a piece, which pleased us both. We played regularly, though first a black bishop and then the white king rolled overboard and we had to improvise substitutes (a salt cellar and a large greasy nut and bolt, respectively).

Holmes won most of the games, but not all. He was a good player, ruthless and imaginative, but an erratic one, for he tended to glory in bizarre gambits and impossible saves rather than the methodical building of defence and thoroughly supported offence. Chess for him was an exercise, boring at times and always a poor substitute for the real game—rather like scales compared to the public performance of a concerto.

One hot afternoon off the island of Crete he came to board with a greater focus than was his wont and a nervous intensity that I found disturbing. We played three half-games, scrapped each time when he was satisfied with the direction each opening gambit had established. The fourth game, though, began with a peculiarly gleeful attitude and opening moves along the very edge of the queen's side of the board. I braced myself for a wild game.

Holmes had drawn white, and he came out, whirling his knights across the board like a berserker with his chain mace, sixteen squares of shifting destruction and disruption that had me slapping together hasty defences at half a dozen spots across the board, summoning and abandoning bishops and rooks, spraying pawns ahead of the fray and leaving them in odd niches as the action stumbled away across the board. One after another he swatted aside my defences, until in desperation I separated my royalty, moving my queen away from the vulnerable king to draw my opponent's fire. For a time I succeeded, but eventually he trapped her with a knight, and I lost her.

"What's the matter with you, Russell?" he complained. "Your mind's not on the game."

"It is, you know, Holmes," I said mildly, and reached forward to move a pawn, and with that move the entire haphazard disarray fell into a neat and deadly trap that depended on two pawns and a bishop. In three moves I had him mated.

I wanted to whoop and leap into the air and kiss Captain Jones on his bristly cheek for the sheer joy of seeing Holmes' consternation and amazement, but instead I just sat and grinned at him like a dog.

He stared at the board like a conjuror's audience, and the expression on his face was one of the biggest prizes I have ever won. Then it broke, and he slapped his knee with a short bark of delighted laughter and rearranged the pieces to replay the last six moves. At the end of it he wagged his head in appreciation.

"Well done, Russell. Deucedly clever, that. More devious than I'd have given you credit for. My children have bested me," he quoted, somewhat irreverently.

"I wish I could claim credit for it, but the move came up in a game with my maths tutor a few months ago. I've been waiting for the opportunity to use it on you."

"I'd not have thought that I could be tricked into overlooking a pawn," he admitted. "That's quite a gambit."

"Yes. I fell for it too. Sometimes you have to sacrifice a queen in order to save the game."

He looked up at me, startled, and then back to the board, and his face changed. A tightness crept slowly into his features until he looked pinched and pale beneath the brown of his skin's surface, as someone does who is stricken by a gnawing pain in the vital organs.

"Holmes? Holmes, are you all right?"

"Hm? Oh, yes, Russell, I am fine. Never better. Thank you, Russell, for such an interesting game. You have given me much food for thought." His hard visage relaxed into the gentlest of smiles. "Thank you, my dear Russell." He reached out, but his fingers did not quite touch my cheek before he pulled them back, stood, and turned to go below. I sat on the sun-drenched deck and watched his back disappear, the victory turned to ashes in my mouth, and wondered what I had done.

I did not see him again until we arrived at Jaffa.

Excursus

A GATHERING OF STRENGTH

✳ 13 ✳

Umbilicus Mundi

. . . it will serve a useful purpose by restoring our courage
and stimulating research in a new direction.

I HAD NOT realised how greatly I desired Palestine until one of its
towns leapt out at me from the list of places offered us, and the
name was on my lips. I had no doubt that some day (next year) I
should make my pilgrimage to the birthplace of my people, but a pilgrimage is a planned and contemplated event of the mind and, perhaps, the heart, which this most emphatically was not. When I was
beset by fear and confusion, when no ground was sure beneath my feet
and familiar places threatened, this foreign land reached out to me,
called me to her, and I went, and found comfort, and shelter, and
counsel. I, who had neither family nor home, found both there.

Palestine, Israel, that most troubled of lands; robbed, raped, ravaged,
revered for most of four millennia; beaten and colonised by Sargon's

Akkadians in the third millennium B.C.E. and by Allenby's England in the Common Era's second millennium; holy to half the world, a narrow strip of marginally fertile soil whose every inch has felt the feet of conquering soldiers, a barren land whose only wealth lies in the children she had borne. Palestine.

At dusk we were making way casually south, parallel to the far-off shore, but when night had fully fallen the captain changed to due east and, engines fast and quiet, we made for land. Holmes appeared, with a nearly flat knapsack and a preoccupied air, and at one in the morning we were bundled onto a ship's boat with muffled rowlocks, and taken ashore. Our landing site was just south of Jaffa, or Yafo, a town whose Jewish population had been forced to flee from Arab violence during the war. Imagine my pleasure, then, when we were summarily shoved into the burnoosed arms of a pair of Arab cutthroats and abandoned. Before the boat had disappeared into the night we had sunk unseen into the war-ravaged land.

They were not cutthroats, or perhaps I should say they were not merely cutthroats. They were not even Arabs. We called them, at their invitation, Ali and Mahmoud, but in a cooler climate they would have been Albert and Matthew, and certain diphthongs in their English exuded public school and Oxbridge. Holmes said they were from Clapham. He also said that although they looked like the brothers they claimed to be, and acted like twins, they were at best distant cousins. I did not enquire further but contented myself with watching the pair of them, hand in hand in the fashion of Arab men, as they strolled the dusty roads, chattering interminably in colloquial Arabic and gesticulating wildly with their free hands while we followed in their wake.

If our two guides were not what they appeared, neither was anything else in the weeks that followed: The drab boat that had brought us from England was experimental, an outgrowth of war's technology; its crew were not simply sailors, despite the presence of the child; even the two of us were not as we seemed, a father and son of dark-skinned, light-eyed nomads. Our very presence in the land had a heavy touch of the unreal about it: For the first two weeks we wandered with no apparent aim, performing a variety of tasks that again seemed aimless. We retrieved a document from a locked house; we reunited two old friends; we made detailed maps of two yawningly unimportant sites. During this dreamy time I had the feeling that we were being observed, if not judged, though I could never decide if someone was testing our abilities, or waiting for a job to appear that we were suited for. In either case, perhaps even coincidentally, a case abruptly appeared to immerse us and shore up our sagging self-confidence with the sharp exhilaration of danger and the demands of an uncomfortable way of life. I soon discovered in myself a decided taste for that way of life, as the sense of daring that the tamer liberty of Wales had given me flowered into a pure, hot passion for freedom. If Mycroft's hidden purpose was to provide us with an exotic form of holiday, it certainly succeeded.

Not that we were under his control, or even supervision: Mycroft's name opened a few doors for us and smoothed some passages, but travelling under his cachet did not mean that we were under his protection. Indeed, our pursuits in the Holy Land took us into some quite interesting situations. However, the dangers we faced (aside from the microbial and insectoidal), although immediate and personal (particularly for Holmes, who at one point fell into unfriendly hands), were also refreshingly direct and without subtlety.

Both of us took injuries, but neither seriously. Indeed, other than being shot at by a strikingly incompetent marksman out in the desert and later set upon by thugs just outside the Church of the Holy Sepulchre, my own most uncomfortable moment was when I was cornered by a trio of amorous and intoxicated merchants in the Arab Quarter. Even the revelation of the quantity of hair beneath my turban did not give them much pause, as they seemed equally willing to pursue a woman as the young man they had thought me. I nearly committed murder that day—not on the merchants, but on Holmes, for the highly amused reluctance with which he came to my assistance.

As I said, I found this combination of unreality and hazard immensely appealing, and indeed it gave me a lasting taste for what is called Intelligence (which is not to be confused with Wisdom, being, in fact, often completely devoid of sense). At the time all I thought about was that we were safe from our shadowy pursuer, and that Mycroft was proving a powerful if enigmatic ally.

This is not the place to burden the reader with a detailed (that is, book-length) account of our expedition to Palestine, for, although it had its own distinct points of interest, it had almost no bearing on the case that had sent us there. It was an excursus, the chief benefit of which was that it enabled us to reconsider the balance in our relationship, and to come to a decision about how our case at home was to be handled, while Mycroft and Lestrade were assembling data for us. That our time of exile changed my life personally, that it endowed me with a sense of the texture of history that has stayed with me to this day, that it moved me to profound wonder and joy and fury, that the sense of Palestine as a refuge made me a Jew more than any one thing apart from the accident of my birth—all these have proven to be of lasting interest to me personally, but of peripheral interest to this particular narrative.

Nor shall I subject the reader to a travelogue of that most remarkable of lands. We stayed for a few days in a mud hut near Jaffa, getting our bearings and perfecting our disguises (which Holmes had used before, in Mecca) before setting off south. We moved into the empty desolation of nomadic peoples and ruined monasteries, where the desert shimmered even in January. We walked and rode across the wilderness to the Salt Sea, and in the dark before the moon rose we floated in its remarkable buoyant waters, and I felt the light of the stars on my naked body. We went north and touched the crumbling remains of mosaic pavements, the delicate stone fishes and twining grape clusters, and walked among the massive remains of temple walls and the more recent remains from Allenby's victories. We slept under Bedouin tents that stank of goat, in caves cut into the hillsides, on warm, flat roofs under the stars, in feather beds in a pasha's palace, under an Army lorry, under a fisherman's skiff, and under nothing but the sky. We drank cold, sour lemonade with Jews in a Zionist settlement, hot, syrupy mint tea with a Bedouin sheikh, and Earl Grey with tinned milk in the house of a high-ranking Army officer in Haifa. We bathed (far too seldom for my taste—there are drawbacks in being disguised as a male, and one of them is public bathing) in a bubbling spring above Cana of Galilee, in a smooth stretch of the Jordan surrounded by barbed wire (under the disapproving gaze of a kingfisher), and in the tin hip bath of an English archaeologist in Jericho, whose passion for preserving her site was matched only by her extreme Zionism.

(She was, incidentally, the only person I have ever met who, seeing me in disguise, knew me immediately and matter-of-factly for what I was. She greeted us with a furious barrage of words from the bottom of her trench, established that we were not about to carry off her beloved potsherds, marched us off to her remarkable home, which resembled a low Bedouin tent made of scrap wood and corrugated iron, and closeted me in a windowless room with concrete walls and an endless supply of gloriously hot water. Holmes she allowed to sluice off under a bucket of cold water in the courtyard.)

We—I—left Jerusalem until nearly the end, circling around it on our way north, coming tantalisingly close twice and shying away, until finally we walked the long dry hills up to the city in the company of a group of Bedouins and their emaciated goats and stood, burnt black and footsore and absolutely filthy (even the normally catlike Holmes) on the crest of Mount Olivet at sundown. There before us she rose up, the city of cities, the *umbilicus mundi*, centre of the Universe, growing from the very foundations of the earth, surprisingly small, like a jewel. My heart sang within me, and the ancient Hebrew came to my lips.

"*Simchu eth Yerushalaim w'gilu bah kal-ohabeha,*" I recited: Rejoice with Jerusalem and be glad for her, all you who love her. We watched the sun set and slept among the tombs overnight, to the consternation of our guides, and in the morning we saw the sun lay tender arms around the city walls and bring her to brilliant, vibrant life. I rejoiced, and I was inexpressibly grateful.

We sat until the sun set the white-gold walls to blazing and dust rose from the road, and we went across and entered the city. For three days we walked her narrow streets, ate food from her bazaars, breathed the incense of her churches. We touched her walls and tasted her dust, and in the end we came away changed, to watch the winter sun relinquish her to the night. We then shouldered our packs and turned our backs on her.

As the sky moved from thick cobalt to limitless black, we walked north, then stopped, made our two fires and pitched our three tents, drew water from a cistern, cooked and ate the inevitable tough goat's meat that seemed to be Ali and Mahmoud's staple diet, and drank tiny cups of Mahmoud's coffee, thick as honey and nearly as sweet, which he boiled and poured and we strained through our teeth. The fires burnt low and our guides went to their beds, and in communicative silence Holmes and I respectively smoked and searched for constellations. When the embers had become mere flecks in the blackness, and the vault of the sky was pierced by a million points of hard white light, I was moved uncharacteristically to song, and with the warmth of the fire on the underside of my throat I chanted to the stars the hymns of Exile, the songs distilled from the longings of a people torn from their land, taken from the home of their God, and left to weep within the boundaries of the conqueror, Babylon, a hundred generations ago.

My voice fell silent. On a distant hilltop jackals set up their eerie chorus of yelps. Somewhere an engine rose, faded. A cock crew. Eventually, filled with that serenity that comes only with a decision reached or a task well completed, I rose to go to my tent. Holmes stretched out to knock his pipe bowl into the fire.

"I must thank you for bringing me here, Russell. It has been a most instructive interlude."

"There is one more place in this country that I wish to see," I told him. "We shall pass through it on our way to Acre. Good night, Holmes."

TWO DAYS LATER we sat atop a windy hill and looked out across the blood-soaked Plain of Esdraelon. General Allenby had caught the fleeing Turkish army here four months before; the Crusaders had met with calamitous defeat here 730 years earlier; various armies across the last three thousand years had struggled here for control over the narrow north-south passage that joins Egypt and Africa with the continents of Europe and Asia. The plain's Mount Megiddo, Ar Megiddo, has given its name to the site of the ultimate battle: Armageddon will begin here. It is a crossroads, and it is fertile: a deadly combination. That evening, however, the only violence was the sound of a dog barking and the distant clamour of goat bells. Tomorrow we would begin to make our way to the Crusader fortress at Acre, where the boat was to meet us and carry us back to the cold of an English January and a resumption of our struggle against an unknown foe. A wearying prospect, seen while sitting here with the setting sun on our backs, the tents flapping gently in the breeze. The past weeks had been a thing apart, and only obliquely had we referred to the events that had driven us here. I knew that Holmes had chafed at being forced to allow others to do his footwork for him, even if the other was his brother Mycroft, but he had managed to control his impatience well. Finally, on that hillock overlooking the battleground, I reached out for the avoided topic and placed it firmly between us.

"So, Holmes. London awaits us."

"She does, Russell, she does indeed." There was a sudden light in his grey eyes that I had not seen in some weeks, the anticipation of a hound long denied the hunt, and I did not think the "she" referred to the city.

"What is your plan?"

He put his hand inside his dingy robes and withdrew his pipe and tobacco pouch.

"First, tell me why you have brought us here."

"To Jezreel? I told you my mother's name, I believe."

"Yes, it was Judith, was it not? Not Mary McCarthy. Refresh my memory of the story, Russell. I try to forget things that I will not need in my work, and tales from the Bible normally fall into that category."

I smiled grimly. "Perhaps this is one story you may see a use for, Holmes. It is one my mother and I read when I was seven. She was the granddaughter of a rabbi, a small woman, quiet, possessed of a remarkable wisdom. Although the story is Apocryphal rather than from the Hebrew canon, she chose this as the first story we studied together because she did not believe that religion should be an easy thing. Also, it involves her namesake."

"The Judith and Holofernes story."

"It happened here, or at any rate the story was set here, in a small town astride the Jerusalem road that we have just come up. Holofernes was the commander of an army from out of the north, sent to punish Jerusalem. This little town barred his way, so he cut off its water and laid siege to it. After thirty-four days the townspeople gave God an ultimatum: Provide water within five days, or we stand aside and Jerusalem can have this army.

"Judith, a wise, upstanding, wealthy young widow, was disgusted with them. She put on her richest clothes, summoned her maid, and left the town to walk out to Holofernes' camp. She told him she wished to be saved from the coming destruction and paraded herself around in front of him for a few days. He, of course, invited her to his tent. She got him drunk, he passed out, and she cut off his head and took it back with her to the town. The invasion fell apart, Jerusalem was saved, and two and a half thousand years later women named for her give their children nightmares with the story."

"A stimulating tale, Russell, though hardly one that I should choose for a seven-year-old."

"My mother believed in starting theological training early. The following year we did the Levite's concubine, which makes the Judith story sound like a nursery rhyme. Still, that is why I wanted to come here, to see where Holofernes arrayed his troops. Does that answer your question?"

He sighed. "I'm afraid so. Then you did see what I was thinking, on the boat?"

"I could hardly miss it."

"And you offer this as an alternative." He waved one hand at the darkening plain.

"Yes." I would not consider the implications, not until I had to.

"No. I am sorry, Russell, but I will not have you place yourself within the enemy camp. I do not believe that you would find this opponent of ours an obliging drunkard."

"I won't be sacrificed, though, Holmes. I refuse to abandon you." I was relieved, but all the same I would not be a coward.

"I am not suggesting that you abandon me, Russell, only that you appear to do so." He rose and went to his tent and came back with a familiar wooden box in his hand. He set out the pieces as they had been in the game we had played off Crete, before my queen had fallen. He then turned the board around to take possession of the black. This time it was I who captured his queen, I who pressed and chivvied him into a corner. The game shifted, however, for I knew his intentions and refused to be drawn in.

The moves lengthened, slowed, as our two diminutive armies clashed. Pieces fell and were removed from the field of battle. The first stars emerged unnoticed, Ali brought over a small oil lamp and set it on a rock between us, and Holmes laid a pincers movement that took my second bishop. I took a rook (a hollow victory; Holmes scorned their stolid directness) and two moves later lost one to his knight. (Holmes' knights were terrible weapons when a certain mood was upon him, more like Boadicea's bladed chariot with its wholesale mowing-down of men than a proper knight on horseback.) Mahmoud pressed tiny cups of syrupy coffee into our hands, watched the board for a time without comment, and went off.

It was a long game. I knew that he intended to duplicate my surprise victory, when I allowed the queen to fall in order to set up a trap in the hands of the commoners, but I refused to be manoeuvered. I drew him out, I kept away from his pawns, and used my queen with great caution, and eventually he seemed to change his tactics and laid another triangle of pincers to drive me into. I danced away from it, he relaid it farther back on the board. Again I avoided it and sent my remaining rook down to place him into check. He evaded it, I brought up my queen in support, and then somehow in the excitement of closing in I overlooked the board in front of me, and the pawn that had been weak man in the first, long-forgotten pincers movement was in my second rank, and then it was before me, newly born a queen.

"*Regina redivivus*," Holmes commented sardonically, and proceeded to tear into the unprotected back side of my offence like a hailstorm through peach blossoms. I fell before his resurrected queen in a complete rout, was mated in half a dozen moves, and then it was my turn to laugh quietly and shake my head before I sobered.

"Holmes, she'll never fall for it," I objected.

"She will, you know, if the distraction is believable enough. The woman is proud and scornful, and her anger at our absence will make her incautious and all too willing to believe that Sherlock Holmes has failed to preserve his queen, that poor old Holmes stands alone, exposed and helpless." He reached out and rocked the crown of the black king with the tip of his finger. "She will swoop in to pick me off," he tapped the white queen, "and then, we have her." He picked up the black pawn and rolled it around in his hands as if to warm it, and when he opened his hands the black queen lay there. He put her back onto the board and sat back with the air of a man concluding a lengthy and delicate business negotiation. "It is good," he pronounced, "really very good." His eyes gleamed in the last flicker of the lamp's wick, with a curious, intense relish such as I had seen on his face the week before, when he was facing a young assailant with a large knife. *Joie de combat*, I supposed, and my heart quailed before this changed Holmes.

"It's dangerous, Holmes," I protested, "really very dangerous. What if she sees what we're doing? What if she doesn't play by the rules and just decides to wipe us both out? What if—" What if I fail? a voice wailed inside me.

"What if, what if. Of course it's dangerous, Russell, but I can hardly spend the rest of my life rusticating in Palestine or tripping over bodyguards, can I?" He sounded quite pleased about it, but now that the time had come, I wanted to hide.

"We don't know what she'll do," I cried. "At least let Lestrade provide some guards at the beginning. Or Mycroft, if you don't want Scotland Yard in on it, until we know how she's going to react."

"We may as well put an advertisement in *The Times* to inform her of our intentions," he scoffed. "You ought to take up fencing, Russell, truly you should. It offers a most instructive means of judging your adversary. You see, Russell, I have a feel for my opponent now, I know her style and her reach. She has made some points off me in the game thus far, but she has also revealed her own faults. Her attacks have all been patterned on her perception of my nature, my skill at the game. When we return, she will expect me to continue dodging and parrying with my customary subtlety and skill. She knows that I will do so, but . . . I shall not. Instead, I shall foolishly lower my blade and walk unguarded into her. She will stand back for a moment, to see what I am doing. She will be suspicious, then gradually convinced of my madness, then gloating before she strikes. But you, Russell," he swept his robed arm over the board, and when he drew it back the black queen stood in the place of the white bolt-and-nut king. "You will be waiting for her all the time, and you will strike first."

Dear God. I had wanted more responsibility, and here it was, with a vengeance. I worked to control my voice.

"Holmes, it is no false modesty to say that I haven't the experience in this—this 'game,' as you insist on calling it. A mistake on my part could be fatal. We must have a back-up."

"I shall think about it," he said finally, and then he leant forward over the chessboard and looked into my eyes with that same curious intensity that he had shown earlier. "However, I want you to realise, Russell, that I know your abilities, better than you do. After all, I have trained you. For nearly four years I have shaped you and tempered you and honed you, and I know the mettle you are made from. I know your strengths and weaknesses, particularly after these last weeks. The things we have done in this country have honed you, but the steel was there to begin with. I do not regret my decision to come here with you, Russell.

"If you truly feel that you cannot do this, then I shall accept that decision. I will not consider it a failure on your part. It will merely mean that you join Watson while I enlist Mycroft's help. It would be inferior, I admit—inelegant, and I think long, but not hopeless. It is, however, your choice entirely."

His words were placid, but what lay beneath them shook me breathless, for what he was proposing would in another man be sheer recklessness. Holmes the painstaking, Holmes the thoughtful, calculating thinker, Holmes the solitary operator who never so much as consulted another for advice, this Holmes I thought I knew was now proposing to launch himself into the abyss, trusting absolutely in *my* ability to catch *him*.

And more even than that: This self-contained individual, this man who had rarely allowed even his sturdy, ex-Army companion Watson to confront real risk, who had habitually over the past four years held back, been cautious, kept an eye out, and otherwise protected me; this man who was a Victorian gentleman down to his boots; this man was now proposing to place not only his life and limb into my untested, inexperienced, and above all female hands, but my own life as well. This was the change I had noticed in him and puzzled about, the intensity and relish with which he was facing the coming combat:

There was no hesitation left. He had let go all doubt, and was telling me in crystal-clear terms that he was prepared to treat me as his complete, full, and unequivocal equal, if that was what I wished. He was giving me not only his life, but my own.

I had long known the intellect of this man, been aware for nearly as long of his humanity and the greatness of his heart, but I had never had demonstrated to me so clearly that the size of his spirit was equal to his mind. The knowledge rumbled through me like an earthquake, and in its wake a small voice echoed, wondering if I had just pronounced his epitaph.

I don't know how long it was before I looked up from the small carved queen into the carved-looking features of the man across from me, but when I did, it seemed that his eyebrows were waiting for something. I had to think for a moment before I realised that he had actually asked a question. But there was no decision to be made.

"When faced with the unthinkable," I said shakily, "one chooses the merely impossible." He smiled approvingly, warmly.

And then a miracle happened.

Holmes reached out his long arms to me and, like a frightened child, I went inside them, and he held me, awkwardly at first, then more easily, until my trembling faded. I sat, safe, listening to the steady beat of his heart until the oil lamp guttered out and left us in darkness.

TWO DAYS LATER the Crusader walls of Acre closed in on us, as unlike the sun-swept stones of Jerusalem, eighty miles away, as could be imagined. Jerusalem's golden walls had sparkled and shone, and the city vibrated with an inaudible song of joy and pain, but Acre's walls were heavy and thick, and its song was a multilingual dirge of ignorance and death. The long shadows seemed like spectres to be avoided, and I noticed Holmes glancing about him sharply. Ali and Mahmoud, in their customary place four strides ahead of us, seemed as unaware of the gloom as they were of anything outside themselves, but even they edged towards the middle of the streets as if the walls were unclean. I tried to push away the mood, but it crept back stubbornly.

"I wonder if these stones would speak with such a bleak voice if I didn't know what the place stood for," I said to Holmes irritably.

"To a mind attuned to observation and deduction, the product reveals the mind of its creator." He squinted up at the great, ponderous blocks that loomed up to hide the sky, and rubbed his hands together slowly. "Take Mozart—frenzied gaiety and weeping put to music. The agony of the man is at times unbearable. Let us go."

We made our way through the streets down to the water, and when we turned a final corner, Ali and Mahmoud had disappeared. I felt shockingly naked without those two swathed backs billowing along in front of me, heads together, but Holmes just smiled and nudged me ahead. As we went past a wooden door set into a wall he spoke into the air.

"*Marhaba,*" he said, and to my surprise added, "*ᶜAlla-M'āq.*"

I echoed his thanks, and the blessing, and we went on to the edge of the water, and we sat drinking mint tea from a nearby stall and watched the waves rub at the remnants of the Crusader pier until dark, when we were found by the crew member who had taken us ashore at Jaffa the month before. Our backs were to the fortress as he rowed us noiselessly towards the waiting boat, our faces turned to England.

We stood on the deck and watched the last lights of Palestine fade. Jerusalem was hidden from sight, but to my eyes there was a faint glow in the southeast, as of stored sunlight. I recited under my breath,

"*ᶜAl naharoth babel sham yashavnu gam-bakinu . . .*
Im eshkahek Yerushalaim tishkah y'mini. . . ."

"You sang that the other night, did you not?" asked Holmes. "What is it?"

"A psalm, one of the more powerful Hebrew songs, full of sibilants and gutturals." I translated it for him.

> "By the waters of Babylon, where we lay down and wept when
> 	we remembered Zion . . . We hung up our lyres,
> for our captors required songs of us, and our tormentors
> 	demanded mirth.
> How can we sing the Lord's song in a strange land?
> If I forget you, Jerusalem, may my right hand wither,
> May my tongue cleave to the roof of my mouth, if I do not
> 	remember you."

"Amen," he murmured, surprising me again.

The land receded to a smear of lights against greater darkness, and we went below.

Book Four

MASTERY

Battle Is Joined

❧ 14 ❧

The Act Begins

Isolate her, and however abundant the food or favourable
the temperature, she will expire in a few days not of hunger
or cold, but of loneliness.

THE SHIP'S ENGINES picked up in pitch even before we
reached the common cabin, and the powerful movement beneath our feet told of some speed. I made for the bath and gratefully
shed my dust-thick, sweat-stiff, pungent, threadbare clothing. One
hour and three changes of water later I arose transformed: my nails
pink and white, my hair freed at last from its concealing wraps, my
skin tingling and alive. I slipped on the long, embroidered kaftan I had
bought in the *suq* in Nablus and, feeling positively sensuous as I glided
across the floor, a female again in my loose clothing after weeks of
squatting, striding, and scratching, I went to make a large pot of English tea. Holmes had bathed elsewhere and sat reading *The Times*,
dressed in a clean shirt and dressing gown as if he had never gone

unshaven, never slept wrapped in goatskins, never concerned himself with the local fauna taking up residence in his scalp. I picked up a delicate bone china cup and laughed silently in sheer delight.

There came a knock at the door, and the captain's voice.

"Good evening, Mr. Holmes," I heard. "Permission to enter?"

"Come in, Jones, come in."

"I trust you had a satisfactory stay in Palestine, sir?" the captain said.

"Simple pleasures for simple minds," Holmes murmured. His words actually startled the good captain into a reaction, causing him to run an experienced eye over the fading green-yellow bruises on Holmes' face and glance for a moment at the neat bandage peeking out from the sleeve of my kaftan. He even went so far as to open his mouth on a comment, but before he could lose control so completely he made a visible effort, snapped his jaws shut, and then turned to close the door. Holmes glanced at me with an expression that looked suspiciously like mischief.

"And you, Captain Jones," he said. "I hope you have had a successful January, though I see you haven't spent too much of it aboard ship. How was France? Rebuilding already, I see." Silence fell, and as I came out of the galley I saw a familiar look of wary perplexity on the captain's face.

"How do you know where I've been? Oh, sorry: Evenin', Miss." He touched his cap.

"No major mystery, Jones. Your skin tells me that you've spent no great time in the sun since you left us, and your new hair pomade and the watch on your wrist tell me you have spent a day in Paris. Don't worry," he said with a chuckle, "I haven't had spies on you. Just my own eyes."

"I'm glad to hear that, Mr. Holmes. If I thought you'd been nosing about I'd be forced to have some gentlemen ask you a few hard questions. Not to offend, sir, it'd just be my job."

"I understand, Jones, and I am careful to see only those things that tell me of unimportant activities."

"That's probably for the best, sir. Oh yes, this packet is for you. It was sent by a courier from London last week, into my own hands—in Paris, in fact." I was standing close to him and reached out for it, but Holmes' voice cut in, sharp, scathing, and utterly authoritative.

"Not to Miss Russell, Jones. This and any future official conveyances will be delivered personally to me, and to me alone. Do you understand, Captain Jones?"

In the cabin's shocked silence Holmes rose and walked forward, coldly took the packet from the captain's hand, and went to open it by the window. Jones stared at his back for a moment, then looked at me in open amazement. A flush of shame crept into my face, and I turned abruptly and went into my cabin, slamming the door. A minute later I heard the outer door close behind the captain. We had begun our play.

In a few minutes I heard two light taps on my door. I stood and went to the window before responding. "Come in, Holmes."

"Russell, this packet is most—ah. I see. The mind was willing but the heart taken aback, I take it?" How he could discern my distress from looking at my spine, I cannot think.

"No, no, it was just the suddenness of it, it took me unawares." I turned to face him. "I was not expecting to begin the act so quickly. However, perhaps it is for the best. The captain is now aware that something is amiss, and I doubt that I could have acted that particular scene. I'm not exactly Sarah Bernhardt." My smile was a bit forced.

"It was indeed most convincing. I fear there will be any number of painful moments before this act is over."

"The lines are written; we must speak them," I said dismissively. "Now, what were you saying about Mycroft's packet?"

"Here, look for yourself. Our adversary has been most prudent. I am filled with admiration for her technique. Were it not that she presses so close in on me, I should relish this case greatly, for I cannot remember one in which such a large number of clues led absolutely nowhere. I think I shall go and fill my pipe."

The packet was a thick one. I put aside for later reading the five fat envelopes with Mrs. Hudson's writing and stamps from various ports of call, and looked at Mycroft's offering. Numerous pages from the laboratories at Scotland Yard described the prints on the cab, the button with its attached bit of tweed, and the analysis of the three bombs, one in grisly detail. It was the description of the hive bomb that illuminated the most, and in fact changed the entire picture. The investigation had found that the charge was ignited, not by Holmes' clumsiness, but by a hair-thin wire that ran from the hive he had been checking, hidden beneath the grass, to the bomb in the next hive. Mycroft's men had found it in the wreckage.

"She never meant to kill you, then!"

"I was glad to see that. The problem had troubled me. Oh, not her murder attempt, but that mine was the first. The whole point of killing you and Watson, as I read it, was to hurt me, but how could I be hurt by your deaths if I were already dead? I was very pleased to see that explained by the trigger. It also confirms that you shall be safe if we appear alienated. I shall have to arrange for a discreet guard for Mrs. Hudson when she returns from Australia, but Watson's protection we shall continue to leave to Mycroft."

The rest of the pages were interesting, but not as important as the fact of the wire trigger. The prints on the intact Oxford bomb were those of the deceased man, and his alone. The cab's prints included those of Holmes, myself, and Billy, its owner and another driver (both of whom Lestrade had interviewed and released), and two others, one of whom had a thumbprint matching the one on the button. This gentleman was well-known to the police record books and was soon apprehended. His colleague made an escape out the back window of his house and was rumoured to have fled to America. The large man in custody was being charged with all the injuries done to Billy and to the cab, but Lestrade was of the opinion that the man would not be threatened into revealing anything concerning his employer. "He does not appear frightened of retribution," wrote Lestrade, "simply very firm in his refusal, despite threats of a long prison term for the assault. It should be noted that his wife and their two teenaged sons have recently moved into a new house and seem to have an income from outside. Their bank account does not reflect any great change, but they have significant quantities of cash to spend. Thus far enquiries have been without result."

I looked up at Holmes through his cloud of grey smoke.

"We have another family man in our group, I see."

"Read on, the plot thickens quickly."

The Yard's next document concerned the dead man, John Dickson, who had bombed Dr. Watson's house. He had indeed been apparently reformed, living happily, to all appearances, with his wife and children and working in his father-in-law's music business. About six weeks before the trio of bombs, he had come into a comfortable inheritance, from a distant relative who had died in New York. According to his widow, he had told her that the inheritance was to be in two parts, of equal size, the second to be received within four or five months. He began talking about University for the young children, and the surgery one of them needed on a crippled leg, and they planned a trip to France the following summer. However, shortly after the first sum of money arrived, he began to become secretive. He put a lock on a back shed and spent hours in there. (The investigation revealed traces of the explosive powder used and clipped ends of wire such as the Oxford bomb had preserved.) He disappeared occasionally for one or two days, returning travel-stained and weary, but oddly excited. He had left the house on a Saturday night in the middle of December, saying that he should be away for several days, but that after this trip he should not have to leave again. The wife and her father tried to persuade him not to go, it being a very busy time of year for the shop, but he was adamant.

In the early hours of Thursday morning he was killed by the bomb, apparently a result of the timing mechanism having been tampered with. One week later a bank draught was received in the wife's name, drawn from a bank in New York. Police there found that the account had been opened some weeks before by a woman who had brought in cash for the purpose. An odd afternote was that the amount of the second payment was exactly twice what the first had been, rather than an equal amount as Dickson had anticipated. The two draughts depleted the account, which was closed. Lestrade concluded by noting that although it was irregular, there was no way to prove that the money was connected to the bombing; therefore, it looked as though the widow would be allowed to keep it.

"What do you make of that second payment, Holmes? Guilt pangs?"

"Cleanliness has affected your brain, Russell. Clearly the murder was premeditated."

"Yes, of course. The original amount was what had been planned for. But possibly not by Dickson."

"Make a note, Russell, to ask Lestrade about Dickson's state of mind at the time of death."

"You are thinking that it might have been suicide? In exchange for a payment to the family?"

"Whatever it is, it adds an interesting facet to our foe's personality. She is a person with international connexions, or so the large quantity of American currency would tend to indicate, yet she carries through on her agreement with a dead man. On top of everything else we know about her, she's a murderer with a sense of honour. Most subtle."

I returned to the packet, which included a faint carbon copy of the bomb report, highly technical and couched in police English, several large, glossy photographs of the cab and the Ladies', and a letter from Mycroft. I glanced at the first, set aside the photographs, and began to read Mycroft's cramped but remarkably impersonal handwriting. The first part of the letter was concerned with the bomb: He agreed that it had been Dickson's work, adding that although the toggle detonator had been manufactured in America before 1909, it had apparently been exposed to London's corrosive air for some many months. He went on to address the problem of the marksman who had shot at us in Scotland Yard, who may or may not have been the same gentleman whom the mother pushing her pram across the bridge had witnessed bundling an elaborate contraption like a street photographer's camera, complete with hood and, in this case, wheels, into the backseat of a waiting taxicab and squealing off. Concerning this he wrote:

I perceive a distinct odour of red herring, as with the fleeing steam-launch, which we discovered was hired—anonymously, with cash—to make off at all speed immediately the captain heard a sound "like a shot."

Concerning the identity of your lady pursuer (continued Mycroft) very little has appeared, but for the following: Three days ago on my way to the Club, an unbelievably unsavoury character with the physiognomy of a toad—and something of the colour—sidled up to me in a manner meant, no doubt, to appear casual, and muttered out of the corner of his flat lips that he had a message for my brother. (I do wish that you might arrange for these persons to send letters. I suppose they are illiterate. Might they be instructed in the use of the telephone?) The sum total of his message was, and I quote: Lefty says there's Glasgow Rangers with buckets of bees in town, the pitch and toss is somebody's Trouble. End quote.

I thought this might be of interest to you.

Incidentally, heartiest congratulations on the success of your Palestinian episode, no more than I expected from you, but the Minister and the PM are immensely grateful. I suppose that when your name finds its way onto next year's lists you will wish me to arrange for its removal. This becomes tedious, and I gather that before too long I shall be doing the same for Miss Russell.

I trust this finds you and your companion well. I anticipate your return (with something of the eager interest of a fox outside a henhouse into which he has seen saunter a cat).

Mycroft

I tore my eyes from the intimations of the penultimate paragraph and looked up from the missive.

"Glasgow Rangers? Buckets of bees?"

"Cockney rhyming slang. Strangers, with a great deal of money— bees and honey—and the boss is somebody's 'trouble and strife.' Wife. A woman."

I nodded thoughtfully, put down the letter, and took up the photographs to lay them out on the low table in front of the sofa, and began to study them carefully. The photographer had taken two full sets of the interior of the cab, the first as it had been originally, the second after I had removed my scraps. With a pang I remembered the pleasure the green silk dress had brought me as I saw a portion of its cuff in one photograph.

"What was the point of this destruction, Holmes? Why attack the clothes, and not us? Even Billy wasn't badly hurt, just parked to one side. Do you mind if I open the window a bit?"

"It is a bit thick in here, isn't it? That's good. Better close it in a minute or two, though, we don't want our voices heard. Why indeed, as you say, might a foe be content with a few clothes and the seat cushions of an old cab? Except to show us that she knew where we were, and that she could as easily have done the same to our bodies as your clothes. And finally, to thumb her nose at me by pulling my own trick of leaving reversed footsteps, and topping it off with Baker Street mud. It was a demonstration, no doubt about that, but was that all? I think not. Look closely at the slashes on the seats, there." He arranged the last set of photographs so that they overlapped, to place the seats in a continuous line. "Do you see something?"

I looked at the shredded seats, the cuts that crossed, met at their lower ends, and ran parallel. I laid my spectacles to one side and squinted hard at the clear black and grey images. "Is there a pattern?" I asked, hearing the excitement in my voice. "Hand me that pencil and pad, would you, Holmes?" The first two cuts crossed each other in the middle, and I wrote an X on my pad. The next two met at the lower edge of the seat, a V. After some minutes and discussion with

Holmes, I had a string of Xs, Vs, and straight lines on my pad that looked like this:

XVXVIIXXIIXIIXXIIXXIVXXXI

"Roman numerals?" I wondered. "Does this mean anything to you?" I asked Holmes, whose steely eyes were studying the page intently. I could see that it did not, so I put on my glasses and sat back.

"A string of twenty-five Roman numbers. Do they add up to something?" I did the simple sum in my head, ten plus five plus ten and so on. "One hundred forty-five, if they make up twenty-five separate numbers. Of course, they could say fifteen, seventeen, twenty-two, twelve, and so forth."

"What would that come to?"

"There won't be much difference, because of the nature of Roman numerals, but it comes to, let's see—143."

"Interesting. And the number between them is 144, a dozen dozen."

"And the two sums added together make 288, which is the number of dollars my father had in his desk when he died. Holmes, these numbers games could go on forever."

"What if we translated the numbers into letters, one of the more simplistic codes?"

We scribbled and thought, but came up with nothing. Reading it as 15, 17, 22, 12, 22, 24, 20, 11 yielded gibberish as OQVLVXTK, and no other combination made any sense either. I finally pushed it away.

"There are just too many variables, Holmes. Without a key we can't even know if it's a word, or the combination to a safe, or a map coordinate, or—"

"Yet she left it for us to find. Where could she have put the key?"

"Judging from her previous style, I should say that the key is both hidden and completely obvious, which is always the most effective means of hiding something."

It was very late now, and my eyes felt gritty. I picked up the conversation where we had left it before the slash pattern had appeared.

"I agree that she was demonstrating her cleverness. She won a number of points in that round. I wonder what her next move might have been had we not been spirited away by Mycroft. Cutting off Watson's nose to show that she could have taken his head?"

"More to the point, what will her move be now, when we walk openly home? For how long will her wariness last before she thinks it is perhaps not a trap, that we truly are divided and the trauma of it has made me an empty wreck? Mere extermination is not what she wants, apparently. She wishes to ruin me first. Very well, we'll give her that, and wait for her to move."

He carefully inserted the papers and photographs back into their oversized envelope and stood looking down at me.

"Well, Russell. Thank you for showing me Palestine. It may be a long, long time before we are able to speak freely. I shall say good night, and good-bye, and we will meet when the prey takes the bait and comes into our trap." His lips gently brushed my forehead, and he was gone.

THUS BEGAN OUR act of alienation. Holmes and I had only a few days to perfect our rôles of the two friends now turned against each other, the father and daughter alienated, the near-lovers become bitterest, most implacable of enemies. It takes time to develop a part, as all actors know, time and an exploration of the nuances and quirks of the person being played. We had to be word-perfect before we reached England for the trap to be effective. We had to assume that we were being watched at every moment, and a slight slip of affection could be disastrous.

It is a truism of the actor's art that one can play only oneself on the stage. To be fully effective the actor must have a sympathy for the character's motives, however unsympathetic they might appear to an outsider. To a large extent, the actor must become the character if the act is to be effective, and that is what Holmes and I did. From the time we rose in the morning we did not *play* enemies, we *were* enemies. When we met it was with icy politeness that rapidly disintegrated into vicious attacks. I grew into the rôle of the young student who had come to view her old teacher with withering scorn. Holmes responded with malevolent counterattacks and the full strength of his razor-sharp sarcasm. We cut each other with our tongues and bled and crawled off to the sanctuary of our individual cabins and came back for more.

The first day was technically difficult, keeping up the persona in front of my real face, continually thinking, What might I do at this point if I really were this way? and How ought I respond to that? It was exhausting, and I went to bed early. The second day it quickly became easier. Holmes never looked out from behind his mask, and mine too was now firmly in place. I went to my room early to read but found it difficult to concentrate. My mind wandered off. What on earth was I doing here? I ought to be in Oxford, not on this boat. I had no business taking off this time of year. Even basic work was impossible in this battleground. Perhaps the captain might let me off in France and I could take the train home. Probably be faster, and certainly more restful. I wonder—

I jerked to attention, horrified. These were not the thoughts of an actor; this was the character thinking. I had become, for a moment, the person I had played throughout the day. I sat appalled at the implications: If this could happen after less than forty-eight hours of play-acting, what would happen after days and weeks of it? Would I be able to shut it off at will? Or, my God, would it become a habit too firm to break? "For what will it profit a man, if he gains the whole world and forfeits his life?" Wouldn't a nice clean bomb be better than losing Holmes? A malevolent voice seemed to murmur beneath the engine throb.

"If I forget thee, Jerusalem, may my right hand lose its cunning." I went out into the common room for some brandy, and Holmes passed me silently as he went into his room. I stood in the dark, looking out at the black sea until the glass was empty, and went back to the hallway. Holmes had left his door slightly ajar, and my steps slowed. I stopped and let my shoulder and head come to rest against the wall, not looking in at the segment of his room that was available to my eyes.

"Holmes?"

"Yes, Russell."

"Holmes, when you have acted a part for some days, do you find it hard to drop it?"

"It can be difficult to shake off a part, yes." His voice was calm, conversational. "When I spent a week working on the docks on a case many years ago, the day after the man was arrested I dressed and went out at the usual time, and walked clear down to Oxford Street before I came to myself. Yes, a part can become habitual. Had you not realised that risk?"

"Not completely."

"You are doing well, Russell. It becomes easier as time passes."

"That is precisely what I am afraid of, Holmes," I whispered. "How long before the part becomes so natural that it is no longer a part? How am I to maintain my objectivity, to watch for signs that the opponent is opening herself up, if I become the part?"

"When the time comes, you will do it. I have faith in you, Russ."

His easy words brought me an element of stability, calm within the storm. "I am glad you have faith in me, Holmes," I said drily. "I bow to your superior experience."

I could feel his smile through the door.

"I shall send you messages from time to time while you are up at Oxford. Obvious ones, for the most part, though if I have the opportunity to send a secure one, I shall do so. You, of course, will write occasionally to Mrs. Hudson when she returns from Australia, and she will leave the letters lying about pointedly."

"You think it will be safe to allow her to return to Sussex?"

"I do not know how I should keep her away. Mycroft had practically to kidnap her to get her on the ship in the first place; Mrs. Hudson is a very determined woman. No, we shall simply have to take on one or two extra servants. Mycroft's agents, of course."

"Poor Mrs. Hudson. She'll be so upset when she finds we've quarrelled."

"Yes. But Mycroft will be a safe liaison. There's no hiding anything from Mycroft. I fear our alienation will also cause considerable pain to Dr. Watson. I can only hope it will not wind on for too many months."

"You think it could go on so long?" Oh, God.

"I believe our foe is a careful and patient individual. She will not act precipitously."

"You are right. As usual."

"Your aunt will be pleased, I fear. Your farm, of course, will necessitate the occasional trip to Sussex."

"No doubt it will." I thought for a moment. "Holmes, an automobile might come of considerable use in this adventure. However, I can no longer borrow money from Mrs. Hudson, and I doubt that my aunt would approve the expenditure. My allowance goes up this year, but not enough for that."

"I think Mycroft should be of help there, in persuading your trustees and the University offices that an automobile is a necessary item. You may even come to my farm once or twice, in attempts at reconciliation."

"Which will, of course, fail."

"Of course." I imagined the quick smile flitting across his features. "This is a good trap we're constructing, Russell, strong and simple. It only needs patience, patience and alertness to the prey's movements. We will catch her, Russell. She's no match for us. Go to sleep now."

"I believe I will. Thank you, Holmes."

I did go to bed, and eventually to sleep, but in the still hours that are neither night nor morning the Dream came for me, with a greater force than it had had in years. I came up from it to find myself huddled on the floor with my arms over my head, a shriek of complete hopelessness and terror echoing off the walls. All the old symptoms washed over me: cold, copious sweat, sour vomit in the back of my throat, heart bursting, lungs heaving. Then the door was flung open and Holmes was kneeling beside me with his strong hands on my shoulders.

"Russell, what is it?"

"Go away, go away, leave me alone." My voice was harsh and hurt my throat. I stood up and nearly fell, and his hands helped me to my bed. I sat with my head in my hands, pushing the dream back into its box, my body slowing. Over the pounding in my veins I was peripherally aware that Holmes was still beside me, tying the belt of his dressing gown, smoothing his hair back from his temples with both hands, and drilling the back of my skull with his gaze. Eventually he left off and went out of the room, but he did not close the door, and was back after a minute with a glass in one hand and his tobacco pouch in the other. He held out the glass.

"Drink this."

To my surprise it was not brandy, but water, cool, sweet water, sweeter than honey wine. I put the empty glass on the table with hands that were almost steady, and shivered from the drying sweat.

"Thank you, Holmes. Sorry I woke you. Again. You can go back to bed now."

"Pull the bedclothes over you, Russell; you'll take cold. I'll just sit for a moment, if you don't mind."

He brought a chair around to the head of my bed and sat down, crossed his pyjama-clad legs, and took out his pipe, and I curled up and listened to the old, familiar sounds of a pipe being filled and lit: the scrape and tap as he cleaned the bowl, the rustle of the tobacco pouch, the rattle of the matchbox, the quick scratch and flare of the match lighting, the suck of air drawing, and several quick puffs of his lips around the stem. The sharp smell of sulphur and the sweet wash of pipe tobacco filled the air, and Holmes sat and smoked, unobtrusively, undemandingly.

My wits gradually returned from the realm of Pan and, as they had a thousand times before, turned to the Dream. This upwelling of my subconscious had driven me to the works of Freud and Jung and the others of the European schools of psychoanalytic theory—countless hours of self-hypnosis, self-analysis, dream symbolism. I had analysed it, dissected it, thrown the full force of my mind against it. I even tried ignoring it. No matter what the approach, eventually there came another night when I was flung again into the hell and the agony of the thing.

The one thing I refused to try was telling someone about it. One morning my aunt had become too persistent in her questions about my "nightmares," and I had hit her in the face and knocked her to the floor. My neighbours in lodgings had commented on my nocturnal disturbances, and I had passed it off as studying too hard. The thought of telling someone, and having to see their face afterward, had always clamped my mouth down on the words, but now, to my exquisite horror and relief, I heard the words trickle from my mouth. Slowly at first, inexorably, they pushed themselves into the dim room.

"My brother—my brother was a genius. Reading by three, complex geometry by five. His potential was huge. He was nine when he died, five years younger than I. And I, I—killed him." My harsh voice faded, leaving the low sound of engines and the burble of the pipe. No reaction from Holmes. I turned onto my back and put my arm across my eyes, as if the hall light hurt them, but in truth it was that I couldn't bear to see his face as I told him this.

"I have this—this Dream. Only it's not a dream, it's a memory, every minute, tedious, horrible detail of it. We were in a car, you see, driving along the coast south of San Francisco. My father was going into the Army the following week. He had been rejected because of his bad leg, but finally he persuaded them to put him into—" I laughed bitterly. "You could guess this, I think—into Intelligence work. We were taking a last family weekend at our cabin in the woods, but I was—being difficult, as my mother put it. I was fourteen, and had wanted to go with some school friends to Yosemite, but had to go to the cabin instead. My brother was being particularly beastly, my mother was upset over Dad leaving, and Dad was distracted by business and the Army. A merry company, you see. Well, the road is bad there, and at several places it runs along the top of some cliffs over the Pacific. A drop of a couple hundred feet. To make a long story short, we were just coming up to one of these, with a blind corner to the left at the top of it, when I started screaming at my brother. My father turned around at the wheel to tell us to shut up, and the car drifted across the centre. There was another car coming around the corner, going very fast, and it hit us. Our car spun around, I was thrown out, and the last I saw was the outline of my brother's head through the back window as the car went over the side. Dad had just filled the petrol tank. There was nothing left of them. Any of them. They scraped together enough pieces for the funeral." Silence.

How could I possibly have thought it right to tell Holmes this? I was empty, dead, the world was filled with a howling wind and the gnashing of teeth. The Dream had escaped my control, my past had freed itself to destroy me and the (yes, I would admit it) love (*the thin wail of my mother's voice as the car went over*) I had for this man.

"I went crazy for a while, kept having to be restrained from throwing myself off things. I finally came across a very good psychiatrist. She told me that the only way I could make up for it was not to kill myself, but to make myself worth something. In effect, though she didn't say it so simply, to be my brother's stand-in. It was an effective piece of therapy, in a way. I no longer tried to jump from high places. But the Dream started that same week." Holmes cleared his throat.

"How often does it come?"

"Not often now. I haven't had it since we were in Wales. I thought it was finally gone. It appears not. I've never told anyone about it. Ever." I lay there and thought of the time, just before I left California, that Dr. Ginzberg drove me down to the cliffs, and I had seen the sparkle of glass and the scorch marks below, and how tempting and

welcoming and cool the waves looked as they pounded themselves to
froth on the rocks far below.

"Russell, I—"

I interrupted him with a desperate rush of words.

"If you're going to reassure me that it wasn't my fault and say that I
mustn't feel guilty about it, Holmes, I'd rather you left, because that
really would finish us off, truly it would."

"No, Russ, I wasn't about to say that. Give me some credit, I beg
you. Of course you killed them. It was not murder, or even manslaugh-
ter, but you are certainly guilty of provoking a fatal accident. That will
remain on your hands."

I could not believe what I was hearing. I took my arm away and
looked at him then, and saw in his face a mirror image of the pain I
could feel on my own, only in his case the rawness of it was smoothed
over, soothed by wisdom and years.

"I was merely going to say that I hope you realise that guilt is a poor
foundation for a life, without other motivations beside it."

His gentle words shook me, like an earthquake, like the tremor I
had felt as the gout of flame came bubbling up over the cliff. I felt myself falling into a chasm that yawned up within me, and all that held
me was a pair of calm grey eyes. Gradually the trembling stopped, the
earth subsided, the chasm fell in on itself and closed, and the eyes saw
it all, and understood. My guilt, the secret that had gnawed at me day
and night for four years, was in the open now, recognised and acknowledged, and no longer would it be swept away to grow malig-
nantly in the dark. My guilt had been admitted. I had been convicted,
had done my penance, and had been given absolution and told to
move on; the healing process could begin. For the first time, the very
first time since I had awakened surrounded by white coats and the
smell of the hospital, a sob tore into my chest. I saw it on the face of
the man opposite me, and I closed my eyes, and I wept.

———

THE FOLLOWING MORNING we resumed our rôles, all signs of the night's revelations banished. It was bearable now, because that night and each successive night after the lights were turned out I would hear two taps at the door, and Holmes would enter, stay for a few minutes, and leave. We spoke of quiet things, mostly concerning my studies. Twice I lit a candle and read to him from the little Hebrew Bible I had bought in the old bazaar in Jerusalem. Once, after a particularly bitter day of verbal duels and bloodletting, he sat and stroked my hair until I fell asleep. These moments made sanity possible. From the time I rose in the morning until I turned off my light, Holmes was my enemy, and the ship rang with our fury, and the men retreated from the ice that spread from us. At night, however, for a few minutes, battle was suspended and, like the British and German soldiers exchanging cigarettes and carols across No-Man's-Land during the undeclared Christmas truce of 1914, we could put away the battle and fraternise, two weary and seasoned veterans.

I grew in strength and pride and, while the weather held, spent hours on the deck reading, turning darker yet, my hair almost bleached white. Holmes, on the other hand, drew in. His scathing attacks began to reveal an undertone of bewilderment and pain, an emotional reaction that his pride would not allow him to show to the world. He rarely left his cabin, where the lights burnt at all hours. His plates were returned untouched, and he smoked vast quantities of his filthy black shag tobacco. When the supplies ran low, he resumed the habit of cigarettes, which he had left some years before. He drank heavily, never showing the slightest sign of its effect, and I suspected he would have returned to his cocaine had he been able to get it. He looked ghastly, with a strange yellow tinge beneath his tan, his eyes bloodshot and rimmed in red, his normally thin frame on the edge of emaciation. One night I objected.

"Holmes, there's not much point in this elaborate farce if you kill yourself before she has a chance. Or are you trying to save her the trouble?"

"It is not as bad as it looks, Russell, I assure you."

"You look jaundiced, Holmes, which means your liver is failing, and your eyes tell me you haven't slept in several days." I was startled to feel my bunk shaking, and then realised that he was laughing softly.

"So the old man has a few tricks left, does he? Russell, I discovered a large quantity of spices in the ship's hold and liberated a few of the yellower ones. Also, various irritants rubbed in the eyes cause temporary discomfort but lasting external effect. I assure you, I am doing myself no harm."

"But you have not eaten in days, and you're drinking far too heavily."

"The alcohol that disappears in my cabin ends up largely in the drains, with certain quantities used on breath and clothing. As for the food, I promise you that I shall allow Mrs. Hudson to feed me when she returns. When I step off the boat, Russell, every eye must know that here stands a beaten man, who cares not if he lives or dies. There would be no other reason for me to return openly."

"Very well. I just want your assurance that you will care for yourself in my absence. I will not have anything damage you, even your own hand."

"For the sake of the partnership, Russell?" The smile in his voice reassured me more than his words.

"Precisely."

"I promise. I shall, if you wish, promise to wash out my socks at night, too."

"That will not be necessary, Holmes. Mrs. Hudson will do that for you."

WE CAME HOME to London on a grey, heavy morning, both of us burnt by the sun and scorched by the fires of conflicts honest and contrived. I stood alone on the deck and watched the city approach, feeling the palpable unease of the captain and men as they worked behind me and belowdecks. Familiar forms stood on the dock as we approached. I could see Watson looking anxiously for Holmes, and Inspector Lestrade standing next to him, equally curious at the detective's absence. Mycroft stood to one side, his face a closed book. They called to me as we pulled in, but I did not answer. When the gangway was let down I seized my bags before one of the men could do so, walked firmly across with my eyes down on the boards, and pushed past the men standing on the dock, to the obvious amazement of two of them. Watson held out his hand and Lestrade called.

"Miss Russell."

"Mary? Wait, Mary, what's wrong?"

I turned to them coldly, not looking at Mycroft.

"Yes?"

"Where are you going? Is something wrong? Where is Holmes?"

A movement on the deck above caught my eye, and I looked up into Holmes' eyes. He looked dreadful. His grey irises stared out like holes in two blood-filled pools. His yellowed skin sagged over his bones, and he was poorly shaven, this normally fastidious individual. His tie was straight, but the collar of his shirt was slightly rumpled, and his jacket was unbuttoned. I squelched any urge to pity or uncertainty and summoned up every drop of the scorn I had spent the last days in distilling, filling my face, my stance, my mind with it, so that when I spoke, acid dripped from my words.

"There he is, gentlemen, the great Mr. Sherlock Holmes. Savior of nations, the mind of the century, God's gift to humanity. Gentlemen, I leave you to him."

Our eyes met in a brief flash, and I saw in them both approval and apprehension, and a farewell. I turned on my heel and stalked away down the wharf. Watson must have started after me, because I heard Holmes' sharp, high-pitched, and infuriating drawl stop my friend and uncle dead in his tracks.

"Let her go, Watson, she'll have none of us. She's off to make her mark on the world, can't you see?" His voice sharpened further into a querulous cry that must have carried to the other side of the river. "And God help any man who gets in her way!"

With these searing words on my coattails I rounded the corner and set off to find a cab. It was the last I was to see of him for two months.

❅ 15 ❅

Separation Trial

She is alone in the world, in the midst of an
awakening spring.

BACK AT OXFORD, I threw myself furiously into my studies.
I had missed nearly a month, and although the Oxford program
is not dependent on classes and attendance at lectures, one's absence is
noted and strongly disapproved. My maths tutor was away, illness of
some kind, and I was secretly grateful not to have that pressure. The
woman who tutored Greek was also away, vanished into maternity over
the Christmas holidays. By dint of working flat out for three weeks I
managed to redeem myself in the eyes of my remaining supervisors and
felt that I had caught up to my own satisfaction as well.

I changed that spring. For one thing, I no longer wore trousers and
boots, but filled my wardrobe with expensive, austere skirts and
dresses. I had, as I feared, alienated Ronnie Beaconsfield, and lacked

the energy to regain her friendship, but instead made an effort to make contact with the other girls in my year. I found I enjoyed it, although after a few hours their talk made me impatient for my solitude. I took long walks through the streets and the desolate winter hills around Oxford. I took to attending church, particularly Evensong at the cathedral, just to sit and listen. Once I went to a concert with a quiet young man from my patristics lecture. The music was Mozart, and well played, but halfway through, the shining genius and the pain of it made it impossible to breathe, and I left. The young man did not ask me again.

My written work changed, too. It became even more precise, less tolerant of other, softer viewpoints, more ruthlessly logical: "Brilliant and hard, like a diamond" was a remark from one reader, not altogether approving.

I drove myself. I ate less, worked invariably into the early hours of morning, drank brandy now to help me sleep. I laughed when a librarian at the Bodleian suggested, only half joking, that I might move into the stacks, but my laughter was a polite, brittle noise. I became, in other words, more like Holmes than the man himself: brilliant, driven to a point of obsession, careless of myself, mindless of others, but without the passion and the deep-down, inbred love for the good in humanity that was the basis of his entire career. He loved the humanity that could not understand or fully accept him; I, in the midst of the same human race, became a thinking machine.

Holmes himself, on his farm in the south downs, was retreating from the world into softness and bewilderment. Mrs. Hudson cut short her expedition to the Antipodes and returned home in late February. Her first letter to me was brief and shocked at the state she had found Holmes in. Subsequent letters neither accused nor begged, but pained me even more deeply when she simply stated that Holmes had not been out of bed one day, or that he was talking about selling his hives. Lestrade had set guards on the cottage at all times. (He had tried to do the same for me, but I had baited him and eluded them and finally he withdrew. I did not believe any of Lestrade's men could guard me better than I could myself, and as time went on I was more surely convinced that the rules of the game had indeed been changed, and that I was not yet in danger. Besides, I found their constant presence unbearable.)

Watson wrote too, long tentative letters, mostly about Holmes' health and mind. He came to see me once in Oxford. I took him for a long walk so I might not have to sit and face him, and the cold and my coolness sent him limping away with his bodyguard.

It was a long, bitter winter after the warmth of Palestine. I read my Hebrew Bible, and I thought about Holofernes and the road to Jerusalem.

In early March I received a telegram from Holmes, his preferred method of communication. It said simply:

ARE YOU COMING DOWN
BETWEEN TERMS QUERY
HOLMES

I read it openly at Mr. Thomas's busy front desk and allowed a short twist of irritation to show on my face before I turned to go upstairs. The next day I sent him a return question.

SHOULD I QUERY
RUSSELL

The following day his response lay in my pigeonhole.

PLEASE DO MRS HUDSON
WOULD ALSO BE GLAD
HOLMES

Mine in return, sent two days later, confirmed that I would come.

The next free day I went to London to see the executors of my parents' will, to lay before them the proposal that I be given sufficient

advance from my inheritance, now less than two years away, to purchase a motorcar. The partner who handled my parents' estate
hemmed and hawed and made several private telephone calls, and to
no great surprise of mine he approved. I went down the next day to
the Morris Oxford garage and paid for it, as well as arranging lessons. I
was soon mobile.

It was at this time, two weeks before the end of term, that I first became aware that I was being watched. I was highly preoccupied, and
often read a book while walking, so it is possible that they had been
present before and I hadn't noticed them. The first time I saw the
man, I was outside my lodgings and realised suddenly that I had forgotten a book. I doubled back quickly to get it, and out of the corner
of my eye noticed a man stoop down suddenly to tie his shoe. It wasn't
until I had my key in the door that it hit me: He had been wearing
laceless shoes. After that I was more attentive, and found that a
woman and another man alternated with the first. All were reasonably
good at disguises, particularly the woman, and I should certainly not
have been able to pick out the nun with no scuffs on her toes or the
man walking the bulldog as being the same person had I not spent
time under Holmes' tutelage.

I had only one problem. If I had truly cut myself off from Holmes,
I would not hide my annoyance at being spied on. However, I hesitated to bring the thing into the open before consulting him. This was
the first time anyone had come sniffing around the bait at my end, and
I was loath to frighten them off. Would the adversary believe that I
was not seeing them? They were far from obvious, but still—

I decided to continue as before, and became even more absentminded until one day as I had my Greek Testament in front of my
nose, I walked into a lightpost on the High Street. I found myself sitting stupefied on the ground while people exclaimed over the blood
on my face and a young woman held out my shattered spectacles.
I came home from the surgery with a large plaster on my forehead, and
I had to wear my spare spectacles for two days while the others were

repaired. As I would probably not have recognised Mycroft Holmes himself standing in front of me with the old ones on, it settled temporarily the problem of whether or not I ought to notice my followers. The doctor who stitched me up suggested mildly that I keep my mind off aorist passive verbs while I was walking, and I had to agree. As an actress I was a good changeling.

When my new glasses came I found my tail still behind me. I decided that I would drive to Sussex rather than take the train, and made prior—public—arrangements with the garage around the corner where I kept my new car, telling them that I would be leaving the next morning for my trip home. I wanted to be certain that I was followed, for I was on their mistress's trail every bit as much as they were on mine.

They used five cars on the journey, which proved the money behind them. I wrote down the numbers from their plates when I could read them, which was in three cases, and noted carefully the cars and all their drivers. (I doubt that the doctor would have considered the exercise less distracting than aorist passives, but I avoided all accidents and do not think I was the cause of anyone else's.) When I took lunch in a pub before reaching Guildford, the young couple kissing in the front of the roadster pulled out of the parking area three cars behind me. When I stopped for tea on the road to Eastbourne, the old man who had replaced the couple twenty miles earlier drove past, but the woman in the old Morris, who was walking a (familiar?) bulldog behind the inn, was soon behind me on the road. Her lights drove on past only when I turned into my own road a few miles from Eastbourne. I breathed a sigh of relief that they hadn't lost me. I wanted them here, to witness my innocent behaviour and report it to their boss.

My aunt was—well, she was herself. In the morning I saw that the farm was looking well, thanks to Patrick. He accompanied me on a tour. We greeted the cows, discussed the state of the barn's roof, examined the new foal that his huge plough mare Vicky had recently borne, and touched upon the possibility of investing in a tractor, which other farms in the area had turned to. I hung over the stable door and watched the beautiful dun colt, with his stubby black tail flapping furiously, nuzzling at his mother in the warm, straw-strewn barn, and knew that I was seeing the end of an era. I said as much to Patrick, but he only grunted, as if to say that he was not about to get sentimental about a horse. He didn't fool me.

It was the first time in well over a month that I'd worn trousers and waterproof boots, and they felt good. I invited Patrick up to the house for tea, but he, having no great love for my aunt, suggested his own little house instead.

The tea was hot, strong, and sweet, necessary for a cold spring morning. We talked about bills and building, and then suddenly he said, "There was some men in the village, asking about you." Not much went unnoticed in a village. These were obviously city people we were dealing with, but then I had assumed that.

"Yes? When was that?"

"Three, four week ago."

"What did they ask?"

"Just about you, where you was from, that kind of thing. And about Mr. Holmes, wanting to know if you was seeing much of him. They asked Tillie, down the inn, you know?" He and Tillie had been seeing each other for some time now, I noted. "She didn't realise they was askin' 'til later, though, 'cause it was just a conversation, you see. Wasn't until she found they'd asked the same questions down the post office that she put the two together, like."

"Interesting. Thanks for telling me."

"None of my business, but why aren't you seeing him anymore? It seems to have hit him bad."

I looked at his honest face and told him what would have been the truth, had I been telling the truth.

"You know that race horse of Tom Warner's that he's so proud of, wants to start a stud farm with?"

"Yes, it's a fine runner."

"Would you hitch it up with Vicky to pull a plough?"

It was such a patently foolish question that he looked at me for a minute before answering.

"You're saying that Mr. Holmes wants you to be a plough horse?"

"And that, right now anyway, I need to run. Nothing wrong with a plough horse. It's just that if you force a race horse to work along with a plough horse, they'll both get upset and kick apart the traces. That's what happened with Holmes and me."

"He's a good man. He came and took out a swarm from under Tillie's eaves last year. Didn't fuss." Not fussing was Patrick's highest accolade. "See if you can hold yourself in long enough to see him. I think he'd like it. His gardener tells me he's ailing."

"Yes. I will see him. This afternoon, in fact."

He mistook the hint of excitement in my voice for nervousness, and reached over to pat my soft scholar's hand with his big, calloused one.

"Don't you worry. Just remind yourself that you're not yoked to him, and you'll be fine."

"I'll do that, Patrick, and thank you."

I HAD ARRANGED to be at Holmes' cottage at four o'clock, knowing that tea was Mrs. Hudson's favorite meal to produce. There was a farm cart overturned on the road, which made me somewhat late, but at a quarter past four I pulled the car into his gravel drive and shut off the motor. The sound of Holmes' violin came to my ears. The violin is by its very nature one of the most melancholy of instruments when played alone; played as Holmes was doing, a slow and tuneless meditation, it was positively heart-wrenching. I slammed the car door noisily to interrupt and retrieved the basket of cheeses and fruits I had brought from Oxford. When I straightened up, the door of the cottage was open, and Holmes was leaning against the door jamb, no expression on his face.

"Hello, Russell."

"Hello, Holmes." I walked up the path trying to discern what was behind those hooded grey eyes, and failing. I stood below him on the doorstep and held out the basket. "I brought you and Mrs. Hudson a few things from Oxford."

"That was nice of you, Russell," he said politely, voice and eyes saying nothing. He stepped back into the room to let me pass. "Please come in."

I took the basket through into the kitchen and somehow survived Mrs. Hudson's welcome without breaking down into tears. I allowed myself to embrace her, hard, and let my lip quiver slightly to let her know that I was still Mary Russell, and then became polite again.

She laid out vast quantities of food for us and talked on and on about the ship and the Suez Canal and Bombay and her son's family while I filled my plate with morsels I did not want.

"How did you hurt your head, Mary?" she finally asked me.

I decided to make a joke out of it, the absentminded undergraduate walking smack into the lightpost, but it didn't really succeed as humour. Mrs. Hudson smiled uncomfortably and said she was glad the glass hadn't hurt my eye, and Holmes watched me as if I were a specimen under his microscope. She excused herself and left us alone.

Holmes and I drank our tea and pushed the food around on our plates. I told him what I had been doing that term, and he asked a few questions. Silence crept heavily in. I desperately asked him what he had been working on, and he described an experiment going on in his laboratory. I asked some questions to keep the flow of words going, and he answered, without much interest. Finally he put his cup down and gestured vaguely in the direction of his laboratory.

"Do you want to see it?"

"Yes, certainly, if you want to show it to me." Anything was better than sitting here crumbling a cheese scone into a pile of greasy bits.

We stood up and went into his windowless laboratory, and he closed the door behind us. I saw immediately that there was no ongoing experiment, and when I turned to question him, he was standing against the door, his hands deep in his pockets. "Hello, Russell," he said for the second time, only now he was there in his face, and his eyes looked out at me, and I couldn't bear it. I turned my back on him, my hands two fists, my eyes shut. I could not see him now, talk to him, and still keep up the act. After a moment two soft taps came on the door, and I smiled in sheer relief. He understood. He pushed a tall lab stool up behind me and I sat on it, my back to him, eyes still closed.

"We have perhaps five minutes without it looking odd," he said.

"You're watched, I take it."

"Every move, even in the sitting room. They've made some arrangement with the neighbours—telescopes in the trees. They may even be able to read lips. Will tells me that rumour in town says they have a deaf person there."

"Patrick says they were asking about me, and you. They are city people, and don't know that you can't hide anything in the country."

"Yes, and they are sure of themselves. I assume you are being watched."

"I only saw them two weeks ago, two men and a woman. Very good, too. Five cars followed me down here. The lady has money."

"We knew that." His eyes studied my back. "Are you all right, Russell? You've lost half a stone since January, and you aren't sleeping."

"Only six pounds, not seven, and I sleep as you do. I'm busy." My voice dropped to a whisper. "Holmes, I wish this were over." I felt him behind me and stood up abruptly. "No, don't come near me, I couldn't bear it. And I don't think I can do this trip again. I'm fine when I'm in Oxford, but don't ask me to come down again until the end. Please."

Silence radiated off the man like heat waves, and the low, hoarse voice that came from him was a thing I had never heard before. "Yes," he said. "Yes, I understand." He stopped, cleared his throat, and I heard him take a deliberate, long breath before he spoke again in his customary incisive tones.

"You are quite correct, Russell. There is nothing to be gained by it, and much to lose. To business then. I had copies of the photographs made for you. I gave the Roman numeral series to Mycroft, but neither of us can make any sense of it. I know it's there. Perhaps you can dig it out. It's that packet on the bench in front of you." I took the oversized brown envelope and put it in an inner pocket.

"We must go back out now, Russell. And in about ten minutes we will begin again, and you will leave angrily before Mrs. Hudson can of-fer you any supper. Yes?"

"Yes, Holmes. Good-bye."

He went back out into the sitting room, and I joined him a few minutes later. Within twenty minutes the sarcastic remarks were be-ginning to escalate, and shortly after six o'clock I slammed out of his cottage door without saying good-bye to Mrs. Hudson and sped off down the lane. Two miles away I stopped the car and rested my fore-head on the wheel for some time. It was all too real.

❧ 16 ❧

The Daughter of the Voice

It is so certain, then, that the new generation . . .

will do something you have not done?

THE DREARY WEEKS dragged on. My watchers remained discreet and I, absentminded. Trinity term began, and I was almost too busy to remember that my isolation was an act. Almost. Often at night I would start awake from bed or chair, thinking I had heard two soft taps at the door, but there was never anything. I moved in a woolly cocoon of words and numbers and chemical symbols, and spent my every spare minute in the Bodleian. Oddly, the Dream did not come.

Spring arrived, hesitant at first and then in a rush, heady, rich, long days that pushed the nighttime back into ever smaller intervals, the first spring in five free from the rumour of guns across the Channel, a spring anxious to make up for the cold winter, life bursting out from four years of death. All of England raised her face to the sun; or nearly all. I was aware of the spring, peripherally, aware that no one in the University save myself and a number of shell-shocked ex-soldiers was doing any work, and even I submitted to a picnic on Boar's Hill and another day allowed myself to be dragged off for a punting expedition upriver to Port Meadow.

For the most part, though, I ignored the blandishments of my former friends and current neighbours and kept my head down to work. That was the pattern for most of May, and it was the case on the day nearly at May's end when the tight snarled threads of the case began to come loose in my hands.

Upon my return from Sussex I was faced with the problem of where to put the envelope Holmes had given me. I could no longer depend on the security of my rooms, and preferred not to carry it about on my person at every moment. In the end I decided that the safest place to hide it was behind one of the more obscure volumes around the corner from the desk where I habitually worked in the Bodleian. It was a risk, but short of buying a safe or visiting the bank vaults with suspicious regularity, either of which would have alerted our enemy that I was up to something, it was the safest risk I could come up with. After all, the general public was not allowed inside the library, so my watchers usually waited long hours outside, and both the hiding place and my worktable were in dim corners where it was easy to see people approaching. Over the weeks I retrieved it any number of times to study the mysterious series of Roman numerals. Like Holmes, I knew our opponent well enough to be positive that this was a message, and like Holmes and his brother both, I could find no key to unlock it.

However, the mind has an amazing ability to continue worrying away at a problem all on its own, so that when the "Eureka!" comes it is as mysterious as if it were God speaking. The words given voice inside the mind are not always clear, however; they can be gentle and elliptical, what the prophets called the *bat qol*, the daughter of the voice of God, she who speaks in whispers and half-seen images. Holmes had cultivated the ability to still the noise of the mind, by smoking his pipe or playing nontunes on the violin. He once compared this mental state with the sort of passive seeing that enables the eye, in a dim light or at a great distance, to grasp details with greater clarity by focussing slightly to one side of the object of interest. When active, strained vision only obscures and frustrates, looking away often permits the eye to see and interpret the shapes of what it sees. Thus does inattention allow the mind to register the still, small whisper of the daughter of the voice.

I had been working hard, I had spent a sleepless night and rose to bird song. I had attended a lecture, finished an essay, and twice taken out the packet of photographs Holmes had given me. I held each one by its increasingly worn edges, studying the mute series of numerals until they were burnt into my brain, every wisp of horsehair that tufted from the crossed slashes, every straight edge of the twenty-five recalcitrant black Roman numerals. I even turned the photographs upside down for twenty minutes, in hopes of stirring some reaction, but there was nothing. All that happened was that I became increasingly irritable at having to cover them with some innocent papers every time someone walked by my worktable.

In the late afternoon the traffic past my table picked up, and after having slipped the photographs away seven times in less than an hour my temper snapped. I had no idea if those accursed slashes meant anything or not, and here I was wasting precious hours on a problem that quite possibly existed only in my mind. I shoved the photos back in their envelope and into their hidey-hole and stalked out of the library in a foul mood. I did not even care what my watchers would think, I was so disgusted with myself. Let them wonder. Maybe there is no goddamned enemy, I thought blackly. Maybe Holmes really has gone mad, and it's all one of his little tricks. Another "examination."

By the time I reached my rooms I had calmed down somewhat, but the look of my desk waiting reproachfully in the corner was more than I could bear. I heard my neighbour moving around in her room next door. I went out into the corridor.

"Hello, Dot?" I called. She appeared at her door.

"Oh, hello, Mary. Cup of tea?"

"Oh, no thanks. Are you doing anything urgent tonight?"

"Going to hell with Dante, but I'd be glad of an excuse to put it off. What's up?"

"I'm so sick of it, I can't face another book, and I thought—"

"You? Sick of books?" Her face would not have registered more disbelief if I had sprouted wings. I laughed.

"Yes, even Mary Russell gets fed up occasionally. I thought I'd have dinner at the Trout and go listen to a harpsichord recital a fellow in one of my lectures is giving. Interested?"

"When do we leave?"

"Half an hour all right with you?"

"Forty-five minutes would be better."

"Right. I'll call for a cab."

We had a pleasant dinner, Dorothy found a friend to flirt with, and we went to the recital. It was an informal affair, mostly Bach, which has the beauty and cadence of a well-balanced mathematical formula, particularly when played on the harpsichord. The symmetry and nobility of the master's music, together with a glass of the champagne served afterwards, calmed my nerves, and I found myself in bed before midnight, a rare occurrence in the past few months.

It was, I think, about three in the morning when I jerked up in my bed, my pulse thudding thickly in my ears, my breath coming as fast as if I had sprinted upstairs. I had been dreaming, not the Dream, but a confusing mixture of things real and imagined. A shadowy face had leered at me from the bookshelf in the corner, half-hidden by blonde hair, and held out a clay pipe in a twisted hand. "You know nothing!" the figure cackled in a voice both male and female, and laughed horribly. His/her gnarled fist tightened over the pipe, which I knew to be one of Holmes', and then opened.

Shards bounced slowly about the floor. I stared despairingly at the shattered pipe and knelt down to retrieve the pieces, in hopes of glueing it together again. Some of the larger bits had rolled underneath the bookshelf, and I had to lie down to reach them. As I felt around, my hand was suddenly seized, and I shot upright in terror with a fading image of the bookshelf in my mind's eye. It had been a section of history, the titles all on Henry VIII.

I groped for a light and my spectacles and lay back until my cold sweat dried and my heart no longer pounded in my chest. I knew that I could never get back to sleep after that, so I reached for my dressing gown and went to make myself a cup of tea.

In a few minutes I was sitting, inhaling the comforting steam, and thinking about the nightmare. It was very rare for me to be aware of dreams, other than the Dream, and I could not remember having another nightmare since my family had died. What was the purpose behind this one? Some of its elements were obvious, but some were not. Why, for example, was the hidden blonde both male and female, when I invariably thought of my adversary as female? The smashed pipe was an easily understood image of my intense, nearing frantic anxiety about Holmes, and bookshelves were such a part of my life that I could hardly imagine any part of me, even a dream, omitting them. But why were the books on history? I held no great passion for recent history, and due to my erratic schooling English history was a relative stranger. What was King Henry doing in front of my eyes? That obscene, gout-ridden old man with his numerous wives, all of them sacrificed to his desire for sons, as if it were their fault and not that of his own syphilitic self. What would Freud make of that dream, I wondered, with Holmes falling beneath the misogynist king, to the echoes of a man/woman's laughter? It was the sort of thing that would have made Dr. Leah Ginzberg lean forward in her chair with a Germanic "Ja, and then?" I sighed into the silent room and reached for my books. If I had to be up at three o'clock in the morning, I might as well make some use of it, Henry VIII or no. I settled myself to work, but all morning the dream kept intruding, and I would find myself staring blankly at the wall in front of me, seeing the spines of those books. Henry VIII. What did that mean?

I worked on, and in the afternoon I went out to take coffee in the covered market before an afternoon lecture, and I ended up ordering a large meal I had not known I wanted until I had walked into the tantalising smell of frying bacon. Two meals, actually, and pudding— more food than I had taken at one sitting at any time since Mrs. Hudson had been feeding me.

Somewhat bloated, I left the market stalls and walked up Turl Street for the afternoon lecture, only to find my steps slowing as I approached the Broad. I stopped. Henry VIII. When in ignorance, consult a library. With few qualms I abandoned the enquiry into Second Dynasty Burial Texts and turned right instead of left. (The familiar loitering and overaged undergraduate behind me emerged from a shop entrance and followed me up Broad Street and past the Sheldonian, but not through the doors of the library.) I called up several books on the period, but they bore no resemblance to my dream image, and leafing slowly through them caused no bells to go off in my mind. Knowing it was hopeless, I retrieved the photographs, laid them out on the desk in front of me, and it was then that the voice spoke to me, and I knew.

Holmes and I had discussed the possibility that the series was based on a number/letter substitution code, in which, for example, 1 might be read as A, 2 as B, and 3-1-2 translates as CAB. Extreme complexity—basing the substitution on a key text, primarily—is commonly used to make the translation from number to letter difficult: A long message in such a code can be broken by a bit of fiddling, but for short phrases, one must discover the key. If the key is something external, such as the words on a page of a book, decoding a brief message such as the one we were faced with may prove virtually impossible.

In this case the numerals used were not our Arabic ones, but Roman ones, and as they had not been spaced or had their divisions marked, it was sheer guesswork to know whether there were twenty-five separate numbers, or only seven, or some total in between. That is where Holmes and I had left off, as we could make no sense in the number/letter result we had extracted.

I had to make a few basic assumptions in looking at the problem. First of all, I had to assume that she had left it there for us to see and, eventually, understand, that it was not just a means of maddening us with tantalising clues that led nowhere. Second, I had to believe that the key to it lay somewhere in front of me, waiting to be seen. Third, I assumed that once the key was found, it would unlock the puzzle fairly quickly. If it did not, I would undoubtedly conclude that this was not the correct key and lay it down again. To give an example, it would call for a boneheaded sort of persistence to unravel the Roman numeral series XVIIIXIIIIXXV through all its possible Arabic equivalents into the numbers 18-13-1-25, and then into RMAY, and then finally to unscramble it to MARY, unless the person already knew what she was looking at. No, the key would not give too much difficulty once it was inserted into the lock. Of that I was certain.

If I was right, the key had been found by the still, small daughter of a voice and laid into my dream for me to find. Henry VIII meant nothing to me, but VIII, or base eight, meant a great deal. If human beings had been born with three fingers instead of four opposing their thumbs, we would count by units of eight instead of tens. A one plus a zero would mean eight, 11 would be how we wrote nine, and 20 would be the same as a base ten sixteen. I wrote it out on a piece of paper, the first twenty-six numbers in base eight with the alphabet underneath:

1	2	3	4	5	6	7	10	11	12	13	14	15
A	B	C	D	E	F	G	H	I	J	K	L	M

16	17	20	21	22	23	24	25	26	27	30	31	32
N	O	P	Q	R	S	T	U	V	W	X	Y	Z

I was left with the problem of dividing up the twenty-five Roman numerals into numbers whose letter equivalent said something. Although I knew them by heart now, backwards and forwards, I wrote them out too as a visual aid:

XVXVIIXXIIXIIXXIIXXIVXXXI

Twenty-five numerals, ones, fives, and tens. Taken at its most straightforward, these yielded a series of Hs, Es, and As, which would be meaningless. My job was to divide that string up so that the letters made sense.

I began with the first ten numerals, XVXVIIXXII. That last *I* might be attached to the following X to make nine, but I should keep that possibility in mind. XVXVI, or 10-5-10-5-1, yielded H-E-H-E-A, which, unless she wanted to show her derisive laughter, made no sense. Taking the first XV as 15 gave me MHEA. X-V-XVII = 10, 5, 17 gave HEO, which was better than the other. Higher numbers gave the greatest variation of the alphabet. I tried using the highest possible numbers I could get from the twenty-five digits, which divided into 15, 17, 22, 12, 22, 24, 31. In base ten this had read OQVLVX. The 31 was a problem because there are only twenty-six letters. However, in base eight that yielded M-O-R-J-R-T-Y. It took me a moment to realise what I was seeing. My pencil reached out by itself and slowly crossed out the figure 12, substituting 11-1, and there it was. MORIARTY.

Moriarty could not have done this. The professor-of-mathematics-turned-criminal-mastermind had died at the hands of Sherlock Holmes, hurled over a huge falls in Switzerland nearly thirty years before. Why then was his name here? Was our foe telling us that the purpose behind our persecution was revenge for his death? After nearly three decades? Or was there meant to be a parallel between this case and that of Moriarty and Holmes? I do not know how long I sat there in the Bodleian while the light faded outside, but eventually the little daughter of a voice whispered for one last time, and I heard myself, talking to Holmes in my room on the night it all began. "My maths tutor and I came across some mathematical exercises developed by an old acquaintance of yours, while we were working with problems in base eight theory." And the whispery voice of Holmes in my ears: "Professor Moriarty . . ."

My maths tutor. She was not the owner of the blonde hairs we had found in the cab; her hair was dark and tinged with grey. However, she had laid Professor Moriarty's base eight exercises before me on the very day the bomb appeared at my door and, I knew now, three days later had slashed that string of ciphers with great precision into the seats of our cab. My maths tutor, Patricia Donleavy, who had left because of an unexplained illness beginning that same week. My maths tutor, a strong woman, a mind of great subtlety, one of the teachers I had found to learn from, who had shaped me, whose approval I cherished, with whom I had talked about my life, and about Holmes. "Another Moriarty," Holmes had speculated, and she herself had just confirmed it. I pushed the implications from me. My maths tutor.

I looked up blankly to see someone standing beside my desk, a desk openly strewn with photographs, calculations, and the translation. It was one of the old library clerks, looking amused. He had the attitude of someone who has waited to be noticed.

"Sorry, Miss Russell, it's time to close up."

"Already? Heavens, Mr. Douglas, I had no idea. I'll be with you in a minute."

"No rush, Miss. I have some tidying to do, but I wanted to let you know before you took root in here. I'll let you out when you come down."

As I began hastily to insert the pages back into their envelope, a very unpleasant thought came to me. How many other people had glanced onto the desk during the evening? I knew I had been careful to hide the photographs at first, but at what point had I become so engrossed in the mathematical detective work that I had simply not seen who came past? I seemed to remember two first-year men who had been searching for a book, and an old priest who coughed and blew his nose loudly, but who else? I hoped no one.

Mr. Douglas let me out with a cheery " 'Night, now" and locked the door behind me. The dark courtyard was deserted but for the statue of

Thomas Bodley, and I walked quickly through the entrance arch to the Broad, which, conversely, seemed crowded and well-lit, and safe. I walked back to my lodgings, deep in thought. What to do next? Telephone Holmes, and hope no one was listening in? Send him a coded telegram? I doubted I could devise one quickly, a message Holmes could read and Patricia Donleavy could not. If I went to him, could I do so without alerting my watchers? A sudden movement on my part could endanger Holmes. And where was Miss Donleavy? How could I find her, and how could we spring a trap on her now?

In the midst of all these whirling thoughts I became aware of some other idea niggling gently at the back of my mind. I stopped dead and tried to encourage it to show itself. What was troubling me? Busy street? No, not even so crowded now. The idea of the telephone? No, wait; back up. Not crowded? The watchers! *Where is my watcher?* And I saw then that I had not been followed since I left the Bodleian, and I knew immediately what it meant that they had been pulled off me. I clapped my hat to my head and ran.

Mr. Thomas looked up startled at the crashing entrance of a breathless undergraduate into his lodge.

"Mr. Thomas, get Holmes on the telephone, I have to talk with him; it's an emergency." I was grateful that the old man did not pretend he didn't know the name of his unacknowledged employer, merely saw my face and reached for the telephone.

I stood tautly, tapping my fingers on the counter, wanting to scream at the slowness of the thing. Connexions were made, exchanges consulted, and then Mr. Thomas's face became still.

"I see," he said, and, "Thank you." He hung up and looked at me.

"The telephone lines seem to be down on that side of Eastbourne," he said. "Some kind of accident on the road, apparently. Can I do anything, Miss?"

"Yes. You can go around the corner and tell the garage to get my motor out. I'll be there in a few minutes." With surprising agility

Mr. Thomas ducked out the door, leaving his post unattended, and I pounded off up the stairs. I had the key in my hand before I cleared the last stair, reached for the keyhole, and stopped. There, in the middle of the shiny brass knob, was a black, greasy smudge.

"Holmes?" I whispered, "Holmes?" and flung open the door.

❧ 17 ❧

Forces Joined

The enterprise is hopeful, but full of hardship and danger.
It would seem to have been conceived by some sovereign
intelligence, that was able to divine most of our desires.

I T'S A GOOD thing there wasn't another bomb here, Russell.
There wouldn't be much left of you." It was the old priest from
the library, sitting in my chair and peering at me with disapproval over
his spectacles.

"Oh, God, Holmes, it is good to see you." To this day he swears
that I thrust his head between my breasts, but I am quite certain that
he was on his feet by the time I reached him. I was reassured that his
musculature had not suffered during his weeks of confinement and enforced sloth, and in fact felt distinctly bruised about the rib cage from
the force of his arms. He of course denies this.

"Holmes, Holmes, we can talk again, it's over, I know who she is, but
I thought she had you, my watchers disappeared and your telephone line

is out, and I was coming up here to get the revolver and drive down to Sussex, but you're here, and—"

Fortunately Holmes interrupted this drivel.

"Very well, Russell, I am flattered that you seem relieved to see me alive, but could you be a bit clearer please, particularly concerning the telephone line and the watchers?" He reached up to reattach his beard, and I stooped to pick up an eyebrow from the floor and absently handed it to him.

"I've been working in Bodley this afternoon—"

"Oh for God's sake, Russell, don't be completely daft. Or has my absence softened your brain?"

"Oh, of course, you were there. Why didn't you make yourself known then?"

"And have a scene like this in the midst of those hallowed halls? I thought you might wish to work there again in the future, so I came here to wait for you. I could also see you were on the edge of something and didn't want to risk knocking it out of your head. I did blow my nose loudly in your ear, if you remember, but when that failed to get your attention I took the hint and left. What did you find? I could see that you were working on the Roman numerals theory, but without peering too closely I couldn't see where your thoughts were taking you."

"Yes, Holmes, it was a code. Roman numerals in a base eight, not base ten. It spelt Moriarty. And do you know who had me working on base eight three days before the bombs were set?"

"I do remember, yes, your maths tutor. But how does—"

"Yes, and she even told me of Moriarty's exercises, though not directly, of course, just mentioned offhand that she had seen some problems in a book and—"

"Ah, I see now. Yes, of course."

"Of course what?"

"Your maths tutor is a woman. I might have known."

"Didn't you know? I thought I told you. But she's not blonde, you see, so—"

"And where is she now? Kindly quit blithering, Russell. I should greatly enjoy catching this woman if she is so kind as to walk into our trap, so I shouldn't have to spend the rest of my life dodging bombs and pretending to detest the very mention of your name."

"Oh. Yes. But she is. I mean, she withdrew my watchers today while I was in the library. She may have guessed what I was doing, or she may have just decided to go ahead, but the telephone lines to the village are down, so I thought—"

"Right you were, Russell, and that means we must fly. Can you put on some more sensible clothing? There may be rough work ahead of us."

I plunged into the next room and into my young man's mufti in two minutes flat, and in another thirty seconds had my boots on and the gun and a handful of bullets in my pocket.

The two of us created quite a sensation clattering down the stairs. The hypochondriac down the hall had just come out of the bathroom when we came running towards her. She screamed and clutched her dressing gown to her chest as we flew past.

"Men! Two men in the hall!"

"Oh, for God's sake, Di, it's me," I shouted ungrammatically.

She leant over the stairwell with several others to watch our descent. "Mary? But who's that with you?"

"An old friend of the family!"

"But it's a man!"

"So I noticed."

"But men aren't allowed in here!" Their protests faded above us.

"Russell, I must use Mr. Thomas's telephone—Ah, here he is. Pardon me, Thomas."

"I beg your pardon, reverend sir, may I help you? Miss Russell, who is this? Please, sir, what do you want? Sir, the telephone is not for public use. Sir—"

"Mr. Thomas, is my car ready?" I interrupted while Holmes awaited connexion.

"What? Ah, yes, Miss, they said they would bring it out for you. Miss, who is this gentleman?"

"A friend of the family, Mr. Thomas. Dear me, I hear Dianne at the top of the stairs. Do you think you should perhaps see what she wants? You know how highly strung she is. No, Mr. Thomas, you go help her; I'll show this friend of mine out. Yes, friend of the family. Very old. Yes. Good-bye, Mr. Thomas, I'll not be back in tonight."

"Or tomorrow night," shouted Holmes. "Come, Russell!"

The car was warmed up and running at the kerb, and the garage man quickly got out when he saw us coming, then paused with his hand on the door.

"Is that you, Miss Russell?"

"Yes, Hugh, thanks a million. Bye." He winced as I squealed the tyres, but after all, it wasn't his motorcar. Holmes did more than wince before we were out of Oxford, but I didn't hit anybody, and only brushed the farm cart slightly. It wasn't his automobile either, and what do men know about driving?

When I had settled the Morris down to a slow blur on the black and narrow road out of Oxford, I turned to Holmes.

"What are you doing here, anyway?"

"I say, Russell, do you think—that is, is this the proper speed for this particular road and these—watch the cow—these particular conditions?"

"Well, I could go a bit faster, if you like, Holmes. I suppose the car would take it."

"No, that was not what I had in mind."

"Then what—Oh, of course, you want an alternate route. You're right as usual, Holmes. Reach behind you and get the maps; they're in that black pouch there. There's a hand torch in the pocket. Holmes, your eyebrow has fallen off again."

"I'm not surprised," he muttered, and peeled off the rest of the disguise.

"You make a fine priest, Holmes, very distinguished. Now, those maps start with Oxford and work their way down to Eastbourne. There's a point in a few miles where we can get off to the left. It's marked as a farm track. Do you see it?"

Holmes claims that night's ride took ten years from his life, but I found it quite exhilarating to be rocketing along unlighted country lanes at high speeds with the man I hadn't been able to properly speak with openly for so many months. He didn't seem to find many topics of conversation during those hours, though, so I had to fill in.

Once, when we slipped by inches through a gap between a hay wagon and a stone wall, losing considerable paint to the latter, Holmes was really quite uncharacteristically silent. After some minutes I asked him if he was feeling well.

"Russell, if you decide to take up Grand Prix racing, do ask Watson to do your navigating. This is just his métier."

"Why, Holmes, do you have doubts about my driving?"

"No, Russell, I freely admit that when it comes to your driving abilities, I have no doubts whatsoever. The doubts I have are concerned with the other end of our journey. The question of our arrival, for one thing."

"And what we shall find when we get there?"

"That too, but it is perhaps not of such immediate concern. Russell, did you see that tree back there?"

"Yes, a fine old oak, wasn't it?"

"I hope it still is," he muttered. I laughed merrily. He winced.

W E SUCCEEDED IN working our way across all the major arteries coming from London on our cross-country flight. Finally we shook them off and straightened out for the last clear run at home. I glanced at Holmes in the pale moonlight.

"Are you going to tell me how you came to be in Oxford? And what your plans are for the next few hours?"

"Russell, I really think you ought to slow this machine down. We cannot know when we will come across our opponent's minions, and we do not wish to attract their attention. They believe you are in Oxford and I am in bed."

I allowed the speedometer to show a more sedate speed, which seemed to satisfy him. Hedgerows and farm gates flew past in our headlamps, but it was still too early for the farmers themselves.

"I came to Oxford by train, a commonplace method of transport considerably more comfortable than your racing car."

"Holmes, it's only a Morris."

"After tonight I doubt the factory would recognise it. At any rate, I regret to inform you that your friend Mr. Sherlock Holmes has taken a definite turn for the worse. It seems that last week he foolishly allowed himself to take a chill and was soon in bed with pneumonia. He refused to go into hospital; nurses were in attendance around the clock. The doctor came regularly and looked grim when he left. Russell, have you any idea how difficult it is to find a specialist who can both lie and act? Thank God for Mycroft's connexions."

"How have you kept Watson away?"

"He did come to see me once, last week. It took me two hours to apply the make-up to convince him, and even then I had to refuse to let him examine me. If he had come bouncing out of my cottage like a cat hiding the feathers, can you imagine what that would have done with the trap? The man never could prevaricate. Mycroft had to convince him that if anything were to happen to my dear friend Watson it truly would do me in, so he is back in hiding."

"Poor Uncle John. We shall have a lot of explaining to do when this is over."

"He has always been most forgiving. But, to continue. I had thought that my grave illness might increase the pressure on the woman and force a move out of her. I was going to speak to you about it when you came down this week, as I knew you should when you got Mrs. Hudson's weekly letter tomorrow—or, rather, today—but it began to move faster than I had anticipated, so I came to Oxford to consult. Only to find that you in turn were coming here."

"What happened to make you come?"

"You know my hillside watchers? They've really become most care-less, glints of light from their glasses and lighting cigarettes in the dark. One of Mycroft's little gifts last month was a high-powered tele-scope, so I've spent a great deal of time behind my bedroom curtains, watching the watchers. Their routine is quite predictable, always the same people at the same times. Then suddenly yesterday, or rather the day before yesterday—Sunday evening it was—as I was watching them watch me, they all disappeared. A man whom I hadn't seen be-fore came from the back side of the hill, they talked for a few minutes, and then off they went, leaving their equipment behind them. I hadn't dared hope for something like that, but given the opportunity I wasn't about to let it go by. I sent old Will up to take a look and bring back what he could find for me. He's retired, but in his day he was the best, and when he doesn't want to be seen, a hawk wouldn't find him.

"He came back two hours later, just after dark, with a fine sack of rubbish for me to pick over. Cheese rinds, an old boot heel, some biscuit wrappers, a wine bottle. I took it into the laboratory, and what did I find? Oxford cheese, Oxford mud on the old heel, and a wrapper around the biscuits from a shop in the Oxford covered market. I smoked a cou-ple of pipes and decided to spend the day in bed while catching the morning train. The doctor, by the way, gave a slightly more hopeful prognosis this afternoon, the night nurse has been dismissed, and the sound of my violin has been heard from behind the bedroom curtains on and off throughout the afternoon. You know, Russell, of all the mir-acles of modern technology, I have found the gramophone the most use-ful. Incidentally," he added, "Mrs. Hudson is in on the charade now."

"You could hardly keep it up without her, I'd have thought. How is she doing at the game?"

"She was absolutely delighted to join in and has emerged as a very competent actress, to my surprise. Women never cease to amaze me."

I did not comment, not aloud. "That explains it until now. What comes next?"

"The signs all point to a rapidly approaching dénouement. Would you not agree, Russell?"

"Without a doubt."

"Furthermore, all my instincts tell me that she will want to meet me face to face. The fact that she has not lobbed an artillery shell into the cottage or poisoned my well is an open statement that it is not just my death that she wants. I have been dealing with the criminal mind for forty years now, and of this I am certain: She will arrange a meeting, so as to gloat over my weakness and her victory. The only question is, will she come to me, or have me brought to her?"

"Not exactly the only question, Holmes. I should think even more important the question of our response: Do we meet, or not?"

"No, dear Russell. That is no question. I have no choice but to meet her. I am the bait, remember? We have simply to decide how best to position you, to give you the best opportunity to strike. I must admit," he mused softly, "I am quite looking forward to meeting this particular adversary."

I braked hard to avoid running over a badger, and resumed.

"Holmes, if I didn't know better, I might think you were becoming quite infatuated with Patricia Donleavy. No, you needn't answer. I shall just have to remember that if I ever want to catch your attention, all I need do is threaten to blow you up."

"Russell! I should never have thought—"

"Never mind, Holmes, never mind. Really, Holmes, you are a most exasperating partner at times. Would you please get on with it? We'll be at my farm in two minutes and you still haven't told me your plan of campaign. Talk, Holmes!"

"Oh, very well. My telephone call was to Mycroft, asking him to bring a few of his most discreet individuals into the area after dark tonight. Last night there were too many people coming around my cottage to allow your Miss Donleavy to make her move, but today my medical friend will announce that I am recovering and need peace and quiet. Mrs. Hudson will take herself to bed early, at her end of the cottage, and we shall lie in wait. I believe your manager, Patrick, is trustworthy?"

"Completely. We can leave the car in the barn and walk to the cottage across the downs. I assume that's what you have in mind."

"You do know my methods, Russell. Ah, here we are."

I drove through the gates and up to the doors of the old barn that lay apart, next to the road. Holmes jumped out and opened the door for me. Once we had shifted a few hay bales the vehicle fit in snugly between the stalls, and Vicky and her various family members peered at the odd black intruder with mild curiosity.

"I'll go tell Patrick it's here, so he'll keep the doors shut. Back in a few minutes."

I let myself into Patrick's house and climbed the stairs to his room, whispering his name at regular intervals so that he wouldn't take me as a burglar. He was a sound sleeper, but I finally roused him.

"Patrick, for God's sake, man, the barns could burn and you'd sleep on."

"What? Barns? Fire? I'm coming! Who's that? Tillie?"

"No, no, Patrick, no fire, don't get up, it's I, Mary."

"Miss Mary? What's wrong? Let me get a light."

"No light, Patrick. Don't get up." I could see by moonlight that the top half of his body was unclothed, and I had no wish to find out about the other. "I just had to tell you that I've hidden my car in the lower barn. Don't let it be seen: It's very important that nobody knows I'm here. Even my aunt. Will you do that, Patrick?"

"Certainly, but where are you, here?"

"I'll be at Holmes' cottage."

"There's trouble, Miss Mary, isn't there? Can I help?"

"If you can, I'll get a message to you. Just don't let anyone see my car. Go back to sleep now, Patrick. Sorry to wake you."

"Good luck, Miss."

"Thank you, Patrick." Holmes was waiting for me outside the house. We set off in silence across the dark downs, empty but for the foxes and owls.

It was not the first time I had walked that way at night, though the setting moon lit the first couple of miles. I was concerned at first that his confinement might have lessened Holmes' normally iron constitution, but I needn't have worried. It was I who breathed heavily at the tops of hills from the hours spent in the library, not he.

Sounds carry at night, so our conversation was low and terse, dwindling to a few muttered words as the miles passed and his cottage neared. The moon had set, and it was the darkest time of night before the stars faded. We stood on the edge of the orchard that backed the cottage, and Holmes leant close to breathe words into my ear.

"We'll circle around and go in through the end door, then straight up to the laboratory. We can have a light in there; it won't be seen. Keep to the shadows and remember there's a guard about somewhere."

He felt my nod and slipped away. Five minutes later the door clicked lightly to his key, and I stood inside the dark cottage breathing in the mingled smells of pipe tobacco, toxic chemicals, and meat pies, the fragrance of home and happiness.

"Come, Russell, are you lost?" His low voice came from above me. I pushed away the feelings of reunion and followed him up the worn steps and around the corner, not needing a light, until my hand touched the air of an open doorway and I stepped inside. The air moved as Holmes swung the door closed.

"Stay there until I make a light, Russell. I've moved some things about since you were here last." A match flared and illuminated his profile, bent over an old lamp. "I have a cloth to tack up over the door edges," he said, and adjusted the flame to give the greatest light, then turned to set it on a worktable.

"My nose tells me that Mrs. Hudson produced meat pies yesterday," I said, shrugging off my coat and hanging it on the peg on the door. "I'm glad she is convinced of your approaching recovery." I turned back to Holmes, and I saw his face. He was looking across the lamp to the dark corner, and whatever it was he saw there bathed his face in dread and despair and the finality of defeat, and he was utterly still, slightly bent from depositing the lamp on the table. I took two quick steps forward so I could see around the bookshelf, and there, dominating my vision, was the round reflected end of a gun, moving to point directly at me. I looked at Holmes and saw then the first fear I had ever witnessed in his eyes.

"Good morning, Mr. Holmes," said a familiar voice. "Miss Russell."

Holmes straightened his long body slowly, looking terribly, utterly exhausted, and when he replied his voice was as flat as death.

"Miss Donleavy."

❋ 18 ❋

Battle Royal

> . . . there being not room for many emotions
> in her narrow, barbarous, practical brain.

WHAT, MR. HOLMES, NO bon mots? 'I perceive you have
been in Afghanistan,' or New York? Well, not every utter-
ance a gem, perhaps. And you, Miss Russell. No greeting for your
tutrix, not even an apology for the inadequacy of your final essay,
which was not only sodden but hurried as well?"

At the sound of her precise, slightly hoarse voice I was overcome,
pierced to the core of my being. Her voice, sweeping me into memories of her dim and opulent study, the coal fire, the tea she served me,
the two occasions when she had given me a glass of rare dry sherry to
accompany her rare, dry words of praise: I had thought . . . I had
thought I knew what her feelings towards me were, and I stood before
her like a child whose beloved godmother has just stabbed her.

"You do look like a pair of donkeys," she said in irritation, and if her first words had left me stunned, her quick ill humour jolted me back into life, an automatic response learnt early by all of her students: When Miss Donleavy snaps, one gathered one's wits with alacrity. I had seen her reduce a strong man to tears.

"Sit down, Miss Russell. Mr. Holmes, while I have this gun pointed at Miss Russell, would you be so good as to switch on the electrical lights I see over our heads? Move very carefully; the gun is already cocked, and it takes very little pressure to set the trigger off. Thank you. Mr. Holmes, you look considerably further from Death's door than I was led to believe. Now, if you would please bring that other chair and place it at the table to the left of Miss Russell. A bit farther apart. Good. And the lamp, extinguish it and place it on the shelf. Yes, there. Now, sit down. You will please leave your hands on top of the table at all times, both of you. Good."

I sat at arm's length from Holmes and looked past the gun's maw at my mathematics tutor. She was sitting in the very corner of the room behind a rank of shelves, so that the shadow cast by the shelves cut directly across her. The overhead glare illuminated her tweed- and silk-covered legs from the knee down, and occasionally the very end of the heavy military pistol. All else was dim: an occasional flash of teeth and eyes, a dull glint from the gold chain and locket she wore at her throat; all else was shadow.

"Mr. Holmes, we meet at last. I have been looking forward to this meeting for quite some time."

"Twenty-five years or more, isn't it, Miss Donleavy? Or, do you prefer to be addressed by your father's name?"

Silence filled the laboratory, and I sat bewildered. Did Holmes know where the woman came from? Her father . . . ?

"Touché, Mr. Holmes. I take back my earlier criticism; you still do a nice line in bon mots. Perhaps you might explain to Miss Russell."

"It was her own name that Miss Donleavy signed on the seats of the four-wheeler, Russell. This is the daughter of Professor Moriarty."

"Surprise, surprise, Miss Russell. You did tell me what a very superior sort of mind your friend has. What a pity he was born trapped in a man's body."

With a wrenching effort I took control of my thoughts and sent them, useless as it might now seem, in the direction of the last plan that Holmes and I had laid. I swallowed and studied my hands on the tabletop.

"I cannot agree, Miss Donleavy," I said. "Mr. Holmes' mind and his body seem to me well suited to each other."

"Miss Russell," she said delightedly, "sharp as always. I must admit I had forgotten how I always enjoyed your mind. And, as you intimate, I had also forgotten that the two of you have become . . . alienated. I must say I often wondered what you saw in him. I could have done a great deal with you had it not been for your irrational fondness for Mr. Holmes."

I pointedly said nothing, just studied my hands. I did wonder why they weren't shaking.

"But now the fondness has turned, has it?" she said, in a voice that was soft and tinged with sadness. "So very sad, when old friends part and become enemies."

My heart leapt with hope, but I kept all expression from my face. If she believed this, we might yet get around her. It was difficult for me to tell, partly because I had to judge solely by her voice and also because my trust in my own perceptions had been badly shaken, but beyond this she also seemed somehow foreign, her reactions exaggerated, fluctuating.

I had little time to reflect on the question, because Holmes stirred at my side and spoke up, his voice flat.

"Kindly refrain from baiting the child, Miss Donleavy, and continue: I believe you have something you wish to say to me."

The round metal circle on her knee began to shake slightly, and after a brief moment of terror I heard her laughter, and I felt ill. She had been playing with me. We might have fooled her for a time, but now

our act was exposed, and even the small chance we'd had with decep-
tion was no longer ours.

"You are right, Mr. Holmes. I have not much time, and you have
robbed me of a great deal of energy in the last few days. I have no great
energy to spare, you understand. I am dying. Oh yes, Miss Russell, my
absence from the college was no sham. There is a crab with its claws in
my belly and no way to remove it. I had originally planned to wait several years for this, Mr. Holmes, but I do not have the leisure now. Before much longer I will not have the strength to deal with you. It must
be now." Her voice echoed in the tiled laboratory and whispered away
like a snake.

"Very well, Miss Donleavy, you have me at your mercy. Let us dis-
miss Miss Russell and get on with the issues between us."

"Oh no, Mr. Holmes, sorry. I cannot do that. She is a part of you
now, and I cannot deal with you without including her. She stays."
Her voice had gone cold, so cold it was hard for me to connect it
with the person who had drunk tea with me and laughed in front of
a fire. Cold, and with danger uncoiling from its base. I shivered, and
she saw it.

"Miss Russell is cold, and I imagine tired. We all are, my dear, but
we have a while to go before the end. Come now, Mr. Holmes, don't
keep your protégée here all day. I am sure you have a number of questions you would like to ask me. You may begin."

I looked at Holmes, sitting less than a yard from me. His hand
rubbed across his face in a gesture of fatigue, but for the briefest frac-
tion of an instant his eyes slid sideways to meet mine with a spark of
hard triumph, and then his hand fell away from features that were
merely bone tired and filled with defeat. He leant back in his chair
with his long, bony hands spread out on the table before him and gave
a tiny shrug.

"I have no questions, Miss Donleavy."

The gun wavered for a moment.

"No questions! But of course you have—" She caught herself. "Mr.

Holmes, you needn't try to irritate me. That would be a waste of our precious time. Now come, surely you have questions." Her voice had an edge to it, and a flash of memory came, of a time when I had failed to make a logical connexion that ought to have been obvious, and her voice had cut deep. In perfect counterpoint came the voice of Holmes, fatigued and slightly bored.

"Miss Donleavy, I tell you, there are no questions in my mind regarding this case. It has been very interesting, even challenging, but it is now over, and all the significant data have been correlated."

"Indeed? Pardon me if I doubt your word, Mr. Holmes, but I suspect you are playing some obscure game. Perhaps you might be so good as to explain to Miss Russell and myself the sequence of events. Hands on the table, Mr. Holmes. I have no wish to cut this short. Thank you. You may proceed."

"Shall I begin with the occurrences of last autumn, or of twenty-eight years ago?"

"As you wish, though perhaps Miss Russell may find the latter course of some interest."

"Very well. Russell, twenty-eight years ago I, not to mince words, killed Professor James Moriarty, your maths tutor's father. That it was self-defence does not contravene the fact that I was responsible for his falling to his death over the Reichenbach Falls, or that it was my investigation into his extensive criminal activities that was the direct cause of his seeking to kill me. I found him out, I exposed his network of crime, and I was the immediate cause of his death.

"However, Russell, I made two mistakes at that time, though how I might have anticipated events I cannot at the moment think. The first was that my subsequent three-year-long disappearance from England allowed the scattered remnants of Moriarty's organisation to regroup; by the time I returned it had succeeded in extending itself internationally, with little structure left aboveground in this country. My second mistake was to allow Moriarty's family—the existence of which was one of his better kept secrets—to disappear from my view. His wife and young daughter left for New York, never to be seen again. Or so I had thought. Was Donleavy your mother's maiden name?"

"Ah, so you do have a question! Yes, it was."

"Minor lacunae, Miss Donleavy, and hardly worth the effort of pursuit. What does it matter, whether the hair you left for me to find was your father's? or, which room in the warehouse across the river the marksman was in before shooting at Miss Russell? or indeed, was it you or some minion who prematurely triggered the bomb that killed Dickson? Peripheral matters left unanswered make for an untidy case but hardly affect its basic framework."

"An interesting statement, from a man who bases his investigations on minutiae," she commented, with some justification. "But we'll let it pass. Yes, it was my father's hair, from the days when he wore it down to his collar. My mother kept it in a locket. This locket I wear, in fact. And yes, my friend with the accurate rifle was indeed in the warehouse, although I understand that Scotland Yard is still looking for the launch. How they can imagine that anyone could aim from a boat on water and achieve any degree of accuracy—And as for Dickson, he knew the risks when he signed on. I was angry with him, for making such a mess of the bomb that incapacitated you, and it made him clumsy. I was generous with his family's compensation, you will give me that."

"What price a man's life, Miss Donleavy? How many guineas is recompense to a widow, three fatherless children?" His voice hardened. "You killed him, Miss Donleavy, yourself or one of your hired thugs, who heard your anger and took it as command. You intended him dead when you opened the New York bank account from which he was paid, last November. And he is now dead."

We sat in utter silence, and my heart beat ten, eleven times before she responded, with grudging admiration and a touch of amusement, and sounding again like herself.

"Mr. Holmes, how generous is the urge to Christian forgiveness in your soul, to perceive the man who nearly killed you and your two closest associates as a poor fellow whose widow and children weep for him."

"John Dickson was a professional, Madam, an artist with fuse and explosive. He never killed, and only once injured, in his entire career, until you brought him out of retirement. I can only assume you held something over him, some threat to his family, I imagine, to force him to engage in wholesale slaughter. Do not play games with me, Madam, with your accidents and your shows of pique; my patience has its limits."

The room's silence was so heavy I was sure she would hear my heart rate accelerate when I saw the end of the gun sag slightly away from me. He had her complete attention now. In a minute her voice came from the dark corner, flavoured with what sounded like respect.

"I can see that with someone like you about a person would never become complacent. You are quite correct: I suppose I did want him dead and tidied out of the way. His affection for those poisonous children of his was a weakness, and he would have exposed me when he had the chance. Ah well; introspection has never been one of my strong points. I have an unfortunate tendency to overlook side issues when I have a goal before me. As Miss Russell could tell you, I think."

The silver muzzle was again aimed directly at me, and I willed my muscles to relax, cursing inwardly. We were all silent for a long minute, two, and when she started again I knew that Holmes had miscalculated, that his successful gambit had, instead of distracting her, only driven her more strongly into asserting her domination over him. I could have told him, but he could not have known. Her countermove was vicious and calculated to take him at his weakest point, where pride met aloof independence.

"I believe," she said slowly, and again she had fluctuated into that slightly "off" manner that made me feel as if I did not know her in the least. "I believe that I shall call you Sherlock. An awkward name, that. What was your father thinking? Nonetheless, we have had such an intimate relationship—admittedly one-sided up to now—for so many years, I believe it is time to make it reciprocal. You will address me please by my Christian name."

Before she reached the end of this bizarre little speech I knew what the strong sense of wrongness was that I had sensed in her. When I had known her at Oxford, she had struck me as a person whose frustrations with the demands of University life would cause her, before too long, to make a break with the University and go elsewhere to exercise her considerable abilities. Indeed, that is what I had half assumed had taken place when she did not return for Hilary term. It was now clear that the break had taken place, but internally: The tightly controlled impatience she had always exhibited had broken free, and the knowledge of her superiority had progressed to a sense of supremacy. Eccentricity had flowered into madness.

It was an almost textbook illustration of dementia, but I needed no book to tell me what my crawling skin knew: The woman was more dangerous than her gun, as volatile as petrol fumes and malignant as a poisonous spider. My frantic thoughts could find no option to grab hold of, could conceive of no way to calm her, or even distract her. I could only sit, still and unimportant, to one side, and leave the field to Holmes' vast experience.

"Madam, I can hardly think that—"

"You ought to think very carefully, Sherlock, before you choose."

I had heard that tone of voice before, on occasions when her reiterated query as to whether I was satisfied with my solution had sent me scrambling for my error before she came down on me like a barbed whip. Holmes either did not perceive the threat or chose to ignore it.

"Miss Donleavy, I—"

The gunshot exploded into the closed room at the same instant that something tugged gently at my upper arm and a piece of equipment disintegrated noisily on a shelf next to the door, and I just had time to hope fervently that Mrs. Hudson would not be brought in by the noise when the pain flared. Holmes heard my gasp and turned to me as I clamped my left hand over the wound.

"Russell, are you—"

"She is fine, my dear Sherlock, and I suggest that you sit quietly or soon she will not be at all fine. Thank you. I assure you that I hit precisely what I intend to hit with this gun. I do nothing by halves, and that includes target practise. And incidentally, you need not worry that your guard will interrupt us this evening; he and Mrs. Hudson are both sleeping very soundly. Now, take your hand away, my dear, and let us see how much you are bleeding. You see? Barely a nick. A pretty shot, I think you'll agree. You know," she said in another voice entirely, that of a woman of reason and compassion, "I am really terribly sorry that I had to do that to you, Miss Russell. I hope you realise that I am not in the habit of shooting my pupils." Her voice tried to coax a smile from me, and the terrible thing was, despite the looming panic and shock, I wanted to give it to her. Wanted to trust her.

"Now, Sherlock, my dear, to return to the topic. What was it you were about to call me?" she said in mock coquetry.

Her voice set my skin to crawling. The surface was light mischief, but just below lay threat and contemptuous laughter and another thing that took me a minute to recognise: a coarse, sly tone of intimacy and seduction from a female completely sure of her power. It made me want to vomit, and then it began to make me angry. With the anger grew control.

"I am waiting, Sherlock." The gun jiggled slightly on her knee.

Holmes' response landed in the room like a glob of spit.

"Patricia."

"That's better. We need to work on the intonation, but that will come. As I was saying, I feel that I know you very, very well by now. Do you realise that you have been my hobby since I was eighteen? Yes, quite some time now. I was in New York. My mother was dying, and in the newsstand outside the hospital I saw a copy of a journal with your picture on the front, and inside a story of how you had not died, but how instead you had murdered my father. It took my mother a long time to die, and I had many hours to think about how I should meet you one day. I inherited my father's business, you know, though I was really more interested in pure mathematics than the organisation. It ran itself, really, while I went to school. My managers were very loyal. Still are, for that matter. Most of them. They occasionally consulted me at University, but for the most part I would tell them what to do, and they would work out the how. Sometimes I made requests, which they carried out most efficiently."

"Such as the unfortunate accidents that befell two of the other tutors shortly before you were hired?" I blurted out, unthinkingly letting loose a snatch of remembered conversation. I felt Holmes tighten disapprovingly beside me, and kicked myself mentally for drawing her attention.

"So you heard about that, Miss Russell? Yes, unlucky, weren't they? Still, I had the job I wanted, the job my father had been cheated out of, and I could get on with my hobby. I collected every word written by or about you. I even have an autographed copy of your monograph on bicycle tyres, one that you presented to the police commissioner. I assure you, I value it more highly than he did. Over the years I have learnt everything about you. I located three of your London hideaways, though I suspect there's at least one other. The one with the Vernet is quite nice," she said casually, "though the carpet leaves something to be desired." She waited for a reaction and, getting none, went on in irritation. "Billy was too easy to find, and following him that night you went to the opera was child's play. I had thought of using him against you, blackmailing him concerning certain incidents in his sister's past, but it seemed cheating somehow." Again the pause, again no response.

"Yes, there is very little I do not know about you, Sherlock. I know about why Mrs. Hudson's son emigrated so hastily to Australia, about you and the Adler woman after my father's death, about the scar on your backside and how you came to have it. I even have a rather fetching photograph of you emerging from the steam rooms at the Turkish Bathhouse on— Ha! That reached you, didn't it?" she crowed at

Holmes' faint exclamation and drove it home. "I even bought the farm up the hill from you several years ago, through an employee, of course, so I might look down upon you, even through your bedroom window." However, Holmes had recovered from his lapse, and she abandoned the attempt to goad him.

"It took me five years to bring seven of my employees into the area, but I enjoyed every move. And then—oh, the delicious irony of it!— your Miss Russell came to me for tutoring. I could not have asked for a more perfect gift: my own intimate link with the mind of my father's murderer. Had I taken up residence in the corner of your sitting room I could not have learnt more about you than I did from Miss Russell. It was truly delicious.

"During the summer holidays I generally spend time with the business, just to keep my hand in. This last summer we decided to follow up a rumour that an important American senator was about to place himself in a remote area, so we borrowed his daughter. As you know, we were not entirely successful, but imagine my pleasure when I realised that you too were on the same job, albeit from the other end. It was almost worth the failure, having that piquant extra, a chance to meet, as it were, to work together.

"From that fiasco came my plan. I decided to kidnap Miss Russell, take her to a place where you would not find her, and play with you, in public, over a prolonged period of time. I laid plans. I bought clothing for her in Liverpool—quite adequate clothing, you will agree, though I gather she did not make use of the things? Pity. One of my lighter-fingered employees removed a pair of shoes from her rooms, mostly to underline the parallelism of the two kidnap cases—ah, I see you missed that point. How disappointing. I planned to take her at the end of term, so my absences might not cause undue comment."

It was extremely disconcerting, listening to her talk about me in this matter-of-fact manner, but I did not react. I was disappearing from her sight now, becoming a third-person reference. My right arm throbbed, and the fingers of that hand were tingling mildly.

"Then in late October everything changed. My doctor told me that I should be dead in a year, and I was forced to review my plans. Did I truly want to embark on a complex and physically demanding project, one that might take six or eight months to do properly, and should involve regular travel to some godforsaken place like the Orkneys? I decided, reluctantly, to simplify matters. I could not bring myself to forego the pleasure of a cat-and-mouse game, but I decided at the end of it I should merely kill you all and have done with it. If I could make public your failure to escape me, so much the better. I had little to lose, after all.

"By the end of term everything was in place. I arranged my medical leave, from which I will not return, hired Mr. Dickson, and, just before I left Oxford, laid some of my father's mathematical exercises in front of Miss Russell. The next few days were marvelous, they truly were, like a complex equation falling into place. I was, as I said, really most annoyed at Mr. Dickson for knocking you about so thoroughly, and had to delay Miss Russell's bomb for a day until I could be sure you were up to defusing it. Then I sat back to see which of your paths I would pick you up on first. I did not need Dr. Watson, though that was amusing, was it not? Doddering old fool. I had a boy watching your brother's room all day, and I knew you were there before you went through the door. The next day I gambled, after you succeeded in throwing off my men, but I put my money on Billy, and it paid off. He led us straight to you and carried on a tedious conversation with me until he fell asleep. I was sorry about your clothes, Miss Russell. They must have cost a goodly percentage of your allowance."

"The money was mine, actually," Holmes volunteered. I felt her eyes leave me and return to him.

"Well, that's all right, then. Did you enjoy my little game in the park? Your articles on footprints were most instructive and helpful."

"It was very clever," Holmes said coldly.

"'It was very clever' . . . ?" she prompted.

He spoke through clenched jaws, to my relief. I had begun to think his anger genuine.

"It was very clever, 'Patricia,'" he spat.

"Yes, wasn't it? But I was most upset when you disappeared on that damnable boat. Really very angry indeed. Do you know what it cost me to keep an adequate watch on the docks? To say nothing of the other ports? I was certain you would come back into London, and instead, weeks went by without a sign. My managers were disturbed at the expense. I had to get rid of two of them before the others would calm themselves. And the time, my valuable time, lost! Finally you came back, and I could not believe it when my man reported how you looked and behaved. I actually took the risk of coming down here to see for myself, and I admit, I fell for it. I did not think that it could be an act. Oh, on your part, yes, that I would have believed, but I did not expect that Miss Russell was capable of that quality of performance; it's a far cry from dressing up as a gipsy girl and slurring your speech. It was not until you both came through that door that I knew for certain it was bogus."

Her voice had become increasingly hoarse, and the gun had drooped casually to one side as she talked. Holmes and I remained still, he with a look of polite boredom on his face that must have been infuriating, I trying to look young and stupid. The blood had stopped dripping onto the tiles, though my right hand was a bit numb. When Donleavy spoke again her voice cracked slightly with tiredness. I waited, invisible, for Holmes to make me an opening.

"Which brings us to the present. Sherlock, my dear man, what do you think I've come for?"

His response was uninterested, obedient, insulting.

"You wish to crow over me, like a cock on its dung-heap!"

"Patricia." The gun rose in threat.

"Patricia, my dear." His sardonic voice turned it into a sneer.

"To crow over you, I suppose, is one way of putting it. Nothing else?"

"To humiliate me, preferably in some public manner, so as to revenge your father."

"Excellent. Now, Miss Russell, do you see the envelope on the shelf to your right? The top one. Stand up and get it please—slowly now, remember. All right, take it back to the table and place it in front of Sherlock. Sit down, hands on top of the table. Good.

"This document is your suicide note, Sherlock. Rather lengthy, but that cannot be helped. If you are curious, the machine it was typed on is downstairs, substituted for your own. Read it, by all means, and lay it in front of Miss Russell if you wish her to see it. You will not touch it, Miss Russell. One never knows how clever the fingerprint people have become, and it would not do to have your fingerprints on such a highly personal document as this. Please, dear Sherlock, you must read it. I am really quite pleased with the effect it produces, if I do say so myself. Besides that, you must never sign any document until you've read it." She laughed merrily, and the madness rang clearly from her.

It was, as she said, a suicide letter. It began by stating that he, Sherlock Holmes, being in his right mind, could simply no longer see any point in staying alive, and it went on to elaborate the reasons. My rejection of him and the ensuing depression it caused were so vehemently denied as to underline my absence as the chief cause of his decision, though I personally was carefully removed from blame. Then the letter launched into a long, rambling, detailed explanation of how the cases as recorded by Dr. Watson had been so entirely wrong. Seventeen cases in all were presented with microscopic attention, pointing out in each one where the credit for its solution had in reality lain: usually with the police, occasionally elsewhere, several times by Holmes accidentally stumbling on the answer, once with Watson. Page after page of it, we read and she sat. Finally came the murder of Moriarty, where it was revealed that the entire story was a deliberate fabrication against an inoffensive professor who had stolen the young woman Holmes desired, and whom Holmes had then hounded to his death by the creation of a totally imaginary crime syndicate. The document ended with an abject apology to the memory of a great man so badly wronged, and to the population in general who had been so misled.

It was an extremely effective piece of writing. The reader was left with the clear impression of a badly unbalanced, severely depressed, drug-ridden egotist who had destroyed careers and lives in order to build his reputation. The simple white sheets with their lines of print, were they ever to get before the public, would create a huge scandal, and very possibly turn the name of Sherlock Holmes into a laughing-stock and the object of scorn. I sat back, shaken.

"You have a definite flair for fiction-writing," said Holmes, his voice cold with revulsion, "but surely you cannot believe I might sign the thing."

"If you do not, I shall shoot Miss Russell, then I shall shoot you, and one of my employees will forge your signature to it. It will appear to be a murder-suicide and will take Miss Russell's name down with yours."

"And if I do sign it?"

"If you do sign it, I shall allow you to give yourself one final injection, one that will prove fatal even for a man of your inclinations. Miss Russell will be taken away and released after the newspapers have found your letter. She has no proof, you see, none at all, and I shall be far away."

"You would give me your word that no harm should come to Miss Russell?"

He was quite serious, even I could see that.

"Holmes, no!" I cried, appalled.

"You will give me your word?" he repeated.

"You have my word: No harm will come to Miss Russell while she is in my care."

"No, for God's sake, Holmes." My attempt at lying invisibly in wait was shattered. "Why on earth would you believe her? She'd shoot me as soon as you were gone."

"Miss Russell," she protested, affronted, "my word is my honour. I paid Mr. Dickson his fee posthumously, did I not? And I support that other worthless family while my employee is in prison. I even sent that messenger lad who delivered the clothing his second sovereign. My word is good, Miss Russell."

"I believe you, Patricia. Why, I don't know, but I do. I am going to take my pen from my inner pocket," he said and, with slow and deliberate movements, did so. I watched in horror as he uncapped it, turned to the last page of the sheaf of papers, and put the pen to the paper. Anticlimactically, the thing refused to write. He shook it, without success, and looked up.

"I'm afraid the pen is dry, Patricia. There is a bottle of ink in the cupboard above the sink."

There was a moment's hesitation as she looked for a trick, but he sat patiently with the pen in his hand.

"Miss Russell, you get the ink."

"Holmes, I—"

"Now! Stop snivelling, child, and get the ink, or I shall be tempted to put another hole in you."

I stared at Holmes, who looked back at me calmly, one eyebrow raised slightly.

"The ink, please, Russell. Your tutrix appears to have us in a position of checkmate."

I pushed my chair back abruptly to hide my surge of hope and went to fetch the bottle. I put it on the table in front of Holmes and took my seat. He pushed the paper away, unscrewed the top of the squat ink bottle, drew the ink up into his pen, and cleared the nib of excess ink by pulling it, first one side and then the other, against the glass rim of the bottle. He then laid the pen on the table, screwed down the lid, put the bottle to one side, picked up the pen again, pulled the final sheet of typescript back in front of him, held the pen over the paper, and paused.

"You know, of course, that your father also committed suicide?"

"What!"

"Suicide," he repeated. He capped the pen absently and laid it on the table in front of him, picked up the ink bottle and fiddled with it for a moment, deep in thought, laid it aside, and leant forward on his elbows.

"Oh, yes, his death was suicide. He followed me to Switzerland after I destroyed his organisation, arranged a meeting at the most solitary spot he could find, and came to meet me. He knew he was no match for me physically, yet he did not bring a gun. Odd, don't you think? Furthermore, he arranged for a confederate to fling rocks at me afterwards, because he suspected that he would not take me with him into death. No, it was suicide, Patricia, quite clearly suicide." In the course of this speech his voice had grown harder, colder, and his lips curled over her name as if he were pronouncing an obscenity. The relentless cadence of his words went on, and on.

"You say you have come to know me, Patricia Donleavy." He spat out her name and wrapped it in scorn, facing her across the table. "I know you too, Madam. I know you for your father's daughter. Your father had a superb mind, as do you, and as you did he left the world of honest thought and turned to the creation of filth and evil. Your father created a network of horror and depravity that exceeded anything these islands had ever before known, a web woven of all that the world of crime has to offer. His agents, 'employees' as you call them, robbed and murdered, drained families through blackmail, and poisoned men and women with drugs. Nothing was too squalid for your father, Patricia Donleavy, from smuggling and opium to torture and prostitution. And all the time—ah, the perverted, filthy genius of it!—all the time the good professor sat in his book-lined study and kept his delicate hands clean of it. Nothing touched him, not the agony or the blood or the stink of terror that spread out from his agents. Just like you, Madam, he was touched only by the profits of all that sordid purulence, and he bought his wife pretty dresses and played mathematical games with his little daughter in the drawing room. Until I came along. I, Sherlock Holmes, with my meddlesome ways. I carved the network into many small pieces and I turned the name Moriarty into a term of derision, so that even his daughter will not carry it openly, and finally, when there was nothing left of his life, when I had driven him into a corner from which he could not escape, I pushed him over the Reichenbach Falls and he died. Your father, Patricia Donleavy, was a festering sore eating into the face of London, and I, Sher—"

With a shriek of animal fury she broke. The gun rose and swung up to face Holmes, and I, my useless right hand lying limp on the table, picked up the heavy bottle of ink and threw it hard and straight at her hand. The room was split again by a flash and deafening report, and the gun flew spinning against the wall. She came out of the dark corner in a dive for the pistol, and reached it a moment, just an instant, before I hit her in a massive, launched tackle that sent us crashing into the shelves, showering us with books and bottles and pieces of equipment. She was immensely strong in her madness and rage, and she had the gun in her hand, but I held her down with my entire body, and my hand hung with all its strength onto her wrist, to turn the weapon away from Holmes, slowly, so slowly against her impossible strength, and then came a confused jumble of impressions, of something slipping and my left hand holding a hot, empty palm just as a third and completely deafening explosion went off beside my head, and the shock of it went through me like a physical jolt. She stiffened beneath me in a curious protest, and coughed slightly, and then her right arm went limp and her left hand came down across my back. I lay stunned in her embrace for a moment until my eyes focussed on the gun, inches away from her arm, and I pushed the gun hard away from me so she could not reach it, and then thought, Oh my God, where had her second shot gone, and turned to see that Holmes was unhurt but something was wrong, something was suddenly very wrong with my right shoulder. And then finally the pain came, the immense, overwhelming, shuddering roar of pain that built and beat at me, and I flung out my hand to Holmes and cried aloud as thunder filled my ears and I slid down into a deep well of black velvet.

Postlude

PUTTING OFF THE ARMOUR

Return Home

Most creatures have a vague belief that a very precarious
hazard, a kind of transparent membrane,
divides death from love.

ENDLESS HOURS, WHAT seemed weeks, washed in a sea of
dark, muttering confusion, a labyrinth of blurred images and
disconnected snatches of voices, speech from the other side of an invisible wall. The Dream without end, horror without an awakening,
casting about for solid ground only to be caught up again by the pain
and flung back into the roaring, hissing blackness. My brother's rumpled hair framed by the car window. Patricia Donleavy, gaunt and sick,
lying in the spreading lake of incredibly red blood. A beaker of liquid
copper sulphate, smashed bilious green and dripping slowly from the
workbench above me. Donleavy again, standing above my hospital
bed and offering to throw me from a cliff. Holmes, so still on the laboratory's tile floor, one lonely hand curled about his head. Cold and

fever burned me, and I lay consumed by a universe of shivering night-mares.

Slowly, stubbornly, my body began to reassert itself. Slowly the fever burnt itself out, flickered, and died; gradually the drugs were cut back; and late one night I swam up towards rationality, to lie on my back look-ing incuriously up into the room from a point just below the surface. A thin, shimmering film was fixed between me and the painted white ceil-ing, the white tile walls, the machinery above my head, the pair of grey eyes that looked calmly, quietly at me. I floated closer, bit by bit, and fi-nally the bubble softly burst, the thin membrane collapsed. I blinked.

"Holmes," my lips said, though no sound entered the room.

"Yes, Russell." The eyes smiled. I watched them for several minutes, remotely aware that they were somehow important to me. I tried to re-construct the circumstances, and though I could remember the events, their emotional overtones seemed, in retrospect, excessive. I closed my heavy-lidded eyes.

"Holmes," I whispered. "I am glad you're alive."

I slept, and woke again to find the morning sun blazing painfully through the window. The fuzzy glare was broken in several places by darker shapes, and as I squinted at them a figure moved to the source of the light, and there was the swish of curtains being drawn. With the room now at a tolerable level of dimness I could see Holmes stand-ing on one side of the bed and a white-coated stranger on the other. White-coat laid firm, gentle fingers along the inside of my wrist. Holmes bent forward and settled my glasses onto my nose, then sat on the edge of the bed so I could see him. I could not move my head. He had shaved that morning, and I could see in intricate detail the pores of his hollow cheeks, the soft, powdery quality of the skin around his eyes, the slight sag to his features that told me he had not slept in some considerable time. But the eyes were calm, and a faint hint of a smile lay at the corner of his expressive mouth.

"Miss Russell?" I took my eyes from Holmes and looked at the doctor's earnest young face. "Welcome back, Miss Russell. You had us worried for a while, but you're going to be fine now. You have a broken collarbone, and you lost a great deal of blood, but other than one more scar for your collection there will be no lasting effect. Would you care for some water? Good. The sister will help you. Just a bit at a time until you get used to swallowing again. Mouth taste better now? Fine. Mr. Holmes, you may have five minutes. Don't let her try to talk too much. I shall see you later, Miss Russell." He and the nurse went out, and I heard his voice going down the hallway.

"Well, Russell. Our trap caught its prey, but it nearly took you with it. I had not intended quite such a generous sacrifice."

I licked my dry lips with a thick tongue.

"Sorry. Too slow. You hurt?"

"By no means, you reacted as quickly as I thought you might. Had you been slower her bullet might indeed have seriously disarranged my insides, but thanks to your father's ideas concerning women on the cricket field, your good left arm saved me from anything more than a bruised rib and a missing flap of skin the size of your finger. I am the one to apologise, Russell. Had I been faster to my feet the gun would not have gone off at all, and you would have an intact collarbone, and she would be sitting awaiting charges."

"Dead?"

"Oh yes, very. I shan't trouble you with the details now, because the white-coated people would not be happy if I raised your pulse, but she's dead and Scotland Yard is happily rooting about in her papers, finding things that will keep Lestrade busy for years. To say nothing of his American colleagues. That's right, shut your eyes for a while; it is bright in here." His voice faded. "Sleep now, Russ, I shan't be far away." The hard hospital bed rose up and wrapped itself around me. "Sleep now, my dear Russell."

LOW VOICES WOKE me in the afternoon. The room was still dim, and my shoulder and head throbbed beneath the stiff dressings. A nurse bent over me, saw that I was awake, thrust a thermometer into my mouth, and started doing other things to various parts of me. When my mouth was free again I spoke. My voice sounded strange to my ears, and the pull of muscles sent twinges into my collarbone. The routine was all too tediously familiar.

"A drink, please."

"Certainly, Miss. Let me raise the bed for you." The low voices had stopped, and as she cranked the handle my field of vision gradually dropped from the ceiling above the bed to include the bed itself and my visitors, rising from their chairs in the corner. The nursing sister held the glass for me, and I pulled methodically at the straw, ignoring the hurt of swallowing.

"More, Miss?"

"Not now, thank you, sister."

"Right-o, ring if you need me. Ten minutes, gentlemen, and see you don't tire her."

"Uncle John, your moustache is almost back to normal." (*Doddering old fool . . .*)

"Hallo, dear Mary. You're looking a sight better than you were three days ago. They're good doctors here."

"And Mr. Holmes. I am happy to greet you more civilly than the last time we met." (Mycroft's expression of jovial bonhomie seemed faintly menacing.)

"Please, Miss Russell, I hardly think that formality is necessary or even appropriate, what with being welcomed into your boudoir and all." The fat face smiled down at me, and I felt so tired. What were they doing here?

"Brother Mycroft, then. And Holmes. You have had a rest since the morning, I think. You look not so strained."

"I have. There is a vacant room next to yours, and I have made use of it. How are you feeling, Russell?"

"I am feeling as though a large piece of lead passed through me and took a considerable quantity of myself with it. How do the white-coats say I am?" (*Why didn't they go? Perhaps it is the painkillers, dulling my interest.*)

Watson cleared his throat.

"The bullet passed through the back of your neck, missing the spinal column by—by enough. It did go through your collarbone and nick various blood vessels before leaving the front of your shoulder and continuing on, to lodge finally in Miss Donleavy's heart. The surgeons have pieced together the clavicle, though there is considerable damage to the muscles in that area. And," his face prepared me for a feeble attempt at a joke to cheer the patient, "I fear you will never care to dress in anything other than high-necked clothing. Though I think you had already resigned yourself to that. Where on earth did you pick up all that scar tissue?"

"Watson, I think—" Holmes began.

"No, Holmes, it's all right." I was so utterly weary, and Watson was peering down into my face with what I supposed was loving concern, so I closed my eyes against the brightness. "It was an accident some years ago, Uncle John. Ask Holmes to tell you the story. I think I'll sleep for a while now, if you don't mind."

They filed out, but I did not sleep. I lay and felt the fingers of my unresponsive right hand, and thought about the walls of Jerusalem, and what my mathematics tutor had taken from me.

I WAS IN that hospital for many days, and a degree of movement gradually returned to my arm and neck. I could not abide the thought of my aunt, and indeed after I was conscious I refused to have her in my room. After some discussion it was arranged that I go home to the spare room in Holmes' cottage, to the great delight of Mrs. Hudson and the concern of the hospital authorities, who disliked the distance, the remoteness, and the poor road I should have to travel. I told Holmes I wished to go with him, and let him fight it out for me.

Once there I ate obediently, slept, sat in the sun with a book, and worked at restoring strength to my hand, but it was an emptiness. I did not dream, though often during the day I would find that I had been staring off into the distance unblinking for great chunks of time. When I had been in the cottage for two weeks I went to the laboratory and stood looking at the clean floor and the restored shelves. I touched the two bullet holes in the walls, and felt nothing but a vague unease; I could only think how bare and cold the tile looked.

Summer wore on, and my body gained strength, but there were no suggestions that I move back to my own farm. Holmes and I began to talk, short, tentative discussions about Oxford and my reading. He was away a great deal, but I did not ask why, and he did not tell me.

One day I came into the sitting room and saw the chess set laid out on a side table. Holmes was working at his desk and looked up to see me standing there with what must have been an expression of extreme loathing on my face as I stared at those thirty carved figures, the salt cellar, and the nut-and-bolt king on their teak and birch squares. I turned on him.

"For God's sake, Holmes, haven't you had enough chess for one lifetime? Put it away, get rid of it. If you wish me to leave your house I will, but don't ask me to look at that thing." I slammed out of the room. Later in the afternoon I came back through to see its box and board sitting closed up but still on the table. I said nothing but avoided that part of the room. They remained on the table. I remained in the cottage.

I began to find Holmes more and more irritating. The smell of his pipe and the odours from his laboratory plucked at raw nerves, and I retreated outside or behind the closed bedroom door. His violin sent me on walks into the downs that left me trembling with exhaustion, but I did not go back to my house. I began snapping irritably at him, but his response was invariably reasonable and patient, which only made me worse. Rage began to stir but lacked the consummation of open battle, for Holmes would not respond. In the last week of July I made up my mind to leave the cottage, gather my belongings, and return to Oxford. Next week.

Into this state of mind fell a letter. I was outside, on a hilltop away from the cottage, a forgotten book in my lap as I stared out across the Channel. I did not hear Holmes come up behind me, but suddenly there he was, his tobacco smell and his gently sardonic face. He held out the envelope between two long fingers, and I took it.

It was from little Jessica, addressed in her childish printing. I had a quick image of her bent over the envelope with a pencil in her small hand, laboriously copying my name. I smiled, and it felt strange on my lips. I took out the single sheet of stationery and read the child's words aloud.

Dear sister Mary,

How are you? My Mama told me a bad lady hurt your arm. I hope it's all right now. I am fine. Yesterday a strange man came to the house but I held Mama's hand and I was brave and strong like you. I have had dreams sometimes and even cry but when I think of you carrying me down the tree like a mama monkey I laugh and go back to sleep.

Will you come to see me when you are better? Say hello to Mr. Holmes for me. I love you.

Jessica Simpson

"Brave and strong, like me," I whispered, and started to laugh, a sour, bitter sound that tore my throat and sent pain shooting through my shoulder, and then it turned to tears and I cried, and when I was empty I fell asleep in the simple sunshine as Holmes stroked my hair with his gentle, clever hands.

When I awoke the sun was lower in the sky and Holmes had not moved. I turned awkwardly onto my back to ease my shoulder and looked up at the bowl of the sky. Holmes reached for his pipe and broke the silence.

"I need to go to France and Italy for six weeks. I shall be back before your term begins. Would you care to come with me?"

I lay watching his fingers fill the pipe, tamp down the black shreds of leaf, strike a flame, draw it down into the bowl. The sweet smell of burning tobacco drifted across the hillside. I smiled to myself.

"I believe I shall take up smoking a pipe, Holmes, for the sheer eloquence of the thing."

He looked at me sharply, and then his face began to relax into the old attitude of humour and intelligence. He nodded, once, as if I had given an answer, and we sat watching the sun change the colour of the sea and sky until the wind came up. Holmes knocked his pipe out against the sole of his shoe, stood up, and reached down to help me rise.

"Let me know when you're ready for a game of chess, Russell."

Twenty minutes later we came to his hives, and he went down the row to check them while I stood and watched the last workers come home with their loads of pollen. Holmes came back and we turned towards the cottage.

"I'll even spot you a piece, Russell."

"But not a queen?"

"Oh, no, never again. You're far too good a player for that."

"We'll start equal, then."

"I shall beat you if we do."

"I don't think so, Holmes. I really don't think you will."

The cottage was warm and filled with light, and smelt of tobacco and sulphur and the food that awaited us.

Discussion Questions

and Author Interview for

THE BEEKEEPER'S
APPRENTICE

Laurie R. King

❦

WARNING!

The following contains key plot points and

spoilers, enter at your own risk!

THE BEEKEEPER'S APPRENTICE is the first in a series of books to follow the adventures of Mary Russell, a gawky, egotistical, recently orphaned young lady who literally falls into the lap of Sherlock Holmes. Though he appears long retired from crime fighting, and is quietly engaged in raising honeybees on his Sussex estate, Russell piques his interest and in short order impresses the detective with her intellect and powers of deduction. Under his tutelage, this very modern twentieth-century woman proves a deft protégée and a fitting partner for the Victorian detective, and in this first volume we witness the formative years of a character who will grow and develop over many books to come.

The Beekeeper's Apprentice also paints a historically accurate picture of what it is like to live as a woman in misogynistic times. Between the strands of the mystery, Laurie King threads her own subtle commentary on how war transforms social status and the mutability of gender roles even under oppressive circumstances. In addition, this novel is a faithful and formally impressive foray into the world of Sir Arthur Conan Doyle, one that carefully evokes the voice of Sherlock Holmes while at the same time presenting him with a new foil, and fresh adventure. King revives the literary tradition of Conan Doyle, and all of its pleasures, but from a distinctly different point of view.

Discussion Questions

1. In an Editor's Preface, Laurie King playfully discloses the "true" origin of the story at hand: that what follows will be the actual memoirs of Mary Russell, which were mysteriously sent to her out of the blue, along with a trunk full of odds and ends. Why does King begin with this anecdote, essentially including herself in the story? Does it bring the world of the novel closer to our own? Have you read any other books (*Lolita*, for example) that begin with a false preface, and what effect does this device have on the rest of the novel? Were you fooled?

2. It is 1915, the Great War is raging through Europe and the men of England are in the trenches. How does this particular period in history allow a character like Mary Russell to take the stage in areas of post-Victorian society usually reserved for men? In what significant ways does she seize these opportunities? Would she have thrived if she were born into a different, more oppressive social climate, say, one hundred years earlier?

3. How would you characterize Mary Russell based on her first opinion of bees? Does her disdain for their mindless busywork and adherence to hive social structure reflect a particular attitude toward the social landscape of England at the time? Do you agree with Russell?

4. Holmes uses the game of chess to sharpen Mary Russell's strategic thinking and intuition. How does chess—and, in particular, the Queen—serve as a metaphor throughout the story? In what ways does King herself use the game to comment upon the master-apprentice relationship?

5. Russell and Holmes don disguises throughout *The Beekeeper's Apprentice*, and their work sometimes requires them to cross-dress. Discuss each point in the novel where either Russell or Holmes takes cover in the opposite sex; what special access does this method of disguise give them to the other characters? Is gender reversal necessary in order to win the confidence of certain people? How does Mary Russell's world change when she dresses as a man?

6. Watson is eternally known as the great detective's sidekick. Who, in your opinion, is a more effective foil for Holmes, Watson or Russell? What different aspects of Holmes's personality emerge in the presence of each? What would happen if Holmes were paired with a different partner, one more timid or less tenacious?

7. At Oxford, Mary Russell concludes that theology and detective work are one and the same. In your opinion, how are the two subjects related?

8. The art of deduction is constantly at play in *The Beekeeper's Apprentice*. Even when Mary notices that Watson has shaved off his mustache, she cares to look closer at the skin and imagine that it was done "very recently." Is Laurie King training the reader's perceptions to be more acute throughout the novel? Does every detail of our lives hold a mystery and a story?

9. What are some crucial differences between the training Patricia Donleavy received from Moriarty and the training Mary Russell received from Holmes? What mental and emotional strengths do both women have in common, and what separates them? Holmes comments: "A quick mind is worthless unless you can control the emotions with it as well." How does this maxim apply?

10. At what point in the novel did you suspect that Russell's adversary was a woman? When you read a mystery, what assumptions do you typically make about the gender of the villain? In what ways does King toy with the readers' assumptions about gender throughout the novel?

Author Interview

1. *The* Beekeeper's Apprentice *is only the first in a long and increasingly rich series of mysteries. Would you give us some insight into how it all started, and where you got the idea for the character of Mary Russell?*

The Russell books began with the thought, What would Sherlock Holmes look like if he were a woman? How would that cold, discerning mind change, and how would it remain the same? And because two similar objects are more interesting when they are close enough to set each other off, I chose a time and a place where the two versions could meet.

The latest Holmes story by Sir Arthur Conan Doyle takes place at the beginning of the Great War, in August of 1914. The society that gave birth to Sherlock Holmes did not survive that terrible war, and the Holmes stories written by Conan Doyle after 1914 were all set beforehand, with Holmes firmly locked into the time of gaslights and hansom cabs.

But what if Holmes had survived the War? What if he had been permitted to grow and change with his country? *Beekeeper* opens in the spring of 1915, when the nation is beginning to feel the War's transformation. By choosing that time, I defined a great deal of what the series would become—the story not only of a young woman, but of an era.

Mary Russell is a woman of the twentieth century; through her, Holmes enters the modern age.

2. *Many people have stepped into Conan Doyle's shoes and performed the difficult task of evoking Holmes's voice. How were you able to make your revival of Holmes more than an act of ventriloquism, and really bring him to life in these pages? Did you feel intimidated by the task of writing an iconic literary character? What emboldened you to accept the challenge?*

If I have succeeded in "restoring Holmes to life," as one reviewer put it, it may be because I did not try to write Holmes stories, but put Holmes in the role of supporting actor. I was free to let him evolve in ways he would not have had I been writing pastiches set in and around his Baker Street days.

At the same time, because he was not my central concern, I did not worry about how I would handle him—I was focused on Russell, and Holmes just slipped through. In a sense, I don't feel I can take credit for the personality that comes across in the Russell books. Perhaps I'm just channeling Conan Doyle. . . .

3. *From films to books, others have tried to create new stories for Holmes. Which are your favorites? What are your favorite film adaptations of Holmes?*

I read very few pastiches, mostly because I'm afraid that my mind will forget that the adventure is not one by Conan Doyle, and I'll work it into a story somewhere down the line. I do enjoy books that take the character and deliberately work him into another time and place, such as Peter Straub's *Mystery*, with his aging detective a clear stand-in for Holmes.

I did read, and love, the two recent Holmes novels that explore the detective's great old age, Mitch Cullin's *A Slight Trick of the Mind* and Michael Chabon's *The Final Solution*. And because it will take "my" Holmes quite awhile to make it there, I don't have to worry about unconsciously adopting the story lines.

When it comes to film adaptations, the Granada series with Jeremy Brett was absolutely superb, both as adaptations and in evoking the man and his time.

4. *What is your favorite Conan Doyle story?*

Why not ask me who is my favorite child? *The Hound of the Baskervilles* for its inimitable (I know, I tried!) atmosphere, *The Sign of the Four* for being a dashing good yarn, "Silver Blaze" for its energy, for its classic Holmes construction, and for containing what is arguably the best Holmes exchange of them all—"But the dog did nothing in the night-time." "That was the curious incident."

5. *Today's murder mysteries in television, film, and books often rely upon meticulous forensic science—readers know all too well what can be done with ultraviolet lights and microscopes. What do you see as the difference between the forensic investigations of past and present, and what are the different challenges of telling a story within those two very different realms of plausibility?*

Cutting-edge forensic techniques were one of the striking innovations of the Conan Doyle stories—Holmes solves a murder based on fingerprints, he experiments with identifying human blood. But on the whole, he solves his cases not in the laboratory, but by seeing, noticing, and thinking. When I wrote a book that was part Holmes, part modern day (*The Art of Detection*), one of the things that came out was how oddly similar the two eras of investigation are. Television dramas may not agree, but, in fact, crime labs are used to prove cases, and only rarely to solve them.

Having said that, Holmes would have reveled in modern technology, from the Internet to DNA.

6. *Along those lines, you are also the author of a contemporary series of books, the Kate Martinelli mysteries. What specifically moves you to write in the two different time periods?*

The Art of Detection is a Martinelli novel, with story lines in both time periods. I find that there are some stories I can't tell within the rather whimsical world of Russell and Holmes, and some that fit into modern times better than they do the early twentieth century.

Beyond that, it's a pleasure to me to write in such different flavors, and reduces the danger of repeating myself. As they say, a change is as good as a break, and alternating between Russell and Martinelli, or Russell and a stand-alone novel, keeps the writing fresh for me. When time comes to start another in their saga, I'm eager to do so, since it's been a year or more since I last lived with them.

7. *Many people are curious about how to construct a mystery. Do you plot it out backwards, knowing the conclusion, or proceed forward and allow the solution to surprise you (as it does the reader) in process?*

Frankly, I'm curious myself.

I'm one of those writers who doesn't outline, who basically doesn't know what she's getting into from one chapter to the next.

When I first started, I needed to know the final scene before I could begin the book. Then I started *Folly*, and got halfway into it before I realized that I didn't have a clue as to its ending. Fortunately, by the time one has written seven or eight books, there's a certain degree of assurance in the process: I might not have known what I was doing, precisely, but I've always seemed to figure it out up to now.

Now, when I start a book, I know what the story's about, who it's about, what the main events are, but beyond that, I depend on growing the novel organically. In practice, this means that the back of my mind seems to know what's going on, even if the front of my mind is in a state of blissful (or not so blissful) ignorance.

8. *How have fans and scholars of Conan Doyle taken to the series so far?*

When I first started writing the Russell books, there was much mistrust among the Sherlockians (or in Britain, Holmesians). From the beginning, however, there were a few of the faithful who saw what I was doing with the series and enjoyed it. Bit by bit, we've won over (or maybe just worn down) the skeptics, to the point that I was invited to speak at the 2007 annual Baker Street Irregulars dinner, and not a single tomato was thrown.

I think they came to see the enormous affection and respect I have both for Holmes and for Conan Doyle. I may have written a series of books in which Sherlock Holmes is the supporting character, but without him, there would truly have been no Mary Russell.